MW00467052

The Living Wood

The Living Wood

Saint Helena and
the Emperor Constantine

by Louis de Wohl

IGNATIUS PRESS   SAN FRANCISCO

Published in 1947 by J. B. Lippincott
Philadelphia and New York

Cover art by Christopher J. Pelicano

Cover design by Roxanne Mei Lum

Published in 2008 Ignatius Press, San Francisco
ISBN 978-1-58617-227-5
Library of Congress Control Number 2007928875
Printed in the United States of America ∞

Contents

BOOK ONE

❧

A.D. 272

CHAPTER 1

THERE WAS FOG in the channel.

The lone man, groping his way over the cliffs, was cursing softly as his feet slid over the wet grass, which was scarce, like the ugly tufts of hair on the bald head of a giant.

Rain came down through the gray atmosphere in a monotonous, hesitant, lazy drizzle. There was nothing refreshing or wild or aggressive about it; it was wet and queasy, an old man's rain.

A hopeless country, thought the man, wiping the drops off his face: a hades of a country. Mad idea to be out surveying this coastline.

Rufus had warned him, of course, and Rufus knew the country, for he had been stationed in Britain these last seven years, poor fellow. But he had not listened; instead, he had barked at him: "Very well, if you're afraid of getting wet feet, you can stay in camp and play dice. I don't need an orderly. I'll go alone!"

And Rufus had made his long-suffering service face and saluted, and he had gone out alone, like a fool.

Damn that grass. Damn the rain. Damn the whole godforsaken country! What was the good of surveying this strip of coast, anyway? No one in his senses would try to invade a country like this, not even the Germans.

Service in any of the districts along the Rhine was sheer joy compared with this land of mist and wetness—to say nothing of Belgium, or Gaul.

It had looked quite different, when the news of his command in East Britain had come through, in the middle of an amusing time with the Fourteenth Legion at imperial headquarters in Milan. Or rather, at the former imperial headquarters. The generals had been taking it easy ever since the Emperor went east—to Egypt, for the campaign against that little Queen in Syria, Zenobia.

Among the younger officers there had been no doubt whatsoever about the purpose of Aurelian's campaign. Let the old warhorses of the staff gibber about the importance of Palmyra as the crossing of the great caravan roads to the east and the south.

Caravan roads! As though an Emperor would think fit to make war for the sake of a few roads! But Zenobia was supposed to be the most beautiful woman in the world, and old Aurelian had always known what was good.

So it had been wine and women and an occasional bit of drill for the Fourteenth in Milan, and there wasn't much future in that for a man of ambition.

It was not bad to be a tribune at the age of twenty-seven; but it was better to be a legate, and you cannot be a legate at that age unless you get an opportunity. And Britain, after all, was an outpost of the Empire and not just the place where oysters came from.

By Pluto, he had actually gone so far as to pull strings in order to get transferred to *this*.

It had been a dismal disappointment, right from the start. A lot of third-rate ruffians, calling themselves the Twentieth Legion! A general who admitted, from the third goblet on, that he was here because he wasn't liked anywhere else—Aulus Caronius, bald, potbellied, and as lazy as a Syrian whore.

"Rheumatism, my dear boy, rheumatism! You'll get it, too, in this infernal climate, don't you worry."

The medicos sent him west to Aquæ Sulis every year to take the baths there.

In the meantime one could try to make soldiers out of the rabble that was wearing the proud name of the Twentieth Legion.

Shadow of Cæsar, if you could see them! Hardly a Roman among them. Gallic hotheads, Belgian good-for-nothings, a few hundred tame Germans, and a sprinkle of Spaniards and Greeks—the dregs of the recruiting stations, with names that twisted one's tongue.

What a life! And where was that damned road now? By Styx, you can't see three yards ahead! By the cold nose of Cerberus, I've lost the direction—a fine thing for an officer supposed to be surveying a potential invasion shore. Blast that cat-livered, yellow-bellied son of a one-eyed mule driver, Rufus . . .

Rocks, fog, and rain.

Standing still, he became instantly aware of the fact that he was soaked through, coat and armor and tunic and all.

He might have left the damned armor at home, at least, but he hadn't. He had wanted to give an example of discipline. Rufus would grin when one came home. That is, *if* one came home. It wasn't at all certain now. This looked more and more like one of the bigger and better labyrinths of hades. Right? Left?

The sea was out of sight, of course, and it would come into sight possibly when it was just a little too late, when a perfectly good Roman tribune was hurtling, head on, through the air, because one of these thrice-blasted chalk slabs had given way under a wet sandal.

"Halt", said an angry voice in Latin. "Stop where you are. Who are you?"

The tribune needed a few moments to take in an entirely new situation. About the last thing in the world he could have thought of was to be challenged by an enemy. There wasn't a war on. True, up in the deep north there always was, with the barbarous painted tribes beyond the wall. But that wall was hundreds of miles away, and this was a quiet British province—as far as he knew, at least.

As for robbers—well, they were omnipresent, of course. But what robber in his senses would choose this rugged bit of landscape for his beat?

He had done what a soldier does instinctively when suddenly challenged: he had thrown his small shield forward and laid his right hand on the sword hilt. But the mind needed more time than the body to sort itself out.

"Who are you yourself?" he asked, more curious than annoyed.

The challenging voice came back: "Never mind that. I'm at home here; you are not. So you just answer my questions."

It was a very angry voice—but also a very young voice.

He laughed. "Have you never seen a Roman tribune before?"

"Stupid", said the voice. "Am I to see a man's rank in this fog?"

The challenger's Latin was excellent, but it had a distinctly foreign intonation.

The tribune was annoyed this time. "Tribune Constantius of the staff of the Twentieth Legion, reporting to you", he said with sharp irony. "And who the hell are you, and where are you hiding yourself?"

"Here I am", said the voice. A shadow became visible through the fog. It was a very slim shadow, and it seemed to be unarmed.

Constantius made two cautious steps forward—the soil was still very slippery; he swung the shield on his back and seized the challenger's slim shoulder.

"Let me have a look at you", he said grimly—and stared into the face of a girl.

She was very young—seventeen, eighteen, perhaps; hardly more.

Many of the native women here were quite good looking in a fierce, dark way, and this girl was no exception. At least that was what he thought at the sight of her fine, well-cut features. She seemed to be well built, too, from what little one could see in this night of a day.

He began to laugh. "My dear girl, you seem to have chosen a bad time for a meeting with your lover—"

"I have no lover", said the girl contemptuously. "Let go my shoulder."

He did, to his own surprise. Her dress was a little more elaborate than any he had seen so far, and she was wearing pearls.

"I've told you who I am", he said. "Don't you think you might tell me who you are, too?"

"I'm Elen", said the girl. "And you may be a tribune, but I know something else you are."

"What's that?"

"You're lost. You don't know where you are. Or else you wouldn't be here."

He raised his eyebrows. "Why not?"

"Because this is sacred ground. Only Druids are allowed here."

Constantius frowned. It was an unwritten law in the Roman army not to interfere with native gods and their worship. It was not so much because of their potential power, though one could never know for certain about that, but rather because it was bad policy. It caused a lot of annoyance with no advantage to make up for it, and Caronius hated difficulties, let alone unnecessary ones. If this was sacred ground—but then, the girl had given him the benefit of the doubt, and an opening, too.

"You are a Druid, then", he said in a bantering tone. "They choose them young, these days."

"Silly", said the girl gravely. "Of course I'm not a Druid. I'm just a girl. But I am allowed here because I am the King's daughter."

This was worse—if it was true. She might get hysterical and scream, and Caronius would have a first-rate scandal to deal with when the news reached him in Aquæ Sulis. "The King's daughter". The only King around here was old Coellus, who resided somewhere near Camulodunum.

"What's your father's name, Princess?"

"Coel—surely you know that? All the tribunes I have ever met before did."

"And have you met many?"

"Too many", said the princess acidly.

He laughed. "You don't seem to like tribunes."

"I don't like Romans. But you mustn't tell my father that I said that. He doesn't like me to tell the truth."

Constantius began to be amused. "Well, he's quite right. It's dangerous."

She flared up. "What nonsense you talk! My father has more courage than any Roman. But he believes in not telling the truth when it hurts people."

"Now that's very nice of him", acknowledged Constantius. "And you disagree?"

She tossed up her head. "I don't mind hurting people when they deserve it."

Promising little lady, thought Constantius. But he remembered what she had said about this being sacred ground.

"You are quite right about one thing, anyway", he said. "I really am lost in the fog, and I am sorry that I came to this place. I swear it by all the gods."

It was difficult to hide a smile. There was little likelihood of the gods taking that oath amiss—after all, he had done nothing else but feel sorry about having come to Britain, these last hours.

The girl gave him a puzzled look. "You've admitted that you are lost, and you have said you are sorry", she stated. "So now I shall help you."

"That's good of you", murmured Constantius. "Let's go, shall we?" She nodded and took the lead.

"How far away am I from the new camp?"

"Five hours at least. You can't get there tonight. I'm taking you to my father."

The tribune thought that over for a moment or two. Old Coellus was supposed to be something of a lone wolf. Of the present garrison, only a very few officers had ever seen him. Caronius had, of course, and two or three others. It was not exactly an agreeable idea to meet him—it might create some sort of a diplomatic entanglement.

But then he shrugged his shoulders. One had become too cautious in the gilded imperial city of Milan, where everything one said or did or didn't say or didn't do would be twisted and turned by the courtiers. Besides, what else could one do? And he was wet and hungry.

"Right, Princess", he said. "How long will it take us?"

"Half an hour the way we're walking now. If I were alone—half that time."

He laughed. "You're carrying no armor", he said.

"And you don't need to", was the quick answer. "There's peace in this country, I believe. But you Romans will go about, tramp, tramp, tramp—" She imitated the long, heavy step of the regular troops, and again he laughed.

"One day you may thank your gods for the step of the legions, child. Wherever they march, they protect the land."

"They're marching in Syria now, aren't they?" asked the girl.

He gave her a quick look—innocence or impertinence?

"That's a punitive expedition", he said slowly.

"Yes—against a woman. I wonder, does she regard it as that?"

"Zenobia? Well, no—she'll probably call it a war of aggression. They all do."

The girl smiled angrily—he could just see it. "She's wonderful. She has beaten armies led by men before, hasn't she? She'll do it again."

"She won't beat the Emperor, child."

"That remains to be seen. She is a great woman—as great as Boadicea was—and Cleopatra—as great as—"

She broke off.

"You've had history lessons, Princess", said Constantius not unkindly. "You'll remember, then, how those women died."

"How did Cæsar die?" she flashed back at him, quickening her step. He stumbled after her in the semidarkness. This was not exactly the moment to insist on the superiority of the male sex.

Still, it was amazing to find a girl with these views here, in Britain, of all places.

"What did you say your name was, Princess?"

"Elen. Maybe one day you will remember it."

"I won't forget it again. Elen—that's Helena with us. You've heard, I suppose, of the story of Helena—*the* Helena—whose beauty caused the death of many men?"

"I don't know about her", said the girl contemptuously. "And beauty is nothing."

Constantius, looking at her, thought not without surprise that she herself looked very beautiful.

CHAPTER 2

KING COEL was a kindly old man with a drooping white mustache, bushy white eyebrows, and unruly white hair. He was sitting in his hall when his daughter led Constantius in, and although there were no servants to announce the visitor, he did not seem to be in the least surprised.

"Welcome, daughter. Welcome, guest", he said. "Here, somebody, a goblet of wine for the noble Constantius."

The tribune looked at him in amazement. "How is it that you know my name, King? We have never met before."

Coel laughed. "My daughter is very young, and she must be told things in only one way. I am very old, and things are told to me in many ways. I am sorry that you have been inconvenienced by my climate. Unfortunately there is very little I can do about it."

A wizened little servant brought the wine, which gave the Roman time to think. He remembered that some people thought that old Coel was a little mad and others that he was a sly old fox, pretending to be mad. He decided to reserve judgment for the time being. The wine, by the way, was excellent—a Massican of good vintage.

"But what I can do is to give you a hot bath, as you strange people like it", went on the King. "I could never

quite understand the idea; it is not hot enough to boil in it
and not cold enough to enjoy it. But then, we all have our
strange ideas and seem a little mad to each other. . . ."

Constantius, caught unaware, jerked up his head.

Coel smiled beatifically. "It's Massican, all right", he nodded. "Now that's wonderful stuff, that blood of the vine of
yours. We haven't got anything like it in this country. Even
when you drink too much of it, it only makes you happy
in the way of poets and singers; not like our mead, which
makes you feel as though you had seven skulls instead of
one. I think I like you. You've got imagination, and you
will go far, but now go and bathe yourself, child. They'll
give you dry clothes, and then we shall all eat together."

A very dignified movement of the King's right hand dismissed Constantius, who bowed and followed the wizened
servant without so much as a murmur; he was grinning
awkwardly. It had been years since anybody had addressed
him as "child".

They were twelve at table: the King; Helena; an elderly
woman whose name sounded like Eurgain and whom Constantius labeled as "Virginia", obviously something between
a governess and a lady-in-waiting; and eight old men, whose
chains, armlets, and badges of office showed that they were
councilors or something of the kind.

Constantius, after his bath, had gently but firmly refused
British dress and slipped back into his military tunic, which
he found was almost dry. He enjoyed the meal: bread; cheese;
eggs; and, as the main dish, roast mutton.

The King ate little, drank less, but talked a good deal in
his queer, high-pitched Latin. The notables had eyes only
for him, although it seemed doubtful whether all of them
knew enough Latin to understand what he said.

Helena was very silent, but whether that was because of the presence of her father or of Virginia, Constantius did not know.

He had, however, a good look at her, at long last—so far he had not been able to see more than a finely cut profile and the potentialities of a good figure. She was tall, taller than her father, and almost too slim. Dark eyes under long lashes, a pale complexion—the mouth still childish and pink. Her hair was dark, too, and formed a curious little peak in the middle of the forehead, baring the beautiful temples. The chin was stubborn. It was the chin alone that showed something of the spirit he had encountered at their first meeting.

She might be Spanish, thought Constantius. Or of Gallic breed. She could even be Roman.

"Elen does look like a Roman girl, doesn't she?" interrupted the King in his disconcerting way of saying what one had just thought. "But she doesn't like the Romans much, you know. She has a very low opinion of anybody who wasn't born on this island."

Constantius laughed politely.

A thin red mounted into the girl's cheeks, but she remained silent.

"I've told her that it is wrong", went on Coel. "One mustn't measure everybody with the same measure. They brought a hunchback before me the other day, and he complained bitterly about the injustice of the gods. I asked him what he complained about, and he said it was because he was so ugly. I said, 'But you are not ugly, friend; you are not at all ugly—for a hunchback.' "

Constantius shifted a little on his seat. He was not quite certain whether the King had made a joke or not.

"Romans will be Romans", said King Coel cheerfully. "And as such they can be appreciated. Elen only looks

Roman. Sometimes I think it is almost a pity that she wasn't born a boy."

"She would have become a great warrior, no doubt", said Constantius.

"But she is", said the King, sipping his wine and enjoying its bouquet with dilated nostrils. "She killed a wolf all by herself only a fortnight ago."

"It wasn't a very big wolf", said Helena with a shrug. "And it was only a male."

"The female is always more dangerous", nodded Constantius. "Wolves are getting scarce here now, I'm told—since the Roman She Wolf has taken over."

Helena bit her lip. Coel seemed amused. "We all have our wolf's age", he said. "Sooner or later we become more peaceful. I used to be quite a wolf myself when I was young. It's a long time ago, though not as long as the life of the She Wolf you were talking about, Constantius."

"You're right, King", said the tribune slowly. "Rome wants peace and peace only."

"Zenobia will be glad to hear it", said Helena sharply.

"The Queen of Palmyra has been exceedingly ill advised", replied Constantius. "We had reports that she intended to make Egypt a Syrian province—and even that was only the first step. Palmyrenes have been talking of a Palmyrene Empire quite openly."

His tone was a little stiffer than he had intended it to be, and he was angry with himself for taking the precocious young woman too seriously.

"Syria", said Coel. "That's the east. The direction from which it all comes nowadays. It itself used to be the west, but that was a very long time ago—no one spoke of Rome in *those* days. Not even the gods who foresee the future. The direction changes, but the message is always the same."

Constantius refilled his goblet. He felt distinctly uneasy. Perhaps the old man was mad after all.

He saw Helena darting a quick glance at him, but her small face remained impassive. She was probably accustomed to her father's ways.

"The message is always the same", repeated King Coel. "And no one ever understands it."

The eight notables went on devouring what was left of the whole sheep on the oblong plate in the middle of the table.

"You have such clever men in Rome and Milan, Constantius", said Coel. "They are reading their tablets and scrolls and parchments and go on adding to them—but they don't understand. And do you know why?" He leaned forward. His simple dress was innocent of any ornament except a heavy golden chain round the neck. Just above that chain the ancient skin sagged a little.

Like a very old dog, thought the tribune. Like the father of all dogs. And he said politely, though a little bored, "Why don't they understand, King?"

"Because they do not believe in fairy stories", said the old man mysteriously. "And fairy stories are the only true stories, you know!"

Mad. Or, perhaps, a bit drunk. He hadn't drunk much, but perhaps he couldn't carry it. It was a thing one had learned in the army, to carry one's wine.

Fairy stories, by Pluto.

"Clever or not," said Helena suddenly, "Romans are not very much interested in fairy stories, Father."

King Coel smiled. "Neither are you, yet", he said gently. "But perhaps you will be, one day. And that will be a great day in your life, child, and a great day in many other people's lives. Pity I won't live to see it—from here. Elen must show you around my palace, Constantius. It's all wood—you have

21

observed that, perhaps. Oak, the royal tree, Constantius. The holy tree."

"It is sacred to Jupiter", said the Roman gravely.

Again King Coel smiled. "It was sacred long before Jupiter was sacred, Constantius. But do you know why?"

"Because it attracts the lightning of the gods, I suppose", ventured the tribune. He was used to being a little solemn when the gods were mentioned—but not too. The Emperors all preferred their officers to be believers in the gods; it was only natural—for was not the Emperor himself a godhead, in front of whose statue incense was burned? An officer who did not believe in the godhead of Jupiter was not too likely to believe in the godhead of Aurelian, and that could have certain disagreeable consequences. Hence it was better to be a little solemn when the gods were mentioned— not too, though, for the reputation of being a pious fool was the next worst thing in the army. It was all a damned nuisance, really, and one would do away with most of it, as soon as one had a commanding position. But the thing was to get that position first.

"Wood is sacred", said King Coel, nodding his heavy head. "Wood is man's disaster and man's triumph. It kills man and saves man. The world as we know it is built on wood, on Yggdrasil, the holy tree, the tree of life."

Constantius tried hard to hide his boredom. "The tree of life", he repeated mechanically. "I think I've heard that before, somewhere. . . ."

"In Egypt, perhaps", said the strange old man. "Or in Germany. Or here in Britain. It is a very old story. The tree that spells death, and the tree that spells life. There is a great mystery about wood, Constantius. It is all in the message I told you about—the message that no one understands. I've tried hard to understand it myself, but

I'm not sure that I do.... The tree of life—the living tree—the living wood ..."

Constantius emptied his goblet. When he looked again, he saw that King Coel had fallen asleep.

"It's his favorite story", said Helena curtly. "But it always makes him sleepy. Have you eaten enough? They have—and I have. Good. Gullo, show the tribune to his room."

She rose and with her Virginia, who had not said a single word the whole evening.

"Must I go to sleep, too?" asked the tribune meekly.

Helena laughed. "You can do what you like—but what else is there to do? The day has come to an end."

"I could talk to you", murmured the tribune. But Helena was already busy chasing the eight notables away from the last remnants of the sheep—a few sinews around the bones. They bowed themselves out, and she turned round.

"We can talk tomorrow, if you wish, Tribune", she said with quiet dignity. "I shall get horses for you in the morning, so that you can reach your camp quicker. Good night."

"Good night, Princess."

"Arbol! Beurgain!" commanded Helena. "Carry the King to his bed. And be careful with him. If you drop him again, I'll have your ears torn off. I mean it. Careful! That's better...."

CHAPTER 3

THE MORNING WAS FRESH and clear. Constantius had found his armor polished and his coat and tunic brushed and placed next to his bed when he woke up in the simple guestroom.

23

The wizened little servant, Gullo, brought him a goblet of wine sweetened with honey. Drinking it, he could not help feeling a little touched. The sweetened morning wine was a Roman, not a British, custom. It was obviously a delicate gesture on the part of either old Coel or his daughter. He pondered a while which of the two alternatives was the more likely one and decided that the odds were heavily in favor of the King. For some reason, that vexed him a little. Why was the girl so decidedly anti-Roman? It could hardly be some silly local patriotism. Britain had been a Roman province for three centuries now. The thing was ridiculous....

He ate a hearty breakfast in the big hall where they had had dinner the night before. Gullo served it: bread, cheese, gull's eggs, and a sound portion of a boar's back. Again the wine was very drinkable, a light Falernian from Fundi, unless he was mistaken. Served in a nice goblet, too.

Quite a pleasant little interlude, all this. Something to talk about when one was back in camp. That reminded him that by now they were likely to be worried about him at the camp. It was time to get home. He rose.

"Where is the King?" he asked.

Gullo blinked and shook his head.

But just then the clatter of hoofs came from the court-yard, and he saw Helena riding toward the entrance, on a very pretty chestnut. She was leading a second horse, a piebald.

The tribune's experienced eye saw quickly enough that she could ride better than most of the men of the three mounted squadrons he had been trying to instruct during the last few months. He sauntered into the courtyard.

"Lovely", he said.

"Yes, they are fine animals", nodded Helena. Not for one moment did it seem to occur to her that he might not have been referring to the horses. "The Legate Bassianus sold them to Father three years ago", she went on.

"Well, that's something good that came from Rome", he teased her.

"They came from Spain. The only animal Rome has introduced is the rabbit, and it has become a plague. Has Gullo given you something to eat? Good. Are you ready?"

"I have not taken leave of the King yet—"

"Oh, Father—he's been out for hours. He always rises early and makes the rounds. You'll see him another time."

"I don't know about that", said Constantius, and she laughed.

"Oh, yes, you will. He said so, you know."

"Oh, well, if he said so. . . ."

She shrugged her shoulders. "You don't know him—I do—a little. If he says so, it will be so. He knows things. Shall we go?"

" 'We'?"

"I'm coming with you. Someone has to bring the horses back."

"I am very much honored", murmured Constantius. Strange girl. Strange old man.

"It's only an hour's ride, when you know the way as I do."

He mounted the piebald, clanking in his armor. Spanish breed all right. Had been in good hands, too.

She turned her chestnut and rode off without looking back.

He followed and caught up with her.

"That's the old Roman camp, over there", she said casually. "Father's building a small town around it. It'll merge into Camulodunum one day, he says. They're calling it Coel-castra."

Constantius remembered what Caronius had told him about the old camp. "Too near to the sea—don't know what was in the mind of my noble predecessor to have it built there. No idea about strategy. Hopeless position."

"We'll cross the river soon now", said Helena. "I know the ford. You are not a bad rider."

Her praise left him speechless. The pupil of the finest Roman cavalry school, instructor of the best cavalry in the world: "not a bad rider". Ye gods!

"You're riding like Hippolyta yourself", he said with twinkling eyes. "She very likely looked like you, too."

"Who was she?" asked Helena suspiciously.

"The Queen of the Amazons."

"Here's the river."

Constantius pulled the reins sharply. Over there, on the crest of a small hill, stood a man motionless. It was too far away to see more than a long blue coat and a head of unruly white hair. It might be a lone old shepherd or a farmer.

But somehow he knew that it was the King.

He wanted to speak of it to Helena, but she had ridden on and was already deep in the ford. So he contented himself with raising his arm in salute to the lonely figure on the hilltop, but there was no response, and so he rode on into the river.

Amid a shower of flying water he reached the other bank, where the girl was now waiting for him.

"I think I saw your father just now", he said. "Over there, on the hilltop."

"Maybe you did", said Helena quietly. "You never know where he will turn up."

She spurred her chestnut into a gallop, and Constantius guessed that she did not want to talk.

About an hour later they reached the camp, from the south. The sentinel at the *porta decumana* gave the salute.

"Come with me to my tent", suggested Constantius. "The horses can do with a mouthful of barley, and we with a goblet of wine."

"I'm not thirsty", replied Helena curtly. "And the horses are not hungry."

Before he could speak again, Quintus Balbus strode up, the immaculate Balbus. "Ah, here you are, Constantius", he said. "Everyone thought you must have had an accident. How right they were, and what a delightful accident it is!"

His voice had the nasal twang the Roman elite affected at the time. He had not been in Britain long enough to forget it.

Constantius frowned. "The Tribune Quintus Balbus", he introduced. "This is Princess Helena, the daughter of King Coellus."

Balbus grinned with delight. "By Jupiter, you do know how to pick 'em, don't you, Constantius? Surveying the British coast by day and a British princess by night, eh? Nice bit of work."

Constantius' face was naturally pale; it became ashen now.

"You must be drunk. You will instantly apologize to the princess for behaving like a lout", he commanded.

The elegant Balbus drew himself up. "There's no need for that sort of tone, friend—just because you've had a good time with this little bit of native vintage. . . ."

Constantius jumped from his horse and clanked up to his fellow tribune. "Are you going to apologize immediately, or do I have to make you?"

But Balbus had all the coward's fear of appearing as a coward. "Make me?" he asked haughtily. "I'd like to know what you mean by that!"

"I'll show you", bellowed Constantius, dropping his shield and grabbing Balbus by the throat. He was in a blind rage. Balbus drove his fist into Constantius' face, but Constantius did not even feel it. His relentless fingers closed deeper and deeper around the hated throat. Only when he heard the wild clattering of hoofs did he look up; there was Helena, galloping away on her chestnut and leading the piebald. Her black hair was fluttering behind her like a flag.

With a curse Constantius loosed his hold on Balbus' throat and sent his fist crashing into his face.

Balbus staggered back and fell—at the feet of a tall, potbellied man in the full uniform of an imperial legate. There were at least a dozen officers behind him, and their faces reflected every emotion: horror, joy, amusement, contempt.

"Charming performance", said the legate. "You will both report to me in my tent in half an hour." He turned sharply and walked away, followed by his staff.

Constantius looked at Balbus, who was being helped by two sturdy centurions. It was quite a business even to pick him up.

"And that's not the last of it, either", said Constantius, his fury unabated, as he marched off. No wonder she didn't like Romans. Of all the damned stupid, foul-mouthed idiots ...

It took him some time to calm down sufficiently to take stock of his own situation. Damned bad luck that Caronius should have come back from Aquæ Sulis at this time; worse still that he had actually seen it happen. And Balbus, though not of a very good family, had a few influential acquaintances in both Milan and Rome. This was *not* going to make life easier, and it could do a good bit of damage to his career.

He wiped his nose and mouth, saw blood on his hand, and grinned. It had been a good thing all the same. He could not remember having been so angry since the day, over seven years ago, when he had been confined to barracks by a practical-minded superior officer who wanted him out of the way because they were both courting the same woman.

Meanwhile here was Rufus, with a woebegone face.

"Well, Rufus, been playing dice?"

The old orderly made clucking noises like a mother whose child has come back dirty and covered with scratches. They had all been very worried about him, a patrol was to go out looking for him in an hour's time, and old Tertius had it from a very good source that the legate had said, "Young Chlorus of all people—my best man!"

Constantius grinned. "He's changed his opinion since, I believe." But it amused him that even the legate knew his nickname of "Chlorus"—Paleface. A nickname, unless it was a decidedly uncomplimentary one, was always a sign of popularity, and popularity helped, to a point. Too much popularity, of course, wasn't good. Everything in life was a matter of quantity—the right doses. However ...

"Brush up my helmet, Rufus. I've got to go and see the legate."

When Constantius entered Caronius' tent, Quintus Balbus had already arrived. He didn't look too good, with his face all swollen and one eye closed. The four guardsmen in front of the curtain separating the entrance from the actual sanctum looked impassive, but Constantius saw an underlip quiver and an eye twinkle a little. This affair was just the sort of thing to amuse them.

The tall, cadaverous figure of Curio, Caronius' aide-de-camp, threw back the curtain. "The Tribunes Constantius and Balbus to the noble legate."

They clanked in, side by side, saluted, and reported themselves present.

Caronius was sitting at his field desk, signing papers. For a while he did not seem to take any notice of them. When he finally looked up, his face showed the acid annoyance of an old schoolmaster who has to deal with a couple of recalcitrant boys.

"Tribunes", he said, "are supposed to be men of education and culture. It amazes me to find you indulging in a common brawl like drunken gladiators."

Both the young officers tried to speak at the same time, but a sharp gesture of the legate stopped them abruptly.

"You were missing this morning at parade, Tribune Constantius", he said. "Why is that?"

Constantius gulped. "I went out surveying yesterday afternoon, sir", he said. "Fog set in, and I got lost. Finally I got—with some help—to King Coellus' place and spent the night at his—house." One could not very well call the smoky old oak hall a palace.

The legate seemed interested. "Did you see the King?"

"Yes, sir. I was received in the most friendly manner. This morning his daughter was kind enough to bring me back to the camp."

"His daughter? The young woman I saw galloping away—"

"That was she, sir. We had just arrived at the *porta decumana* when Tribune Balbus came up and insulted the lady in the grossest way—"

"I only said—"

"Quiet, Tribune Balbus", roared the legate. His heavy face was flushed and his eyes suffused with blood. "Proceed, Tribune Constantius."

"Balbus insinuated that I had slept with the lady—"

The legate rose. "Could she hear what he said?" he asked anxiously.

"She couldn't have missed a word, sir. She speaks and understands Latin very well, and Balbus stood as near to her as he now stands to you."

The legate began to pace up and down. "Then what did you do?" he asked.

"I ordered Balbus to apologize to the lady, and he refused. So I proceeded to teach him manners, and—you know the rest, sir."

The legate stopped in the middle of his tiger-in-the-cage performance. "By hades, yes", he said. "I know the rest. But you don't. Tribune Balbus, what have you got to say for yourself?"

"I didn't say that Constantius had slept with the girl", sulked the elegant tribune.

"He didn't say you did", snapped Caronius. "He said you 'insinuated' it. Did you?"

"Not in so many words, sir."

"I understand. You thought fit to show your cleverness. You made a spirited little joke. You were witty. And your wit may cost Rome very dearly. The Princess Helena is the only child of King Coellus, of an ally of Rome, who can command fifteen thousand men in the field—and you made her the butt of your wit, you stupid clown."

Balbus looked thoroughly crestfallen. Even Constantius was taken aback. His conception of old Coellus had been that of a landowner rather than of a ruler and commander of a sizable army.

Caronius seated himself and wiped his forehead. "Tribune Balbus, you will leave this afternoon for the north, for the Great Wall. You are not suited for service in this part of the country. Up there you can try your wonderful wit on the Picts and Scots, if you wish. But I'd be careful, if I were you; they haven't much of a sense of humor. No need to report to me before you leave. This is your leavetaking. You may go now."

The wretched Balbus saluted and withdrew.

The legate sank into a reverie. Constantius stood still, as stiff as a ramrod.

Then the aide-de-camp cleared his throat, and Caronius came to. "Idiotic thing to happen, now of all times, Curio."

"Most inopportune, sir."

"We better tell him, Curio."

"Yes, sir."

Caronius swung round. "Sit down, Tribune."

"Thank you, sir."

The legate fixed him steadily. "Everything I'm telling you now is in the strictest confidence, Tribune."

"Of course, sir."

"Well, then—there's been extremely bad news from Gaul."

Constantius raised his head. "An insurrection, sir?"

The legate's eyes widened. "How did you know?"

"I didn't. But I know Gaul—a little. There's a deep rift between the Gallic landowners and the peasants—"

Caronius nodded. "That's just it. You seem to keep your eyes open. So much the better for what I have to say to you. It's insurrection, all right. That's why I had to come back from Aquæ Sulis so suddenly. Went north to Eburacum first, and saw Petronius Aquila. We've been ordered to send the Thirty-Fifth over immediately."

"An entire legion!" exclaimed Constantius. "We'll be thinned out below minimum strength."

"Exactly", nodded the legate. "But it must be done. You'll understand now how important it is that we entertain the most friendly relations with all the tribes in the province. I don't know, and no one knows, how long this Gallic business is going to last, and we're not likely to get reinforcements from elsewhere. We've just got to hold the fort and pray. A conspiracy of half a dozen tribes could be fatal for us. And at such a moment that blithering young fool goes and insults King Coellus' daughter! We shall have to make amends, of course. I'll send a delegation over with a letter for the King. Must scrape up some presents for him, too. Wish I knew what."

"Something made of wood", said Constantius. "He loves wood. It's sacred to him."

"It is sacred to Jupiter", said Caronius solemnly.

"Quite, sir."

"I'll think of something. I'd go myself, but I can't. I've got my hands full with collecting shipping for the transport of the Thirty-Fifth. Hades of a business. So I'll send you instead."

"Me, sir?"

"Of course, you!" roared the legate. "You seem to get on well with the old man—and with his daughter. Ceremonial visit, my boy. Come and see me about it tomorrow after parade."

"Very well, sir."

"By the way—"

"Sir?"

The legate blinked a little. "Did—eh—the princess see you hit that young whippersnapper?"

"Oh, yes, sir. Bound to. She must have seen at least the beginning of the scrap."

Caronius grinned. "Splendid! Splendid! You may go now." Constantius rose, saluted, turned smartly, and left. He was beaming.

CHAPTER 4

KING COEL was sitting on his favorite stone in his favorite forest. Helena was sitting at his feet, looking straight ahead, across the clearing toward the faraway hills. Thus they had been sitting, who knows for how long, and no word had passed between them.

"I don't want to marry him, Father."

"No?"

"He is arrogant and condescending, and he treats my will as though it were a plaything."

"And is it?"

She blushed deeply. "My will is my will. It is mine."

"So it is—*if* it's for the good."

She took a deep breath. She wanted to ask "what is good?" but she had asked that before, and she still remembered his answer: "Good is what the heart says and not the desire. You know it, but sometimes you betray your knowledge." She said nothing.

The King chuckled. "You are angry because you cannot rule him. But if you could rule him, you would despise him. What is good about that?"

She gritted her teeth. "I want to be as Zenobia is. I'm not made to sit at home and gossip with the servants and rule over little things."

"If you cannot rule little things, how can you rule big ones?"

She looked up eagerly. "Then I shall rule big ones, Father? You never told me. Shall I?"

"Not if you want to be Zenobia, Elen."

"But she is great, Father—and she ruled her husband, too. She is a real Queen. I do want to be like her."

"I wonder", said the King, and she could feel that he was smiling a little.

"Anyway, I won't marry Constantius", she said angrily. "He's treating me like a child, and he is a child himself. And he doesn't believe in his own gods, really—or in anybody else's."

"You always want everything at once", said King Coel enigmatically.

"I've treated him as he deserves, Father."

"Let your mind be quiet", said the King kindly. "How else can you hear your heart speak?"

She made an impatient gesture, but her arm dropped, and she sat quite still.

"He's come every other day, all these weeks now", said the King.

"Presents", Helena shrugged her shoulders. "Presents to keep you in good humor, because they need you. They're playing their clumsy game. Presents when they need you— the iron rod when they don't. You know."

"Every other day is much", said the King, quite unperturbed.

"He only thinks of his ambition", said Helena bitterly. "It's Rome and the Empire all the time. I told him last time he should not waste his precious hours on polite visits. He'll be in command now that Caronius is going away again. It's bad for the troops when their commander is absent too often. He won't come any longer."

The King did not seem to have heard her. "Parul tells me they're in trouble at their village in the south", he said. "The gale last week smashed eleven boats and damaged many houses. I shall go there this afternoon, but I shall be back tonight. Go now—and I've given orders to Gullo to have a state meal served one hour after sunset."

She looked up in blank surprise. State meals were solemn occasions, with at least fifty notables and ladies of high rank. She wanted to ask what the occasion was and who was invited. But the King's head was drooping on his chest, and she saw that he was sleeping again, as he so often did lately.

She rose silently, breathed a swift kiss on his unruly white hair, and walked away into the clearing.

It was quite safe to leave him alone in the forest. Even a wolf would not harm *him*; she knew that. As for her, she was armed—she had a spear and a short dagger.

After a while she looked back. She could still see him, old and white and almost as wizened as Gullo. It occurred to her that he might die soon, and the thought gave her physical pain.

I don't want him to die, she thought furiously. I need him. He is the only one I need.

After the clearing came a strip of forest, at the end of which one could look down on the main road, along the river.

Something was coming up the road, still far away, something like a glittering beetle. He was coming after all. . . .

They met near the palace. He was alone, and as he jumped off his horse, she saw that he was excited, as though he had had good news.

"Well, Tribune, what leads you, again, away from your duties?"

"You do", was the immediate answer and he showed all his teeth in a smile. "No, don't say anything, Helena. You are quite right. Yours is a very bad influence on me, without doubt. And what is worse still, it is increasing daily."

They walked toward the palace, where a burly servant took charge of his horse.

"Is your father at home, Helena?"

"No. He is visiting a village to the south, where the gale has done damage."

"He is a father of his people", nodded the Roman. He took off his helmet, with its bronze eagle of the Twentieth Legion, to which he was now attached.

"Solid", said Helena casually. "And nicely worked."

"Oh, just regulation", shrugged Constantius. "They're making them in Treveri now. Armor and swordhilts and spears are made in the Narbonensis, town called Massilia. Biggish place. The blades come from Spain."

"Is there anything left to be manufactured in Rome itself?"

There, again, was that sarcastic tone he never quite knew how to cope with. But today he didn't seem to mind it.

"But then, of course, you are an empire", she went on. "We are only poor little people—and to you we are barbarians, I suppose. Yet we pride ourselves that we live on our own land and from our own land. My spear and dagger were made by my father's armorer. We do not make other people work for us, and we do not make others fight our wars for us—as Rome does."

He stopped, and there was a sharp line between his eyebrows.

"Why do you hate Rome so much, Helena? I've always wanted to ask you that. It is not because this or that Roman did not know how to behave to King Coellus' daughter. You are above that sort of thing. But what is it?"

She looked straight past him. "I do not hate Rome", she said slowly. "I love my own country. Rome means nothing to me."

"And yet you are part of Rome", he teased her. "This soil we're standing on—"

"Is Roman soil? Really?" She drew herself up to her full height. She was as tall as he was.

"Yes, it is. Or are we again on sacred soil—as when we met first?"

Her eyes were burning. "Yes, we are, Roman. But you would not understand. The soil of this country is sacred soil. There are spirits in the air above, spirits in the waters around it, and spirits in the soil itself. You have been here for many a generation now—and how firm is your rule? It may slip from your fingers any day, like the reins from the hands of a bad rider. Whoever comes to this country of mine will either be absorbed or rejected. There is nothing else. You will not be absorbed—you are too proud of being Romans. Be rejected then!"

He shook his head. "Who taught you all that nonsense?"

She laughed angrily. "My father, whom they call 'the Wise' all over Britain. You were the first to come here, other than peacefully—except for the robbers from the outer islands in the north and east. And they only attack our coasts; they do not dare to come inland—they cannot fight unless they are still in sight of their ships. You were the first to treat us—as you have treated all the rest of the world. There will be others after you, my father says. But they will be absorbed, one after the other, and it will be that mixture of blood that one day will give us strength second to none. We are at our beginning—you are nearing your end."

But he had not listened. He had been far too busy gazing at her. She was never more beautiful than when she was roused. What did it matter what she said when she could look like this?

"You are very lovely", he said. "You are quite incredibly lovely when you are angry with me."

The blood rushed into her face.

"And what is more," he went on, "I want to marry you."

She took a step backward, as though an invisible hand had pushed her. "Rome must be in a bad way," she jeered, "for the noble Constantius to sacrifice himself for her glory by marrying a mere Briton. Are you marrying me or my father's army? There is trouble in Gaul, I believe—just as there is in Syria."

Constantius exploded. "By Hercules, Rome would indeed be in a bad way if I'd take that from anyone—even from you! You needn't worry too much about us, Princess. News came through this morning: Palmyra has fallen, and Zenobia is the Emperor's prisoner. He has spared her life. She will march in his triumphal procession in the Eternal City in a few months' time. The Syrian legions are free."

"Zenobia—a prisoner?"

Helena gripped the shaft of her spear, as though to find support in a world crashing to pieces around her.

"The Emperor is merciful", said Constantius coldly. He seemed to tower over her, with the shoulders and arms and neck of the god of war. All her strength was drained from her body. Penthesilea may have felt like that when Achilles stood face to face with her on the battlefield of Troy. Zenobia—a prisoner.

A more sensitive man would have seen the tremendous upheaval in her, would have sensed that she was standing at the feet of a fallen idol. But he had not the key to her mind and would not have it for many years to come.

He walked up to her, armored and terrible. "But if war is what you want, you can have it", he said with eyes blazing.

She looked up as one looks up at a thundercloud, trying to guess from where the next stroke of lightning might come. Zenobia had fallen, and Rome was once more the strongest force on earth.

At this moment her pride destroyed itself. The strange and morbid desire of the fugitive to give himself up, out of sheer fear that he will be caught; the unwitting drift of the weak toward the strong; the dark urge to reconcile threatening power—there was all this and more, though none of it was conscious, not even the physical movement, as she fled toward him, to hide herself in the very thundercloud from which the lightning would come.

Her face, upturned, was stained with tears, and her lips were moving. When he kissed her, she responded at once.

He began to laugh, the deep, happy laughter of a man who has succeeded, he knows not why, when all seemed lost.

She managed a smile, and it was kissed off her lips.

But her eyes saw something over his shoulder, and, turning, he too saw servants, carrying a large wooden bench. It took him some time to realize that they were standing in the hall, with servants all around them trying to set benches and tables together, and that they had been obstructing their path, oblivious of anything around them, immersed in their war and defeat and victory.

Now the external world was flooding back upon them.

He grinned. "It's public now, Helena—too late to say no."

"I didn't say no", said Helena. And with a feeling of wondrous fear and relief she realized why her father had ordered a state meal for tonight.

BOOK TWO

❧

A.D. 274–289

CHAPTER I

THE GREEK PHYSICIAN tiptoed into her room and sat down at her bedside. He was a slight man with a laurel wreath of untidy gray hair round a bald head, with a snub nose like Socrates and a broad mouth whose lips were perpetually in motion.

Helena knew he was there, but she did not stir; her lashes lay darkly on her lower lids; her black hair was painting wild designs on the cushions. She had been half awake for hours, imagining herself to be a fish, round and white and heavy bellied, slowly sinking into the soft sand of the bottom of the sea, deeper and deeper; yet when she opened her eyes, the imprint of her body on cushions and mattress had not deepened, and she quickly closed them again to regain that lovely soft sinking feeling.

She had disliked the physician from the very first. "He is so polite, Constantius, so sickly polite—I can't bear it." But Constantius had smiled and insisted on Basilios, who was famous for his knowledge far beyond the boundaries of Britain and besides had been the physician of the consular legate's wife when *her* child was born.

"I don't need a doctor at all—not for having a baby. It's absurd. Any experienced woman will do."

"My dear, that may be the custom of the Trinovantes—it is not Roman custom, except with the lower classes."

She had made faces at him, as always, when he teased her about her "tribe". The Trinovantes had long ceased being a tribe; they were a people now, had been a people

43

for many a generation. But Basilios had become a frequent visitor during the last months of her pregnancy. He had smiled at her changing moods, was overcourteous when she felt petulant, and never gave her an opportunity to let herself go. Once she had thrown a vase at him; he had calmly bent down and started picking up the pieces.

Now she was determined to make him think that she was asleep. But when he took her hand to feel her pulse, she wrenched it away.

"Can't you see I'm tired? Leave me alone."

Basilios did not reply, and she suddenly felt angry with herself. It was true he was only a slave, but it was not good form to treat slaves badly. Only the newly rich did that, to avenge themselves for their own humiliations—and people with really nasty characters. Perhaps I am a really nasty character, she thought, and for a brief moment enjoyed the idea. Then she dropped it. It was small and stupid. Instead she tried to return to the lovely feeling of sinking into soft sand. She was quite unaware of the new expression in the physician's eyes. Basilios was worried. She did not cooperate, and she seemed to have lost most of her energy in the last three days.

And there was that small pelvis. . . .

He left, again on tiptoe, and the smile with which he tried to reassure Constantius in the corridor was a little forced.

The tribune saw it. "It will be well for you if all goes well", he said harshly. "Otherwise . . ."

"All will be well", assured Basilios hastily. "I have had more difficult cases before, noble Tribune—no, don't enter now, the Domina wishes to sleep, and she will need all her strength. . . ."

He took his leave, and Constantius returned to his study, the last room of the right wing of the house. It was built,

44

like most of the more elegant villas, of wood on a stone foundation. The rooms were rectangular, the walls covered with painted plaster for ornament. Hypocausts heated three of the eight rooms; there was a large corridor in front, another, smaller one at the back of the house. The garden was well kept and shaded by trees and encircled by a stone wall covered with green tiles.

There was no noise, or almost none, although one was not more than half a mile from the *Domus palatina*, where the consular legate resided, in the very heart of Eburacum. And the Domus palatina was not only the heart of Eburacum: it was the heart of Britain as a whole. At least under Petronius Aquila it was. Under his predecessors there had been something like a division into halves: Eburacum had been the capital of the north, Londinium that of the south. It was not that Petronius Aquila was a particularly strong nature—though he was stronger than Caronius and superior in rank to him, as well. It was, really, because the Emperor did not take much interest in Britain for the time being. The division into halves was simply a matter of imperial policy. Split the country, and you split the army of occupation. Which means that if an ambitious commander in Britain has certain plans of his own, he won't have enough troops to put them into action.

Well, nothing of the kind was to be expected from Petronius Aquila. The Thirty-Fifth Legion had never come back from Gaul, where it had been sent a year and a half ago, together with three cavalry regiments and a number of auxiliary troops; nor had there been any replacements. There was one full legion in the north, another in the south, twelve cavalry regiments and perhaps twenty-five thousand auxiliaries, and a motley crowd they were, too. Not even forty thousand men, all told. You can't get ambitious on that. Not if you have any sense, and Petronius Aquila had sense.

It was just as well. There was no more stupid stroke of fate than to be forced into a rebellion by an ambitious superior—unless he was a military genius and succeeded. In most cases it meant a few months of cheerful conquering—that always happened at the initial stage—then a pitched battle, a resounding defeat and the end of a military career, and possibly worse than that. No, that sort of thing should be undertaken only at the right moment by the right man with a sufficient number of troops.

Constantius smiled thinly. Nice thoughts, for a mere tribune.

But a tribune need not stay a tribune all his life—especially not when he has earned the esteem of his superior, and Caronius was not getting any better in Aquæ Sulis. It was all very well for old potbelly to order the Twentieth about, have the men live in camps as though there were a war on instead of enjoying themselves in Londinium or Verulamium or Camulodunum—*he* was miles away taking his precious baths. He did not share their training—and he did not know what they said about him. But it all came here, to Eburacum, faithfully reported by the secret service. Caronius would last only a matter of six months—or a year at the utmost. . . .

Then the command of the Twentieth. Get real order into the rabble; Caronius was an old schoolmaster and moody—sometimes too sharp, sometimes too benign. A commander must be more balanced, and he must have a strong sense of justice. The officers will feel that at once, and so will the troops. Just treatment makes all the difference—and so does a sense of humor. Besides, as commander of the south one could set the damned lazy *coloniae* into motion and make them do things. Verulamium, for instance, was in a shocking state—if Aurelian or his successor should suddenly get the idea of making an inspection, there would be hades to pay. As for the coast defenses: Isca was practically useless, and so was Segontium. A string of entirely new fortresses would have to be built to safeguard the island against trouble—oh, stop it. We have not got there yet. Never mind—we'll get there. And then . . .

If only the child were a son! Basilios said one could not be sure, though it was likely. Likely, why? Because it was the father's wish? He had such a shifty look in his eyes, the blasted Greek. He's had more difficult cases before, he said. Why was this a difficult case? Helena was a healthy woman, she was young, she wanted the child more than anything else—she had said that time and again. Idiotic arrangement of nature—much easier with a horse or cow.

Seemed to have tamed her, this business of having a baby. . . .

That was something. But then, she would have come to see reason in time, anyway, the little firebrand. She'd never be popular with the wives of superiors—especially when they tried to be hoity-toity like Petronius Aquila's old hag, with her silly pride about being a member of the Marcian family. But she needn't be. Some fellows may try to get their step by making use of an attractive wife, but it was not the thing to do. To hades with it.

If only the child were a son! It might be born any day now, any hour, really. Durbovix, the Gallic butler, had told him that they were praying for the Domina in the servants' quarters. Well, that was the custom; Durbovix had only forestalled his orders, which showed that the man was clever.

For an instant Constantius thought of the statues of the *Lares* and *Penates*, the house gods, in the atrium. But then he dismissed the idea. He would burn some incense on the little altars when Helena's labor had started; it was the thing to do. The Gallic servants were praying to Hesus—Teutates, or Epona—no, that was the goddess of horses; and the British servants were praying to the Three Mothers, of course, and very likely to the whole host of minor deities: to Camulus and Ancasta and Harimella, to Vanauns, Viradecthis, and whatnot. Well, maybe they existed, and maybe they didn't. How was a man to know? As for Helena, she never spoke of these things. Better than jabbering about them all the time like Caronius' wife, who was so superstitious that at one time she had been suspected even of leanings toward that Jewish cult of Jesus, or whatever the man's name was, whom they had executed in Tiberius' time, or was it Caligula's? Well, what did it matter? Helena very likely had some odd ideas of her own, trust old Coellus for that; the Roman marriage ceremony in the little temple of Juno in Camulodunum had not impressed her much—the only thing that seemed to have mattered to her was the prayer her father had murmured over them both, in the old oak hall near Coel-castra. Some queer gibberish.

By Jove, it was difficult enough to believe in anything—except Fate, perhaps, or the three old girls who spun the thread of destiny; the Germans believed in them, too, called them the Norns or some such thing. Perhaps they were the same as the Three Mothers and they again the same as the Three Parcæs.

Well, all of you, what matters to me is that I get a son!—a strong, healthy son, to whom I shall leave a thunderous good job, one fine day. In thirty years' time, perhaps, or still better, in forty. There's no hurry. . . .

Here was Virginia, as pale as a sheet. What? It has started? "Where's Basilios? Send for him, at once. I'll kill the man

48

if he's not back before I can count to a hundred. Run, woman! Run!"

He ran himself, over to the left wing of the house; he pushed the slaves aside right and left and crashed into Helena's room. She was lying quite still, did not look at him, stared up at the ceiling. Only her hands twitched a little.

"Absurd", she said. "It's only started. It will take hours—and hours—and hours...."

Her voice was dry and toneless. Constantius began to talk, but he had no idea what he was saying. Then Basilios came and took over. Constantius saw that he was worried; it was quite obvious that the man was worried. Constantius began to utter threats, and Helena smiled a little. Virginia, the goose, began to howl.

All went well up to about midnight. The labor quickened, and Basilios made his patient stand up and clutch the curtains. Helena obeyed mechanically. The waves of pain had electrified her body into action; she had tried to suppress the urge to scream, but Basilios insisted on it. "Don't resist it—give in to it—all women scream at this stage, and even Jupiter himself screamed when Minerva sprang from his head...." She had wanted to laugh, but the pains did not allow her enough breathing space.

Constantius was now threatening the Lares and Penates on their altars in the atrium. He had given up threatening Basilios; the man was doing all he could, anyway.

Then, shortly after midnight, the labor ceased suddenly. At once Helena felt drained of all strength, of all will to fight. She wanted to sleep, to die, anything—it did not matter what happened so long as she could lie down and close her eyes. Basilios murmured incantations, prayers, curses; he was deadly pale, his forehead glistening with perspiration. A slave ran to fetch another medicine chest. There was a rare herb whose juice was supposed to make the labor start again, if one rubbed it over the belly. But he knew that this was not the only danger. The narrow pelvis . . .

At four o'clock in the morning the situation had become desperate. Despite all efforts labor had not started again; Helena was lying in complete apathy, motionless; her eyes were wide open, but she did not seem to see anything. When Constantius, beside himself, shouted her name, she did not answer. He had spent the last hour on his knees beside her bed. Now he rose slowly and looked at Basilios. The physician began to tremble. "The gods are against us, Domine", he whined. "I've done all I could—I am doing all I can—I—"

"Death to you", said Constantius in a low voice. "I wish you could die seven times, you dog."

"Domine, Domine, it is not my fault. The child is very big, and it is pressing against the pelvis—the labor is frustrated—and I can't get at it, as it lies—"

"What does that mean?"

"Domine, I may have to kill the child to save the mother—and even so—her pulse is weak, very weak—"

There was a flash and almost immediately a stroke of thunder.

Constantius took a step backward. With glassy eyes Basilios saw him drop the dagger. Two women slaves began to cry.

Lightning—thunder. Lightning—thunder.

Was Basilios right? Were the gods hostile? Generations of superstition stirred in his blood. He looked at Helena, just as another flash, another thunderclap occurred. She did not move.

He tried to think and could not. He did not know that neither could anyone else in the room; that they all were filled with a simple feeling rushing along the channels of their nerves—fear.

Rain began to splash outside, but that was not the only noise; nor was it thunder again, though it sounded not unlike it. It was earthly thunder, the thunder of hoofs in full gallop; and the rolling of wheels, louder and louder; and then silence.

Fear still hung over the room, and with it was its father, helplessness. No one seemed to be able to move; everyone's feet were glued to the floor; it was like one of those dreams in which one would like to run away from the most terrible danger and finds that one cannot. Another flash, weaker than the others—but, instead of the thunder, footsteps could be heard outside in the corridor.

A slave rushed in. "Domine, a visitor has—"

The thunder, rumbling at last, cut him short.

An instant later, the visitor entered the room. He glanced sharply at Helena, took a deep breath, and then looked at the rest of them and made a short, imperious gesture. "Leave me alone with her, son."

In Constantius' eyes a glimmer of hope came and went. "Father, we have—"

"Obey, son."

Constantius hesitated—but it was only for a short moment.

Then he bowed and left the room, making a sign for the others to follow him. Basilios alone risked another instant of hesitation; a look from the visitor's eyes chased him away like a whipped dog.

Alone, King Coel walked straight up to Helena's bed. He did not uncover her. He just bent down and made a few passes over her eyes and her forehead. When she awoke, she smiled a little. He, too, smiled. "Get up, child", he said.

"I—I can't, Father."

"Get up, child."

She got up. He did not even help her. "Walk toward me", he commanded. As she did so, he slowly drew backward. She began to moan. "My back, Father, my back—I—"

"Walk toward me—"

She walked clumsily, step by step. There was a large table at the end of the room. King Coel brushed Basilios' medicine chest off it, some goblets and plates, even the rug that covered it.

"Lie down on this, child."

She obeyed, but this time he had to help her. The table was high. He laid a gnarled old hand on her swollen belly with a gesture of infinite tenderness, and she felt that he blessed her and that she was home and at peace. The room seemed very deep and silent. She was staring at the ceiling, but there was an expression in her eyes now—a new expectancy, the forerunner of joy.

"Stand up", said King Coel.

Action was demanded; it was the same tone in which he had ordered her to stand up when he brushed her hair, years and years ago, when she was a little girl. He had always brushed her hair before she went to sleep and when she got up. "You have no mother", he had said once—only once. "So I must brush your hair." She had never forgotten the voice in which he had said that—soft and clear like a woman's. And then he had said, "Stand up", in quite a different tone, just as he did now—hard and strong and like iron.

"Stand up! On the table!"

She stood on the table; her head was very near the ceiling, and she felt a slight dizziness. Her back began to ache again, more violently than before; her feet were unwilling to support her weight. It was impossible to conceive that once she had run through the forest, jumped brooks, danced. . . .

"Bend backward, child!"

He was standing behind her now. She could feel his presence like that of a friendly army, backing up the fighter. But she could not bend backward; she could not.

"I am here—my arms are open, child—bend—bend!"

He caught her, and she felt herself drawn backward, very slowly. Suddenly he gave her body a vicious jerk from left to right, and she screamed, screamed so that it chilled the blood of all those huddled in the corridor.

"Stand up again!" thundered the old man. "Stand up, Elen! I have sired royal blood, have I not?"

She stood. There was blood on her underlip, but she stood.

He came into sight now, huge and erect, his eyes blazing. He opened his arms.

"Jump, Elen!"

She looked down. The floor was far away; it was an abyss, a chasm, bottomless, the void. This was the end. Her head spun; she raised her arms like a bird's wings, laughed, and jumped down, into his arms. Her feet gave; it seemed to her as though she were sinking to the middle of the earth; but beyond her own scream she heard, she heard the victorious roar that came from King Coel's mouth: "Enter— all of you!"

Then at last she fainted.

When she came to, she saw Constantius' face bent over her in anxiety. She saw him, but her eyes were fixed with magic force on the cradle where her son lay.

King Coel was sitting beside the cradle, quietly gazing at the child. The curtains had been drawn, and daylight was flooding into the room.

"Give him to me", she said. "Give me my son."

The old man lifted the little bundle with great care and brought it over. "It is good breeding", he said. It did not seem to surprise him in the least that she knew about the child's sex.

Her eyes were eating and drinking.

"He was born at sunrise", said King Coel. "What are you going to call him?"

"Constantine", said Constantius quickly.

The King laughed. "Constantine—the *little* Constantius. It is well that he should be called after his father, for he will do as his father, though he will be greater than the father."

The tribune wanted to reply, but Helena laid a tired white hand on his arm. She had seen her father's eyes.

"He will own all the land he rides on", said King Coel softly. "He will be bliss to his mother and death to his son. And he will live to see the Tree of Life."

CHAPTER 2

"UP, SHIELD," said the centurion. "Higher up—up! That's right. Only the eyes must be above it. When the enemy's sending a salvo of arrows over, you needn't raise the shield—just bow your head an inch, and you're safe. Like this—see?"

"I'd never do that", said the boy angrily. "Why, the enemy'd think I was afraid of him!"

The giant centurion grinned. "Would he be right?"

The boy flushed deeply. "Of course not! How dare you—"

"That's easy, then", said Marcus Favonius—they called him "Facilis" in the Twentieth, because everything was easy to him. Stalk a Numidian patrol in the desert: easy. Build a camp with first- and second-class defenses after a march of fourteen hours: easy. Clear an inn of a dozen drunken gladiators who have got troublesome: easy. "You're not afraid, but the enemy thinks you are. Excellent! You couldn't be in a better position. You've completely deceived the enemy about the true situation—a very definite advantage. An enemy befuddled is an enemy half beaten."

But the boy shook his head vigorously. "I don't want anybody to think that I'm afraid", he persisted. "Watch out—I'm going to attack you!"

"Very old-fashioned, that", grunted Favonius. "We don't announce an attack; we just attack these days—and anyway, keep that shield up, or I'll get you before you can get me—there you are!"

The boy stumbled back, as the centurion's spear ripped the shield off his arm. Instead of trying to retrieve it, he lowered his head and attacked again, ram fashion. He was so quick that the veteran soldier only just had time to throw his shield forward, and again the boy stumbled back, holding his head.

"Metal is harder than bone", said Favonius phlegmatically. "Who taught you barbarian tricks like that, Constantine? I'm sure I didn't. Come on, pick up that shield and fight like a Roman. It's easy."

The pair in the pergola overlooking the lawn were sitting quite still, watching it all. Constantius saw a glint of anxiety in his wife's eyes. "It's all right", he said. "Favonius knows his job."

"Of course he does", was the reply. "I'm not worried about that. But Constantine's still uncontrolled—that temper of his will get him into trouble one day, and he will not keep his guard up. There he goes again, the silly little fool."

Constantius smiled contentedly. He had chosen Marcus Favonius as his son's military tutor—but it had been Helena's wish that he should do so. She was a magnificent mother. He couldn't help comparing her with the set of Roman ladies he knew in Milan and Rome and Naples. Helena was much more a Roman matron than any of that lot: Domitilla or Sabina or Vipsania. Helena might have belonged to the time of the Republic, when women were men and men half-gods. Today women were lap dogs or bitches, and men were women.

"That's better", said Helena. "He'll learn it yet. Did you see that? Nice thrust. And he's tenacious, too. What are you grinning about, Legate Constantius?"

Her husband laughed outright. "That's easy, as Favonius would say. I'm grinning because I'm happy. I'm happy because I have got you and that brat over there. Look out, he's going wrong again. There, he got it. Serves him right for laying himself wide open, the little ass. He's bleeding, too."

"He's not crying", said Helena with satisfaction. But she moved uneasily in her chair.

The Greek pedagogue came hurrying up, with a stern expression on his wrinkled face. "Domine, Constantine is already late for his literature lessons. And now I see him prostrate and bleeding—how can he learn his Pindar, his Anacreon—"

"I don't approve of Anacreon", said Constantius.

"I don't think much of literature", murmured Helena.

The Greek began to plead, to entreat; how could he be responsible for the education of the young master if he did not have the support and appreciation of his master's parents; how could a boy of almost thirteen years of age—

"Twelve and four months", said Helena.

"—of twelve years and four months be expected to become a scholar, when he spent all his time in hitting a fully grown man and being hit by him in return—"

"I don't want the boy to become a scholar. I want him to be a soldier like his father", said Helena. "Go away, Philostratos—I want to watch this. He's picking himself up at last."

"Go, friend", nodded Constantius, and there was a twinkle in his eye. "Go and tell Homer and Pindar and the rest of them that the world cannot consist only of those who write about heroic deeds—there must also be a few who are capable of performing them."

The unfortunate pedagogue withdrew, smiling unhappily.

"Poor old Philostratos", said Constantius.

"They should have given him another name", ventured Helena. "'He who loves the army' is singularly inept. Ah, very good! He's learned it now. Lovely!"

The boy's renewed attack had been perfect. "I'm practically dead", said Favonius. "See? That was just right. Once you know the trick, it's easy. That'll do for today."

"Once more, Favonius, only once ..."

"Enough. Come along, soldier."

The boy beamed. Favonius never called him that unless he was really satisfied. They marched up to the couple in the pergola.

Helena saw at once that the wound was only a scratch, and she looked at Favonius with smiling approval.

The centurion saluted with his spear. "Training time up, sir", he said. "Progress satisfactory."

Constantius nodded. "I've seen it, Favonius. Go to old Rufus in the kitchen and tell him I've sent you. He'll know what to do."

"Thank you, sir", said Favonius gravely and marched off. Rufus, formerly Constantius' aide-de-camp, was now inspector of the household, much to the annoyance of Durbovix, the butler. Rufus and Favonius had served together in the Twentieth and were old friends.

"Tired, Constantine?" asked Helena.

An almost contemptuous "no" was stopped at the last moment; "yes, a little" was being pondered; then the boy said somewhat sulkily, "Not really."

"What is 'truth' in Greek?" asked Helena innocently.

"*Aléteia*", answered the boy mechanically.

She nodded. "You know it in Greek—and you know it in life, too. You needn't have your Greek lesson today, if you don't want to. Father and I are going for a ride. Care to come with us?"

Her eyes were dancing. Constantine threw his arms around her neck. "Mother is so funny, Father. She always reads me."

"She reads me, too", laughed Constantius, meeting her eyes. "Poor Philostratos, what chance has he got against that combination of powers?"

Constantine frowned deeply; then his little face lit up.

"We could buy him a piece of sea gold", he said. "There are many in Bojorix' shop in the Via Nomentina. He likes sea gold. I've still got that silver piece you gave me last week."

"Bribery and corruption", laughed Constantius, but Helena was pleased. "That's a very good idea. We'll do that."

As they were walking along the patterned pavement toward the house, Constantius began to wonder a little where Bojorix had got the sea gold. It was not to be found in Britain, but came from a country far away in the northeast— Estonia. The Estonians exchanged it for wine and leather goods. There was a lively trade going on with some German tribes across the Rhine; the sea gold, or "elektron" as they called it in the south, came into Gaul and into the lands of the Belges, Jutes, Frisians, and Angles. But it was from Gessoriacum that the stuff got into Britain, and all the ships arriving from or departing to that port came under his own jurisdiction. He saw the lists with the cargoes of every single ship. There had been no elektron among the cargoes for the last year or more. How could Bojorix' shop be full of it? Had the goods been shipped across the straits in secret? And if so, what other goods had been shipped across? Arms, perhaps?

The military situation in Britain was a joke. It had been bad enough under Petronius Aquila. It was far, far worse now. Just when he had got the Twentieth into shape, half the legion had been ordered away to Gaul, where they were still battling with insurrections. A legion and a half of regular troops for the whole of Britain! Auxiliaries, too, had been ordered to various other provinces, and the Emperor's agents in such matters had a knack of picking the best material.

If there was any arms smuggling going on, and if it was more than one little chieftain or other having a bit of fun, then something had to be done and done quickly. He decided to pay a visit to Bojorix' shop and to ask a few friendly questions.

But when they entered the house, Durbovix came up to them, bowing. Constantius saw that the man was deadly pale and that he was perspiring profusely. "What's the matter with you, man? Are you ill?"

The butler took a deep breath. "An imperial envoy to see you, Domine. The Prefect Allectus."

Constantius' mouth twitched a little, but his voice was perfectly calm as he replied, "Very well, Durbovix, show the Prefect in."

Durbovix retired on somewhat wobbly legs, and husband and wife looked at each other.

"In other times," drawled Constantius, "this might have meant—er—something rather unpleasant. But Diocletian is not Nero or Commodus."

"Do you know the envoy?"

"Allectus . . . I don't really remember. Anyway, that settles my riding, I'm afraid."

Constantine made a long face. "Why don't we take him with us, Father—perhaps he would like to get some sea gold, too. . . ."

"Quiet, Constantine", said Helena.

"You ride with him", suggested Constantius. "I shall have to work with Allectus. I suppose he'll want still more troops."

"Let me stay with you", she begged.

He shook his head, smiling. "He's come to see me here, at my house rather than at the office. Therefore both of us must receive him. But then he and I shall have to work."

Durbovix reappeared, ushering the envoy in. The Prefect Allectus was a tall man, well built, with the head of a bird of prey. Helena saw a pair of cold, gray eyes and a mobile, sensual mouth. As he was carrying his helmet under his arm, she could see his hair, which was of a clear brown, with a reddish tinge. Perhaps he had some German blood in him—there were quite a number of Germans serving in the armies of Rome.

She did not dislike him until he smiled, after Constantius made the introductions—a gray, twisted smile, as false as the sea. And he had long, yellow teeth, like those of a horse.

"You will wish to discuss important matters", she made herself say. "My son and I beg to be excused."

The prefect bowed to her; she acknowledged it with a little nod and swept past him, beckoning Constantine to follow her. The boy had behaved very well, with a natural dignity that filled her with pride, and she had been happy to see the ghost of a proud smile on the lips of her husband, too.

"Come, Constantine", she said. "We are going to the stables. You can choose your own horse, today."

To her surprise there was no outburst of joy, yet she knew how keen a rider he was. Horses meant everything to him. It was, of course, a great disappointment that his father could not come with them; it was to her, too.

"I don't think much of him", said Constantine severely. "Favonius could beat him easily, don't you think so, Mother? He's got hair like a fox. Why has he come, Mother?"

"I don't know, Constantine."

"I hope he'll go away soon", said the boy with some bitterness. After a while he added, "I could beat him, too, in a year or so, I'm sure."

But then they reached the stables, and he forgot all about the rest of the world. It was sheer pleasure seeing him choose his mount; he could ride like a centaur. Time and again she had thought of her father's strange prophecy on the day of the boy's birth: "He will own all land he rides on." She had reminded him of that, when they paid him a visit in Camulodunum, three months ago, but he had only nodded silently. He was very old now, but men still came from all parts of the land for his advice or his help. They got it, too.

She and Constantius had watched him once for three solid hours, settling disputes, arranging and rearranging the affairs of obstinate, quarrelsome, stupid people, with infinite patience, tact, and wisdom.

"What an Emperor he would have been", was Constantius' verdict. She could still see him, sitting on a simple chair in his courtyard, with his unruly white hair flowing in the wind. Next to him stood that young man, Hilary, "his aide-de-camp", as Constantius said, but he was more than that—he was his valet, his staff, and his bodyguard all in one; a beautiful, honest face with the eyes of a dreamer. It was good to know he was looking after the old man.

"Which is your horse, Mother?" repeated Constantine for the third time. She awoke. "I'll have Boreas", she said.

Constantine gave a sigh of relief. When Mother became dreamy like she had just now, there was always the danger that she might change her mind about something. But she hadn't, and Boreas was a good horse. He approved of the choice. It was going to be a ride. . . .

Constantius was reading the imperial letter standing, as was the custom; he knew that Allectus was watching him like a lynx, but it was easy to show the desired reaction. The letter was in the nature of a manifesto announcing to the Divine Emperor Diocletianus' commanders in the field, garrisons, and provinces that the Divine Emperor had deigned to elevate the most illustrious Cæsar Maximianus to imperial rank with the title of Augustus; that Maximianus Augustus would be supreme ruler of Italy and Africa, of Spain, Gaul, and Britain, whereas Diocletianus Augustus would be as before supreme ruler of Thrace, Egypt, and Asia; that the commanders of all troops in the regions and countries delegated to the rule of Maximianus would make their troops swear loyalty to the new Emperor. The rest was a panegyric about the virtues and qualities of the new co-ruler. The letter was written in the customary purple ink and sealed with the Emperor's hand seal.

"This is indeed great news", said Constantius slowly. "The Divine Emperor has deigned to follow the example of Nerva and of Marcus Antoninus—an example that has always proved a blessing to the Empire."

"Quite so", said Prefect Allectus.

"He could not have made a better choice", went on Constantius. "The first statesman and the first soldier of the Empire: What better guarantee could there be for the safety and well-being of the state?"

"Quite so", said Prefect Allectus.

"I shall give orders to the troops under my command to assemble for the necessary ceremony. I take it that you will wish to be present—unless your duties call you to proceed to Eburacum in order to inform my colleague there ..."

"Before I answer that", said Allectus, "permit me to present to you a second imperial message."

"A second message?"

"Here it is."

Constantius bowed as he received the heavily sealed scroll; when he had cut the strings, his first glance was for the signature: it was that of Maximianus. The new Emperor did not lose much time. It was gratifying to see that he could write his name—which was more than one could expect from the son of a peasant. But then, Diocletianus himself was even less than a peasant's offspring. His parents had been slaves in the house of a Roman senator, Anulinus. They came from Dalmatia; Maximianus had been born in Sirmium, like Aurelian, of late and lamented memory. And now the son of a slave and the son of a peasant were co-rulers of the Roman Empire.

The letter was short: "Maximianus Augustus to the Legate Constantius, greetings. We are expecting you at the earliest convenience in Rome for the discussion of urgent affairs of state. You will choose the commander to represent you during your absence." That was all.

"When do you think you can leave for Rome, Legate?" asked Allectus. He knew, then, the content of the letter; well, that was natural. One did not send a man of rank to deliver a message blindly.

"As soon as the troops have taken the oath, I suppose", drawled Constantius. "That's in three days' time——"

But Allectus shook his head. "Unless the elements themselves are against you, the Divine Emperor will not be pleased by such delay. My orders are to place my own ship, the *Titan*, at your disposal; she is a fast post ship."

Constantius raised his brows. "Have you come all the way from Rome in the *Titan*, Prefect?"

There was a moment of hesitation before Allectus replied. "No. I traveled by land up to Gessoriacum."

Constantius was interested. "You have seen the admiral of the fleet there, I take it."

"I have seen Carausius", nodded Allectus.

"A very great man—in his own way, I'm told."

"A devoted servant of the Divine Emperors", said Allectus stiffly. Constantius saw that his eyes were glittering strangely.

"Of course", he said searchingly. "Although it is said that he comes from very simple stock——"

"A man from simple stock can go far, these days", said the prefect, with a dangerous smile. "You have some imperial blood, Constantius—I believe you are related to the late Emperor Claudius; perhaps you do not approve of men who make their way up from the ranks?"

64

Constantius smiled back. "Such disapproval would be worse than stupidity, Allectus; it would be folly. A man does not set fire to the ladder on which he is standing."

The prefect changed the subject. "Whom are you going to appoint commander in your stead?"

"The Tribune Gaius Valerius."

Allectus raised his reddish brows. "Do you regard him as sufficiently experienced for the command of so great a number of troops?"

Constantius lost his patience. "If I didn't, I wouldn't appoint him. You will, I hope, credit me with sufficient knowledge to handle my own affairs."

The prefect was alarmed. "Nothing could have been further from my mind than to offend a commander whose very merits make his advice so valuable to the Divine Emperor that he cannot wait until he sees him to receive it. But surely it is unusual to put a tribune, however experienced, in command of a full legion and perhaps fifteen thousand auxiliaries. . . ."

Constantius laughed outright. "If the Emperor has an adviser in me, he most certainly has a courtier in you, Allectus. But surely you know that my command does not embrace—"

He stopped himself; there was something like greed in Allectus' face, something that wanted to be fed, to be satisfied, saturated, fulfilled—what was it? At the same time the natural precaution of the military commander was aroused, though only for the fraction of a moment. The figures were secret, naturally, but just as naturally they need not be concealed from an Imperial envoy. It was hardly credible that he did not know that himself. Yet, he had talked of a full legion, as though he did not know that Constantius had only half a legion under his command. The figure for the auxiliaries for the southern part of the province was wrong as well, too high by about five thousand men.

On the other hand, Allectus might well be more of a courtier than a soldier—in which case he would not have troubled much about the actual figures; his job was to deliver a message to Constantius and not to check up on the army lists. It was quite absurd to be suspicious; there simply was no motive. But perhaps Allectus wished to imply that the command of all troops stationed in Britain should be given into the hands of the commander in the north—and that was Curio now, Caronius' former aide-de-camp. Ah, that was it, of course! Allectus was worried lest he might insist on a split command during his absence. Yet, surely as a prefect he was soldier enough to know that Curio as a legate and commander of a legion was automatically superior in rank to a mere tribune like Valerius.

All this went through his head in a flash—so quickly that the pause was almost imperceptible, before he went on.

"—My command does not embrace the troops in the north. The Legate Curio will be the soldier highest in rank during my absence. He has got seniority even over me, though as you know that does not imply too much. But you were going to tell me whether your mission will lead you to him, also."

"I shall have to go to Eburacum in due course," nodded Allectus, "but I would be grateful to you, if you would kindly introduce the Tribune Valerius to me before you leave."

"That is simple—he will dine with us tonight."

The prefect was delighted. "And you, Constantius? Do you think you will be able to leave tomorrow? The Divine Emperor was most insistent about it—"

"Where is your ship? Or, rather—my ship?"

"In Anderida. They are taking foodstuffs on board already."

"Very well. I shall leave tomorrow. In the meantime I hope you will accept my poor hospitality. We are provincials, my Allectus, and we cannot offer you the luxuries of Rome—"

The prefect tittered into his hand. "You are too kind; I am only a simple soldier—and I have spent the last weeks either on horseback or in Gallic wagons. The gods alone know what I have done to merit the punishment of traveling in those wagons. I couldn't get decent horses most of the way. The province is in an abominable state. Your house is a haven of peace, noble Constantius—a haven of peace. . . ."

Constantius wondered a little whether there could be such an animal as a stupid fox.

CHAPTER 3

HE WILL COME TO ME, thought Helena. He will come, and I want him to come, more than ever before I want him to come, and yet I know that it would be better if he were gone; much better. I am tired and dumb and laden with fear and the loneliness of the future. He will remember me tired and fearful and pathetic.

She tried to be angry with her thoughts, but her will did not obey her. She dismissed the two Gallic slave girls who had helped her undress and went over to the large window.

There was the garden, the lawn where Constantine had fought with his trainer; there was the pergola where they had sat watching them, this afternoon. It seemed years ago.

It was in another life. It was another woman who had been happy.

Now the garden seemed strangely small and dark; one, two, three steps and there was the end of it and the road and the trees behind the road and the fields behind the trees and a river and houses and again fields and then the coast and the sea, like another, darker sky. Water and water and water, she knew all about it—the stormy gulf and the Spanish coast and the Pillars of Hercules and the Mediterranean. And somewhere at the end of endlessness, Ostia, the port of Rome, and Rome itself. He had come from Rome, and Rome was taking him back.

It was an unbearable thought that he had not yet gone— that this night and the farewell and all the pitiful show of fortitude and serenity were still in front of her. Perhaps he felt it, too, and would not come to her after all.

Perhaps, if he came, it would be because he thought that she expected him to come.

She rose in flaming anger against her weakness; pride was flowing through her veins in a glowing stream, and she felt her beauty renewing itself and with it a new expectancy.

There was no moon over the garden and but few stars. Why don't they shine tonight, she thought fiercely, and she raised her arms as though to invoke them to appear before her, as the Druids did on the feast of the Three Mothers.

When Constantius entered he found her gazing at the sky with a strange intensity. "There are more now", she said. "Many more. But one has gone."

Her body yielded to his arms in tremulous surrender, but when he, at last, withdrew his lips from hers he saw that her eyes were starless, and he felt that if he knew her for a thousand years there would still be something in her, a dark, tranquil light, a flame without heat, that no man could understand.

She was watching his sleep as she sometimes did her child's sleep. Constantine was growing more like him every day. There was that same curve between lip and chin, self-willed and yet ready to laugh at the slightest provocation; there was the way his hair grew, dark brown and glossy and thick, and the firm outline of the eyebrows, almost straight.

He had talked to her, and she had listened, thinking of many things that were her own and of which he would never know—yet she had heard every word he said. The invitation to Rome was what he had been waiting for ever since he had started on the road to the top. It had to come, and now it had come.

His first wild passion had gone out of him and he was at one with all the world, happy and childlike; he talked of Rome and Allectus and Maximianus as a boy talks about a game he loves. "Allectus is a stupid fox—both stupid and a fox; he thinks he's clever and stumbles all the time over his own cleverness. A snooper, of course—they always send that type, and then the type goes and writes long reports which no one ever reads; certainly Maximianus won't. Our new Divine Master is almost illiterate—I don't think he's read more than half a dozen letters in his life, and certainly not a single book. All he knows about is soldiering, but there he's great. Funny how we always seem to raise to the highest rank these men who have had only soldiers' training. It's the old She Wolf's instinct, I suppose; she has always had it—"

Fox, yes, but not only fox; and was he stupid? During the meal he had repeated Roman gossip, for her benefit, as he thought; his mobile, sensual lips forming bubbles of scandal, each of which was followed by that awful smile, like the painted smile of a courtesan. Sturdy little Valerius had hardly said a word, though it was obvious that he had been vastly impressed by the elegant guest from the Imperial City. Even the way Allectus praised Helena's hospitality had had a slightly condescending note. And his eyes always remained cold and observant.

She hated him: he was an enemy, dangerous and treacherous, the more so as Constantius underrated him. She hated him because he had stolen her last evening with Constantius and because he was in Constantius' thoughts even now, when he was lying next to her. Un-Roman as Allectus was, he was the symbol of Rome, always dividing happiness in order to rule. She felt rebellious, as in the old days, when the very sight of a Roman tunic had made her grit her teeth. Constantius had overcome all that, and Allectus had brought it back.

It was wrong, wrong, wrong! She was confusing the issue all the time. She was simply unhappy because he must leave her, why not face it?

Then Constantius had grown more serious; he had spoken of his plans, and she knew that he had never spoken of them to anyone else but her, and she was proud and happy again. She had been his wife for over thirteen years, and she had given him a son; they were part of each other. His greatness was her greatness, and if his greatness was Rome, then so was hers. Rome had long ceased being Roman in the narrow sense of the word. How many of the Emperors had been Romans? Diocletianus was a Dalmatian; Maximian, like Aurelian, came from Sirmium; Carus and Probus had been born far away from Italian soil. Their careers had always been the same in a sense—they had been army men. If Constantius—

It was no good playing hide-and-seek with oneself. Yes, she had considered it possible that he, too, might one day achieve the absolute top, and it was possible. With men of his stature and character everything was possible. This was the age of opportunity, and the only outside factor was chance.

When she was very young she had looked at every single one of his brother officers as a potential danger to his career. Constantius had never tired of teasing her about it; that was the time when she had tried to scheme and intrigue; he had not been amused, and once or twice there had been wild scenes.

It had not been easy learning the way to be the wife of a Roman officer. It was such a tiny sector of the whole, life in a garrison town: Eburacum first, when Constantius became first aide-de-camp to Petronius Aquila; then his present command as legate of South Britain. Many a time when he had gone over to Gaul to hunt with old army friends, she might have accompanied him and did not. And when he had gone far north for the expedition against the three Caledonian tribes who had, for once, united to stir up trouble, he had stayed away for the better part of six months. She had been worried, of course; she had fretted, and it had not been an easy time—but it was, somehow, quite different from now. Now he was going to Rome. . . .

The Caledonian expedition had been pure soldiering. Curio, the legate in the north, had been ill, and Constantius had had to do the job for him and had done it. Done it so well, in fact, that the grouchy frustrated old legate could not but send a glowing report to Rome. Probus had been Emperor, then; they changed so quickly, these days, one almost lost count. And most of them were murdered—almost all of them were murdered. But that would not happen to Constantius, and she knew who was going to see to that.

She wanted him to get on top—wanted it, wanted it. She smiled back at the time when she saw herself as a ruler like Boadicea, like Zenobia. Woman was not born to rule—directly. Cleopatra had been wiser—at first. But she had not played a clever game later on; Marc Antony was not the sort of man on whom one could rely. He was loyal enough—but too fond of pleasure. And Cleopatra had not known how to measure her own pleasures. She had been too greedy. But then, she had only been infatuated with him; she had not really loved him. She had loved Cæsar—perhaps.

"Do you think that Cleopatra really loved Cæsar, Constantius?"

But he was asleep now. Father used to say that when a man was asleep, his mind was traveling either into the past or into the future, but that he forgot either when he awoke, except for a moment or two. Perhaps Constantius' mind was soaring forward into Rome, where he would talk with the new Emperor—or back to the time when he and she had first met, in the fog, near the coast.

It was difficult to think that she had been that girl who hated all that was Roman and who wanted to be Zenobia. If it was difficult for a man in power not to despise those under him, it was almost impossible for a woman. But to rule through the man one loves, that was different. Constantius was going to Rome—that was the first step to real power.

It was a thing to be glad about. And he would not be away any longer than when he had gone to fight the Caledonians, and perhaps much less long. Of course, the Emperor might give him a command somewhere else. But in that case she would be allowed to follow him. It was a thing to be glad about. Why wasn't she glad?

She was sending part of herself to Rome, to wrestle for power and honors. She was sending her own right arm, part of her own brain. There he was, next to her, a tall, pale man, resting. Her right arm. Part of her brain. Go—get the prize. I want it. Do you know how much I want it? Do you? Maximianus, the son of a peasant. Diocletianus, the son of slaves. You are more then they, aren't you, Constantius?

From far away in her mind came a roar, the roar of an old, old voice: "I have sired royal blood, have I not?"

Blood tells, Constantius. Go and get the prize.

She bent over him as though to breathe her thoughts into his mind. Her body, still smooth and slim, had the tautness of a cat about to jump.

You and I, Constantius—let's rule the world, shall we? Imperial blood of Rome and royal blood of Britain: What chance has a peasant's son, and the offspring of slaves? You have never said it in so many words, but I know the thought is in you, and it is not slumbering. It is a hidden flame as it is in myself. Go and get the prize . . . even if it takes you years to get it—it will take you years. We can wait, you and I. We are young. But don't let us wait too long. There are the first few gray hairs on your temples, husband. There are none in mine, yet—but soon there may be. Let us get power when we are still able to enjoy it.

He stirred in his sleep, and she drew back. But he did not wake up. Was there a chill in the room, suddenly? It was long after midnight—only a few hours between now and his departure. What had come over her? What madness, what insane dream—she had thought she had banished it, years ago, back into the glittering depth from which it had come.

Power. Could she have been happier, as Empress, as the ruler of the whole world, than she had been all these years? Who was that woman who had been breathing thoughts into the ear of a sleeping man?

She rose and glided to the window. Over there, to the northeast, were Camulodunum and her father's house. Perhaps he could hear her thoughts, as she had often thought he could, when she was little. Am I two women, Father, instead of one? One who wants power and another who wants her husband and her child and does not care for the rest of the world? Did the gods breathe twice into me when I quickened in my mother's womb?

But he had never answered questions about the gods.

And the gods never seemed to answer questions about themselves.

I shall go to see Father, she thought. As soon as Constantius has gone, I shall go to see Father. It is weakness, of course; it is the same weakness that makes men kneel at the altars of so many gods and goddesses and ask and hope for an answer even when they know so well at the bottom of their hearts that there is no answer and that their own question, their own prayer is being thrown back at them like an echo.

She looked around at the sleeper; she could hear him breathe, deeply and regularly—and yet she felt that he had gone already, diving into the glittering depth to get the prize; that her wish had been an invocation—as irrevocable as an arrow that had left the bowstring; and that she was alone—alone and fearful.

CHAPTER 4

"THE NEW CEREMONIAL," said the imperial chamberlain nervously, "introduced by their Divine Majesties, the Emperors Diocletianus and Maximianus, may the gods give them long life and immortal victory, is as follows: you will enter the Inner Court at a distance of five paces behind me—you will be introduced to the prefect of the Domestic Guards. You will enter the Circular Room, where we shall be joined by other visitors. We shall then ascend the Great Staircase to the Audience Room—what did you say your name was?"

"I am the Legate Constantius."

"Of course, of course; I have your name here—" The imperial chamberlain fidgeted with a large gilt-edged scroll. Constantius saw that it contained hundreds of names, so that the question was more or less excusable. Inexcusable was the fact that the imperial chamberlain had the movements and mannerisms of a frightened old lady and that he used cosmetics. "Very well then, Legate Constantius; your place in the formation at the Great Staircase is between the Legate Bassianus and the Legate Terentius. We shall—"

"Aulus Terentius? Of the Fourteenth?"

The painted face became sulky. "Yes, yes—but I most urgently entreat you not to interrupt me. The new ceremonial is somewhat complicated, and I have many duties to attend to and very little time to do so. Where was I? Oh, yes—from the Great Staircase we shall proceed to the Audience Room. In single file, if you please. In the Audience Room the chief chamberlain, Sempronius, will take over the introduction. His Imperial Majesty may or may not enter the Audience Room—if he does, you will prostrate yourself to the ground as soon as the signal is given by the sound of a trumpet."

Constantius could not believe his ears. Roman legates to prostrate themselves like slaves? The chamberlain was rattling on, but he paid no attention. What on earth had become of Rome! There had been a good deal of grumbling in army circles about the Empire going to the dogs, but that was what disgruntled officers always say when things do not work out as they want. Bribery, underhanded methods, scheming, corruption—yes, certainly. But an imitation of the worst oriental manners—why, not even Heliogabalus had risked this sort of thing. He had imitated the Orient only to the extent that he liked dressing up as an oriental female for his disgusting practices; he had surrounded himself with his kind of lovers and distributed high offices in proportion to their amorous qualities. But Heliogabalus had never dared to encompass the army in his oriental nonsense.

The chamberlain was still jabbering about "formal address" and "official title" and what could and could not be said in the presence of the Divine Emperor.

"Very well", snapped Constantius. "That's all I can digest in one lesson. I've come here to report, not to learn oriental gymnastics."

The chamberlain shrugged a tired shoulder. "Suit yourself, noble Legate—but don't blame me when things go wrong. Our Divine Emperor is not always lenient."

"I haven't heard of Maximianus being lenient, ever", grinned Constantius. "Now then, lead me to it. The Inner Court was the first thing, wasn't it?"

The Inner Court was the first thing. The chamberlain's mincing steps made Constantius itch to give him a resounding kick in the region where his seat was hidden by a long, beautifully embroidered cloak. Perhaps the chamberlain knew he evoked that sort of feeling, and that was why he insisted on a distance of five paces. . . .

Hannibalianus, prefect of the Domestic-Guards, was a big, burly fellow in a uniform resplendent with gold. "How's Britain?" he asked gruffly, as though to show that he knew all about the visitor. He did not wait for an answer, however, but turned back to inspect the sentries placed at equal distances all along the walls.

The chamberlain was mincing on through a broad corridor, also studded with sentries, into the Circular Room, where about a hundred distinguished people made distinguished noise.

Constantius recognized Terentius and sailed straight into the crowd. "Greetings, dear old Pigface", he said warmly. "Been a lifetime. You look just the same. How is the old Fourteenth?"

"By Jove," said the energetic little officer, blinking, "if it isn't young Constantius; and you haven't changed either—how long is it?—no, I think I won't figure it out. But you disappoint me, Constantius; I thought you'd come back all nice and blue—they do paint themselves with woad, don't they?"

"Easy now, Pigface", laughed Constantius. "I married a British girl, you know. Got a son, too—he's almost thirteen and will hold his own against the best rider in the Fourteenth ... unless the rascals have changed a lot since I saw them last."

"They haven't", grinned Terentius. "Never will. Just as well, too. So you've gone native, eh? Well, I don't see why you shouldn't. Nice about your son. Send him to me, when he's old enough, and I'll teach him a few tricks. I picked up one or two new ones in the Egyptian campaign, must tell you about it. There wasn't much to it, it's only a preparation, cleaning up for things to come."

"Persia, you mean?"

"Yes. They are due for it."

"You mentioned my having gone native—but it seems to me that you all have, here at home, from what my exquisite friend, the chamberlain, tells me!"

"Of course we have. We're all damned orientals now." Terentius looked around, but there was no one near enough to have heard what he had said; everybody was prattling away, with little groups spread all over the room; the chamberlain had disappeared.

"They can't help it, you know", murmured Terentius. "They know they are simple men—to make a big show is their only way to hammer it in that they are divine. We've taken over Persian ceremonial—it's the only Persian conquest we've made so far."

"Any idea who is going to have the command?"

"Well, it's not really our affair—we're Maximianus' babies; Diocletian will deal with it; but the old man won't go himself, take it from me. My tip is Galerius."

"Whose father was a shepherd."

"Oh, but you're wrong, friend. Galerius himself was a shepherd. No one knows what his father was—not even Galerius."

They both laughed. "It's good to have you here", said Constantius. "This oriental nonsense depresses me."

"Pigface and Paleface rubbing their noses in the imperial carpet", growled Terentius. "It's a fine state of affairs. Any idea why you have been ordered away from Britain?"

"Not the slightest. Had a visit from one Allectus, prefect of something or other, with a letter from the Emperor—"

"Maximianus?"

"Yes—saying 'come here at once', I boarded a ship and sailed off. My orders were to go to Rome, and we landed in Ostia. There I heard that the Emperor wasn't in Rome at all, but here, in Milan, so off I went again."

"We were in Rome—for a week or so. The old man hates the city, and they don't like him there much, because of the increased taxes."

"Oh, he's increased the taxes, has he?"

Terentius whistled. "Just you wait over there in Britain—you'll get it, too. Someone's got to pay for the oriental ceremonial and all the rest of it."

"I see. And what is 'all the rest of it'?"

"Well, there is the victory celebration, for one—"

"For what victory?"

Again Terentius whistled. "What's the matter with you, man? Where have you been that you don't know?"

"I told you—on board ship. It called itself a post ship, but it was the slowest old boat that ever ambled past the Pillars of Hercules. I fretted and fumed, but nothing I said would make it go any faster. I told the captain I'd be a broken old man when I arrived and called him Charon; he didn't mind. He was always drunk, anyway. But what's the victory we are celebrating?"

"The insurrection in Gaul is over at last."

"Some victory! Over half-crazed, undisciplined peasants—"

"Easy, friend. It's a new jewel in the diadem of our Divine Emperor—"

A gold-glittering official was sweeping past them.

"Sempronius", whispered Terentius. "The highest paid spy of the court. In official life the chief chamberlain, blast him. Oh, you'll love life in Milan. But I do understand your anger against the Gallic business. They've ordered some of your troops to Gaul, haven't they? Friend, it was a rough business, believe me. Peasants roused are the worst enemy one can have. A man will always fight better for land than for money—especially when he has grown up on the land he is fighting for. Whenever we got them down in the west, they promptly rose in the east. But four weeks ago we captured Ælianus and crucified him, and that was the end, more or less. He was a gifted man—cost us about twelve thousand helmets before we got him. Of course, the whole show would have been over long ago, if it weren't for bloody Carausius—"

"Carausius? How does he come in?"

"Well, he's the admiral of our fleet—"

"Stationed in Gessoriacum, I know. My miserable old ship was part of it. I suppose he wanted to get rid of it, and I was a welcome opportunity. But what's he got to do with the Gallic peasants?"

"Everything and nothing. The peasants needed arms, didn't they? And the Franks had arms, see? And in order to get them from where the Franks were to where the peasants were, you had to pass Carausius' men somewhere. Well, he let them pass. Made a pretty penny out of it, too."

"Nice work. And old Maximianus did nothing to stop that?"

"Stop Carausius? You don't know the fellow, I can see that. He commands the whole fleet—about twelve thousand men, apart from sailors and slaves. Has auxiliaries of his own, mostly Franks. And every single man under him is ready to cut anybody's throat at so much as the blinking of his eyelid. He has a peculiar talent for making himself popular—"

Constantius nodded. "That fellow Allectus seemed to be quite enthusiastic about him, too—"

"There you are. But it won't last long, now. Not with the war over, it won't. Unless I'm very much mistaken, Carausius is on the blacklist, and once you're on that—"

"—you don't live long. Heard of it. Well, there goes Carausius. Only thing I wonder about is how one's going to get at him if he's surrounded by enthusiastic friends. . . ."

Terentius wrinkled his nose. "I think we can leave that safely to old—"

"Attention!" barked a voice. It was that of Hannibalianus.

Everybody fell silent. The chamberlain had returned and was now standing at the foot of the big staircase, scroll in hand. "The visitors will go up now," he said suavely, "in the order in which I proclaim their names. The Princeps Senatus, Marcus Trebonius Victor; the Chief Legate, Publius Cornelius Mamertinus; the prefect of the Domestic Guards, Hannibalianus—"

"A noble serpent creeping up the stairs", whispered Constantius, and his friend swallowed a guffaw with some difficulty.

"—the Legate Licinius; the Legate Bassianus; the Legate Constantius—"

"Up you go."

"—the Legate Terentius; the Legate Aurelius Cotta—"

Name after name was called up—many of them resounding like trumpet calls, names that had spelled victory, two, three, five hundred years ago and whose bearers were now to prostrate themselves before a peasant in a purple cloak.

The Audience Room was enormous and already half filled with officials, officers, and guards. Chief Chamberlain Sempronius was standing in the center, staff in hand, as immobile as a statue.

A slight movement of his staff directed each newcomer to his place. There was not a sound in the huge room, except for the steps of those who had just entered.

"He's got an easy job, today", whispered Terentius. "You should have seen him three months ago, when Diocletianus was here, too. Two Emperors in one palace! Poor Sempronius was sweating his entrails out to solve the problems of etiquette. Even I felt sorry for him. There was one day, when the two masters were to make a joint proclamation. It was impossible to have them come in side by side, because one of them would necessarily be on the honor side. So Sempronius had the ingenious idea of having them come in from opposite sides, but exactly at the same moment. I'm told he rehearsed it for hours with the Domestic Guards. It worked out beautifully, too. Diocletian was very pleased—he loves that sort of thing. Old Maximianus loathes it, but thinks that if he gives in on a point like that, he needn't give in on another. By all the gods, look!"

The curtain at one end of the room was being pushed aside vehemently, and a huge man appeared; a round head, bearded, on the neck of a bull; the hair, still full, seemed a little dishevelled. He wore a purple tunic, but no cloak; in one hand he was brandishing the larger part of a roast pheasant.

The sudden appearance seemed to freeze the entire assembly. Only a few people prostrated themselves. The unfortunate chief chamberlain looked as though he were going to faint.

"Where is Mamertinus!" roared the Emperor. "Where is Constantius!"

"Here, your Majesty."

"Here, Sire."

"Come in, you two! Send everybody else away, Sempronius!"

"Y-yes, your Majesty."

In the midst of the turmoil, the two officers walked up to the cloakless man. Maximianus bit into his pheasant, turned round, and disappeared behind the curtain.

Mamertinus and Constantius followed and found themselves alone in a smaller room, where a solitary guardsman stood with a silver trumpet in his hand; he did not seem to know for certain whether he should blow it or not. He decided to come to attention instead. On went the two officers, through a small corridor into still another room, and here stood Maximianus—still holding his pheasant—in front of a table on which a large map was spread. With him were a number of high-ranking officers: Constantius recognized Galerius, whom his friend had mentioned as the most likely leader of the Persian war to come, and Vatinius, the legate of the Twenty-Second Legion, well known for being the most elegant man in the Empire; there was also young Maxentius, the Emperor's son—he had inherited his father's jutting chin and very likely his ambition also.

To his satisfaction, Constantius saw that the chief legate, instead of prostrating himself, just saluted stiffly, and he followed his example. This was obviously a military council, not a court audience.

Maximianus wanted to acknowledge the salute and found himself raising the pheasant; he threw it into the middle of the room. And so tremendous, so terrifying was his rage that there was nothing in the least comic about that gesture. His face was almost blue—he looked as though he might have a stroke at any moment. The veins on the low, broad forehead were like pulsating cords.

"You are the legate commanding in southern Britain, Constantius", he said hoarsely. "Therefore it will be of interest to you to know that the province of Britain has been occupied by the enemy!"

CHAPTER 5

FOR ONE SHORT MOMENT Constantius thought that the Emperor had gone stark staring mad. Some historians had suggested that Tiberius had been temporarily insane when he was in a rage. But if this were the case with Maximianus, the attitude of the men around him would have been different. They would have looked afraid of him; instead they were looking downcast, infuriated, gloomy.

The province of Britain had been occupied by an enemy—what enemy? If Curio had revolted—but Curio would never do that, there was not enough ambition in him; besides, the Emperor would have said a revolt. The Danes? The Franks? The latter were more likely; they had a good-sized fleet of swift brigantines, and it was precisely against those that Carausius' fleet had been stationed in—Carausius' fleet! Was it possible that Carausius—? Yes, by Jove, it was, and that was it!

"Carausius, Sire?" he asked. Constantius' head was ready to reel, but he did not allow it to move. Instead, he saw causes and consequences standing out in relief with an almost uncanny clarity: Carausius, the man who was on the blacklist—the man who was surrounded by faithful troops, who was in possession of a large fleet of excellent ships all stationed at the very doors of Britain. He must have got wind of the Emperor's plans concerning him, and all he had had to do was to flee—to Britain. But fleeing to Britain meant conquest of Britain, if one was Carausius. Poor little Valerius hadn't a dog's chance against such an attack coming out of the blue. As for Curio, he had never been a man of action. The only dangerous high-ranking officer in Britain—dangerous for Carausius—was the Legate Constantius, and the Legate Constantius was safely out of the danger zone when it all happened. Was that accidental? He remembered Allectus' strange interest in the number of troops under his command, his anxiety to have him start immediately, the desperately slow journey of the *Titan*—it all seemed to fit in—

In the meantime Maximianus had been swearing like a mule driver. His huge fist crashed and crashed again on the table, while curses and obscenities proceeded from his mouth with breathless speed. Carausius, of course, Carausius! Who else but Carausius, that misbegotten bit of scum, that son and grandson of one-eyed whore mothers? Had he not always said that he was a traitor? Had he not insisted, entreated, beseeched the commander of Gaul to get that poisonous mushroom, that filthy piece of carrion, behind bars? But all he had said had been spoken into the winds, of course; they all knew better, the commander in Gaul and the commander in Britain!

Vatinius, commander of northern and western Gaul, began to look uneasy. Constantius made himself look quite impassive. He banished any thought of Helena or Constantine. Get the facts, that was what mattered now, get the facts out of this irate, apoplectic man who commanded half of the civilized world.

"And then they come to me with victory celebrations", raged Maximianus. "Victory over Ælianus, poor little monkey! Victory over half-starved beggars, rot your bones! Victory over the carps and the hake is nonsense. What have I done that I am condemned to rule a lot of dithering halfwits who don't know a viper when they see it!"

He can't be just a stupid old man, thought Constantius. Diocletian is much too clever to make such a bad choice. He took a step forward and stood at attention again.

The Emperor cleared his throat and spat. "Very well", he snapped. "What do you want to say?"

"The Legate Constantius, commander of south Britain, reports himself present, as ordered by Your Majesty", said Constantius. "I sailed within twenty-four hours of receiving the order. The ship, chosen by Your Majesty's delegate, took sixty-three days."

Maximianus opened his mouth and closed it again.

"I believe the fellow rebukes me", he ejaculated. "By Hecate, you don't lack courage, I'll say that for you."

"If I did," answered Constantius calmly, "the Divine Emperor would not have sent for me. Your Majesty tells me that Rome has lost a province. I hope I shall be allowed to get it back where it belongs."

Galerius, watching the Emperor's face, permitted himself a low chuckle. But he had miscalculated.

"Glad someone is amused", snapped Maximianus. "What do you know about what happened in Britain, Constantius?"

"Only what Your Majesty has told me so far", was the unruffled answer. "But as Carausius is the criminal, I have a fair idea how he did it."

"Let's hear the 'fair idea'", growled Maximianus.

"May I ask one question first, Sire?"

"Yes. Make it short."

"Did Your Majesty send the Prefect Allectus to me with two letters?"

"I sent for you, yes. Don't know who went as messenger. Who went, Mamertinus?"

"The Tribune Strabonius, Sire. But I know that Allectus very well—he's one of Carausius' officers."

"I thought so", nodded Constantius. "That is why he was so interested in getting me off quickly. He said I would incur Your Majesty's disfavor if I waited even until the troops had been sworn in for you. Carausius must have got hold of Strabonius when he arrived in Gessoriacum to cross over to Britain. He very likely was suspicious, knew that the Emperor was—not very fond of him; knew also that the peasant war was in its very last stage, that it was practically over, and figured that he himself was the next on the list to be disposed of. Here was a tribune with the first orders of the new Emperor. It was vital for him to know what they were and if they affected him. Well, as it happened, they didn't. But he had the idea of getting the commander of south Britain out of the way quickly, and he slowed up my journey to Italy by giving me a particularly poor ship. I was to be on the waters when Carausius struck: I think he must have struck on the Calends of last month—"

"That is correct", nodded Maximianus. "How did you know?"

"The tides were favorable for him, then, Sire. There is nothing more important to consider by anybody trying to invade Britain. Carausius is supposed to be a capable man— therefore he is likely to have split his forces for the attack. His spy Allectus could provide him with most accurate information about the strength and disposal of the Roman troops—he very likely tried a bit of bribery, too. Now if I had had such information in Carausius' position, I would land in Anderida, whose defenses are practically nonexistent—"

"Why?" asked the Emperor crisply.

"Because Anderida was supposed to be protected by that selfsame fleet that attacked it, Sire. I would send another part of my fleet up the estuary of the Tamesis and send cavalry into Londinium and from there to Verulam. The rest is easy."

"Excellent", said Maximianus. "It's exactly what Carausius has done—" And suddenly he roared like a bull, "And it is easy, is it, Legate Constantius? You were entrusted with the defense of south Britain—and you have the effrontery to tell me that it was easy for any blustering, pig-begotten, verminous pirate to conquer it! What in the name of all the gods have you been doing all these years?"

87

"Protesting in vain against the systematic thinning out of the army of occupation", was the cold answer. "There are no more than three thousand regulars in the whole of the south, and ten thousand auxiliaries whose fighting value is decidedly small. I have launched complaints eleven times in the last six years."

Mamertinus felt that the time had come for him, as chief legate, to exculpate himself. "We always get these protests, Sire", he murmured lamely. "If we gave in to them, it would be quite impossible to withdraw troops from any station in the Empire. There was no reason to assume any necessity for maximum military strength in Britain."

"So it seems", jeered the Emperor.

"Britain", said Constantius, "has been conquered by the Roman fleet whose job it was to assure that Britain should not be conquered."

"Your triumph over the peasants in Gaul", said Maximianus, "has been paid for very dearly, Vatinius. No, don't apologize—it is not your fault. It isn't Constantius' fault either."

He had calmed down visibly. "I'm damned hungry", he said. "Why's that? Oh, I know—the blasted messenger interrupted me at my meal. Well, we won't reconquer Britain within the next half hour: we'd better go back and eat something. Give the orders, somebody. You may stay and have a bite with us, Constantius—you, too, Mamertinus. And if anybody pronounces the name of Britain within the next half hour, I'll bite his head off. Come along."

It was only now that Constantius saw the huge dinner table at the other end of the room. There was not a single slave in sight—they had probably been ordered away when Maximianus, startled by the British news, had improvised his war council.

—But—the table was not quite deserted. There were two solitary figures still sitting at it—a young woman and a little girl. Mad, thought Constantius. The whole thing is mad—as mad as a dream. Perhaps—perhaps it was a dream; and he would wake up any moment now and still be on board the old *Titan*, rolling to and fro in a breeze on her endless voyage. The Persian ceremonial—the Emperor with his roast pheasant—Britain conquered by mutineers—and then everybody sitting down with a girl and a child and having dinner. Certainly it was much more like a dream than anything else. Perhaps it was a moment like that, he thought, that made some of those philosopher fellows think that life was not actually real at all, but only an illusion. So far, his own attitude toward that sort of philosophy had been to offer the philosopher a sound crack on the jaw, to give him an opportunity to find out. . . .

But now Maximianus had sat down again, and the officers followed his example. Swarms of slaves appeared from nowhere, and dish after dish was being placed in front of him; and the way in which the Emperor started eating was so utterly real that any idea of a dream had to be relinquished.

Constantius found himself face to face with the young woman. Mamertinus at his side had murmured an introduction, and he had bowed, and she had smiled. The Emperor's daughter, Theodora—or, rather, his stepdaughter, though he could not remember who her father had been. Attractive woman. Very elegant, of course. Priceless pearls. Had one to make light conversation?

But she came to his aid. "It must have come as a great shock to you", she murmured, with a shy glance toward her father, who was now devouring a dozen larks in a sauce that had made famous the cook who invented it. "Please don't think you must talk if you don't feel like it. I quite understand."

Constantius gave her a grateful smile. "You are most kind, Domina." She had beautiful, dark eyes, with long lashes, almost like Helena's. . . . Where was Helena now? What had happened to her in the storm that had rushed across Britain? And to Constantine . . .

The little girl next to Theodora leaned over the table.

"I'm Fausta", she said earnestly.

She had a sweet little face with black cherry eyes and an obstinate little chin; she was about six or seven years of age. He did not quite know what to answer to this self-introduction, so he nodded gravely and bowed a little. By now other ladies—either guests or ladies-in-waiting, or both—had joined the table, without anybody taking much notice of them; the situation was very much as it must have been before the alarming news arrived, except that there were two more guests and that all of them shared what to most parts of the Empire was still a secret. Constantius knew that he had got to banish any thought of Helena and Constantine until he was alone; that he had to watch the Emperor—the incalculable, irascible old man might give the vital command for counteraction to Galerius or Mamertinus or even to his son, inexperienced as he was—and the reconquest of Britain was *his* affair and no one else's. It would not be easy, he knew that: for a few instants he had thought of asking permission to leave at once, with whatever troops he could be given, with whatever ships were immediately available—half a dozen, or three, or even one—to sail for Britain, land somewhere up at the northwest coast, where he was least expected, and then see what could be done; if Curio were still out and about with some of his men, one could join forces and march south—but all that was sheer lunacy. It was ten to one that Carausius would have set up spies everywhere by now; that every ship sailing past the Pillars of Hercules would be reported to him and that his ship or ships would find Carausius' fleet ready for them. After all, Carausius' fleet was Rome's best fleet! Besides, Curio was not the man to go on fighting for long, and even if he wanted to do so, he could not get far with his handful of men.

No, it was impossible to reconquer Britain with a bit of cavalry impudence.

The little girl opposite him pounded the table with her tiny fist. "I'm Fausta", she said again. "I'm important. Don't you see? I shall be an Empress when I'm older."

"Shhh, darling", said Theodora sweetly; her eyes apologized to Constantius.

"But it's true", protested Fausta. "You know it's true. I shall be an Empress." She was staring at Constantius all the time. "And when I'm an Empress," she went on, "I shall marry you."

Theodora laughed outright.

"What's it she said?" asked the Emperor with his mouth full of lark and mushrooms. Theodora repeated it, to both Fausta's and Constantius' embarrassment, and Maximianus grinned, with an appraising look at the ex-legate of south Britain.

"I'm afraid I shall be much too old for you by then", said Constantius. "Besides, I am married, you know."

"It doesn't matter", said Fausta magnanimously.

Everybody laughed this time; Theodora alone did not join in; there was even a shadow of fear in her lovely face. She leaned forward. "Is—your wife in Britain?"

He nodded. "My wife and my son."

91

She looked aside hastily. The slave behind her seat drew nearer with his amphora of wine, but she raised her hand with a declining gesture. When she turned back toward Constantius there were tears in her eyes. "Poor man", she said. "How dreadful for you!"

Constantius stared in front of him.

Vatinius upset his goblet of wine and flushed with anger, as Galerius laughed into his face.

The Emperor, still eating with undiminished appetite, took it all in. No one could know what he was thinking.

CHAPTER 6

"WE SHALL BE HOME SOON", said Helena. "We're quite near now."

"I'm not tired, Mother." Constantine tossed up his head.

The Centurion Favonius grinned. He was dog tired, and so were all of them, the Domina, the young master, old Rufus, and the miserable little bunch of soldiers they had picked up on the ride. But that was the proper way for a trainee of Marcus Favonius to talk.

He was probably the only one who was thoroughly enjoying the present situation. Things had been pretty dull, all these years, but they were certainly not dull now.

No, no one could say that things were dull. It was like being back in the good old days; there was fire in the air, and iron and blood, and one had to keep one's eyes open.

Pity there weren't any better horses for the soldiers—but beggars can't be choosers, and for stolen horses they weren't that bad, really. Old Rufus wasn't in too good a state—lack of exercise, that's what it was. Well, he'd get into shape again in a couple of weeks—if he could live to see them, which was a bit doubtful, as was always the case when things were not dull.

He looked back. "Close up, you", he barked toward the end of the little column. "Can't have stragglers. Pull yourselves together, men—it's easy."

They closed up sullenly, and Favonius rode up to Helena.

"May I say something, Domina?"

She turned a pale, drawn little face toward him. "Yes, Favonius, what is it?"

The giant centurion swallowed. "Something I learned many years ago, Domina—learned it from a great soldier, too. In wartime, when you're on the ride, don't think. Make your mind a blank. It helps. When something turns up, you'll think all right. But in between, don't. It saps your strength."

She smiled wanly. "Thanks, Favonius. I'll try to remember."

He nodded gently and rode on. The wind was charging to the wood, and he sniffed cautiously. There was a fire somewhere in the northwest. Time they got to Coelcastra. But it was lucky that most of the way was forest; nothing worse than riding in a vast plain when one can't afford to fight.

Make your mind a blank—it helps. Helena shuddered. She could not get rid of the sight of Durbovix, staggering up the stairs to the house, with an arrow in his throat, vomiting blood. When he saw her, he had paused and made a touching attempt to stand to attention. "Domina— perhaps—it would be—advisable ..." And then he had crumpled up and died, as though the attempt to give advice to his betters had been too much for him.

She had run into the house and shouted for help, and searched for Constantine, who was having his training lesson with Favonius. The picture of what happened after that was blurred: servants came from all quarters; Rufus turned up, armed with a long kitchen knife, which had made Favonius laugh—

And then Allectus had come, with six men; he suddenly stood there, in the back entrance of the house, very polite, smiling. He had made a little speech to her, but from his manner it was clear that he was addressing all of them. These were great times, he said, and in great times great leaders arose. The great Carausius had landed in Britain with one hundred thousand men. He had taken Londinium without resistance—which was fortunate for Londinium—for resistance against Carausius was certain death.

Then he went on talking about what a great man Carausius was and how he would make Britain independent of Rome, an island of freedom and plenty. He had finished by saying rather pompously that he was proud to announce such good news.

She had seen that two of his men were archers and that the arrows in their quivers had red feathers. It was an arrow with a red feather that had pierced poor Durbovix' throat.

Constantine was listening, wide eyed; she could feel how he became more and more impatient. When Allectus paused to get his breath, the boy's voice shrilled, "What's Father going to say to this?" And Favonius laid a huge arm on his shoulder and whispered, "Wait, soldier."

She found herself entering the house—the servants remained huddled in the garden—and alone with Allectus she spoke her mind. "This is mutiny against the Emperor, Allectus. You and your accomplices will pay for it." He laughed that hateful laugh of his and said, "There is only one Emperor whom I recognize: Carausius. He is the greatest man of his time. Maximianus and Diocletianus are just so much dirt."

"You have spoken of wonderful times", she jeered. "They have started already, I believe—one of your men has murdered my butler."

Allectus apologized politely. It was a regrettable mistake. The country was not safe at the moment—some of the imperial troops were marauding and looting and had to be stopped. Postbattle activities were dangerous, and sometimes an innocent man might have to pay for the guilt of others. He assured her that she and her household were perfectly safe, as long as they obeyed the new government. As for him, he would do everything in his power to make her life agreeable. After all, she already had reason to be grateful to him for getting her husband safely out of the way, and just in time, too—

This with an impudent smile, followed by an even more impudent action. She hit him in the face, and he cursed and jumped at her. She saw his hateful face close in front of her own; she could feel his breath; he clawed her dress off her shoulder.

She fought him with all her strength, but it was good that an enormous fist suddenly came from nowhere and dragged him away from her. "Oh, no, you don't", said the Centurion Marcus Favonius Facilis, and he hit Allectus in the face and hit again and again.

The prefect managed to draw his sword.

"Excellent", jeered Favonius. "Now we shall really have a bit of fun, we two." And he, too, drew his sword, and Helena saw that it was not the blunt thing he used in training with Constantine—he must have had time to go and fetch weapons from the armory.

Allectus, meanwhile, was shouting at the top of his voice for his men. "Don't trouble yourself", recommended Favonius. "They've been taken care of. It's you and I alone—I'm sure you like it much better that way. Swords and no shields—it's easy."

Under the banter she could hear a fierce anger in the centurion's voice.

"I'll have you flayed for this!" screamed Allectus.

"Why don't you do it yourself?" asked Favonius. "Here I am. Start flaying!" And he marched into his retreating antagonist, raining blow after blow upon his defense.

That was the moment Constantine entered the room; there was a smear of blood on his cheek, and he was brandishing a dagger.

Favonius saw him out of the corner of his eye. "Watch out, sonny. Don't interfere. Are the six men secured?"

"Yes", said Constantine breathlessly. "I say, let me have a share in this one, please—"

Favonius laughed. "It would be too much of an honor for him, sonny. I'll deal with this rat."

He lunged out, jumped back, lunged again—and a dark, moist patch appeared on the prefect's tunic sleeve, just underneath the first shoulder plate. It was the left arm, but Allectus made an instinctive gesture toward it with the sword arm, and Favonius thrust at his face, swift as a lightning. He hit the forehead, and immediately the prefect's face was a mask of blood. He dropped the sword and fell, crashing on the tiled floor.

"And that is that", said Favonius with no mean satisfaction. Turning to Constantine, he added, "You will have observed, I hope, that he bowed his head a little—wanted to take it on the helmet, but I had made allowance for that."

Then to Helena, "Sorry about messing up the room, Domina—"

"Thank you, Favonius", was her answer.

And thus the first attack of the forces of Carausius had been beaten off by the villa of the absent commander of south Britain.

Outside, in the garden, they found most of the slaves—about twenty of them—in a truculent mood. Allectus' six men had been bound and gagged, and Rufus stood in front of them, with his long kitchen knife, telling them with many details exactly what he was going to do to them. "You don't know this country", he said contemptuously. "You've only just arrived here. I've been living here practically all my life. This is a very humane country, if you want to know, and particularly fond of dogs. Not the sort of dogs you are, my dear friends—better dogs, real dogs. And we give them nice chopped meat for breakfast every day. Now you look all quite well fed, my friends, and—"

Here he saw Helena and Favonius coming, and he stopped and saluted with his kitchen knife. "Six prisoners under escort, Domina", he reported.

"They didn't put up much of a fight", explained Favonius. "Can't blame them, really. We were too many for them. Two of our men got a few scratches, that is all. Shall we lock them up in the cellar, Domina?"

She agreed to that, and Rufus and a dozen slaves carried out the order.

There was an atmosphere of triumph—but it was not to last long. A message came through from Tribune Valerius—the messenger had been shot at five times on the way, but insisted on riding back immediately. It was short:

Half of my men have gone over to the mutineers; the other half will soon follow. I advise urgently to go north and put yourself under the protection of Legate Curio. Hurry. Londinium has already been occupied by the enemy. If you see the Legate Constantius again, tell him that I capitulated only to death, not to Carausius.

The gods be with you.

Gaius Valerius

Poor little Valerius, so proud of his first command!

The letter arrived in the evening. There was a red glow coming from the direction of Londinium. Valerius was right. There was no time to lose. Allectus seemed to be an important man with these people. They were bound to search for him. He was not dead. Favonius had reported to her that he had lost a lot of blood, but was still alive and might even recover.

"We shall leave at once", she said. "But I am not going north; I am going to my father. Have horses saddled, Favonius. We shall need rugs and some food and weapons, of course, but nothing else. I shall give money to the slaves and let them go wherever they want to. They cannot afford to be found here after what they have done to Allectus' men."

The centurion nodded. "You are wise, Domina. But I think, if you will allow me to suggest it, we might take old Rufus with us. He is not a bad soldier." She nodded assent, and Favonius hurried off.

She had gone to her rooms, unlocked the heavy iron boxes in which she kept money and jewelry, filled a leather bag with their contents, and dismissed her maids despite their desperate pleadings. "You will be much safer if you are not with me", she told them. "Here is money enough to keep you for a year at least; take it and go to Londinium or Verulam. I don't think anybody will harm you. I am the

98

wife of the imperial legate—they might want to keep me as a hostage. Go, girls—we shall meet again one day. This cannot last long. Rome will claim her own."

Half an hour later they had started their ride, she, Constantine, Favonius, and Rufus, who was leading a spare horse, laden with rugs and food and a few other necessities. It was night, and they knew the roads—there was a good chance that they would get through. The enemy was likely to concentrate on the bigger towns and the important road junctions. All they had to do was to keep away from the towns and to use shortcuts as much as possible.

Just before they reached Trinovant territory they came across a dozen soldiers—the survivors of a lively skirmish somewhere near the estuary of the Tamesis. Most of them were men of the Twentieth Legion and knew both Favonius and Rufus, to whom they gave a ragged cheer. Favonius spoke to them. "Look here, boys, there's no doubt that this vermin has got the better of us for the time being. Therefore you'll probably be killed if you join us—sometime between now and the next four or five weeks. You can, of course, go over to them—in which case you will probably live, until the Emperor takes over again. Then you will be killed, that's certain. Now what do you prefer: probably to be killed, or certainly to be killed? Take your choice." They decided to remain loyal. They had blood to avenge, anyway. Favonius chuckled. "You are not half so stupid as I always thought you were, boys. Now your uncle Favonius will go and pinch some horses for you. It's easy."

As a horse thief, Favonius was in a class by himself. He managed to steal twelve within three hours.

And now they were riding through the Trinovant forests, and it would not be long until they had reached Coelcastra—if it still existed.

"Mother—"

"Yes, Constantine."

"When do you think Father will come and chase them out?"

"I don't know, Constantine—but he will come."

The boy looked at her. "Of course he will come", he said hotly. "But when—? Do you think it will be months?"

"It may be even longer than that, Constantine. I don't know."

They rode on in silence. Yes, it might well be longer than months—for Constantius was in Rome, with the Emperor, and who could say what the Emperor would decide? He might send another general—he might even hold Constantius responsible for what had happened. It was impossible to foresee. Only one thing was certain: at the present moment, neither Constantius nor the Emperor knew anything about what was happening in Britain....

Gorse bushes. Pines. One more hour, and the sun would set.

But she knew that group of trees over there—she had known it all her life. Oaks, they were: Father's favorite trees. And on the other side there was a large stone of a peculiar size and color—not even Father knew how it had got there; it was his favorite stone, however, and this was his favorite forest.

Was there a glint of something white between the trees?

Favonius, at the head of the column, raised his hand, glancing forward. They all halted. But Helena rode on, beckoning Constantine to follow her. "Someone's sitting there", whispered Favonius. She only nodded and rode into the clearing where the oak trees stood like sentries.

"Welcome, daughter. Welcome, child", said King Coel.

Hilary, who had been sitting at his feet, got up and bowed.

Helena slid from her saddle and rushed up to him.

"It is good", said the old man, as she buried her face in his lap, sobbing her heart out. "You have come in time. Let the boy come to me, too. Hilary, lead the officer and his men to the house and give them food and drink. Then come back to fetch us, and bring my musicians with you—and one of the small carts. We shall be tired."

Constantine shook his head. He did not approve of his mother's crying like a little child; women did cry easily, though Mother wasn't at all like that, usually. But what he could not understand was that Grandfather had mentioned "the officer and his men", although Favonius and the soldiers were not in sight yet—and he was sitting with his back to them, and even if he had turned round, he could not have seen them because of the big trees just behind him.

Only now they came, and Hilary, with a friendly nod to the boy, went up to Favonius. Constantine jumped off his horse and sauntered over to his grandfather. King Coel's bushy white eyebrows twitched a little. "Sit down, boy—here, on the moss."

He obeyed, after pressing a shy kiss on the old man's wrinkly cheek, as dry as old parchment. He saw Hilary, leading Favonius' horse across the clearing; Rufus and the soldiers followed in single file. Then they were alone.

Under the touch of the King's hand on her head, Helena calmed down. "You know what happened, Father", she whispered. "Of course you do. When will it end? What shall I do?"

"Conquerors come and go", said King Coel. "Only the message is eternal."

She looked up at him in sudden fear. "But Rome—surely Rome has not gone—for good?"

He gave the little chuckle she knew so well. "I remember a time when you were hoping that it was so, Elen—do you?"

"I was a child, then."

"You are a child, still, Elen. You have learned little. Soon you will learn more."

I have learned much, she thought. Here, in this very place, sitting at his feet as she was sitting now, she had dreamed her dream of Zenobia and of personal power, and he had smiled at her dream: and told her she was not going to rule if she wanted to be like Zenobia. But now when she wanted power for Constantius, he had lost his power and left her defenseless. Was her very wish enough to bring about failure? "Let your mind be quiet—how else can you hear your heart speak?" But her heart had spoken. She loved her husband. She wanted him to have power because she loved him. . . .

"Are you truthful with yourself, Elen?"

He had not said it, but she felt that he thought it and that the thought already contained the answer.

"I love him, Father", she said fiercely. "I love him."

"He is thinking of you—now", said the King. "But he may not always think of you. If you love him, love him with all your strength. It will make you strong, too. Love him where you cannot understand him. Love him beyond disappointment and sorrow. It will bear fruit, when the time comes. Let love be stronger than pride—don't forget that: let love be stronger than pride, when the time comes."

She did not understand; but she felt a hidden warning, a dark shadow of things to come, and she sighed deeply. "What am I to do, Father? Can I stay with you? Will it be safe for the boy?"

"No, Elen, you cannot stay; nor can I, though our road will not be the same."

Again she looked up. "But, why not, Father? Surely we—"

She broke off. She had seen his face, and though he was smiling she knew that his days, perhaps his hours, were numbered.

"Father—"

"Peace, child. I am a very happy old man. You wouldn't spoil my happiness, would you? Now, listen: whatever you do—and I know your proud heart and your loyalty—don't let my people suffer. Do not incite them to resist the invader. It is too early. Even Rome needs time to build a fleet. Let this storm pass over their heads as it passes over a field of wheat. Conquerors come and go. Only the message is eternal. Soon now I shall understand it. Promise me that you will not let my people suffer."

"I promise", she whispered.

He nodded. "It is good. I cannot ask you to bow to the invader. You owe loyalty to your husband and to Rome. You must do what you must do. I cannot give you the arms of my people; but I can give you a gift more potent than that—a mind of the kind that is rare. My servant Hilary will be your servant forthwith. No King has left a better heritage to his child. Trust him as you have trusted me."

"I will, Father. I like Hilary."

The old King chuckled again. "Hilary is wise, for one so young. He will be what the strong centurion cannot be. Go north—but not beyond the Great Wall. You have no friends there; Rome has seen to that. There are forests in the north—and forests are kind to Coel's daughter. Forests are wood, living wood, Elen—though not *the* living wood. The tree of life has not grown in our forests."

There it was again—he never seemed to be able to get away from his favorite story.

"Wood, Elen, wood. The woods will shield you against your enemies. On wooden keels come vengeance, too, and joy and sorrow. When he was born—" the gnarled old hand was caressing the boy's dark hair—"do you remember, Elen? I made you lie down on wood, didn't I? And from wood you jumped to victory. There's a strong tie, daughter, between you and the boy—stronger than blood—stronger even than mother love, which the poets say is the strongest force on earth. You and he—together you will find the Tree of Life, yea—the living wood itself. . . ."

His voice had become almost inaudible. As so often before, he fell asleep. His breathing, though weak, was regular.

Helena's eyes fell on Constantine. The boy, too, had fallen asleep, overtired from the long ride. She smiled compassionately and went on sitting quite still, so as not to disturb either grandfather or grandchild. They are all tired—tired and weak, she thought. I must be strong for them.

Nature itself had become very still around her. Once she thought she saw the head of a stag appear between the trees, but perhaps she had been mistaken. It was getting rather dark. . . .

Then she heard the music. It seemed to come from very far, short, abrupt notes and then a little cadenza—and again short, abrupt notes. Father's fiddlers, she thought. War was flooding over the island, men were killed, houses burned to the ground—but King Coel had asked for his fiddlers.

Never before had she felt herself more remote from her father. This was not the hour of aged wisdom, of prudent renunciation—it was the hour of fight. She was sorry already for the promise she had given him, not to incite the Trinovantes. And she had not come to hear for the thousandth time the story of the living wood. . . .

Now they became visible: Hilary first; then the musicians, three of them; and a little cart drawn by a heavy-hoofed horse. The musicians had ceased playing.

She saw Hilary's first glance, full of deep anxiety; it went beyond her and did not seem to find consolation in the old King's quiet breathing. Then he looked at her and at Constantine. He bent down and touched the boy's shoulder; it did not waken him. With an almost motherly gentleness he lifted him bodily. She followed him slowly, saw him putting her son to bed on the soft rugs that filled the cart.

Wizened old Gullo was the driver. He was over eighty now and grinned at her with his toothless mouth. Good old Gullo.

Hilary turned round, and his smile warmed her heart. He walked back toward the King; but suddenly he stopped, and she saw his face become tense. His hands trembled a little; he bowed his head.

She stared at him—then jerked away her eyes, wildly. . . .

King Coel was sitting on his favorite stone as before. But there was a silvery pallor over his face, and she knew that he was dead.

An eternity passed. . . . No one moved. All dreams had come to an end. The sun itself had gone into hiding. The dreadful stillness of nature drowned all feelings—not even remorse was left to her. She stood and stood. . . .

A deep groan made her turn her head toward the cart. There was old Gullo, still holding the reins, with tears streaming over his wizened little face.

She raised her arm to the musicians. "Play", she said in a voice that was not her own.

And they played the Royal Song, as old as man's memory; the King has come home from the ride—from the long, long ride o'er his merry land—the King has come home from the ride—

When the song ended, on a high, triumphant note, Hilary, at last, approached the holy stone and, bowing deeply, lifted the burden that the King had shed and carried it, as he had carried the King's grandchild.

The fiddlers followed him, and after them stamped the heavy horse, drawing the cart with the sleeping boy, and after that Helena walked, alone, across the clearing. There was no thought left in her, but she felt a dull, barren pain. Britain had fallen.

CHAPTER 7

"GOOD HUNTING", said Legate Terentius.

Constantius readjusted the fibula of his cloak; took it off; readjusted it again. "What do you mean, Pigface?"

"Exactly what I said, friend. Good hunting."

The fibula—malachite and gold—was in the correct position now. The cloak was falling in just the right folds. The tunic had been freshly pressed. The sandals, with their little malachite buttons, were decidedly elegant. Constantius gave a short nod to his orderly, who saluted and withdrew. "I don't know what you're talking about", he said stiffly. "I'm going to a little reception—"

"—on the invitation of Domina Theodora. Of course."

"Mamertinus will be there. And there is just a chance that the Emperor himself is going to pass by—"

"Old Maximian is far too busy with his taxes to have time for receptions."

"He is far too busy to have time for the British campaign", said Constantius bitterly. "Almost a year—and nothing has been done."

Terentius sighed. "You are doing your best, Paleface. No man can do more. But I'd keep off Mamertinus, if I were you. I don't think he'll last long as chief legate. The direct way is the best, my boy, believe me."

"As I said, there's just a chance that the Emperor—"

"O ye gods, give me patience. When I say the direct way is the best, I don't mean the Emperor. Pretty name, Theodora—'the present of the gods'."

Constantius stamped his foot. "I wish you wouldn't make silly innuendos like that, Pigface. The princess is a very gracious lady and has shown me much kindness."

"That", said Terentius entirely unruffled, "is exactly what I mean. And she is supposed to have an enormous influence on her father. And I think you are an intelligent man, although you sometimes talk like a vestal virgin. Good hunting."

Constantius wanted to reply, but his friend was suddenly very busy: he shouted for his orderly, asked for the papers with the quaestor's report, gave orders for the training in the riding school to be an hour earlier as from next week—in short, he was very much the legate commanding the Fourteenth Legion—and nothing else. And this was his house, and it was damned decent of Terentius to have given him hospitality during all these months. Just the sort of hospitality he cared for, too—that of a soldier.

Still, Terentius had a way of teasing him about the Emperor's daughter that could be just a little annoying at times.

Constantius left the room without another word. One of the legate's chariots was waiting outside for him. "I shall drive myself", he said curtly, mounting. The charioteer gave him reins and whip and jumped down. He drove off.

Milan had grown considerably, these last seventeen years, and even the core of the city had changed a good deal, especially recently. Diocletian seemed to have building fever. New temples, new palaces, a new court of justice, everything new. No wonder he had to increase taxation. His co-ruler, newly in command, could not afford to stop the imperial building program. And the wretched provincials could not afford to pay for it. In the meantime Rome had lost a province to a mere mutineer.

No good thinking such thoughts when driving a chariot with two fiery bays through overcrowded streets. What a sea of people, and what a noise they made in honor of the great god Profit! Shopkeepers and their customers, hawkers peddling almost anything; the houses were like giant cubes of cheese, whose maggots were milling about in the open. The air was full of their stink. Thousands and thousands of jostling, pushing, clamoring people, litters ramming their way into defenseless backs, thieves and prostitutes going about their business, shrill screams of cart drivers intermingling with the music of flutes and tambourines, the smells of butcher's meat, seething with flies, and of spices and wood fires.

Was there anyone among them who would give one thought to a province lost? All they cared for were profit and pleasure—to fill their pockets, fill their bellies, and sleep with something rounded and soft. It was the same in Rome itself, and in Naples and Athens and Byzantium and Alexandria and everywhere else in the Empire.

Soldiers were the only men to think in terms of the Empire, the only men to whom frontiers meant more than a difference in uniforms and customs. Even among them many were thinking only of their own power, but some, at least, had Rome herself in mind, Roma Dea, and a thousand years of glory.

They made peasants into Emperors—but they expected their Emperors to keep the Empire together. Maximianus would have to make up his mind. It was sad indeed that one had to waste one's time on social visits, in hopes of getting action in the matter; that it might possibly be important to be seen here and seen there; that this and that officer had a favorable impression of one's views; that even imperial ladies had to be waited upon. It was more than sad—it was the next thing to being disgusting; but if it helped, it had to be done. Pigface could make it a little easier by not smirking and jibing as though one were having a love affair with Domina Theodora, who was a perfectly charming woman and fairly intelligent, too.

The outskirts made driving easier, and he cracked the whip over the heads of the bays. If only one could get some news out of Britain. The whole island seemed to be sealed off, hermetically. Some agents had managed to escape in ships during the first few weeks, but since then there had been a grim, leaden silence. What had happened to Helena—to Constantine—?

Come on, you've promised yourself not to think of that. Come on! He cracked the whip again.

"Good looking, isn't he?" said Domitilla.

A slave was filling her goblet with snow-cooled wine. It was done very gracefully, but the majordomo frowned a little, for a slave should not have eyes for the wrists and ankles of his betters, even if, like Domina Domitilla, they were married for the sixth time.

Vipsania was helping herself to another and still another of the luscious little honey cakes. Her figure was past spoiling, so why not enjoy life. "Who is good looking? The ex-legate of Britain?"

"Constantius? With his pale face and perpetual frown? Nonsense, my dear. Vatinius, of course."

"Oh, well, everybody knows that. Don't look too close though, dear, or you yourself might fall in love."

"Why not?" said Domitilla nonchalantly. She had been drinking a little too much, and her pretty face was flushed under the makeup.

Vipsania giggled with her mouth full of honey cake. "Why not? My sweet, you haven't got a chance in the world. Not with Vatinius."

"I've done better than that", shrugged Domitilla.

"Yes, but it's some time ago, dear."

"In any case," drawled Domitilla, "I haven't yet been reduced to making love to my own slaves."

But a woman who weighs double what she weighed ten years ago is not easily nettled. "You'll come to it, too, darling", said Vipsania with a broad smile. "And believe me, it does save one a great deal of unnecessary preliminaries. But I wasn't really being horrid to you about Vatinius—on the contrary. I wanted to warn you. The competition is too dangerous. . . ."

"Oh", Domitilla was interested. It was true Vatinius had been seen pretty often with Princess Theodora lately— but then, there had always been a swarm of officers in their first, second, and even third youth around her. She was careful, though. So far it had been quite impossible to say anything certain about her, ever since her husband had died. She had even acquired the reputation of being a *univira*—a one man's woman. That, of course, was nonsense. There was no such animal as a univira. Horrible idea . . .

"Vatinius", said Domitilla, "can have any woman he wants—and he knows it."

"He can't have me", declared Vipsania. "I hate exertion."

In another corner of the garden, under the shadow of a group of palm trees, Senatus Proculeius was talking shop with the Princeps Senatus Trebonius Victor. There was no doubt that the Emperor had certain—certain disinclinations toward the Senate; Proculeius complained bitterly that his last five—five!—suggestions concerning fixed prices for Egyptian grain had never been taken up, because of the fear of the senators that it might rouse imperial disfavor. The princeps senatus smiled coldly. "It is a pity that you were not born at the time of Cato, my Proculeius", he said.

"Because at that time senators had character, you mean?" Proculeius was most flattered.

"No. No. That's not at all what I mean. Because I didn't live at that time." The cold smile became withering. "I would go warily, if I were you, my Proculeius. You are quite right. Their imperial majesties have not much use for us, these days, and if there should be a reorganization—"

"Unlike some of my colleagues," hissed Proculeius, "I have a good conscience."

"Perhaps you have," the princeps senatus emptied his goblet, "but you also have only one neck. Be economic with that, rather than with Egyptian grain, my Proculeius."

On the lawn, near the fountain in the middle of the garden, loose groups of young people were chattering and laughing. A Gallic juggler and a Syrian contortionist were showing their tricks.

There was a large circle of guests around Princess Theodora's table in the center of the terrace. Constantius had

had a short interview with the gray-haired chief legate. Mamertinus had been entirely noncommittal. He was an old courtier rather than a soldier, and he had spent thirty years of his life being evasive. Few people could boast of having pinned him down, and still fewer had reason to feel happy about it. Of course the Emperor would have to take steps about the reconquest of Britain—it was only a question of time. Actually ships were being built with all possible speed. The trouble, naturally, was that so few troops were available at the present time. If Constantius only knew how difficult it was to make levies nowadays. The provincial governments showed precious little zeal in the matter and had always such excellent excuses: one could not expect them to draft thousands of men into the army and at the same time to get the harvest in, and if they didn't get the harvest in, there would be a famine, and grain would have to be dispatched from Egypt or Pannonia or Africa—in ships. And ships were needed for Britain. It was a vicious circle. It was the most thankless task being the chief legate. All very well for the young commanders to urge and press—not that he minded it; on the contrary, that was just as it should be. Commanders had to be eager and zealous; it was their duty just as his was to keep as much order as possible in the gigantic military machinery of the Empire. The time would come for the reconquest of Britain, certainly it would come. Yes, yes, it was the most natural thing that Constantius was keen on leading the expedition; he could be quite sure that he would keep it in mind. Everything depended, of course, upon the decision of the Emperor. The position of the chief legate was not what it used to be. But he would keep it in mind; of course, he would keep it in mind. . . .

All very benevolent, very friendly, very charming—and very slippery. Worth absolutely nothing.

And Princess Theodora was not so friendly as usual. True, she had greeted him with the same dazzling smile that had made him hope some weeks and even months ago that she really liked him. But most of her conversation was directed to Vatinius. What on earth she could find enjoyable in the fellow was beyond him! He was what was called a "golden soldier" in army circles—a man who had seen more garrison life than service at the front. He had not done too badly as a young officer under Aurelian, it was true; but that had not been much of a campaign, anyway, against that strange girl, Zenobia of Palmyra. Laurels won against a woman—well, it seemed as though he were out to win more laurels of that sort. Preening himself like a peacock. Silk tunic, silk cloak, perfumed hair like an exquisite.

Constantius was angry with himself. Instead of spinning thoughts like an aging retired officer he should be trying to make himself agreeable to the princess—flatter her, be brilliant.

But Theodora was so obviously wrapped up in her conversation with that silken whippersnapper. He rose and sauntered over to the lawn. He could not help looking back once—and he saw Theodora's eyes following him with a strange, veiled expression. Perhaps someone had told her some lie or other against him—or like most women, she could not bear to have the circle of men around her diminish. Who could tell? Women were a strange race.

He helped himself to a goblet of Cæcuban wine from the silver tray of a graceful slave girl and emptied it in one draught. To hades with garden parties. To hades with women. What was he doing here? Wine. He must have more wine. Well, there was plenty of that about, here. That was something.

If only the Emperor would come. The right word at the right moment with a man of Maximian's caliber and one had the command.

There was a new attraction on the lawn, now: a magician. He was a clever fellow, too, producing endless streams of ribbon from the nose and ears of a pretty Circassian girl, a gigantic bunch of flowers from the tunic of a pompous old senator, and a dozen writhing snakes from his own hair. When the ladies became frightened, he uttered an incantation in a weird sort of gibberish, and the snakes seemed to shrivel up and become rigid and were little wooden sticks, which he set on fire. Brandishing his thin arms wildly, he made the fire glow and shrink as it pleased him, and when he uttered another magic formula, it went out altogether.

Very clever, these tricksters. Constantius felt a light touch on his arm. He turned round. It was Livonia, one of the ladies-in-waiting of the princess, a charming creature with pouting lips and smouldering eyes. "One hour after sunset", she whispered. "At the little garden door." Domitilla and Vipsania approached, and Livonia immediately disappeared in a group of spectators.

Charming woman, thought Constantius. But what audacity to pick up a potential lover in such a way. He had another goblet of Cæcuban. He felt flattered, as any man will, when a pretty woman shows him that she desires him. But he was not going to start an affair with her. Oh, no. He had to concentrate on his task, and that was all that mattered. No nonsense.

Bit heady, this wine. The thing to do was to slip out and drive the chariot at a thundering pace. That would do him good. No one would miss him, and these garden parties were informal, anyway. . . .

The next morning, at breakfast, Terentius was at his most inquisitive. He wanted to know everything, every single detail. It was most unusual; as a rule, the legate of the

Fourteenth had already two hours of stiff work to his credit when he sat down for his breakfast, and he contented himself with wolfing tremendous quantities of food and giving little grunts as answers to a guest's questions.

"It wasn't a very interesting party", said Constantius. "Mamertinus was as slippery as an eel; the princess showed much interest in the golden boy Vatinius; the Emperor did not turn up, just as you said he wouldn't; and I drank too much Cæcuban. I came back before sunset, had a bath and my evening meal, read a bit, and went to bed."

"Silliest report I ever heard", said Terentius, munching. "You wouldn't keep anything from me, would you now, Paleface?"

"I tell you, that was all there was to it. There was a fairly good magician at the party, doing some tricks I had not seen before, and a pretty girl wanted me to come and see her after sunset, if that's of interest to you. . . ."

"Well—" Terentius yawned a little and began to tackle a bowl of stewed apricots—"and why didn't you see her—if she was pretty? Who was she?"

"I wasn't in the mood for that sort of thing", said Constantius. "Besides, I am a married man, as you know, and—"

Terentius roared with laughter. "Wonderful! oh, wonderful! He's a married man. He's got a son of thirteen. Holy Juno, would you believe it! Dear old Paleface. Life in Britain must be a sad affair. . . ."

"Not at all." Constantius felt annoyed and embarrassed at the same time. "I haven't met any woman here who is half as attractive as Helena—"

"Touching," nodded Terentius, "really touching. But, man, even if your good lady is the very spirit of Venus—she isn't here! Do you mean to say that you intend to remain faithful to her until you've reconquered Britain? Say yes, just dare to say yes, and I'll tell that story to Berontius, who is always in need of material for a new poem. Well, never mind, friend, don't get angry with me, it isn't worth your while. But tell me, who was your pretty admirer?"

"You are an indiscreet old woman, Pigface."

"Come, come, what are you trying to do? Shield the maidenly honor of a little trollop, just because she's had sense enough to find you attractive? You can take it from me, there were not two girls or women at that party of whom I couldn't tell you stories that would make an elephant blush! Who was it? Domitilla? Metella? Fulvia? She's a cute one, is Fulvia, but she has such a nasty habit of becoming a widow when she's getting tired of a husband. Paula? No, can't be her, she's only just started an affair with Rhesus, the singer. He isn't much of a singer, really, but the women are after him in close formations, they just faint when he squawks away on a high note. Marcella? You wouldn't find much competition, if it's Marcella. Only old Æmilius, who thinks she is faithful to him because he's senile, and young Gabinius, who thinks the same because he underrates old Æmilius, and Marcus Pollio, who doesn't think. Never did. Not Marcella? Well, perhaps it's Celia. She's the eighth wonder, our Celia. Bit too much competition there, even for my taste. There's dear Senator Proculeius, pompous ass, and Varro, Strabonius, the poet Berontius I told you about, and the officer corps of the Numidian cavalry regiment. Yes, our Celia."

"This is disgusting", said Constantius. "I want to eat my breakfast, Pigface."

"Well, I've enumerated practically all the eligible women who were at the party. Can't see dear old Vipsania trying to make love to you. She has become a hippopotamus and has wisely given up the struggle. All the others are a bit beyond the limit, and you did say she was pretty. There are the ladies-in-waiting, of course, but that is out of question—"

"Why?" asked Constantius innocently.

Terentius stared at him. "Well, obviously, because—" he swallowed noisily, poured himself a goblet of wine.

"What's the matter with you, Pigface?"

The legate's face was a shade paler, as he asked. "Look here, friend, I won't ask you for the name of the lady, as you are so discreet, but will you tell me exactly what she said to you?"

Constantius shook his head. "No harm in that", he said with a shrug. "She touched my arm and murmured something about 'one hour after sunset—at the little garden door'. Then someone approached, and she slid away."

Terentius' face was tense now. "Just one more thing", he said. "*Was* she one of the ladies-in-waiting?"

"Well, yes. Why?"

"Oh, Jupiter", groaned Terentius. "Oh, Pluto. Oh, Paleface."

"*Will* you tell me what is the matter with you?" pressed Constantius.

"With me? Nothing is the matter with me, I assure you. It's you I'm worried about! Yes, you—you incredible, impossible father of innocence. Has it never occurred to you that the message of your pretty lady may not have been her own message?"

"Wh-what?"

"Yes! What do you think she's a lady-in-waiting for? That's what I meant when I said that it could not be a lady-in-waiting. None of them would dare to start that sort of thing under the very nose of her mistress, especially when that mistress has made it pretty obvious that she enjoys the company of the man in question. She was giving you a message from her mistress—that's what she was doing! And you, like a fool, like seven legions of fools, went home, had your dinner, read a bit, and went to bed! Oh, ye gods, give me strength! The Emperor's daughter wants to sleep with him, and he goes home and reads a bit. Was it a good book, my Constantius?"

"But—she spent all the afternoon talking to Vatinius—I hardly got a word in edgeways."

Terentius laughed. "That shows that she's a clever woman, Paleface. She was playing about with him, for everyone to see. Excellent cover. And then she sends for you. And you— oh, all ye holy furies! There goes the command of the British expedition. . . ."

"That isn't the way to get a command, anyway", growled Constantius.

Terentius gave him a compassionate look. "I don't know what Britain's done to you," he said, "but if you think that you have the slightest chance now, with Theodora an implacable enemy, you're just mad. You're out, friend. And you had victory within reach—what do I say?—you had it handed to you on a silver platter."

"Whom are they going to send?" muttered Constantius, crestfallen. "Whom can they send?"

He got the answer a week later, when it was officially announced that the Legate Marcus Vatinius had gone to Massilia, to inspect the ship building there and to take over command of the Nineteenth and Twenty-Seventh Legions, which were to be concentrated for special purposes.

Terentius was right. He was out.

He went to his room. At a large table near the window he sat down and gazed at the strange labyrinth of clay that covered it. He was not exactly a sculptor. His model of Gessoriacum was more than primitive, but the distances were exact enough. Here was the town, the knolls near the coast, the port, the fortifications of which he knew and those that Carausius was likely to have built, so as to make the town secure from the land side. For Carausius was still in possession of Gessoriacum, whose harbor contained a large part of his fleet. It was a strong fortress. Now if one were to build a mole, an artificial stretch of land across, here!— one could do that even in the face of the enemy—a huge mole; one could cut the harbor off, seal off the whole town. It was a good idea. Yes, it was an excellent idea. Unfortunately it would remain an idea only.

The whim of a woman had put Vatinius into command. On such things depend the fates of empires.

He swept the clay off the table. Out. Out. He was out.

CHAPTER 8

"CAREFUL, NOW," warned Hilary. "The rocks are slippery. Hold tight—"

"Are you all right, Constantine?"

"Of course, Mother", was the indignant answer. "It's easy."

Favonius chuckled; it always amused him when the young master used his favorite expression. Between them they half pushed, half carried the lean, lanky old man down the cliff.

"Descent into hades", murmured Legate Curio. "I don't think I can make it, Centurion."

"Oh, yes, you can, sir. Just lean on me."

From below the sea was singing up to them. A pale moon, half hidden in the clouds, was their only light.

Helena slipped, and at once an arm caught her round the waist. "It's all right", said Hilary; his quiet smile was worth a king's ransom. She smiled back at him. "I know I shouldn't have come", she said. "But I had to come."

"Of course", said Hilary.

"Can you see the boat, Constantine?"

"Not yet, Mother."

"By Jupiter, we've done it", said Curio. "This is the place, isn't it?"

"Yes, sir. The torch, Constantine!"

The flickering little flame grew.

"I can see the boat now, Mother."

"Eyes like a hawk", muttered Favonius.

"I've got a word to say, before I go, Domina Helena", said Curio. There was an almost rapt expression on his cadaverous old face. "You have done wonders, you know. I'm not easily given to admiration—but I never met a woman like you before, and frankly, I don't think there is one. It certainly isn't your fault that this island has not been reconquered. The attack was badly led."

"It was not led by my husband", said Helena calmly. "When you see the Emperor, tell him that sooner or later he will have to put Constantius in command, and the sooner it is, the better it will be for Rome. I have done nothing. I might have been able to do something, if the attack had not failed."

"I will tell him", said Curio. "But once more, Domina— will you not change your mind and go instead with me? It is easy to see that your husband will be doubly strong, having you at his side."

The ghost of a smile. "There is only room for one on board", said Helena.

The old legate looked at Constantine and understood.

"Besides," said Helena, "the Emperor has more need of an experienced officer than of me. And I must keep our men together—for the next attack. Just as well that so few of them have been exposed, though it's a pity about every one of them who was. That man Vatinius has much to account for."

Hilary and Favonius were trying hard to get the boat alongside the little platform of rock on which they were standing. There were six men in the boat, all sailors.

"May the gods keep you, Domina Helena", said Curio. "You came north to ask for my protection, and it all ended in you protecting me—you and your faithful ones. And if it were not for Hilary I'd never have known anything about this ship."

"Farewell, Curio. I think you can rely on captain and crew. They are smugglers, yes; but they, too, like their lives, and Hilary has told them from me that I'll have them flayed if anything happens to you. They'll do their best, poor as it may be. You'll land in Gaul, near enough to safe territory. And—give my husband my love, Curio. . . ."

"I will", said the old legate, simply.

"Ready for you, sir", cried Favonius.

"Right. Farewell, Constantine. I'll tell your father he can expect to find his son a man when he lands. Goodbye, Hilary. Goodbye, Favonius."

He had not yet sat down when the boat was pushed off. Smugglers have no time to lose, and their goods were already safely on board—they had been instructed to come for the passenger only in the very hour of departure.

The little group on the rock waited until the boat was out of sight and then began to climb back. Favonius first, then Constantine, then Helena and Hilary. It was much easier than the descent had been. A quarter of an hour later they had reached the top of the cliff and the bushes where Rufus was waiting with the horses.

"Nothing, Rufus?"

"All quiet, Favonius."

"Off we go."

An hour's ride took them back to a solitary farm, where a lean old man in a simple blue dress joined them and mounted the spare horse that Curio had used. Silently they rode on. Six persons had left the little town of Iuviacum, and six persons returned.

Carausius had too many eyes not to make precautions advisable.

A fortnight later they were back in the little villa at the outskirts of Verulam, where "the widow Zenia and her son" had been living these past few years. People did not know very much about her—except that "she had come from somewhere in the north"; and with her, her son, her majordomo, Hilary, and a big, burly bear of a man who was supposed to be the head gardener. He was called Marcus and could lift a fully grown man with each arm at the same time. There were also a cook, named Rufus, and a number of other servants.

The widow Zenia was leading a very quiet and retired sort of life; she was paying much attention to her beautifully kept garden and to her stable—for she was very keen on good horses, and her son was an excellent young rider, who would one day be a fine soldier in the army of the great Carausius; the neighbors knew that from a very good source—the chief gardener Marcus himself.

It was strange, perhaps, that the widow Zenia, a dignified woman and still very beautiful, changed her servants so often. Not the main servants, they always stayed on—but the waiters and dishwashers and undergardeners, and there had been a time when the chief of police in Verulam, Rutilo, had made some inquiries about it. But the result seemed to have been satisfactory, for ever since Rutilo had greeted the widow with great respect when they met accidentally in the streets. And why should he not, after all? She was a lady of good birth, everybody could see that, she paid her taxes regularly to the newly installed tax collector in the Via Capuana, or rather Via Carausia, as it was called now, and her majordomo had an open hand for the poor. Besides, she did not show off her clothes, and there were no female slaves in the house, except for two elderly women who were serving as her maids . . . a very sensible thing when one has a young son of sixteen or seventeen.

It was said, though, that the young man had been seen more than once with little Minervina, whose parents were living in a neighboring villa. Empty gossip, very likely— why, the child was only fifteen, and a sweet little thing she was, too, with her large eyes. It was a pity, of course, that she was Roman by birth, and not Celtic or Frankish; but, surely that was not her fault. It was a misfortune rather than a fault, to be of Roman descent, times being what they were. Quite a number of them seemed to think that the Emperor of Rome might reclaim and reconquer the island of Britain, which was pure nonsense, of course. There had never been such an army as Carausius' army, and it was growing stronger every day; the Franks, the Frisians, the Danes sent contingents in such numbers that the Carausian officers could pick and choose the best and send the others back where they came from.

Fresh fortifications were being built all along the coasts, and never before had the frontier in the north been defended with so much vigor. Trade, too, had looked up after the inevitable lull in the first period after the invasion.

And if any doubts could still have persisted in some hearts, the resounding victory over the Roman fleet had dispelled them. The Romans had not even succeeded in landing a single man! The gods themselves had come to Carausius' help, for a storm, unusual at this time of the year, had battered the imperial fleet, pursued by the victorious ships of the defenders. . . .

"There is no need to worry at the moment", said Hilary. "I have seen Rutilo—talked to him for over an hour; he is not the man to conceal much that is on his mind. There is no suspicion against us. Thrax and Boaldus are dead, and they did not talk before they died. Our entire net is practically untouched. How long it will keep like that may be another question."

The widow Zenia raised the chin of Coel's daughter. "It will keep until my husband comes", she said in a hard voice. "I am glad I did not give the sign for the attack prematurely—it's your merit, Hilary, not mine."

"You were against me", smiled Hilary, "only as long as you did not know that Constantius was not in command of the imperial fleet. It was fortunate, perhaps, that we found that out so early. Unfortunately Carausius is a great man."

She flared up. "I don't like you saying that, Hilary. He is a usurper, a mutineer—he took a glaring opportunity."

"I disagree", was the calm reply. "It was a brilliant military stroke. I don't call him a great man because he defeated the Roman fleet. His own fleet was the best the Romans had, and he was their best admiral . . . before he decided to play his own game. It is not greatness to defeat the second best if one has the best. And the Roman fleet had to be built in a great hurry, and it was badly led, as Legate Curio said. But look what Carausius has done in the few years he has been in power. In spite of being an invader, he has made himself liked as well as feared. The frontier in the north is safe; the Caledonians are filled with a healthy respect. And his fleets are carrying his name even beyond the Pillars of Hercules. He rules the channel with complete sovereignty, and that means ruling Britain. No, don't frown at me, Domina; I know he is a usurper and that we must fight him, and fight him we will—but it's no good minimizing his worth—it means minimizing our own effort and with it our own merit."

"Always just, Hilary, aren't you?" smiled Helena.

"Trying to be, Domina. I learned it in a good school."

She sighed. "Father—he died in time. Something broke in me when it happened, Hilary. But he died in time."

"In a way we all do, I believe", said Hilary thoughtfully. "I've come to think that we die when our task is up. And that, you see, makes me hopeful."

"What do you mean?"

"I mean that Carausius' greatness may well be in our favor."

"You are talking in riddles."

Hilary's dreamy eyes were half closed. He was sitting opposite her—when they were alone, she often dropped the formality between mistress and servant nowadays. "His rule is built upon too slender a foundation", he said slowly. "It is built upon his own greatness. It is a one-man system. There is no one to replace him—if he dies."

"Why should he die?"

"He will die—when his time is up. But it's impossible to say when that will be."

"Except", she broke in quickly, "if his death were brought about by some—accident."

He shook his head, smiling. "Still the wild, wild Queen", he said. "Zenobia rather than Zenia."

She smiled, too. It was true that she had chosen the name because it was like an abbreviation of the Palmyran Queen's.

"I wasn't thinking of any action on our side", he went on. "But conquerors rarely die in their beds. We must wait and see. By now Curio must be in Rome. We have our organization—it is small, and we shall never be in the position of giving battle. But we can do a good deal, once the Romans have landed. We have the Christians on our side, too."

"Not exactly of much fighting value, from what I have seen of them", said Helena, pursing her lips. "They are mostly women and slaves; and no wonder: it's a religion for the weak, not for the strong."

"I'm not so sure", murmured Hilary, his eyes fixed on the floor. "I have seen odd things—and I know something about their history. When they believe in something, they'll die for it rather than give it up. And they do believe in authority and the law. They will never revolt against lawful authority. They will always support it. And that's why they are for Rome and against Carausius, whose authority is not lawful."

"They have been good to us, when we sorely needed it", admitted Helena.

Hilary nodded. He thought of the time when they had lived in the woods, far up in the north; when Favonius and he and Constantine had been laying snares for wild rabbits and the soldiers had been searching for berries and making soup of wild herbs and mushrooms. More than once they had been near starvation. But there were two soldiers who always seemed to manage to get food from the nearest village or town simply by asking for it. For a long time they would not tell how they did it, despite the curiosity of their friends, but finally it leaked out—they were Christians, and all they did was get in touch with some person of their own faith, who then informed other members of the community. It seemed to be the law with them always to help one another. And they had certain secret signs by which they would recognize each other immediately. He remembered well that the matter had been rather distasteful to him. He had hated secrecy all his life—well, all that seemed a very long time ago now. It was a long time ago. It was before he had met Albanus. It made all the difference in the world whether one had or had not met Albanus.

"Have you heard anything from your friend Albanus lately?"

Hilary looked up in surprise; then he smiled. "Sometimes I forget that you are King Coel's daughter", he said. "Yes, I was thinking of him. I was thinking that it makes all the difference whether one knows him or not."

She shook her head. "It's no good leaving things to the gods or to a God, as your friend does. One must work them out oneself. I have no wish to meet Albanus—nor do I think it would make much difference if I did."

Quick steps sounded outside, and Constantine burst into the room like a gust of wind. "Mother—Hilary—big news!"

She looked at him severely. "You are a man, now, son; no news is big enough to justify such an entrance."

The young man's body stiffened, almost as though he had caught himself in midair. He bowed a little. "Sorry, Mother."

"Well, then—what news have you got?"

"Carausius is going to pass through Verulam tomorrow afternoon."

There was a sudden flash in her eyes, but her voice sounded quite calm and even a little disappointed as she said, "What of it? He is not coming to see me! Who told you about it?"

"Old Scapula—I mean Aulus Scapula. He has it from the Governor himself. And they are preparing the streets for him now. I'd like to see what he's like, wouldn't you?"

"You have seen Minervina?" came the relentless question.

The boy's face changed to the color of peonies. "Y-yes, Mother."

She nodded. "Remember that she is the daughter of people of good standing; if you see her too frequently it will be harmful to her. There will be talk and gossip. Use discretion and remember that we, too, must not be talked about. No, I don't wish to hear anything from you now. Think it over. Leave us alone, son."

There had been a moment, thought Hilary, when Constantine really looked like a man, but no one looks like a man for long with her.

Then, as he saw her face, he knew instantly that there was danger afoot. He had come to learn the signs; he was not often wrong. She was not thinking of Constantine and his first love—that, in her opinion, had been dealt with. She was thinking of something entirely different. He remembered the casual way in which she had treated the news of Carausius' imminent arrival in Verulam: "What of it?"

She was thinking of Carausius' arrival, too. He remembered his own words; there was no one to replace Carausius when he died. And suddenly he knew that she was thinking of how Carausius should die. . . .

Two hundred cavalry made the vanguard; their armor, rough breastplates, large shields, winged helmets, and long lances were Frankish in style. Carausius, as everybody knew, had a great liking for the Franks; he even dressed like one himself, and so did most of his officers and all his bodyguards.

The streets were strewn with flowers, and many of the houses had carpets hanging out of the windows and little emblems in blue and silver, Carausius' colors.

After the cavalry came a light Gallic wagon, surrounded by fifty picked horse guards. Then another two hundred cavalry; then another Gallic wagon.

The young man in the shadow of the open door took careful aim—back went the bowstring—and then a huge hand clamped down on it, and a familiar voice said, "No good, sonny—and it's the wrong man, too."

"Favonius", hissed Constantine. "Leave me alone— you're mad. Oh, ye gods, I had him—I had him cold—"

"Steady, son. It's all over now. Stop it, I say. Do you want to see us all imprisoned, your mother included?"

"Mother has nothing to do with this", muttered the young man. "I don't know what gave you the idea of spying on me—"

The giant centurion grinned. "When one of my best bows disappears from the armory—and when you go about with such a beautifully casual air, as though you couldn't hurt a fly even if you tried—well, it makes a man think. . . ."

The last detachment of cavalry had clattered past, but there were still agents among the crowd. Favonius closed the door. "It was a damn fool's plan, son", he said severely. "Nothing good could have come from it, whether you succeeded or not. And the man you aimed at was Allectus, not Carausius."

"Doesn't he deserve to die?" argued Constantine. "He is a traitor, isn't he? I haven't forgotten what he tried to do to mother four years ago—even if you have."

"Who knocked him flat, then?" Favonius chuckled. "I may not have made a thorough job of it," he said, "but at least no harm has come to your mother because of what I did. Had you shot him just now, we'd have had the soldiers in here in no time, and can you defend this house against several hundred men? It was a boy's prank, Constantine."

"I would have killed a dangerous enemy of the Emperor."

"At what cost? Is Allectus worth your mother's life? Now you be sensible, boy—it's easy. A great soldier I knew used to say greatness lies in doing what is essential, not what is agreeable."

All the time he went on looking at the street through the small oval opening used by the *ostiarius* to inspect and challenge newcomers.

"Carausius was in the first wagon", he said. "I suppose he was too quick for you; difficult to get an arrow in, too, with all those bodyguards around him. This sort of job should not be done by one man alone—if it must be done at all. But even Carausius—"

He broke off suddenly and drew a quick breath. "All right", he said in an unsteady voice. "Put that bow back where it belongs and stop this nonsense. I won't tell on you, you know that. But I want your word that you won't do anything like this again."

"All right", said Constantine sulkily.

Favonius saw him sauntering off; when he was out of sight, the centurion opened the door and slipped out. He could still see the last little group of riders; they were walking their horses. There were about a dozen of them and, yes, the three in the middle were Roman officers. . . .

From her window in the first floor of the house, Helena had been watching Carausius' cavalcade, and Hilary had been watching her.

"The head of a bull", she said, "and the neck of a bull. Did Father ever tell you the story of Brengan, who was so strong that he could sever the head of a bull with a single stroke of his axe?"

"I wonder", said Hilary, "what he would say to your thoughts at the present moment. . . ."

"The man in the second wagon was Allectus", she went on. "He really has recovered, then."

"He is a big man now", said Hilary. "The chief tax collector. Some say he is the second man of the realm. But he is not a great man. And I wish you wouldn't think the thoughts you are thinking."

"Tiresome, aren't you, sometimes, Hilary?"

"It is madness, Domina. It is not the way it should be done. Look at it from whatever point you wish, it is still murder."

She swung round. "How dare you—"

Hilary dropped on his knee. "Forgive me, Domina. But I had to say it."

"Get up", she ordered curtly. "I hate seeing a man on his knees. But I wish you wouldn't try my patience too far—"

He rose slowly. "When we are in doubt whether an action we plan is right or wrong," he said in his usual clear voice, "the best thing we can do is to try and think what the best man we know would think of it. And if I think of your father—or of Alban—"

"Alban? Is he the best man you know now, Hilary? I didn't know it went quite that far with you. Are you a Christian, then?"

To her amazement he hesitated. Was it really possible that he, Hilary, with his clear brain, the disciple of King Coel, had been caught by the strange lore of that Jewish prophet? Weak-minded women and slaves, both by rank and by nature—yes. But Hilary?

"I don't know", said Hilary. "I'm not sure yet. It is very difficult. There are many things I do not yet understand. I have not seen Alban often enough."

"It seems to me that you've seen him far too often", she exclaimed. "And applying your own rule, Hilary—I wonder what my father would say to this!"

He nodded with great enthusiasm. "So do I, Domina. I've been wondering for some time about that. It is what I regret perhaps more than anything else—that King Coel and Alban never met."

She gave an impatient shrug. "Hopeless talk. What I have to think of is what my husband is thinking of—the cause to which we owe our loyalty. I am thinking of Rome. Carausius is going to spend several days at the governor's palace. The widow Zenia could easily obtain an audience with him. You yourself said that his government rests on him alone. If something happens to him, Rome would—"

She saw Hilary raise a finger to his lips.

A moment later a slave slipped in. "Domina, the chief gardener wishes to see you. He says it's urgent."

"Show him in."

Her eyes widened when Favonius entered. She had never seen him look so pale.

"What is it, Favonius? Don't stand there like a silly statue. Speak up, man. What is it?"

But he waited, listening to the footsteps of the slave; it seemed a long time before he raised his head, and his voice sounded strangely hoarse as he said, "I saw a group of riders passing our house. Oh, not Carausius' train, but separately. There were three Roman officers among them, in uniform. I followed them."

"Roman officers?"

"Yes, Domina. A legate and two tribunes. The others were nobles of Carausius' Court and a few bodyguards."

"Carausius' Court—as if that scoundrel were a crowned head!"

Favonius swallowed hard. "I am afraid he is, Domina."

"Are you mad?"

"I wouldn't be surprised if I were, Domina. I went up to them—couldn't resist it—and asked them what they were doing here. They weren't prisoners, you know: they carried arms. They didn't answer, but one of the nobles said, 'Out of the way, dog. These noble Romans have come to make the peace with our master and to recognize him as Emperor of Britain in the name of Rome.'"

Helena stared at him. "It is not true", she said tonelessly. "It can't be true. He lied."

But Favonius shook his head. "I thought that, too, Domina, and I looked at the legate, and the legate bowed ..."

"Rome", said Helena. "Rome."

"The noble said all these things in a pretty loud voice", went on Favonius. "He wanted people to hear about it; he wanted them to see that the Romans did not contradict him. Hundreds have heard it by now; the news is spreading all over the town."

"Carausius, Emperor of Britain", said Helena. "Recognized by Rome as Emperor of Britain. My husband must be dead."

Favonius had tears in his eyes.

But the bitterest pain was Hilary's. He, to whom Rome meant little, saw grief transforming the woman he loved to stone. Yes, loved. The rigid discipline he had established over himself sufficed no longer to shield him against the searing, despairing pain—he could resist no more. He loved her. And loving her, he embraced her grief with a lover's ardor and made it his, and it was his without consolation or hope.

BOOK THREE

❧

A.D. 294–296

CHAPTER I

THEY WERE BUSY all over Britain preparing for a festival such as had never been before, "the Festival of the Seven Years".

For seven years now Carausius had been ruling Britain—for three of them as Emperor of Britain.

There would be official programs of celebration in all the cities and towns; speeches and garlands, banquets and fireworks, theater performances and parades; and all that was to last for seven days and seven nights.

Almost the only building in which no one seemed to take much notice of it was the palace at Londinium.

Everybody in the city knew the row of windows in the upper floor of the left wing of the building, where the Emperor worked. During the day the palace was silent and forbidding; at night, dim light shone through the windows. But day or night—Carausius was always at work.

There was nothing in the least unusual in the fact that the chief tax collector had an audience an hour before midnight. Nor was it unusual that he should bring his entire staff with him—the heads of the various departments with their chief clerks and advisers.

"The whole galaxy of bloodsuckers", thought Liudemar, stretching himself a little and crossing his hands over the sword hilt. The chief of the Emperor's bodyguards was a Frank almost seven feet high; the bodies of at least two men seemed to have been used in order to form his. He always wore a bear's skin over his shoulders, winter and summer, and Carausius' favorite joke was that Liudemar had skinned it off his own body so as to feel less hot.

The Chamberlain Theudovec went to announce the visitors; he, too, was a Frank, and so were more than half the higher officials of the palace. During the years in which he had been fighting them at sea, Carausius had acquired a good deal of respect for his enemies; now they formed the shock troops of his army and navy and most of his bodyguards.

Figures, thought Liudemar, and he would have spat, had he not in time remembered that the Emperor had pulled him up for that last week. Figures all the time. Adding. Dividing. Making a nice profit for himself and a nice mess for the Emperor. Bloodsucker.

This time he was thinking of the chief tax collector personally. Hawkface. Vulture. Giving himself airs. Bloodsucker. Every time he went in to see the Emperor, the old man was in a nasty temper. Today he had got himself plenty of helpers—perhaps he'd need them, too.

There was not much room for intuitive feeling within the thick skull of the Frank, but enough to sense that there was trouble in the air. The whole day had been troublesome. When he had got up in the morning, his sword had fallen out of the scabbard and got stuck in the floor; now that was a bad sign, as everyone knew. He had made a vow to Wodan: a bull calf, not later than one day after the next payday. Sometimes that sort of thing helped; sometimes it didn't. One never knew with Wodan. He was as moody as Carausius. Well, his day was almost over now, and what trouble there still might be was not his concern but other people's. But the Emperor had been ill tempered all day, like a bunch of nettles.

Chamberlain Theudovec came back. "The Emperor will see the chief tax collector alone", he announced.

Allectus gave him a smiling nod and walked into the cabinet.

Theudovec took his place next to Liudemar. "I wouldn't like to be Allectus tonight", he whispered.

"Or any other time", said Liudemar contemptuously.

Theudovec hid a grin. "The old man hasn't been in a good mood all day, as you know," he murmured, "but it's far worse since that messenger came in."

"Which one? There were half a dozen in succession."

"The last one—with the secret badge. He's done it."

"What was his news?"

"I've no idea. But it must have been trouble."

"Perhaps the Caledonians are getting difficult again."

"Perhaps. Well, the old man will deal with it."

Meanwhile, Allectus had walked up to the large desk at the end of the large room, come to attention, and saluted.

Carausius took no notice. He was reading a letter. The Emperor of Britain, on first sight, seemed to have much in common with Maximianus. There was the same robust frame, the same bull's neck and jutting chin under the brown beard. But there was an expression of strange melancholy on the massive face, and it was that more than anything else that made men sometimes so uneasy in his presence; it was a melancholy that seemed to say that nothing really mattered very much—and certainly not the life of a man; he had not always had that expression; there had been a time, not even long ago, when he could roar with laughter at a bawdy joke, drink throughout a night and a day, and sail out for pirates the night after, enjoying it all with the same primitive joy as Liudemar. He had changed. Not that he had become old, or tired. He was at fifty-two as strong as ever; seventeen hours of daily work came easy to him. Nor had it gone to his head that Diocletian and Maximian had acknowledged his emperorship and addressed him as "Augustus" in their letters. He had needed their acknowledgment for political reasons, that was all. He cared little for official ceremonial.

Yet it was his emperorship that had brought about the change in him, because it had taught him that fundamentally a man is alone. For to birth and death, emperorship adds a third, loneliness, perhaps more frightening than either of the other two, because it is longer lasting in consciousness.

Allectus stood waiting, tall, erect, and elegant. He is taking a long time reading a very short letter, he thought. He has learned play acting after all. How much does he know?

It was quite futile to ask oneself that question. It did not matter how much he knew. The plan was fixed, irrevocable. Nothing could alter it. The sand was running out.

At long last Carausius looked up. "I shall keep it short", he said in his deep, quiet voice. "I have more important work to do than dealing with you."

Wrong, thought Allectus. Very wrong. But never mind. Spit it out.

"Too many complaints", said Carausius. "I can overlook that for a while, when it's about a man I like and trust. I cannot overlook it indefinitely. You have brought half your staff here— that was quite unnecessary. I have made my own investigation."

"I know—Sire", said Allectus.

"You do? So much the better." Carausius' mouth showed contempt. "You have raised a full tenth more taxes than you were ordered, and they are not booked. I am not asking you what you have done with the money because I know what you have done with it."

Allectus smiled. "What have I done with it—Sire?"

Carausius raised his massive head. "You have raised the nucleus of a private army", he said calmly. "There are five thousand men in your private pay. They will be disarmed and banned from Britain within a week."

"Will they?" asked Allectus. His gray, twisted smile was too much for the Emperor, and he rose.

"You have always been a fool, Allectus, but I didn't think you could be as foolish as all that. I wanted to spare you, but you've made it impossible. Liudemar!"

It was the roar of a lion.

But the Emperor's chief bodyguard did not enter. Instead a tumultuous noise arose in the anteroom. And Allectus still smiled his intolerable smile.

Carausius understood at last. His hand flashed out to the little table next to the desk, but his sword was not in its usual place. He felt a searing pain in his side. In utter surprise he saw a large metal button sticking out of his tunic; it had not been there before—what was it?

Then he saw Allectus throw a second dart, tried to sidestep it, found that he could not move, and felt the impact full on his armorless breast. He slumped back into his chair with its two crowned lions.

"Who is foolish?" asked Allectus softly. Cautiously, like the experienced hunter he was, he approached his prey. "You have done your work, Carausius", he said, always smiling. "The rough work that had to be done by a man of your sort. The fighting work. You have done it for me. And now I am taking over. The time for admirals and generals has passed; the time for the statesman begins. Did you really think I was trying to cheat you of a tenth when I can have the whole without cheating? You've always underrated me. . . ."

Outside the tumult had died down. Allectus knew what that meant. Not even Liudemar could fight fifty men singlehanded—and they were picked officers, dressed as clerks, with their swords hidden under their cloaks. Liudemar was dead. Theudovec was dead. And five hundred men, drawn in batches of thirty, fifty, and more, were converging on the palace from all sides, to make sure that the bribed officials did not go back on their word.

He went on staring at the dying Emperor; somehow he could not keep up his gloating smile. And suddenly he knew why that was so. It was because Carausius himself was smiling now. Allectus' first reaction was stark fear—he even looked back over his shoulder, as though Carausius' smile could only mean that there was help coming in the door, noiselessly, behind his back; but there was no one—and the Emperor's life was draining away quickly—each of the two wounds was mortal. What had he to smile about? Or was he already delirious? He was not. His eyes were still open, and their expression was—was—a sort of gigantic hilarity; he looked as if he were going to burst into a tremendous, long-rumbling laughter that would shake the foundations of the palace, the city, and the island. And as though he felt pity for his murderer's bewilderment, the poor man did not understand the marvellous, the uproarious joke of it all, and had to have it explained to him. Carausius opened his mouth to speak. A stream of blood shot forward over the papers and scrolls on the desk. The Emperor's face became a distorted, horrible mask; he spat more blood and spat again, and his mouth came to look like a bubbly, frothy scarlet thing—and yet he still smiled, and now Allectus could hear a sound, a sigh more than a word, raucous and derisive—

"—fool!"

Then Carausius' eyes became fixed toward eternity, and head and neck and shoulders slumped again in the high chair.

At last, thought Allectus. He took a deep breath. He had won—he could breathe, and Carausius could not. He had won. At last. The great hulk in the chair was food for the worms. This very moment his blood had started to coagulate in his veins.

But even now, yes, even now there was that grin, that supreme expression of sovereign and contemptuous joy on the dead face.

Drawn as by magic force, Allectus approached the body and saw that it was still holding that letter; it was not crumpled—and the dead hand held it as though for him to read, for him alone to read.

And he read the secret, his face only an inch distant from the dead face with its frozen grin.

He screamed.

At once the door opened, and they crashed into the room, three, five, ten, twenty of his men; they had been waiting for his call; he had given a strict order not to interfere with "his last audience with the Emperor" before they heard his voice.

They had heard, and here they were; and they stopped in their tracks, so suddenly and vehemently that there was confusion among those behind them, wild clanking of arms, a few curses—and silence.

They found Allectus, just as he had found Carausius only a quarter of an hour ago: with his eyes fixed on a small letter in his hand, reading it and reading it again.

It was Rome's declaration of war.

CHAPTER 2

SIXTY HIGH-RANKING OFFICERS rose when the Cæsar entered the tent. He acknowledged their salute with a nod and took his seat at the head of the war council.

The four standard-bearers in front of the tent gave witness of the fact that Rome, this time, had spared no effort. Four regular legions were an army, and an army had been necessary to reconquer Gessoriacum. Even they, and the thousands of auxiliaries with them, would not have succeeded, had it not been for the gigantic ally they themselves had created during many months of work.

There it was, visible even from the entrance of the tent, stretching across what seemed to be the entire horizon: the biggest mole in all military history. Many a time they had thought they would never be able to drive it through. But the Cæsar had urged them on, cajoled them, threatened them, and on went the mole, relentlessly, despite hundreds of counterattacks on the part of the besieged Carausians—until the day when the mole had served its purpose, had cut off the Carausian fleet in the very harbor that had been its stronghold. War council after war council had been held in Gessoriacum, and always the mole had been the first point on the agenda—once they had realized the purpose for which the Roman general had had it built. It had become an obsession with the Carausians, that tremendous serpent of stone, whose embrace was to strangle the life out of the hapless town. They could not, they dared not send their ships out of the harbor—they knew that the Roman fleet, all newly built ships, was waiting for them. And the main force of the Carausian fleet was over there, across the channel, in the various ports of the isle of Vectis, and did not stir. And the serpent of stone grew and grew, despite all their ingenious attempts to destroy it. Then, when the terrible mole had reached the very harbor entrance, the Roman general had attacked in full force. And the town had fallen.

An overwhelming mass of war material had fallen into the hands of the Romans, including over a third of the

Carausian fleet, virtually intact. And immediately the attackers had gone to work on the ships; they were made seaworthy, and they were painted sea green all over. Hundreds of workmen had to mix paint for days.

The Cæsar had shown the most incredible clemency. True, most of the Carausian officers were sent to southern Gaul under heavy guard. But some of them he allowed to enter his own army, and with them all the ranks who wished to do so. The others were made to work. Burned houses had to be rebuilt, harbor installations reconstructed, streets cleared of rubble—for the Roman siege machines had caused much damage. Huge food transports arrived over land, and the price of grain was fixed on a low level, so that everybody could afford to buy it. Wine, too, was cheap and plentiful, and all looting was strictly forbidden. "This is the Divine Emperor Maximian's town. Looting here is the same crime as looting in Milan or Rome."

Perhaps the people of Gessoriacum would not have become Roman minded so quickly, despite the Cæsar's clemency, if Carausius had still been alive. He had been the virtual Emperor of Gessoriacum long before he had become Emperor of Britain. But Carausius was dead, and the new Emperor was not well known. There were many who had never even heard of Allectus before the astonishing news came that he had killed Carausius in open combat and was now Emperor in his stead.

Perhaps the name of Carausius would have overshadowed that of the Cæsar, although he was a mighty man indeed and the son-in-law of the Roman Emperor himself. They might have feared Carausius' return, for he, they knew, was not a man of clemency. But now Carausius himself was a shadow. Gessoriacum became enthusiastically Roman.

In the tent, the Legate Asclepiodatus reported that all was ready. The ships were seaworthy and fully manned. The regular troops had received the necessary replacements, and so had the auxiliaries. The latest reports from the enemy showed that he seemed to expect a landing somewhere on the coast of the Cantii or Regni tribes, possibly near Anderida. His fleet was still hovering off the isle of Vectis, ready to strike. The tides were favorable for the attack, and so was the weather—the sea was as smooth as a mirror.

"Give the word, Domine—and within two hours we sail."

But the Cæsar shook his head. "I do not agree with you about the weather being good. Your calm sea will cost us five thousand helmets and may spoil the entire plan."

Asclepiodatus, a capable soldier, understood.

"It is just in such weather that the enemy will expect us to strike", said the Cæsar for the benefit of the others. "You will remember the military principle: to come when you are unexpected is half the victory. Even a storm is better than a smooth sea—but the best thing of all would be fog. I have been in Britain long enough to know what fog means. Why, we could practically land before we are seen. Legate Aurelius!"

"Cæsar?"

"I want barrels of the sea-green paint put aboard each ship. As soon as the signal for attack is given, all the men on board must paint themselves sea-green all over: armor, tunics, faces, and all. It will reduce their visibility and save many lives. Legate Asclepiodatus!"

"Cæsar?"

"You will lead the first squadron independently. All ships stationed at present in the mouth of the Sequana are yours. You will sail northwest, bypass the isle of Vectis, and land on the western part of the south coast, in the district of the

Durotriges. Your task is to draw the enemy—the enemy on land, not their fleet. I want to avoid a sea battle. Whoever attacks Britain must do his utmost to avoid a sea battle. They've got a pretty good fleet and experienced sailors. As soon as you have landed—burn your ships."

"Burn them, Cæsar?"

"Burn them, I said. We have come to stay. I want every soldier of your force to understand that. Make it a nice big fire, too. The wider it can be seen, the better. What matters to me is that Allectus should think you are the main force. If we're lucky, he'll believe it and rush over to the west to stave you off. As for me, I shall land exactly where he now thinks that we shall land—at Anderida. I must have Anderida: it's the only serviceable port, and I can make a shuttle service between there and Gessoriacum, to get my auxiliaries over as quickly as possible."

Asclepiodatus nodded. "Lovely", he said. "What are my orders when the ships are burned, Cæsar? Do I give battle, or do I play the old cat-and-mouse game until we have him between us?"

The Cæsar gave him a slight bow. "You are in full command of your squadron, my Asclepiodatus. You will do whatever the situation requires."

Asclepiodatus' eyes sparkled. "It's a pleasure to serve under you, Cæsar", he said.

The Cæsar smiled and rose. As he walked out, everybody stood to attention.

Outside the four standard bearers gave the salute.

He acknowledged it and walked past them. Six aides-de-camp fell in with him. He gave a last satisfied look to his giant mole and mounted his horse; the aides did likewise, young men, all of them, eager and wiry, the highly bred products of the best military education in the world.

A quarter of an hour later they reached the government house, once Carausius' headquarters.

"My wife?" asked the Cæsar curtly.

The majordomo bowed. "The princess is awaiting the Cæsar."

"Very well." And, to the aides, "Ten pounds of gold to the first man to report bad weather to me—twenty to the man who reports fog."

They grinned, showing all their teeth. They loved him, all of them, as one loves a superior being. He was aware of it, and it did him good. But there was an expression of indefinable sadness on his face as he sauntered toward the rooms where Theodora was awaiting him.

CHAPTER 3

THE PERGOLA WAS STILL THERE; the lawn had become a wilderness, but that could be seen to; the house was untouched. It really was like a miracle, after all these years. Even most of the furniture was still there—which was, perhaps, due to the fact that Allectus had claimed and received the villa as a present from a grateful Carausius, almost ten years ago.

Almost ten years ago . . .

It was unbelievable. It was like yesterday.

Helena wandered restlessly from one room to another, from one memory chain to the next: here was her own room, the room where she had dreamed of things to come— the window through which her thoughts had traveled across fields and rivers and the sea to Rome.

She knew that Allectus had never inhabited the house, although he had kept a skeleton staff there; perhaps it had not been big enough for him—or he had preferred to keep closer to the various palaces of the man who was then his Emperor.

Thus, only her own thoughts and memories and feelings were nesting in walls and corners; it was her house she was taking possession of again. It was her life she was taking possession of again. She was being reborn, that was it. Reborn into the moment when she had opened her arms for the last time to life.

The ten years between were not real. She had dreamed that ten years had passed, when all that had happened was that Constantius had gone to Rome and was now coming back. Here were she—and the house—and the garden— and the trees, looking gravely down at their shadows, as she had gravely looked into her mirror this morning.

She was still young. Silver disks do not lie. There was a streak of white in her hair now—a little to one side of the curious peak he had always loved so much—about the breadth of a finger; as though some malicious little spirit had touched her while she was sleeping and drawn the life out of her hair with its touch. But it did not make her older, really. There were a few wrinkles, very few, round the corners of her eyes, hardly visible. And perhaps it would be evening when he came—or even night. She had been here only a few hours, but she had thought of that at least a dozen times. Oh, no, much more often. She laughed a little at herself. Always rushing ahead of time, she was.

It had been the most incredible audacity to come here, really, with the battle for the reconquest of Britain at the stage at which it was, or at least had been, then. But when the news had come through that "Emperor" Allectus was marching westward with all the troops available, to stave off the Roman attack, she just could not wait any longer. The little groups of resistance she had formed in the north and east had received the signal to act independently as the situation might require. It was all she could tell them at the present stage.

She herself, with Constantine, Hilary, Favonius, Rufus, and about twenty slaves, had set out for the south. Even Hilary's cautious nature had given in to her drive. He had held war council with Favonius, first—the old war dog had a sixth sense where battle and danger were concerned. He had found that not even a full legion could have prevented Favonius from action. He had given in, then. If they ran into Allectus' troops, they would pose as fugitives from the Roman attack. Helena would still be the "widow Zenia".

She herself had thrown all caution to the winds. This was the time she had been waiting for—there was to her not the shadow of a doubt that Constantius was in command, despite the fact that scarcely any news from Rome had reached them during the last years. For Carausius had closed off Britain hermetically.

She had no proof—a few very general rumors could hardly be called proof—and she had no doubt.

Constantius was in command, and that meant that Allectus was lost and that his flimsy, adventurous game was up.

One rumor said that Gessoriacum had fallen to the Romans—it came just before the news that the Romans had landed in the west. That had been three days ago—no, four—in the morning after that stormy night, followed by a dense fog.

Fog was lucky to her—she knew that. It was in fog, and owing to fog that she and Constantius had met. . . .

When Favonius, with a grin of unbelievable dimensions, said, "They've landed under the cover of fog, Domina", her mind was made up in a flash. She was not going to wait until Verulam was again occupied by Roman troops. She would go straight south, to the coast, to see for herself. "There will be a second landing, Favonius. I know my husband. Often enough he told me how he would invade Britain—he had worked it all out. 'My task is to defend Britain—therefore it must be my object to try and think with the brain of a potential enemy trying to attack Britain.' I can still hear him!"

But Favonius insisted on a detour. They had to avoid Londinium at all costs—for there they might run into Allectus himself, and he would know instantly who the widow Zenia was! True, he was supposed to have gone west, but one could not be sure of that, and, anyway, it was an entirely unnecessary risk.

Even so they encountered huge masses of troops, all going westward, some in orderly formations, others in wild, confused waves like the barbarians they were.

"The man's crazy", said Favonius, meaning Allectus. "He's denuding the whole country of troops. If you're right about that second landing, it won't meet any opposition."

"Constantius", was all she answered. She was so proud of him; she could have wept with pride.

The last enemy troops passed them during the night of that day. They were mixed troops, cavalry and infantry, Franks, most of them, with huge wooden shields and winged helmets; they were singing their dreary, guttural war songs.

A day later they had reached the coast; there was no sign of a second landing—not a single sail was in sight.

"Never mind—he'll come."

The Cantii living here were sullen and quiet; they obviously did not know what attitude to take. There was no news from the west yet. And then the news came—and what news!

Allectus had been too eager to gather laurels. He had hurried his troops westward in the hope of attacking the Romans before too many of them had landed. The result had been that he arrived on the battlefield with little more than his cavalry—the infantry was far behind. The Roman commander had seized his opportunity and attacked at once. Instead of withdrawing toward his approaching infantry, Allectus had given battle.

Fire signals were flaming the message of the outcome of that battle all along the British coast ... the burning roofs of houses, the pillars of smoke slowly rising from conquered villages, like the spectral legs of giants, whose bodies and heads were hidden in the clouds, stalking from west to east. Allectus had been beaten. He had fled. No, he had been slain. No, he had been taken prisoner by pursuing Roman cavalry. His troops were now marauding the countryside, looting while the going was good.

It was then that Helena had decided to return to the villa where she had lived ten years ago. Whenever and wherever the second landing came—Constantius would look for her where he had left her.

"I am going where my lord will find me", she said to Hilary. "I must not make it difficult for him."

They had arrived at night and found the villa deserted. They had installed themselves as best they could and—slept.

At least the men slept, even the sentries, whom Favonius had posted near the main and back entrances.

Constantine had kept her company for a while.

"I know you are dissatisfied with me, son—"

"Am I, Mother?"

She caressed his dark hair. "Of course you are—do you really think I don't know what is going on in that big head of yours? You are dissatisfied because you wanted to do a bit of fighting on your own and I would not let you. You think: Now I shall forever be condemned to say that Rome has liberated Britain, and I, Constantine, have not even drawn my sword, because my mother wouldn't let me."

He blushed. "Well, and isn't that true, Mother? I am almost twenty-two—"

"Just over twenty-one, but we won't quibble about a few months. You are a man now, son, and that means carrying responsibility."

"That's just it, Mother, I—"

"And what would be your judgment about yourself—what would be your father's judgment of you, if you had gone to fight some little detachment of Carausian troops—and in the meantime something had happened to me?"

"You had Hilary and Favonius and his men, Mother. Of course I would never have left you without protection."

She laughed contentedly. "Ask Favonius. He will tell you that our little expedition was as dangerous as anything you could have undertaken on your own. It's sheer luck—or, as seen by you, very bad luck indeed that we did not have to fight our way through at some point or the other. Let's think it through, Constantine—what could you have done, if you had had your wish?"

"I would have gone westward—with a dozen men, with three—alone, if necessary. I would have found the Roman army—"

"You would *not* have found the Roman army. Your way west would have led you along the path of Allectus' troops. You'd have been killed before you'd got anywhere near a Roman helmet. And even if you had got through you'd have come too late for the battle. Yes, you might have had the chance of killing a few Carausian marauders on their flight back—not exactly the deed of a hero, my Constantine, and not a glorious start of a military career. Nothing to be proud of—"

"I see what you mean, Mother, but—"

She sat up on her couch. It was very dark. The little oil lamp old Rufus had found for her room—"it's better than nothing, Domina"—was painting wild and exaggerated shadows on the wall. There was a giantess sitting up to talk to her giant son. "Listen to me, Constantine. You are not the son of cringing townsfolk who know so little about life and death that they would rather commit an ignoble act than expose themselves or their children to danger. You are of the blood, because your parents are. Had you been in command—no, had there been the slightest chance for you to do something that mattered in this battle—why, I would have sent you to it, even if I had known that it meant my certain death. Do you believe me, Constantine?"

"Yes, Mother", said the young man gravely. "I believe—that you really think it would not have made any difference whether I fought or not."

"And you don't agree?"

"No, Mother, I don't. I would not have remained alone, even if I'd set out alone. I'd have collected men—some of our own men, some of the old legionaries of the Twentieth near Spinae or Calleva Atrebatum. There are over five hundred of them in Spinae alone, I'm told. Arms would have had to be taken from the enemy. Oh, it's childish, really, I know—it's playing war, not waging war—but in three days or four we would have had arms, believe me. And five hundred armed men harassing a fleeing enemy can do a lot of harm. I wouldn't have given battle, of course; just harassing, in-and-out attacks. Slow them up. Give the pursuers a chance to catch up with them quicker."

"It's madness", cried Helena. "But you are a soldier, I believe, son."

"I know I am, Mother."

She bowed slightly. "I apologize to you," she said. Her eyes were shining with unutterable pride. He kissed her tenderly.

"You must sleep now, Mother. You've been riding all day—at your age. You must be dreadfully tired."

"Good night, Constantine." She was hiding a smile.

"Good night, Mother."

The young giant withdrew, and she was alone in the house of memories. He would be proud of his son. She knew he would be.

Tomorrow she would have to put the house in order—a strange thing to think of with Britain in flames. Weed the garden—clean the house—get maids—servants—

What if the beaten enemy came this way? But she felt that this was a futile thought, not worth consideration. Allectus has shown himself to be the worst type of general—impulsive, stupid, even ignorant. It was one thing to conspire against a real leader and quite another to beat a real leader in the field. A stupid fox, Constantius had called him. Perhaps there never would be a second battle. Had Allectus—or whoever now was in command—withdrawn toward the north, the war might have been prolonged. But he could not afford that. He had to think of his fleet off the isle of Vectis.

Again a futile thought. No good trying to play at being a general when one is a woman. An old woman—in the eyes of Constantine. "At your age, Mother." But all that

Constantius had loved in her was still there—she had kept her slim figure, and her face wasn't bad yet. Had he changed?

Perhaps he was landing now—or tomorrow morning—no, it was more likely that he would land at night. And that would be the end of the Carausians; they were caught between two fires then.

She could still see the endless columns of Frankish soldiers marching westward, singing their dreary barbarian songs. They looked fierce and uncouth and strong—but they did not look like men marching toward victory. There was an air of diffidence about them—it was difficult to say why. They were like water running out, like a wave running up the shore; some of the water would die in the sands, and the rest would be carried back into the sea. . . .

She had felt it, then. And Rome was coming into her own again, Rome and Constantius. What a pity, what a terrible pity that they had had to acknowledge Carausius at all—if only for the time they needed to build a new fleet. But then, history was like that. How puny her own efforts looked now—her little conspiracies in the north and east! Still, she was glad she had done what she had done. . . . Then she thought of Constantius.

In the afternoon of the next day there was news of the second landing. Favonius brought it to her—he had heard it from the refugees passing on the nearby main road from Anderida to Londinium. The glint of admiration in the eyes of the old soldier did her good, but all she showed him was a measured smile of acknowledgment. She had known it all the time, hadn't she?

"Why refugees?" she asked calmly.

Favonius grinned. "It's the first trickle—there'll be a stream in a few hours. It's always better to go out of the way of an army—Roman or otherwise."

She had raised her brows and gone back to her work of setting the house in order. It had begun to take shape by now—though it would be months before the garden would be anything like what it had been. Hilary had gone to see whether he could borrow some utensils from some of the neighbouring villas; Rufus had got hold of half a dozen farmhands to help in cleaning the house. Many things would have to be bought, of course, but it was no good trying to send anybody to Londinium, where everything was bound to be in a turmoil. It did not seem quite clear where the second landing had taken place—perhaps right in the estuary of the Tamesis, perhaps somewhere near Anderida—or at both places at the same time.

Well, the Cantii were not likely to resist it—not in the mood they'd been in. They were simple people and had long been accustomed to Roman rule—many of them had Roman blood in their veins. But they were peasants and disliked having their harvest stamped into the ground by marching feet, to whomever the feet belonged.

They did not care much about the idea of the Empire—that was natural; they had never seen it, except in the form of soldiers and tax collectors. The peace it had brought for almost three centuries they had come to take for granted, as man will take a good thing for granted when he has had it long enough. . . . The Cantii would stick to their little houses.

The refugees of whom Favonius had spoken were likely to be townsfolk, from Lemanae or Dubrae or Anderida—some of them afraid, perhaps, because they had held office or worked too closely with the Carausian regime, all of them afraid of burning and looting. It was no good being too patriotic about it: some of that always happened in the first wake of an invading army. There was something repulsive about these people all the same—at least about the men. It was the same thing that made the peasants, who stuck it out, so attractive. But on the whole they were just pathetic. She could see some of them from the little knoll at the end of the garden—she need not even go out on the road, as Favonius had done—bedraggled creatures, trailing along in the dust of the road, carts with wailing wheels, drawn by oxen, by horses, by the people themselves. It was a sorry sight, and somehow it hurt her. This was the hour of triumph, or redemption, of the victory of right; and these people marred it.

She turned her back to the road and walked toward the house; the poor garden—that hurt, too. But perhaps it was just as well. Constantius must not think that everything had been so smooth and easy, in all these years. She found that she hated the expression "all these years". It seemed to create an uncertain, pale light in her spirit, like the light that comes from a rotting tree; and in that light the years between were alone lit, as if they alone had been reality. It was a time she was eager to forget, to nullify, to annihilate. He had left her yesterday; he was coming back today.

She had dressed for him; she was even wearing jewelry. She had had to dress alone—if only Hilary succeeded in getting her a few maidservants. Constantine had given her a look of such blank surprise when he had seen her in the morning that it had made her laugh. For years he had seen her only in the simplest of clothes—certainly it was one of the reasons why he thought her to be old. But then, a mother was always old in the eyes of a grown son—of any son. It was an old dress, of course—and the gods alone knew what they were wearing in Rome now—but it was the best she had, and she had only worn it once before ... at that last dinner with him and Allectus and poor little Gaius Valerius, who had died so valiantly a few weeks later.

With him and Allectus! Who could have foretold the way in which they would meet again, the one as the Roman commander in the field, the other as Emperor of a barbarian empire, on the last day of his emperorship. That was history now—history made by Constantius.

She entered the house. Come, she thought, with a ferocity that made it almost an incantation, come to me—come!

Two hours after noon the first Roman troops passed by on the road to Londinium. They were cavalry, and they seemed in a great hurry. An hour later infantry followed. Favonius counted two cohorts and concluded that more troops must be on the way to Londinium by other roads.

The sight of their uniforms made him feel so good, he could have shouted with joy. Now another detachment was coming along; it seemed a mixed one—there were horsemen and infantry and several Gallic wagons. A centurion rode at the head of the little column, which swung off the main road and came toward the villa.

Favonius beamed at the centurion. "They were always bad riders in the Twenty-Seventh", he said. "I suppose you'd hate to be an exception."

The officer stared at him, and Favonius' grin broadened. "Good to see you, old man. You might have come half a dozen years earlier, though. Too busy polishing your armor, were you?"

"Halt!" ordered the centurion, raising his arm. He was a big, burly fellow with a double scar over one cheek. The column halted. He gave Favonius another stare. "What legion?" he asked.

Favonius laughed outright. "The Twentieth, of course," he said. "Where do you think this is—Africa?"

At last the centurion grinned, too. "You seem to have kept your sense of humor; you'll do well to be a little more economic about it. The Twentieth, indeed! The little babies that Carausius gobbled up for breakfast. I suppose he found you indigestible. You live here?"

"This is the Legate Constantius' house."

"I know that. And he's Constantius Cæsar to you."

"Brother," said Favonius, "this is the best bit of news you could give me. If you weren't a man and if you weren't so dirty and if I weren't so worried about your reputation, I would kiss you."

"I prefer honorable death", said the centurion drily. "We've come to occupy the house and put it right as quickly as possible."

"You mean, he—the Cæsar is coming here?"

"He'll be here any hour, and maybe any minute. *He* doesn't travel with snails on wheels as I had to."

Favonius rubbed his hands. "My friend, I don't know where I shall get it from, but I shall get you a cask of Falernian, if I have to pinch it from the quaestor himself. The Cæsar's wife is living here, you know."

The centurion stared at him again. "I know", he said. "But how did *you* know she's coming? It's supposed to be a secret! Anyway, open that gate now, friend. I've got to get busy."

"Coming?" asked Favonius. "What do mean, coming? She's here already!"

But the centurion had turned round to the column; raising his arm again, he barked a command. Favonius beckoned two gaping slaves to open the gate, and the column began to pass through.

At that moment he saw Hilary galloping along the road; he reached the gate just as the last men, marching behind the second transport wagon, were passing through, and jumped off his horse. There was something wrong—he had never seen Hilary look like this.

He came up to Favonius, breathing heavily. "What's the matter with you, man? You look like death! What's happened?"

"Everything", gasped Hilary. "These troops here—does she know? Curio is on the way here—ah, there he is. Must have had a very good horse—to—catch up with me. Does she know?"

"Know exactly what?"

But before Hilary could answer, the Legate Curio had arrived, at the head of a group of aides. "Old friends, I believe", he said warmly. "I shall recommend—" He broke off. He had seen Hilary's face.

"Sir," said Hilary, "the Princess Helena and her son are in this house."

To Favonius' complete bewilderment the old legate became ghastly pale; and just like Hilary before, he asked, "Does she know?" But he gave himself the answer, too. "She does not—of course not. If she knew, she would not be here, would she? Hilary, what are we going to do?"

"Tell her", said Hilary. His eyes were burning. "At least she has a right to know, don't you think, sir?"

The old man was terribly upset. "You don't know all, yourself, my dear fellow. They are both on their way here—both!"

"No!" exclaimed Hilary. "No!"

"It is a matter of a quarter of an hour—perhaps less", groaned the legate. "And she—the princess—she does not know anything—I shall never be able—"

"I shall do it," said Hilary, but he staggered and would perhaps have fallen if Favonius had not supported him.

The old legate drew himself erect. "It's my business to tell her", he said in a voice he tried hard to make steady. "Lead me to her."

"For old times' sake," murmured Favonius, "for the sake of my poor head, tell me, Hilary—what is all this!"

"It's the most terrible thing, Favonius. The Domina will need—oh, there she is. Grit your teeth, man, and whatever you may believe in, pray to it, as you've never prayed before."

The world's gone mad, thought Favonius. The whole world has decidedly gone mad. But such was his respect for Hilary that he actually thought of Mars Repulsor, to whom a soldier prays—or should pray—when warding off the attack of an enemy superior in strength; and a little even of Jupiter the Best and Greatest. Hilary was looking at the entrance of the house as if he were expecting it to be hit by lightning or crumbled by an earthquake.

Helena stood in the entrance—she had not seen Curio yet, or Hilary or Favonius—she was looking at the soldiers, unloading the heavy transport wagons. The centurion, supervising the unloading, had recognized a lady of rank and given her a polite salute, to which she responded with a gracious little nod, without taking her eyes off the many things, the many magical things—carpets and vases and dainty chairs inlaid with ivory; dresses of Chinese silk and of rare Indian wool died with Phoenician purple; golden goblets and plates—all of which the soldiers were now carrying into the house. He had thought of everything, it seemed—and he had sent it to the villa almost with his shock troops, as though he could not wait to see his house—their house—coming to life again. It was not the splendor of the things—it was the fact that he and she both had had the same thought, which moved her so deeply that there were tears in her eyes.

Then she saw the soldiers snap to attention and turned a radiant face toward the garden; but it was not Constantius, it was Curio who was walking over to her, his golden helmet under his arm.

Quickly she banished her disappointment and gave him the smile one gives to an old friend. "Curio," she said, "you are very, very welcome."

Only then she saw that his face was ashen and his lips pressed firmly upon each other. Was he wounded? Ill? But his eyes, fixed upon her with a strange intensity, claimed no attention for himself. It was not he who was wounded, not he who was ill—it was she. She looked at him, dumbly, and then felt the inrush of danger and worse than danger. Her hand flew up to her heart. She could not speak.

The old, anxious man before her bowed deeply. With his balding head, surrounded by wisps of iron-gray hair, he resembled a priest bowing before the altar. She was not a goddess. Was she, then, a victim?

He looked up. "Domina Helena, I am bringing grave news—may we go inside?"

She made a step toward him. "My husband—"

"He is alive and well", said Curio. She breathed her relief.

"It is all that matters, Curio. Speak here. What is it?"

She heard him talk, then. It did not seem to make sense, though. She had been out of communication with Rome these last years—she was not aware of the changes that had happened there—of the most grave and decisive changes, necessary for the very life and existence of the Empire—

No, she had not. She was not. What was all this about?

The two Emperors—Diocletian and Maximian were both old men—had felt that youth and vigor were essential for many immediate tasks, and that was why they had decided to raise to the rank of Cæsar the two men to whom they felt they could safely entrust such tasks. The two men, subject and responsible to the Emperors alone, were Galerius for the Orient, Constantius for the Occident.

Constantius for the Occident. Constantius Cæsar. Subject only to the Emperors. Immense, immense power. Why grave news?

Curio's voice became a whisper as he continued. It was an exceptional situation, an emergency—she understood that, didn't she? It had never happened before—just like that. It was essential to the Emperors that their first servants, their co-rulers, almost, should be tied to them with a special loyalty—a loyalty, stronger even than that of the most sacred oath: the loyalty of kinship. Therefore Cæsar Galerius had been obliged to repudiate his former wife and to marry Emperor Diocletian's daughter, Princess Valeria.

Helena nodded. In the next instant she became aware, in a flash, of the blow that was to descend on her; it was the word "repudiate" that opened the chasm. For one brief moment she lost all control; she looked like a frightened child. But when Curio, thinking that she was going to faint, made a gesture as though to come to her aid, she drew away from him, and her body became rigid.

"Proceed, Legate Curio", she said.

The old man swallowed hard. "Constantius Cæsar, too, was obliged to—to do likewise, in order to marry the daughter of Emperor Maximian, the Princess Theodora."

"Yes", said Helena.

She was surrounded by staring faces; the soldiers had stopped unloading and stared; the centurion stared; no one could have heard a word of what Curio had said, but everyone realized that something very great and terrible was hovering in the air. Favonius, who had at last succeeded in getting the facts out of Hilary, was looking about, ready to kill: somebody had to die for this, that was clear. Hilary had dropped on his knees, praying to some god or other. But this was the moment where all gods had withdrawn their faces in utter shame of their creation. Favonius turned abruptly and left.

Constantine, thought Helena. He must not know. They must not tell him—

Curio had had almost forty years of service. He had grown gray under the helmet, but these last minutes had exhausted his courage. It was impossible to look any longer at the woman with the face of snow. Yet he knew that he had to deliver the rest of the message.

"It was not possible to inform you of—what happened", he said with his eyes fixed on the soil. "There was no way of getting news into Britain, until now. Your—the Cæsar believes you to be at Verulam. I myself told him that you were living there. He chose this villa as his present headquarters, and he is on the way here now—"

She took a step backward.

"—the princess is with him", went on Curio. "They will be here any time now." There—he had said it all. The chalice was empty.

"Hilary", said Helena in a clear voice. He was instantly at her elbow. "Fetch my son, Hilary. I wish to leave."

"I am here, Mother", said Constantine.

Curio saw that he was standing behind her; he must have been inside the house, he thought. Had he heard it all? Yes, he had. The old legate bowed again. "You are your mother's shield, Constantine."

"I know who I am", said Constantine.

Favonius appeared from nowhere, with Rufus—they were leading five horses between them.

Helena gave him a look he was never to forget. "You see, Curio", she said. "There is still faith in the world."

The old legate began to sob.

They mounted.

"Attention!" roared Curio. "The—imperial—salute!"

Dumbfounded, his aides and what soldiers there were in the garden stood to attention and gave the salute.

Slowly the little cavalcade rode out.

"The imperial salute", murmured one of the aides, a young tribune, the carrier of a great name.

Curio swung round. "Yes, Agrippa. Nothing less. You needn't report it; I shall do so myself."

From afar, the sound of a trumpet announced the arrival of the Cæsar.

CHAPTER 4

"A FRIEND OF MINE has come to see you, Domina", said Hilary.

The woman in black remained immobile, her eyes fixed without sight on the gray tiles of the roof opposite. Gray tiles. Gray tiles seen through the window. The same tiles. The same street. The same life. A friend?

"What does he want?"

"To see you, Domina", repeated Hilary gently.

"I will see no one. Who is he?"

"Albanus, Domina."

"Albanus . . ." She turned her head toward him. Her lips twitched in their approach to a contemptuous smile. "What a fool you are, Hilary, to think that I could—very well; show him in, your Albanus."

There was a dangerous gleam in her eyes now; he saw it well, but he only bowed and withdrew.

She was going to meet him, that strange man who seemed to have such a strong influence on Hilary's mind. Men were fools. Either fools or traitors. This Albanus was a fool; she was going to whip him in front of his disciple.

She could hear his step now. Now she could see him in the corridor—a slight figure, gray-haired, in the simple dress of a craftsman. His salute had dignity. She nodded and beckoned him to sit down. When Hilary, behind him, made a movement to withdraw again, she stopped him with a short gesture, and he remained standing, as he always did in the presence of a third person.

I should have left this Albanus standing, too, she thought. It was foolish to offer him a seat as to an equal, but now it was done. How old was he? Sixty, perhaps, hardly more. Sensitive hands—she remembered that Hilary had told her he was a wood carver. Well, his face seemed to have been carved in wood, too; a strong nose, broad forehead—but eyes and mouth were mild, though not so mild as Hilary's. It seemed almost a pity to crush the gentle, birdlike little man.

"Well, Albanus—we meet at last."

"You did not wish to meet me earlier, Princess."

She raised her chin. "And what makes you think that it is my wish now?"

"It is not your wish, Princess. It is God's wish."

She gave a short laugh. "Do you always know what God wishes, Albanus?"

"Yes, Princess. He always wishes the Good."

She felt, more than she saw, Hilary's smile and became irritated.

"If that is so, he cannot be a very powerful god, this God of yours—he does not exactly see his wish fulfilled very often, does he? Look at the world!"

"Distinguish two things", said Albanus calmly. "God's wish—and God's will. He always wishes the Good, but he does not always impose his will. We have been given a will of our own, and God respects his present to man and will not easily override it."

"Clever", said Helena cuttingly. "That way your God is quite safe, isn't he?"

"Oh, yes," said Albanus, "but we are not."

She shifted a little in her seat. "Who is this God of yours—he's the Jewish God, isn't he? What makes you think that he has got any power other than in Palestina or Syria? Didn't the Jews regard themselves as the chosen people of their God? And if that is true, can you see Romans or Britons take second place, and third? You are a Briton yourself—I am surprised to find you praying to a Jewish deity...."

"The Jews were the people chosen by God", explained Albanus patiently. "It was necessary that there should be one people to carry the truth of the One God through the centuries—of the One who alone can say "I AM" because he always was and is and will be. And the Jews were a particularly well-chosen people—for when a Jew has got hold of a truth, he will not let go easily. They carried on magnificently, on the whole; a little people, surrounded by hostile tribes all praying to many gods, Baal and Melkarth and

Astarte and Nergal and Marduk and whatever their names were. The Jews clung to the One God, whose very name was so holy to them that they would never utter it. And their holy men, their prophets, foretold that one day the Christ would be born in their midst—and born of a virgin—he who would come to save the world through his life and death."

Helena nodded. She had heard the story before. "The Christ," she said drily, "'the Anointed One'—I know; then he came—it was three hundred years ago, I believe—and he collected a handful of simpleminded men around him and went about preaching simple things to simple people—and finally got himself mixed up with the law and the authorities and was arrested and put to death—crucified, I believe—"

Albanus sighed deeply. "Yes, Domina", he said. "He was crucified—for you!"

"For me!" exclaimed Helena, genuinely shocked and disgusted. "What an absurd thing to say, Albanus."

"For you", repeated the old wood carver quietly. "And for me; and for Hilary here—and for your son; for the Emperor in Rome and for the last beggar of his empire; for the German over the Rhine and for the Negro in Africa. For all men, Domina—even for those who do not live yet—for all the countless generations to come—and yet for every one of us alone. You see, he took the curse off us."

She was seething with annoyance. "A curse indeed— what curse?"

The old man shook his head. "The curse from which we all suffer, Domina. When one of us does something wrong, we often say—in kindness, as we think—'Oh, well, it's human, isn't it?' And that is right to some extent—it is human to do wrong. Yet the legends and myths of all peoples tell us of an age long past, a golden age when it was not human to do the wrong thing—when there were peace and goodwill on earth—until something happened that changed it all. We are told of it in our Book, too. It was an act of disobedience—an act by which we cut ourselves off from the one Source of happiness—and ever since the world has been what it is now. . . ."

"A very poetic legend", said Helena indulgently.

"Legends are the really true stories", said Alban.

She swung round. "Who told you that?" she asked fiercely. "Was it Hilary? Admit that it was Hilary!"

The old man looked genuinely surprised. "Hilary? I have never talked to Hilary about legends, Domina."

"He knows nothing of your father, Domina", said Hilary.

She beckoned him to be silent. No, the old man did not look like a common liar. But what was he after? No one did anything without a reason. What did he want of her?

"Our Celtic gods", she said slowly, "were cruel at times—I remember the one my ancestors made, of wicker. They filled him with life—with human lives: prisoners or slaves were shackled and herded together in the god's interior; then they were burned to death. Cruel, wasn't it? But not as cruel as your God is, Albanus. He seems to have condemned the whole of mankind—because of the disobedience of a few men sometime in the gray past."

Alban sighed. "When a father is imprisoned for a crime he has committed—will not his family suffer? When a tribe leaves its hunting grounds and migrates through the desert because the council of elders has so decided—do not the children suffer thirst as well as the elders? When mankind decided to leave God, was it not natural for it to suffer, generation after generation, until we shall find the way back to him? Man is one tribe, one family, Domina. Every man is Adam, the first man born—and every woman is Eve. Only one Man was not Adam; and one woman was not Eve."

"Riddles", shrugged Helena. "Who were they? A couple?"

"They were Mother and Son", said Alban.

"Two gods?"

"There is only one God, Domina. The mother was human, but as she said herself, 'all generations shall call me blessed.' For she gave life—human life—to God."

"Madness," said Helena, "but beautiful madness like a poet's."

The old man went on, as though he had not heard her. "It was the greatest thing that ever happened—far greater than Creation itself", he said dreamily. "We shall never cease wondering about it—it is the song of all songs—not Solomon's, but God's own song. He had given man free will and therefore free choice—man had misused the gift and had fallen—and God became man in order to dissolve man's guilt and make us ripe for real life. He partook of our humanity so that we can partake of his divinity. He became a man of flesh and blood—and it was his blood, his holy blood that he sacrificed for us on the Cross. Have you ever seen a man crucified, Domina?"

"No", said Helena. "Not a man . . ." She closed her eyes.

"There is no more barren thing than a cross—" Alban's voice became almost a whisper. "It is a horrible thing, wood crossed with wood so that a man should die on it in pain. But under the touch of the Holy Blood the barren wood became the Tree of Life—"

Helena jumped up. "Who are you? Who told you—all that? By my father's shadow, if you are mocking me—"

Alban's thin hand stopped her with a gesture of command.

"I am a servant of Christ", he said. "And Christ is God. And God is Love. How could I be mocking you—"

"Love", said Helena. "Love, is he your God? Well—then I have believed in him, too, once; like so many other foolish women. Now—I know better. It is a fool's happiness you are telling me about, Alban. The curse is still there— your Christ has not taken it away, believe me. That which happened to him is happening every day."

For the first time Alban smiled. It seemed to make him incredibly young—almost like a child. "You are quite right, Domina", he said. "It happens every day, praise God."

But his words were lost. "The God of love", jeered Helena. "He can't take away curses. He *is* a curse himself. He makes us blind and stupid—mad—until reality stares us in the face like the Gorgon and turns us to stone. Where was he, your God, when my love was killed? Where was he, when my son was made a bastard? What have we done, my son and I—that this should have happened to us?"

Alban, too, rose. "Rejoice", he said. "Through suffering you are coming nearer to God. Lift up your suffering in your two hands and sacrifice it like the live thing it is—an unblemished sacrifice, if your love was true, that is: unselfish. If your soul is being hammered, it is because it is true gold."

But her face remained dark, and there was no life in her eyes.

"Your message is not for me, Albanus."

"No?" His voice was very gentle now. "Why not?"

"Because I have no aim left in life."

"What was your aim?"

"Love—and power", she said abruptly. "And I shall answer no more questions."

"The message is for you, then", said Alban quietly. "And you could not have received it earlier—for until now you were not ripe for it. You had built your world upon a foundation of illusion—the illusion that it is God's duty to make us happy in exactly the way that pleases us; you have asked him to comply with your standards, to subordinate his wisdom to yours."

"I don't know why I am still listening to this", said Helena between her teeth.

"Because you are big enough to bear the truth", was the calm reply. "Your foundation was an illusion; therefore it dissolved when you were faced with reality. So far you have loved selfishly—you have loved for your own sake, and you expected a reward; you have loved power, too, for its own sake. Only now that you do not expect anything—now that you have lost everything, you will gain love—and you will have power. Give away—and you will have more than you ever dreamed of. Keep nothing for yourself, and you will be rich. That is the message. The peace of our Lord be upon you."

When the curtain had closed behind him, Helena turned toward Hilary; she opened her mouth to speak, but as she looked at him, the words would not come, and even her thoughts fled to hide in the shadow. For she saw in Hilary's face or about his face something for which there is no word in the human tongue; it was not an expression, nor was it a look; it was not a gleam or a radiancy. But she saw it, and as she saw it, she knew that both he and Alban were going to die.

The days went by very quietly in the little house in Verulam. To the good citizens of the town "the widow Zenia" had returned from a journey. She had probably been afraid of the Roman invasion, which was not surprising, at least not in those first days, when no one really knew what was going to happen. But then the armies of the Emperor conquered—the real, the Roman Emperor, of course, not that wretched adventurer—and they conquered with such ease and in one single battle. Within a few days Roman helmets were omnipresent. The Carausians capitulated everywhere or even simply threw away their armor and badges of rank and pretended that they had never been anything but peaceful citizens; some of the Carausian tax collectors fled with their money, but others delivered it, together with their books, to the Roman authorities, as though it were the most natural thing in the world. The fact that their coins showed the head of Carausius did not seem to disturb them in the least. The transfer, or rather the return, of authority went on with a smoothness that would have been unthinkable had Carausius himself still been alive. Little bands of wild Franks went on fighting for a few weeks more, but there was no organized resistance anywhere; certainly there was no resistance on the part of the Britons, not even among those who had acclaimed the Carausian revolution ten years ago.

It was entirely natural, in such circumstances, that the widow Zenia should resume her life in Verulam; she and her young son, who was again seen pretty often in the garden of neighbor Scapula—with little Minervina. Perhaps it was a really serious affair, after all, between those two ... and a nice-looking couple they were, he so tall and proud and soldierlike and she like one of the fairies of the woods, tiny and dainty and of good old Roman blood—could there be a better mixture?

"If it were not for your letter," said Helena, "I wouldn't have received you, Curio."

The old legate nodded. "I thought as much, Domina Helena—fortunately I could afford to write that letter; I really am coming as an old friend of yours—not as envoy or messenger from anybody, and I wished to make that quite clear."

He lied, of course—and Helena knew that he lied. But in his letter one sentence had stood out that had made all the difference. "As an old friend I feel that I have a right to share at least some of your worries; and it might be of advantage for your high-spirited son, if his mother would think fit to discuss her plans with an old officer like myself."

A slave had brought some wine; they were sipping it quietly.

She has grown thinner, thought the old legate; thinner and, yes, older. Much older. The Princess Theodora would sleep more peacefully if she knew that. But it isn't I who am going to tell her.

I am not going to ask questions, thought Helena. Hilary was right—it was necessary to receive this old man for Constantine's sake; Hilary only said what I felt, anyway. But I am not going to ask questions.

The legate began to speak about the political situation. Britain was returning to normal very quickly, he said. Even the Caledonians had thought fit to send out peace feelers to Eburacum. There was a great deal of planning—many of the bigger towns would have to be reorganized, coastal fortifications erected. Eburacum was seething with activity.

Her stony face made him feel more and more uncomfortable. Like many old men he found it difficult to come to the point—the more so as he knew that it was just what was expected of him.

Constantius had looked very tired when he had met him, last week, in the Domus palatina. "Try your best, Curio. You are the only man I can send who has at least some sort of a chance of being listened to."

He, too, had looked much older. Ambition was a terrible rider. A Cæsar was half a god, perhaps—but a mortal has to pay a heavy price for becoming half a god.

"There are many military changes, too", said the legate. "The army will soon be split up into three commands, and there is a new coastal service against smuggling—"

She suddenly felt very sorry for the rambling old man. "Enough of Britain", she said gently. "I have ceased to be interested in things military or political. But you mentioned my son in your letter—"

He swallowed. "Yes, Domina—"

"Let us understand each other, Curio. My son is of age and free to make his own decisions. There is one thing he will never do—and that is to accept favors from—the Cæsar. Therefore, if anything of that kind is in your mind, you might as well forget it straight away."

"I know that, of course", said Curio hastily. "As I said before, I am coming on my own entirely. But it cannot be your intention to keep a young man of his rank and blood here in Verulam—"

"Constantine has no rank", interrupted Helena acidly.

"But he should have", ventured the legate. "And what is more, he can have. It has nothing to do with—the Cæsar. The Cæsar is not the Emperor, and Britain is not the Empire. That's just it, Domina. Why not allow him to join the army of the east? There is always a place for young officers. Now I have a few good friends at the court of Cæsar Galerius who would be delighted to have him nominated for a minor command to start with—he would be a tribune, I suppose—the little formality of putting his name on the list is easily dealt with. He would be stationed in Bithynia, or perhaps in Thrace, and my friends over there would keep an eye on him and see to it that he gets on. What do you think?"

She closed her eyes to hide their expression. So that was Constantius' plan—to send his son to the east. Was he sincere about wishing him to get on in life? Or—or did he have other reasons? Reasons of state, perhaps? Galerius was his opposite number in the east; and the two Emperors, Maximian and Diocletian, were getting old: there were even rumors that they might retire, in which case the two Cæsars would take their place, more or less automatically. When that happened—if that happened—and Constantine was in the east, serving under Galerius, what would be his position? That of a hostage, perhaps? Yes, most likely that of a hostage. Surely Constantius could see that as well as she did. Did he want his son to become a hostage? That woman had given him children already—was he trying to get Constantine out of the way?

After what he had done to her, it was quite possible. No! No! It was not possible. She had not been thinking his thoughts—she had been thinking her own hatred. And it was the only way out for Constantine. He would not and could not serve here in Britain or in Gaul, which was also under Constantius. It was either the east or nothing for Constantine. Here, he was only squandering his time running after the little Scapula girl.

She was a nice girl—but it was not good for Constantine to get tied up too early. Let him make his way first.

For herself it would mean utter loneliness, of course. There was a strangely pleasant bitterness about that thought. First her father had gone—then Constantius—now Constantine. She had been stripped of all that made life worth living. What was it that Albanus had said? "Now that you have lost everything, you will gain love—and you will have power." What nonsense! Love—power—these things had gone for good. But there was one picture that haunted her, had haunted her ever since she had seen it—the picture of herself and Constantine and Hilary, Favonius and Rufus, caught up in the stream of refugees when they had left the villa, just before Constantius and that woman arrived. The milling, sweating, seething mass of miserable people, clogging the roads, blocking their way, fleeing from real or imaginary danger, hollow eyed, stricken, panicky. That was what happened to those who gave up and ran away.

She remembered how she had suddenly felt that she herself was one of them, she and her son—that they, too, had lost everything and had become nothing, that all these wretched people were nothing but symbols of herself and of Constantine.

It did not matter much for her. But Constantine ...

She could go on sitting here in Verulam, running her house, thinking her thoughts; she was growing old, she knew that.

But Constantine had the right to live.

"I shall ask him", she said at long last.

The legate blinked. He had been waiting patiently—it had seemed, almost, as if she had gone to sleep over the answer.

"It's for him to decide", she went on. "He is of age—and he has a will of his own."

"He is his mother's son", said Curio and knew already as he said it that he had made a dangerous mistake.

She did not spare him. "Yes, that is all he is, Curio. It will be up to him to change that."

"I didn't mean—"

"I know." She restored his peace of mind with a faint smile. "Shall we call him in now? Very well—you will find him changed, too, Curio. He is very—manly."

She sent a slave to look for him; it took almost a quarter of an hour before Constantine entered, tall, athletic, and with a sullen expression.

"You wish to see me, Mother—"

"We have a guest, Constantine."

The young man bowed his head. "I know the Legate Curio", he said curtly.

The old soldier felt that it would be something of a task to teach this young thoroughbred the rules of the game; well, there were a few commanders in the east who would know how to deal with him, and Galerius himself was not the sort who would stand any nonsense. He saw, not without pleasure, that Helena, too, was not very pleased with her son's lack of civility, and decided to leave the opening of the conversation to her.

"Constantine, our old friend the Legate Curio has been kind enough to take an interest in your future."

The young man's face remained unchanged—it was as if his mother had told him that Curio had come to see what sort of weather they had in Verulam.

"He suggests", went on Helena, "that you should join the armies of the east—"

"A regular legion or nothing", said Constantine at once. "I will not serve in any auxiliary force. There are eighteen legions under Cæsar Galerius—"

"Nineteen", said Curio.

"Eighteen, sir", maintained the young man. "The First, Third, Seventh, Eleventh,—"

"A new legion was formed five months ago under the command of Marcus Licinius", said Curio gruffly. "Sometimes we in the army have fuller information than civilians."

Constantine bit his lip. He said, "I am sorry, sir."

Curio went on, "They are short of young officers, I believe. And I happen to know Licinius pretty well. Old friend of mine."

Constantine breathed heavily. But he could not make himself say anything.

Curio saw the expression in Helena's eyes and decided to come to the obstinate young man's aid.

"Shall I write a letter to Licinius and recommend you for a tribuneship?" he asked almost casually. "It does not matter that your name is not yet on the list; I can easily see to that."

"You are—being very kind—sir." The few words seemed to cost the young man a tremendous effort.

"That's all right, then", said the old legate, hiding his relief. "I shall write to Licinius tomorrow—he's stationed in Bithynia. And I daresay you need not wait for his answer here in Britain, unless you want to. If I were you, I should travel to Byzantium straight away—next week or the week after—and expect Licinius' answer there. He is not likely to say no to me."

Helena alone observed the short moment of hesitation before the young man answered, "I shall travel to Byzantium in a few weeks' time, sir."

"Excellent! excellent!" Curio got up. "I shall leave you together now", he said gently. "I am staying in Verulam until tomorrow morning. Then I must go back to Eburacum."

At the mentioning of Eburacum mother and son stiffened, and Curio knew that he had made another mistake. Eburacum meant the Domus palatina, and the Domus palatina meant Cæsar Constantius.

"I am still on active service", he said calmly, "though I have very little say. In fact, I think my days in Britain are numbered."

"May I inquire about your future plans?" asked Helena with cold politeness.

The old man smiled ruefully. "Future plans? I'm nearing seventy, Domina, and I have been a legate these last thirty years. My future plans are to plant cabbage on my little estate in the Sabine hills."

"It is your misfortune that you are an honest man", said Helena. "And for an honest man the rank of legate is the top of the ladder."

It was a terrible statement—even Constantine darted an anxious glance at Curio. But the old legate only gave a silent salute and retreated.

Mother and son were alone.

"He came from—him, didn't he?" muttered the young man.

"He is a soldier, obeying orders, son", said Helena. "You too will be a soldier soon now—won't you?"

"Yes, Mother—but not—"

"I know. You will be Cæsar Galerius' man."

Galerius, too, had repudiated his lawful wife, to be Cæsar of the east. Men were all the same. Father alone would not have acted like that—and Hilary—and that man Albanus. What was the key to men like that? What would Constantine do, if—

"Mother—"

"Yes, Constantine?"

"There is something you don't know, Mother—and I must tell you now—"

Her heart began to beat so quickly, she turned away, as though he might see—

"What is it, Constantine?"

"I—I can't leave—just like that."

She gave him a courageous smile. "You must think of your future, son. It will be—"

It would be hard without him—without the last, the most precious tie with life, but she did not finish the sentence. She had seen his face and knew that he was not thinking of her. The tiny wrinkles around the corners of her mouth deepened and made it the mouth of an old woman. Of course he had not been thinking of her.

"I am thinking of my future, Mother", said Constantine sullenly. "I want to take Minervina with me—as my wife."

He looked up, and she saw in his face an expression of such determination that she shuddered a little.

"I want her", said Constantius' son. "You won't make things—difficult for us, will you, Mother?"

"No", said Helena tonelessly. "Of course not. Why don't you bring her to me?"

His strong young face became radiant. "I knew you would understand, Mother. She is a wonderful girl. And I have brought her—she is outside—waiting. May I call her in?"

"Do", said Helena, smiling. "Do bring her in."

He raced away. She found herself clutching a chair. Minervina—the Scapulas—it was a good Roman family. If Constantine had been Curio's son, she could be just the right choice for him. A young married tribune—garrison life—gradual promotion—with a bit of luck he would have a legion, in ten or twelve years be a legate. And then he would remain a legate for the rest of his life. For an honest man the rank of legate is the top of the ladder. She had said that only a minute ago, hadn't she?

She gave a short laugh. This was the end of ambition, once and for all. Good! It was just as well. For once, Father had been wrong. Constantius had married royal blood of Britain, and it hadn't been good enough. Constantine contented himself with a little slip of a girl. What would Constantius say when he heard it? Perhaps it would please him.

It would certainly please *her*—that woman. It would reassure her that no danger threatened her brood from her husband's first marriage.

Then Constantine came back with the girl. Frail little thing. Nice walk. Nice movements. The way she bowed was pretty, too.

She had never seen her face to face before—in fact, she had carefully avoided meeting her; she did not wish to sanction this—these goings on. Once or twice she had pulled the boy up—the Scapulas were too good a family to be trifled with, and they weren't good enough for marriage. But the boy had gone on; he would have it his way.

And now this little thing would marry him and go east with him and share his life. She would have influence over him—she had that now. It was she with whom he would discuss his plans and with whom he would share his troubles and his joys.

Here she was now. Look at her. What did her face convey, what did her eyes say?

Helena looked. There was no triumph in the girl's face—and no fear; she stood alone, slim and white and obedient in a quiet dignified way; her eyes responded to the older woman's query, but they did more than that; they, too, queried. And they did not ask for consent or judgment, nor did they reject either. They spoke a language of their own, longingly and with a confidence that had no kinship with self-assurance. It was this confidence that touched Helena more than anything else. This girl had not her strength, not in mind and not in body; yet she was confident, she believed that she could walk through fire and through water and over clouds as well as on the safe good earth. She believed all that because she was willing to give and to live on giving and through giving.

Helena opened her arms, and the girl at once responded to her love; she was so ready for it, it was so natural to her. Her hair was fine and silky.

Helena could feel the girl's heartbeat. Over her head she looked at her son. Constantine smiled broadly and a little sheepishly; he was very much relieved. Mother obviously liked her, though why she looked at him like that now— like—as if she wanted to ask him something. No, rather as if he had hurt Minervina and she was reproaching him for it. But then a man could never understand what was really going on in women's heads.

BOOK FOUR

&

A.D. 303–306

CHAPTER 1

THE MAIN HALL of the Domus palatina was filled with a glittering assembly—more than three hundred officers, legates and tribunes and centurions of the first rank, all the officials of the Cæsar's household and chancellery, all the heads of the administration.

There was a good deal of nervous tension, for no one knew why this assembly was taking place. It was quite obvious that something important had happened, and there were rumors that a special envoy from the Emperor had arrived in the morning; but not even an inkling of the envoy's mission was known to anybody but the Cæsar himself— except, of course, his chief secretary, Strabo, who was in charge of all confidential mail between Eburacum and imperial headquarters. And Strabo was paid—very well paid— for keeping his mouth shut.

If it had not been for the arrival of the envoy, the odds would have been on Princess Theodora having given birth to yet another child. She was good at that—there were five children already in only eight years of marriage. But as it was, the news was more likely to be political. It could hardly be military—the Persian war had been won last year, and both Diocletian and his Cæsar, Galerius, were resting on their laurels in Nicomedia; and except for occasional frontier incidents, there was peace also in the western half of the Empire. Maximianus was in Africa on an inspection tour.

For once even the best brains were stumped; there was only one thing most of the assembly were fairly certain about, and that was that the news was not likely to be good. The Cæsar's Court was provincial, but it was still a court, and courtiers acquire a special instinct for news. There was danger in the air.

Something of the nature of the danger became clear as soon as the Cæsar made his entrance. For with him were only Strabo and—Velleius, the protonotarius, head of the juridical department, a tall, thin man, bald headed, with the profile of a vulture. A new law, then?

Constantius, pale and gray haired, acknowledged the salute of the assembly and sat down. His throne was a broad chair of ebony, with gilded ornaments; all the rest of the assembly remained standing.

"My friends," began the Cæsar, "I have this morning received a new edict of our Divine Emperor, Diocletian, countersigned by my eastern colleague, the Cæsar Galerius. The Protonotarius Velleius is now going to acquaint you with it."

Old Velleius cleared his throat and started reading from what seemed to be a very lengthy document.

The enumeration of the titles of the Emperor alone took some time—but almost immediately afterward the purpose of the edict became abundantly clear. The Emperor stated that the nefarious and treacherous activities of a certain religious sect whose impiety was notorious and the cause of grave upheavals in all parts of the Empire had become intolerable; that the Emperor had deigned to summon a council composed of some of the most distinguished persons in the civil and military departments of the state; and that the conclusions of the aforesaid council were the basis of the present edict, which was to take effect immediately in all the provinces of the Empire.

The adherents of the sect in question, calling themselves Christians after their head, a Jewish criminal who had been executed under the glorious rule of the Emperor Tiberius, were trying to set up a state within the state; they renounced the gods and the institutions of Rome; they refused to worship the *Genius* of the Emperor and tried to set up a sort of republic of their own, under leaders of their own to whom they professed to owe unlimited allegiance. These leaders, or bishops as they were called, made laws of their own and appointed magistrates of their own; they collected community treasures and used them for the spreading of their doctrines. This movement had to be suppressed before it could undermine the army or set up its own military force.

By now the tension of the audience had eased considerably.

The majority of them knew that the edict did not concern them, although most of them at least knew of some people who were Christians.

The monotonous voice of the protonotarius continued.

Therefore the Divine Emperor had decided that severe measures had to be taken against that sect, and he deigned to give orders as followed: the bishops and presbyters of the sect were to be commanded to hand over all books and scriptures in their possession to the magistrates; the magistrates were to be commanded under penalty of death to have the aforesaid books and scriptures burned in the public marketplace and in their presence. All property of the Christian church was to be confiscated and sold and the proceedings delivered to the imperial treasury.

Such individuals as persevered in the belief and activity of the sect would be declared unfit to hold office or to be employed by the state; slaves adhering to the Christian faith could not be freed; no Christian was allowed to go to a court of justice, except as an accused person. And any churches of the sect were to be demolished down to their foundations.

"Given at our palace in Nicomedia," read Velleius, "on the day of the Terminalia Festival in the year one thousand and fifty-six of the foundation of Rome."

There was a long pause.

The Cæsar rose.

"You have heard the will of our Divine Emperor", he said somewhat drily. "My chancellery will draft the necessary orders to the magistrates in Britain; until that is done, everybody will refrain from taking measures on his own account. I hope this is quite clear! But it is also clear that the execution of the imperial orders must start in my own household and administration. So far I have paid no attention to the religious beliefs of others. It seems that from now on I shall have to. I know that a number of you are adherents to the Christian faith. This must be a heavy blow. I give you two days to decide whether you wish to remain Christians or whether you are willing to give up such dangerous beliefs. I want you all to be here again the day after tomorrow, at the same hour. An altar will be erected to the *Genius* of the Emperor, and I shall ask all those present to burn incense in his worship. My friends—your fate is in you own hands. That is all." He gave a short nod and left the room.

Slowly the assembly began to disperse. There was hardly any comment—but some faces showed grief, deep anxiety, even despair; others were smiling. A number of valuable posts were going to be vacant the day after tomorrow.

Cæsar Constantius returned to his study. "Where is the confidential dossier, Velleius?"

"Here it is, Cæsar."

Constantius studied it for a while. Beside the names of eighty-two persons of the household and the administration was a little cross.

Forty-eight hours later the assembly had gathered again. The large room looked different. An altar had been built, no more than five steps from the side of the Cæsar's ebony throne, and crowned by a marble bust of the Emperor. It was not a very flattering bust; the features of Diocletian remained common however much the sculptor tried to ennoble them; his beard was carefully waved and set—but it only looked as though he had been to a hairdresser for the first time in his life.

In front of the bust, in the middle of the altar stood a small tripod and a vessel with incense.

The Cæsar spoke a few words; then he approached the altar and threw some grains of incense into the tripod. The smoke curled up into the impassive face of the God-Emperor.

Velleius and Strabo followed the Cæsar's example and returned to their place near the ebony throne. Six body-guards behind the throne were next. When they, too, had returned to their places, the Cæsar spoke again: "Let all those among you professing the Christian faith step forward."

An icy silence followed. Then a number of men began to move, slowly, through the throng, like alien bodies ejected from a healthy organism; two, three, ten—fifteen—twenty—

"Form a group on this side", ordered Constantius. His face did not show the slightest emotion; it was as impassive as that of the bust on the altar. Officers of various ranks, officials, freedmen, slaves of the household—it was the first time in their lives that they had formed a group in the Cæsar's house.

—thirty—forty—fifty—

The assembly looked on with a strange mixture of horror and admiration. But no one uttered a word.

—sixty—sixty-three—sixty-four.

Constantius frowned. "Note their names", he ordered, and Strabo did so. When he had finished, he gave the list to his master, who compared it with another list.

"There are eighteen names missing", he said calmly. "The Tribune Quintus Sarto, the Centurions Marcus Niger, Lucius Pallio, Gnæus Calvius—"

He pronounced name after name. Only the Protonotarius Velleius and Strabo knew that there was one name he omitted.

"Those I have just named will form a second group", ordered the Cæsar. "Both these groups will wait until the rest of the assembly have sacrificed to the *Genius* of the Emperor. Velleius—note all those who have sacrificed. Proceed."

For a long time he sat quietly watching, while one man after the other threw his grains of incense into the tripod. The smoke thickened.

At last only the two groups apart remained.

Tribune Sarto made a step forward.

"Yes, Tribune?"

"We wish to declare that we have given up a belief contrary to the safety and well-being of the state, Cæsar", he announced monotonously. "We are ready to sacrifice to the Divine Emperor."

Constantius nodded. "Do so, then", he rasped.

Sarto's hand was shaky as he threw his incense into the tripod; there was a leer on some faces, but the spectators kept silent.

Niger, Pallio, Calvius, and the others followed Sarto's example.

"Now the Christian group", commanded the Cæsar. "The Tribune Flavius Rutilus will sacrifice."

The officer stepped forward. "I cannot do so, Cæsar", he said, saluted stiffly, and stepped back.

"The Tribune Caius Vindex", said Constantius, unmoved.

"I beg to refuse, Cæsar", said Vindex politely.

"The Primipilar Marcus Priscus."

He was a giant of a man, but his voice sounded surprisingly soft. "I can die for the Emperor, but I cannot worship him, Cæsar."

"The Aquilifier Titus Balbus."

The eagle bearer stood smartly to attention. "It is written: render unto Cæsar what is Cæsar's and unto God what is God's."

Constantius, who did not know the quotation, waited; but the man did not move, and he called out the next name.

After the officers came the officials. There was less military stiffness with them, but no less determination.

Fat old Gubates, master of the *horti*, the palace gardens, was crying like a child; he could not utter a word, but shook his head vigorously. He had an ailing wife and four children to look after.

Tuscus, the chief waiter, vacillated. He was a good chief waiter, and it had taken him twenty years to become one. When his name was called, he broke into sobs and made a few staggering steps toward the altar.

At that moment the door at the end of the room opened, and the Legate Curio walked in. Everybody stared at him. He had been ill in bed these last two weeks, they all knew that. He was ill now.

He marched up to the Cæsar's throne, gave the salute, turned round, and—joined the Christian group. He took the place that Tuscus had left.

The chief waiter saw it. He gave a hoarse cry like a hurt animal, swung round, and staggered back to the group. Curio smiled at him and pressed his hand.

There was no more vacillation after that. One man after the other voiced his refusal.

Then silence.

The Cæsar rose. "Thank you, my friends", he said quietly. "It was a good test of loyalty—indeed it was." There was a glint of humor in his pale face. "I need not say that all those not belonging to the two groups will remain at their posts as before. They have always acknowledged the gods of Rome and the *Genius* of the Divine Emperor, and they are doing so now."

He paused; the assembly sensed suddenly that this man in the short purple cloak had the strength as well as the power of his office.

"Surely," said Constantius slowly, "what the Emperor wants to know is whether or not he can rely on the loyalty of his subjects. That and nothing else is the spirit behind his edict— and that and nothing else was the spirit behind this ceremony. Now I, for one, cannot believe in the loyalty of those who are ready to forswear their faith as soon as their posts are in danger—and therefore the group around the Tribune Sarto is herewith dismissed from my service."

A gasp went over the assembly. Tribune Sarto fell on his knees and hid his face in his hands. The men around him were thunderstruck.

"But these men here", continued the Cæsar, always in the same dispassionate voice, "have proved that they can and will resist any pressure, when their faith is at stake. Men such as they do not need to sacrifice to the *Genius* of the Emperor—their ordinary oath of allegiance, even their simple word, is good enough for me. These men will retain their posts; the officers among them are transferred to my bodyguard. I know that with them my life is as safe as the honor of the Emperor. The assembly is closed."

"Long live the Cæsar!" roared the Tribune Rutilus; almost the entire assembly was in an uproar of enthusiasm; the majority felt that this was good sport, that the Cæsar had played a shrewd game and that he was just.

Constantius raised his hand. When they had become silent, he said with a pale smile, "Just in case there should be one of you who does not agree with my verdict and feels compelled to write to the Emperor about it: his address is still the imperial palace in Nicomedia. I should know—I wrote to him about my verdict yesterday, and the messenger is well on his way."

Respectful laughter greeted the sally. Constantius nodded. "Legate Curio!"

The legate disentangled his hand from Tuscus' grip—the chief waiter, tears in his eyes, was trying to kiss it—and stepped forward.

"Cæsar?"

"Come with me, old friend. To my study. You should not have got up, you know—you are still not well. This test was not meant for you. . . ."

In the study, Constantius dismissed Velleius and Strabo with a friendly nod and made Curio sit down in the most comfortable chair.

"That was magnificent, Cæsar", said the old legate gravely.

Constantius laughed. "I rather liked it myself. Have a sip of wine—it's good: a Massican almost as old as yourself. You need it. Well, friend—when Emperors go mad, the Cæsar at least must keep his head cool."

Curio gave him a searching look. "You don't agree with the edict, then?"

"I should say that's fairly obvious, Curio. I shall have to carry it out, though."

"I suppose so", said the old legate wearily.

"Yes. I can, perhaps, afford to twist it around a bit when it comes to giving posts to my household—I can even point out where my sympathies are. But that's all I can do, and it may be too much as it is. Fortunately my venerable father-in-law does not care much what anybody believes, and I am his Cæsar rather than Diocletian's. And it's a long way from here to Nicomedia. But orders are orders."

Curio nodded. "I am afraid we have been soldiers for too long, you and I, Cæsar."

Constantius blinked. "Not too old to change our views, apparently", he said, just a trifle irritated by the older man's polite reproach. "I knew, of course, that you had Christian leanings—but what on earth has made you go in for that sort of thing? A man whose ancestors fought at Zama and Gergovia and Pharsalus. There was a Curio at the storming of Jerusalem, if I remember rightly—"

"There was", acknowledged the legate. "I don't quite understand why that should deter me from accepting the truth when I meet it."

Constantius shifted in his chair. "The truth—the truth—you all seem to have a special right in the truth. I have talked to these—to people of your new faith before, Curio. As far as I can make it out it is a noble enough philosophy, but—"

"It isn't a philosophy", disagreed the legate. "It is a number of facts. Once you have become aware of that, you have to act accordingly. I did."

"'A number of facts'", repeated Constantius. "I must say, I found it a bit bewildering. As long as they say 'behave to others as you want others to behave to you', I can follow;

that's more or less the core of every decent philosophy of morals. Even when they say that there is only one God, one might be inclined to agree with them—we have far too many gods and far too few serious believers. Perhaps it would be better to have it the other way round, though just one is a little drastic for my taste. I cannot imagine one God because I cannot believe that Good and Evil have the same source."

"There is a perfectly good explanation for that—"

"No doubt, no doubt," interrupted Constantius. "Don't let us go too much into detail. But there are two points where I cannot see eye to eye with them—and, frankly, I don't understand how you can. There is that—forgive me—crazy belief in a God turning man, performing all sorts of miracles, and finally even rising from his tomb. I suppose that's what the simpler minded among your—sect— believe, just as there are simpleminded people who believe in Jupiter transforming himself into a bull or a rain of gold. *You* don't believe that sort of thing, do you, Curio?"

"I do," said the old legate, "and I know very well what you are thinking at the moment: you are thinking that old Curio is really very old now and that he can't think straight any longer. I'd probably think the same, if I were in your place."

"You amaze me", said Constantius.

"In reality," went on Curio, "I'm simply being logical about it. Yes, logical. If God is God, he can perform miracles. If he has created the laws of nature, he can suspend them."

"But why should he?"

"That's a different story altogether, Cæsar, and it has nothing to do with facts. I'm a practical old man—I'm not given to speculations, least of all speculations about the intentions and plans of a Being vastly superior to me. Facts are all I'm interested in."

Constantius began to drum with his fingers on the table of citrus wood before him. It was a little annoying to be told off dialectically by this dear old miracle believer.

"You haven't seen these miracles yourself", he said.

"Nor have I fought at Pharsalus or stormed Jerusalem under Titus", shrugged Curio. "But does that mean that I am credulous for believing that Jerusalem has been stormed?"

"But, man—these are historical facts—"

"I know. That's just it. So are Christ's miracles. Historical facts. Reported by eyewitnesses. I can see no reason why I should believe Flavius Josephus when he tells me about the destruction of Jerusalem but not the Apostle John when he tells me about the miracles of Christ. I have no reason whatsoever to doubt either author's sincerity."

"You are the most irritating logician", exclaimed Constantius. "Surely everybody can convince himself today of the fact that Jerusalem has been stormed: the ruins are still there, though part of the city has been rebuilt. You can go and see it with your own eyes. Your analogy is absurd, friend."

"Jerusalem is far away", said the old legate, smiling. "If both of us had to prove our case to a judge in court, you'd be in a far worse position than I."

"What do you mean?"

"Well, you would say: come with me to Jerusalem, two months', three months' journey by sea, and have a look at the ruins. I, on the other hand, would say: stay right here in York. Perhaps your ruins are still there—but most certainly Christ's miracles are still there—and they are not in ruins, either. You have just seen old Gubates stick to his faith in Christ, despite the fact that he knew—or thought he knew—he was going to lose his job. He's got a sick wife at home and I don't know how many brats. He can keep his job, by just throwing a few grains of incense into an old tripod. And he doesn't do it. He would rather lose his job. Friend, you may prove to me that Jerusalem is in ruins—but I *have* proved to you that Christ's miracles are very much alive."

Constantius' eyes narrowed. "Very well", he said. "Maybe he did perform miracles. Maybe your Apostle John is as reliable a witness as Flavius Josephus. But I've seen a good many clever tricks in my life—wizards and jugglers who did the most astounding things. I saw one in Milan, some years ago—perhaps your Christ was a wizard—a sorcerer—I don't know. Why must he have been a god?"

"Because he said so", said Curio gently.

Constantius looked at him in utter amazement. Then he began to laugh.

"'Because he said so.' That's wonderful. I say I am a god. Therefore I am a god. And you call that logic!"

"It is perfectly good logic", smiled the old legate. "Figure it out yourself, Cæsar. When a man says that he is God—how many logical possibilities are there?"

"One. He is mad."

"I disagree. There is also the possibility that he is a criminal—a scoundrel, trying to hoodwink simpleminded people."

"True and logical", nodded Constantius.

"And thirdly," continued Curio, "there is the possibility that he speaks the truth. It may be a fantastic possibility—it may be the least likely of the three—but it is a possibility from the point of view of sheer logic."

"Granted—theoretically", smiled Constantius.

"Therefore we have three possibilities," nodded Curio, "and not merely one. Now I have taken the trouble to study the life of this man whom the Jews called Yeshua or Jesus; I have studied what he said. Friend, if that is a lunatic, I should hate to be called sane! Some of his words have such depth that I felt as I did on the day when I first saw the Alps—you know what I mean. Others are just simply sense—good and honest sense, and you feel that it's time that they are said. No, I had to drop the possibility. Whatever this Jesus was, he was not mad."

"Well?"

"So I had a look at the second possibility. A criminal, trying to delude others. But in that case there must be a motive. No one is a criminal just for the sake of being one. What did this Jesus want to get out of it all? Money? He despised it. Throughout his life he lived as a poor man. Women? He never touched a woman. Power?"

"Most likely."

"Impossible. It was offered to him—the Jews wanted to accept him as their King. They were ready, thousands of them, to follow him into battle. He refused. Said his kingdom was not of this world. Do you know of another motive? I don't. Therefore he wasn't a lunatic, and he wasn't a criminal. So there remains only the third and last possibility—that he really was what he said he was."

"Clever old logician", smiled Constantius. "You've worked it all out. But I can see a fourth possibility."

Curio leaned back. "Your brain is far better than mine", he said. "I am most curious. What is it?"

"The fourth possibility", said Constantius slowly, "is that your Jesus never said he was God! And that only some of his followers said so. I have seen what can happen to reports when they are going from mouth to mouth. I say here and today, I have made levies, and now I have three legions under my command. Tomorrow they'll say in Gaul that I have five, in Illyricum that I have ten, and when the news comes to Nicomedia, I have twenty-five new legions, and that means I am bound for the conquest of the whole Empire. Surely, you too know what rumors can do."

"Rumors are not facts", said the obstinate old legate. "I insist on dealing with facts. A fact is that this Jesus was condemned to death because he insisted on being God. He was condemned for blasphemy. Another fact is that his first followers, his disciples, were executed or tortured to death because they insisted that he was God and that he had said that he was God. The Scriptures you are supposed to have burned contain copies of the letters of some of Jesus' first disciples and a description of his life by four different authors. One of them was a disciple of Jesus himself—another the disciple of a disciple, a physician by profession—a man called Lucas. Now when men die for their belief, they may have the wrong belief, but there's no doubt that they believe it! And that settles your fourth possibility."

Constantius did not reply. He was not so much interested in old Curio's logic, but it impressed him tremendously that an officer of the legate's rank and descent should become a convinced follower of that strange sect; many another sect had come from the east—western people were not imaginative enough to invent anything of the kind—and Rome had absorbed them one after the other; there was the cult of Isis, of Mithras, even of the Jewish God who knew no statues and whose name was not to be pronounced; but all these had been like fashionable fads in Rome. No Roman legate or tribune would be ready to give up his rank or post for Isis' or Mithras' sake. This thing was different.

Perhaps—perhaps the Emperor was right, and it was a dangerous thing after all?

He cleared his throat. "I remarked that there were two points on which I could not see eye to eye with this religion of yours", he said. "We have discussed the first only."

"Well—what is the second?"

"When Christians refuse to sacrifice to the *Genius* of the Emperor—well, I can understand that; even Diocletian knows perfectly well that he is human. At least I hope he does. It is—shall we say: a little stiff necked, and just a trifle exaggerated on the part of your—co-religionists; after all, there is not much harm in throwing a bit of incense into a tripod. But let that pass. However, when Christians refuse to serve in the army—when the Centurion Marcellus throws his arms away and declares that he will only serve Christ, the King of Kings; when the recruit Maximilianus refuses to be enrolled and to swear allegiance—"

"He didn't."

"You know the case?"

"I know both cases, Cæsar. Marcellus and Maximilianus refused only what I, too, have refused this very day. They refused to commit blasphemy by giving the Emperor honors due only to God. One can be a Christian and a soldier, believe me. Christ detested violence, that is true. But he never condemned soldiering as such. He had words of high praise for a Roman officer—the commander of our little fort at Capernaum. No, what he hated were hypocrisy, hardheartedness, and vice. What he preached were love and justice."

"Justice—" Again Constantius shifted in his chair. "Of all the goddesses of Olympus she is the most difficult one to serve. I don't like this edict, Curio. I shall give orders to be clement in the handling of the matter. It's sheer nonsense to demolish perfectly good buildings. I don't believe in the burning of books and scriptures either. Justice must needs be cold, of its very nature. It has nothing to do with burning."

"There is still another justice—"

"I know. Don't say it. Not all I have done in my life has been just. Don't remind me. I have never thanked you sufficiently for what you did for me, five years ago—in Verulam."

"You needn't thank me", said Curio gravely. "I did it for her—not for you."

Constantius gave a somewhat embarrassed laugh. "No one can call you a hypocrite, my Curio."

"I hope not. And I hope that your wish, to have this horrible edict handled with clemency, will be fulfilled. But will it? It gives the little chiefs such a beautiful opportunity to show off their power. It's an unjust edict, you see—and I very much fear that no amount of clemency can turn injustice into justice."

"You should pray to your Jesus", said Constantius with his pale smile.

"I shall do so", said the old legate.

CHAPTER 2

THE LIGHT GALLIC WAGON was speeding along the road to Verulam.

Awakening, Helena shivered a little; it was getting colder now—the leaves in Father's forest had been brown, and many of them had covered his favorite stone, under which he was buried as had been his wish. She had spent a full day there, all alone, as she did every year.

He has been the last King of the Trinovantes, their father rather than their King. There was no need for a successor—the once so warlike tribe had long since become peaceful, and the Roman administration was good on the whole. Perhaps the very name of the Trinovantes would soon vanish, but King Coel was not to be forgotten. Long processions of people made pilgrimages to his tomb. There were many who said that he was still watching the destiny of the land from the Beyond and even some who prayed to him, as to the country's protecting spirit. The town of Camulodunum had grown in size and encompassed now the old site where the Roman military camp had been—Coel-castra. There was talk that the name of the town should be changed to Coel-castra altogether.

Perhaps it would, one day. But what mattered more was that King Coel's memory was alive in the hearts of the people.

More than once Helena had thought of giving up the little house in Verulam and retiring to Camulodunum; in Father's forest she felt at peace—and Verulam meant painful memories only. But then she would have had to reassume her name and rank, and she did not want to do that. Besides, Hilary was happy in Verulam, where his Albanus lived. If only he would be a little more cautious about his Christian activities. When the imperial edict had come out, eight months ago, a number of arrests had been made, and the government had confiscated several houses that the Christians used to hold their assemblies and religious ceremonies in. Things had quieted down a little since then, but they could flare up again at any moment—whenever something went wrong, the Christians were always a welcome scapegoat for the municipal authorities.

Perhaps the worst thing was that Christians were practically outlawed—they could be accused, but they could not accuse. Which meant, of course, that they were cheated and imposed upon all the time. Even if they had been superstitious people, intolerant of other people's beliefs and bad citizens—this treatment—wholesale and without discrimination—would have been wrong and unjust.

That woman could not have a good influence on—on the Cæsar if things like that were possible under his rule. She had given him another daughter, last month. Six children he now had from her. Three boys and three girls. He had seen to it that Rome would not lack rulers. . . .

Let them rule, then. What did it matter who wrote unjust edicts or carried them out? It seemed as if the word *rule* itself implied injustice. It was not like Constantius—no, it was not like him—to make innocent people suffer—for nothing. And he could hardly believe that the Christians were dangerous people. Perhaps he did not know how his measures were being carried out. No ruler could ever know that for sure, unless he had ideal subjects. Now, if everyone would live up to Hilary's standard and principles—

The wagon swerved a little, and she leaned out of the window to see what was the cause.

"Something burning over there, Domina", said the coachman. "Perhaps we'd better take another road."

"Over there" were the first houses of Verulam. Helena saw a thick pall of smoke hanging over one of them.

"Very well, take another road."

Half an hour later they reached home. Favonius came running from the garden, wiping his big hands on his tunic, his huge face beaming.

"All well, Favonius?"

"All well, Domina."

"A letter from my son?"

"No, Domina."

She nodded to him and to Rufus, whose toothless grin welcomed her at the door, and began to mount the stairs.

No letter. It was almost five months now since Constantine's last letter had arrived. Minervina used to write more often than her husband, but now she was pregnant again—perhaps it would be a daughter this time. Her firstborn child was now almost five years old—little Crispus.

If only she could have him here.

No letter. Of course, he might be at the Persian frontier, where men did not find time to write letters. Or perhaps he was on one of those long hunting expeditions in the mountains of Cappadocia.

He might write a little more often, though. He did not like writing. Soldiering was the only thing that interested him—and even that had to be in the field rather than at training schools.

His letters were respectful, but—yes, deadly dull. Dutiful sentences, truisms, dry reports about his activities.

He should write more often, all the same. Favonius missed him, too—he was pining for him, poor old man.

Ah, here was Hilary at long last. She was so glad to see him again that she almost forgot how angry she had been with him for not having come with her. It was the first time that he had let her go alone to Coel-castra and her father's tomb. "I can't, Domina—and please don't ask me why not." She had not asked; it was quite clear to her, anyway. He was getting deeper and deeper into his Christian activities. One day she would have to talk to Albanus about it.

Then she realized that his tunic was torn in several places and that he was covered with grime.

"What have you been doing, Hilary?"

"Trying to help extinguish a fire, Domina."

"Near the Porta Londinia?"

"That's right, Domina. A house was on fire there."

"I saw it. What has it got to do with you?"

He avoided her eye. "It is—was—an assembly house, Domina. So they burned it down."

"And—the authorities?"

"Helped, Domina."

"To extinguish?"

"To burn, Domina."

She stamped her foot. "Really, everybody is being as troublesome as can be; the authorities are behaving like rabble, and you, of course, must be mixed up with it."

"Not with the rabble, Domina", said Hilary smiling.

She, too, had to smile, and it annoyed her. "I do so wish you would give up this—this sort of activity, Hilary. It's dangerous. Nothing good will come of it." She felt how utterly irrelevant her words were, and it increased her annoyance. "A man may hold a belief and deem it sacred—he need not, for that reason, go and shout it from the rooftops. He need not join clandestine meetings. He need not sneak about like a hunted criminal—"

"You know quite well, Domina," said Hilary, "on whose side lies the crime."

"Yes, yes—I know; but I hate to see you like this—there's blood on your arm! Let me attend to it—I'll—"

"It is nothing," said Hilary hastily, "just a scratch. Please, don't worry about me, Domina. I assure you it is nothing. I've only just come in, or else you wouldn't have seen me in this state. I'll go and wash now, if I may."

He almost fled. There was something—something virginal about him. Strange man. Strange belief. But at least he believed in what he believed, and he lived what he believed, too. If only there weren't so many slaves and women going in for this thing—people who were weak and needed the support of the invisible; people whose lives were hardship and sorrow and disappointment and who were only too ready to believe in the promise of a better sort of life after death. They were clinging to their illusion with a tenacity. . . .

Yet Hilary was neither woman nor slave—and there was that man Albanus, gentle, birdlike, a simple man; he had been a soldier in the Roman army for seven years before he took to wood carving—what gave a man like that a power of speech and demeanor as though he had been born with royal blood in his veins?

For the hundredth time she discovered that she was thinking of Albanus against her will; he put himself back into her mind as though he had a right there—as though he had sent her a letter that she had not answered. He was like a duty unfulfilled, an annoying obligation. She turned abruptly and went over to her old place at the window.

When Hilary returned, he found her sitting with her back toward him, staring out into the street. He knew that she had gone back to the past once more—the place at the window was like a magic circle, within which she felt safe.

"Domina—"

There was no answer.

"Domina, I have been serving you for sixteen years now—"

Her body stiffened. She had thought that she had lost everything. Now she knew that this was not so, and she knew it only because she was going to lose more. Hilary was going to leave her. He had left her already. Once more she felt the presence of shadows in the room, dark and deadly—as on the day when Albanus had come to visit her.

"Domina, the time has come to tell you at long last what the King, your father, kept in his innermost thoughts."

"My father? What do you mean?" She did not turn.

"The story of the living wood, Domina. The story of the Tree of Life."

The living wood. Wood is sacred. Wood is man's disaster and man's triumph. It kills man and saves man. The world, as we know it, is built on wood, on Yggdrasil, the holy tree that gives life. It is all in the message—the message that no one understands. The living wood.

And then Father fell asleep. It was a story without a beginning and without an end. It had haunted him all his life. It had been his last thought. "You and Constantine—together you will find the living wood, yea, the very tree of life—"

"He never told you the end of the story", said Hilary. "He couldn't. He did not know what I know—now."

"What do you know?"

"The story of the living wood is as old as mankind, Domina. King Coel knew the legends told in the north. He had heard of the Egyptian tree of life, but he did not know—though he saw it in his own way—what I am going to tell you now."

"Who told you?"

"Albanus, Domina. And he heard it, a long time ago, in Syria, when he was serving in the army."

Albanus. Again Albanus. Always Albanus.

"Very well—tell me."

"Thus runs the legend, Domina. When the first man and the first woman, Adam and Eve, had lost paradise— what the Greeks called 'the golden age'—they lived in exile. The day came when Adam was to die. And as he lay dying, God sent a winged messenger to earth—a great and powerful spirit, whose name was Michael. And Michael appeared to Seth, Adam's son, and gave him a tiny seed—the seed of a tree. When Adam had died, Seth planted the sacred seed in his father's mouth. And a tree grew upon Adam's grave. Thousands of years later, the tree stood in the courtyard of a royal palace—the palace of King Solomon, the wise ruler of Israel. But wise as he was, he knew nothing about the origin of the tree. Until one day, a great Queen came to visit him from the south, the Queen of Sheba. And she knew about the tree and its secret, for Seth had been her ancestor, and he had passed it on to his son, and he to his son, and so on from generation to generation. And the Queen of Sheba told King Solomon that this tree was sacred because the Savior of the World would die on it. The King had the tree hewn down, and the timber was buried deep in the ground, near the precincts of the Temple. The pit they dug filled with water, and it was there that the sacrificial animals were washed for many generations. But at the appointed time the pit dried up, and the timber was found again."

"The appointed time?"

"The time when the greatest of all sacrifices took place. That of which all sacrifices had been a symbol."

Suddenly Helena remembered. "There is no more barren thing than a cross", Albanus had said. "But under the touch of the Holy Blood the barren wood became the Tree of Life. . . ."

"Hilary—do you believe that story?"

"I believe in the meaning of it—yes. I believe that it is no coincidence that all the peoples in the world have heard of a tree of life. I believe there is a reason why all the peoples have legends about a golden age that has gone, because something went wrong with us. I believe that there was once a golden age, and that something did go wrong with us; that from then on a whispering went from mouth to mouth, from generation to generation, that one day the world would be saved through the tree of life. Each generation, each race and each people added a little to it, or forgot something about it, and thus we have innumerable stories—of the world ash, supporting the earth, of a magic key, of Osiris killed and Attys slain—and all pointed to the Cross to come. Your father knew almost all these stories—except the one I have told you now. How he would have loved it!"

"Yes", said Helena.

"King Coel the Wise was a forerunner—" Hilary's voice was as soft as a woman's—"time and again he would point to the tree of life to come—"

"But—don't you believe that it *has* come, then? Your Christ died on the Cross three hundred years ago."

"Yes, Domina. And ever since his teaching has spread, from country to country and from generation to generation. But it is said that it will encompass the Roman world only when the Cross is found again. For it has disappeared—and no one knows where it is."

Suddenly and for no apparent reason, her heart began to beat tumultuously; she could hear the beat like a wild gong, thundering and thundering a flaming appeal; louder and louder, until there was nothing but that beat, filling the room and the world. She herself was nothing but that beat, and there was nothing in the world that was not that beat—

It was all over before she was really aware of it, like a chariot thundering by so quickly, one could catch only a glimpse of manes and tails and wheels as it vanished in a cloud of dust.

That afternoon Hilary told her that he had become a Christian priest. It did not come as a shock to her now; she only nodded—she understood at once why he had not come with her, as he had all the years before, to visit her father's grave. He had done better than that—he had made it his life work to serve the Tree of Life. And she was touched by the manner in which he told her—shyly and reluctantly as though to spare her feelings. It did not make her feel small, strangely enough.

She inquired how it had happened, and he told her about Bishop Osius, who had passed through Verulam a few days before and had ordained him. It seemed to be a solemn little ceremony, ending in the "laying on of hands", and it had taken place at night, in the house she had seen burning.

"It would have been my church, that house", said Hilary, and his brave attempt to hide his grief made her forget her own feelings.

"Do you mean to say that you now have no place in which to hold your meetings or services?"

"We shall meet at Albanus' house, tomorrow morning. But it's a small house, and it won't do to assemble there regularly—it would arouse suspicion quickly enough. The next time it will have to be somewhere else."

She looked up. "This house is at your disposal, Hilary", she said simply, and she smiled happily as she saw a thin red rising in his cheeks. "I am not a Christian," she said, "and I don't think I ever shall be—but I hate injustice. You know, of course, what they say about your secret meetings—that you are sacrificing the flesh and blood of little children and that you insist on adoring the head of an ass. I don't know about your sacrifices—but *if* you adore the head of an ass, you are doing exactly what they all do—although I find it difficult to understand why you should refuse to worship the *Genius* of the Divine Emperor, in such circumstances."

Hilary laughed, and she laughed, and the atmosphere of the room seemed strangely light and unreal.

"In one respect the rumors are right", said Hilary then, and his face grew serious again. "It is true—we do sacrifice the Flesh and Blood of an innocent victim."

She shook her head. "Now what do you mean by that, Hilary?"

"It is not easy to understand", he said. "When the Lord and his disciples assembled for the last meal before his captivity and death, he changed bread and wine into his Flesh and Blood. They tasted like bread and wine—but it was his Flesh and Blood, for he said it was. And he asked them to do likewise in his name and in his memory."

"A lovely allegory—"

"No", said Hilary, and there was hard metal in his voice. "It is not an allegory. It is a fact. Reality."

"Hilary!"

"Why should it surprise you that the supernatural happens when the supernatural is at play?"

"It's three hundred years ago, Hilary—perhaps you believe now what was not believed then?"

"The great Irenæus mentions it clearly in his treatise against the Marcionites 120 years ago, and so did the saintly Justin more than 150 years ago. We are not dealing with loose allegories and symbols in Christianity, Domina—with us it's hard facts. Even two hundred years ago, Bishop Ignatius of Antioch mentions 'the medicine of immortality, the antidote that we should not die, but live forever in Jesus Christ'."

"Indeed you have become a priest, Hilary."

"Yes, Domina—and that means that my lips can call down the all powerful God to our altar. As God descended into the world of matter and became flesh, so matter is now changed into God. And we eat his Flesh and drink his Blood,

213

so that we may partake of his divinity, as he partook of our humanity."

Magnificent madness, she thought. And she said with sudden determination, "I want to be present at one of these—sacrifices. I shall come with you, tomorrow morning."

Almost at once she regretted having said it—but she did not want him to feel hurt.

"It is not without danger, Domina—the edict—"

That sealed it. "At what time tomorrow morning, Hilary?"

At dawn.

Four little oil lamps were burning in the room, which was packed with people. Most of them had been there when Helena entered with Hilary and Albanus, who had greeted them at his door. He did not seem to be surprised at her coming, she noted, nor was anyone else. She was just one more person in the room.

She saw one or two faces she knew—the wife of a rich merchant in the Street of the Silversmiths and the owner of the shop where she used to buy her cosmetics. Most of those present belonged to the poorer classes, but then, Verulam was not a rich town, and it did not even try to be elegant, like Aquæ Sulis, for instance.

There was something that they all seemed to have in common: it was difficult to define, and it showed in different ways, but they all had it. It was an eager expectancy, a powerful longing—as though they had all *hurried* to this place and were still a little out of breath; and now they were waiting as people wait at the gates of a palace, to hear a beloved King say that the war has come to an end—anxiously and yet in a strange sort of triumph.

It was fascinating to see the tremendous influence that Albanus had over them all; though he was not a priest, he seemed the natural leader of the little community. They all knew him, and to know him seemed to mean that they expected him to direct them. Tightly packed as they were, he managed to pass from one to the other with ease, and he had a few words, a smile, an encouraging gesture for everyone.

But perhaps Albanus had some sort of rank after all—for it was he who commanded silence, first by raising his hand, then by making a mysterious sign, first touching his forehead, then his heart, and finally the left and the right side of his chest. The community imitated his example. Then the old man bowed to Hilary and produced a tattered old scroll, from which he began to read.

"When Jesus saw how great was their number, he went up on to the mountainside; there he sat down, and his disciples came about him. And he began speaking to them; this was the teaching he gave. Blessed are the poor in spirit; the kingdom of heaven is theirs. Blessed are the meek; they shall inherit the earth. Blessed are those who mourn; they shall be comforted. Blessed are those who hunger and thirst for holiness; they shall have their fill. Blessed are the merciful; they shall obtain mercy. Blessed are the clean of heart; they shall see God. Blessed are the peacemakers; they shall be counted the children of God. Blessed are those who suffer persecution in the cause of right; the Kingdom of heaven is theirs. Blessed are you, when men revile you and persecute you and speak all manner of evil against you falsely, because of me. Be glad and lighthearted, for a rich reward awaits you in heaven; so it was they persecuted the prophets who went before you. You are the salt of the earth—"

At that moment the door burst open, and the red glow of torches shone into the packed room.

"No one moves", bellowed a voice. Bare swords glittered in the entrance. A few women screamed.

"Extinguish the lamps!" came Albanus' voice in ringing tones. The men next to the oil lamps obeyed instantly. The soldiers could not prevent it—the room was so full that they simply could not enter.

The torches alone were not strong enough to disclose more than a pandemonium of wrangling, terrified people, an almost compact mass.

Helena did not move. She felt angry rather than frightened, and she was looking toward the door to see whether she could make out an officer ranking higher than subaltern among the intruders—someone to whom she could give a piece of her mind. It was outrageous to disturb a peaceful gathering in such a manner.

The dark figure of a man loomed up in front of her. She recognized Albanus, and she heard him say quickly to Hilary, "Flee at once—that way! They are not likely to know about the little door at the side."

"I don't want to leave my—"

"You must. We cannot afford to lose another priest. And take this—hurry."

"What is it?"

"You know—! For the Lord's sake, hurry."

But he had not forgotten her. "Come, Domina."

They managed to slip behind a curtain, along a small corridor. A tiny door opened, and they made their way out into the bleak morning, too dark still to see anything except a few yards of pavement and the sullen shadows of suburban houses.

From inside the house came hoarse commands, thudding noises, and then one long-drawn agonized scream.

"Where are we going, Hilary?"

He did not answer; she could see, dimly, that he was clutching something tightly to his chest; it was the thing that Albanus had given him—it looked like a large goblet.

Through the mist the armor of a soldier became visible; no, two soldiers—they had been seen.

A vulgar voice barked an order, and as they walked on, faster and faster, they heard the soldiers break into a run.

It was like a nightmare, and just as in a nightmare she had often made an end to it by a sudden, wild action, she did so now, turning round and facing the pursuers.

At once, Hilary too stopped.

The soldiers arrived, panting.

"What do you want?" asked Helena imperiously. "Have you nothing better to do than to run after a lady and her freedman?"

"Are you Christians?" asked the taller of the two, in a strong Gallic accent.

"Don't be ridiculous", snapped Helena. "Who is your officer in command? The leader of the cohort, I mean, not of the maniple."

They looked at each other, dumbfounded.

"Well—when are you going to answer me?"

"The Centurion Marcus Tervax—Domina", growled the soldier. "But he isn't in charge today."

"I have no dealings with centurions, but I shall have a word with his legate about this. Now go away."

"You'd better go back to your house, Domina", said the soldier. "This is not a good time for you to be about—we are searching houses all over the place for these Christian rabble rousers."

"I *am* going home", said Helena disdainfully. "I've seen quite enough of you. Come, Hilary."

They walked on, without looking back. The whole street was awake, of course, and something like a chase was going on: screams and wild curses and laughter—it was like in a conquered town. There were very few soldiers about; most of the people were scum from the worst quarters.

At the corner of the next street they saw that there were two houses burning.

"Christian houses?" asked Helena curtly. Hilary nodded without saying a word. His face was a tragic mask.

"This is a day of shame, Hilary—but not for the Christians."

They were near the end of the street when a big, burly fellow with rough features obstructed their path; he was carrying a large bundle—loot, most likely.

"Here, you, give me that thing there. What is it—gold?"

And he clawed at it, with his free hand. Hilary stepped aside and walked on; perhaps he thought the man would not try to run after him, heavily laden as he was—or that the man was just drunk.

But Helena saw the fellow drop his bundle, and she called, "Look out, Hilary!"

The thing for him to do, of course, was to drop what he was carrying and fight this lout—he was much bigger than Hilary, but she knew that Hilary was strong. For some reason, though, he would not drop the thing Albanus had given him; he only clutched it still tighter to his breast and with the other arm tried to ward off the attack. Desperate, she looked about for the nearest soldiers—but the only one she could see was running madly after a screeching young woman; he caught her, too, and Helena turned sharply away. Hilary and the looter were grappling with each other; he seemed to be holding his own—but now she saw a dagger gleam. She knew at once what she had to do and also that it was too late to do it; yet she did draw the sharp stylus from her writing tablet and rushed up to the two and thrust out, with all her strength. The stylus cut, two inches deep, into the arm of the looter, and at the same moment Hilary fell to his knees. The looter, roaring with pain, dropped his dagger and clutched his arm, and as she was raising the stylus again, he turned and ran.

"Are you hurt, Hilary?"

Still he did not speak; but as she was helping him up, she saw his eyes shining with an unutterable gratitude, an abandonment of gratitude, the like of which she had never seen—she was just going to repeat her question when there were terrified screams, followed by a rumbling crash. Looking back, she saw that one of the burning houses had collapsed.

"Come, Hilary—do you think you can walk?"

But she had to lead him, and she felt his weight heavier and heavier on her shoulder. It seemed an eternity before they reached their own neighborhood; and the nearer they came, the more his weight increased. She did not dare to let him sink down while she ran on alone to the house to fetch help. He was holding onto her like a drowning man. The morning mist was beginning to lift, and the birds were singing. The street was empty and peaceful.

The last fifty yards were the most difficult; she had almost to carry him. He seemed far heavier than one might expect of a man of his size. When at long last she reached the door, she was utterly at the end of her own strength; her heart was beating wildly, and her head was spinning. She gave the knock, and then, while she was waiting, she felt something wet and sticky on her arm and shoulder and saw that her dress was covered with blood.

The slave who opened the door shouted for Favonius, who appeared from nowhere, fully dressed. He lifted Hilary bodily and carried him to his room. The sun was up now, and she could see clearly that it was too late for help. He had been bleeding and bleeding; his face was waxen and empty, the eyes almost closed. Favonius had sent slaves to fetch any physician they could get hold of; he had tried to take the thing out of Hilary's hand, but found it impossible. The dying man was clutching it with a terrible force; all the sinews and muscles of his arm stood out—it was as though all the life still in him were concentrated in that one arm that could not relax.

So Favonius had cut open his tunic instead and there was the wound, in the shoulder. He got busy with it.

Helena stood transfixed; her eyes were humble beggars entreating and rejected.

No, not rejected. For Hilary's lids were drawn back like the curtains of a temple, and he saw her and recognized her. For one last time his body obeyed his will, and slowly his cramped arm relaxed and stretched forward. She saw his lips moving and fell on her knees to be closer; all she could hear was:

"You—keep—safe—"

The thing was a golden goblet, covered with a lid. Only now could she see it clearly, and as she stretched out her hand to receive it, his fingers opened, and it fell into hers.

Hilary was dead.

She remained where she was, on her knees, the golden goblet in her hands, staring at his bloodless face; there was, on his lips, the ghost of a smile of such serenity as one might see on those of a happy child. He is very beautiful, she thought.

Then Favonius helped her up and led her to her own room, and she opened the lid of the goblet; it contained a thin wafer of unleavened bread.

All she could think was, Father gave me Hilary—and Hilary gave me this. . . . She closed the lid reverently and locked the goblet away. This is not going to leave me—ever, she thought.

She could not cry.

CHAPTER 3

"LADY TO SEE THE CÆSAR", reported the soldier Davus.

The centurion of the watch gave him a cold stare.

"You gone mad, you son of a cross-eyed whore mother?"

"Lady to see the Cæsar", repeated the soldier Davus sullenly.

"Why", said the centurion of the watch, "why must I be punished by the gods; what have I done to deserve a command over jibbering lunatics! A lady to see the Cæsar! What do you think this is, you offspring of camel droppings? An amusement hall? A tavern? This is the *Domus palatina*, you putrid carrion. This is the *palace*. There's an audience list for those who want to see the Cæsar—if the Cæsar wants to see *them*. This audience list is the business of the chamberlain, and when someone with an audience is expected, one of the chamberlain's clerks comes down at the appointed time. Nothing to do with us. Have I been understood? No, I have not been understood. I must make myself clearer, must I? Tell the good woman to go away, see what I mean? Tell her to write to the Cæsar's chamberlain or in Jupiter's name to the Cæsar himself. Stating her address, age, and business. Off!"

"Lady to see the Cæsar", said the soldier Davus.

Only now did the centurion of the watch look up; he saw the silent despair in the soldier's eyes—and he saw the tall figure of the lady standing almost immediately behind him. He jumped to his feet.

"I am Princess Helena", said the lady icily. "You will instantly go and inform the chamberlain that I am here to see the Cæsar."

"Yes, Domina", said the centurion of the watch, saluting. There was a huge man of military bearing standing behind the lady; he now took a step forward. "*And* get the princess a chair", he growled. "If this is a palace, there should be a chair somewhere."

"A chair for the princess", said the centurion of the watch to Davus. "Go and fetch it. Take mine here—no, go and get one in the blue room, there are better ones in there."

Davus ran. The centurion saluted again and walked off with a briskness that satisfied even Favonius. Then Davus came back with a chair and placed it against the wall of the guardroom.

"You really are mad", said Favonius. "Is this a room for the princess to wait in? Carry that to a decent room."

They followed him, as he carried the chair back to the blue room. It was a private audience room of the chamberlain.

Helena sat down. She was tired, tired to death. They had made the journey to Eburacum in three days; she had hardly slept at all; and all the time she had been haunted by—no, not again; not again the pictures of her thoughts, ferocious and snarling like live animals. The blood on her hands, the blood on her dress; the smile on Hilary's face and the cool, steady sheen of the goblet; the flames of burning houses and the scream of a woman in deadly danger—She could not stop them; they came back, all of them, again and again in one long whirling procession. The face of Albanus as he read from the scroll—Albanus! The pain in her heart as she stood before the commander of the troops! Poor embarrassed little man, what else could he do but what he was told? It was not he, the municipal authorities had these matters in hand, would the Domina get in touch with them? But it was not a wise thing to do; one only made oneself suspect. No, he could not advise her to go and see them. Some time ago, most of these Christians had been poor people, little people, but lately there were rumors that even people of good standing had joined that sect, and no one was entirely above suspicion. He himself did not care at all what a man believed, but what could he do, orders were orders! And when the municipal authorities asked him for some detachments of soldiers for this sort of—work—well, his orders were to provide them. It was most regrettable. Most regrettable.

Then the municipal leaders; they would not tell her at first what had happened to Albanus and to all the people who had been at his house. Instead they asked her who she thought had been there—and had she, perhaps, been there herself, too? Not on that day, of course, because all the people who had been there that day had been arrested. Or did she, perhaps, know of anybody who had not been? What was her interest in the matter? These people were criminals, and they had been caught red-handed, so to speak, in the middle of their blasphemous activities. Surely it was as much to her interest as theirs that the honor and safety of the Roman Empire should not be endangered?

Her servant had been murdered? This was, indeed, most deplorable. Could she tell the circumstances in which it had happened? Where was it? What was he doing when he was attacked—and had she been with him? There were so many cases, these days, the sifting alone would take weeks and possibly months. Over twenty people dead, and more than fifty wounded, in that one night. And there was no end to it—these sectarians were most insolent. As soon as they were driven out of one hole, they would gather in another; and they never talked, even under torture one could not get much out of them. Fanatics.

Now that bunch they had caught in the house of Albanus! Seventy-four people—and not one of them would say who their priest was. There was bound to be a priest around; they always flocked together when a priest was about for the conduct of their blasphemous rites.

But then, of course, some of them might not have known who he was—although that was rather unlikely. That man Albanus, however, was bound to know. And he would not speak! All right, she might as well know it—they had been put into prison, and Albanus, as their leader, had been executed this afternoon. Did that upset her? Why should it upset her? Was she, perhaps, a Christian?

No, she was not a Christian—but the municipal authorities were doing their very best to make her one.

The high-born lady was speaking in jest, surely? Perhaps she had known Albanus, bought some of his wood carvings? Well, it would comfort her to know that he had died the death of a Roman citizen; he had been decapitated, a clean death. He had been lucky, really. For there had been an assault on the prison, the night after, on the part of the roused population; they had overcome the guards and burned the prison with all the prisoners in it. Most deplorable, certainly—but that sort of thing would happen when a decent town harbored members of a fanatical religious sect. There had been women and children among the imprisoned people, true. Very, very deplorable.

Favonius' startled face, when she came home and gave orders to saddle the horses. To Eburacum? Yes, to Eburacum. He had not asked any more questions. He was the sort that would go to the other end of the world without asking questions.

It was that sort of man that had made the Empire great; men like the leaders at Verulam would see to it that it went down. And there was one Favonius in a hundred thousand.

This brutal persecution had to be stopped.

Yet there had been a moment when she had hesitated—after having given the orders to saddle the horses. She had been alone in her room, with her traveling cloak in her hand. She had stopped.

What was it she was going to do? Go to *him*—whom she had sworn never to set eyes upon again? What would he think? Perhaps he would not even receive her! Very likely he would not receive her. And she—that woman—she was with him. Perhaps they would laugh at her, as she stood, waiting for an audience.

The thought made her double up with a twisting, physical pain.

She could not face it—not that.

She could not quite fathom what it was that had made her do it, after all. So many things had crossed her mind at the same time; there was Hilary's smile, of course, and Albanus' eyes, and even more his voice as he read from the tattered old scroll, blessing after blessing; there was a sudden, violent contempt for her own pride: the pride not to be proud—if there was such a thing; there was the urgent, the demanding voice calling for action. And she was not going to give counterorders, of course. Never give counterorders.

She flung the cloak around her shoulders and left abruptly.

Then, in the rolling, staggering, groaning wagon the doubts came back, and she let them in, ate them and drank them and slept with them.

But the wheels were turning, and she was drawing nearer and nearer to Eburacum. And now she was in Eburacum, in the Domus palatina. And they were calling on the Cæsar.... The Princess Helena to see you, Cæsar—

It was the Cæsar she had come to see, not Constantius.

A chamberlain appeared, a fairly young official, polite and most embarrassed. Could it be, could it really be the Princess Helena herself? If only they had known she was arriving everything would have been prepared for a suitable reception. It was unforgivable, even so, that a lady of her rank should have been made to wait—

"Has the Cæsar been informed that I am here?"

The chamberlain was in despair; an hour ago special envoys had come from Milan, with news of the utmost gravity— affairs of the state, of course. He himself did not know what it was about. The Cæsar had received them alone, and after five minutes the order had been given not to disturb him. Where had the august princess taken quarters? He did not dare to disobey so strict an order, but at the first free moment, the august princess could rely on it, at the first free moment the Cæsar would be informed of her arrival in Eburacum....

"I have taken quarters here, in this room," said Helena, "and I intend to stay here until I have seen the Cæsar."

Imploring hands, polite despair. Surely the august princess would understand—it all depended upon the Cæsar; it might not be possible to inform him before late in the evening; why should the august princess endure unnecessary hardship? If no other quarters had been taken so far, he would do his best to make suitable arrangements without delay, and he would send a messenger as soon as the Cæsar was free—

"The Cæsar", said Helena. "All I want is to see the Cæsar. And I am not moving from this room until I have seen him. You don't know me, young man."

The chamberlain withdrew, murmuring profuse apologies.

Helena waited. There was nothing to be done but to wait.

Grave news—affairs of the state. These court officials always took things very seriously. The only grave affair of the state was injustice done, from within or without. Nothing else mattered. It was she who was bringing—how was it?— news of the utmost gravity. This thing had to be stopped. Constantius had to stop it; the Cæsar had to stop it. Or no one could ever be happy from Britain to Persia. For such happiness was paid for in tears and blood and despair.

Was that the true picture of the Empire? A surface of marble and triumph, of splendor and valor, of wealth and power—and rows and rows of dungeons underneath, where all the horrible vices were let loose?

Somehow the phrase "whited sepulchres" came into her mind; she could not remember where she had heard it before. Perhaps Hilary had mentioned it—he had often said surprising things, incredibly good metaphors—it was a pity he had never written them down.

Hilary. Hilary. It was true what Father had said of him: no King had left a better heritage to his child. She had lost that heritage as she lost all the rest.

And here she was—and had not even the right to speak to her own husband; another woman had that right, had all rights. And she might walk in here, any moment, and tell her to go. . . .

Who is that woman, insisting on having an audience with my husband, the Cæsar? That British wife of his, repudiated years and years ago? What does she want of him now? Money? Or a fat post for her bastard son? Her time is over, was over long ago. Turn her out! The impudence of her coming under *my* roof.

She might say that. Any moment now she might come in and say that. And she only need to speak one word, and her orders would be obeyed instantly.

Helena groaned. And her heart missed a beat as at that moment the door opened.

But it was a man who came in, slowly and a little bent, an old man. His hair was iron gray and dishevelled; his face was heavily lined, and there were pouches under his eyes. It was Constantius.

She rose; she had prepared every word she was going to say to him, as soon as she had bowed to the Cæsar, the representative of the Emperor. But she did not bow. Instead she said, "You look dreadfully tired, Constantius. Are you ill?"

"I am not too well", he said. "A little overworked, that is all."

But it was not all; she knew that. And she knew that he knew it, too. He sat down cautiously, as old men will. "You, too, look tired, Helena. With me, it is understandable. I am sixty, next month. But you——"

"I'm fifty-five myself", said she with the ghost of a smile. "But I am sure I am looking worse than I should; I have not changed dress for three days. I had to speak to you at once. Or rather—I had to speak to the Cæsar."

She was deadly serious again; but now it was he who smiled.

"Then you are unfortunate, Helena. There is no Cæsar any longer."

She stared at him, wide eyed. "What do you mean?"

"Both Diocletian and Maximian have abdicated; Galerius and I are their successors. At least we both think so."

"You mean—you are the Emperor now?"

"Yes, Helena. The proclamation is being written out now. Except for the envoys and Strabo you are the first one to know."

He was gazing into the void; she saw that his tunic was stained. They are not looking after him properly, she thought. He had taken to biting his fingernails, too.

Suddenly her thoughts came back with a rush. "But this is excellent news", she exclaimed. "This will make things much easier."

His eyes were veiled. "Will it? Which things?"

She made an impatient little gesture. "What I have come for, of course. As Cæsar you might have got into trouble with the Emperor. But now—"

"An Emperor has more troubles to fear than a Cæsar", said Constantius quietly.

"The thing an Emperor has to fear most is injustice", said Helena. "Injustice committed in his name."

He sighed. There was the shadow of a disappointment in his face, as he said, "And who has committed injustice against you, Helena? But, then, I know the answer of course. I did."

Again the impatient little gesture. "You're just as obtuse as you used to be, Constantius. What I have to tell you has nothing to do with you and me—not with you and me personally. I thought I'd made that clear when I said I'd come to see the Cæsar."

"What have you come for, Helena?" asked Constantius cautiously.

"That edict, Constantius. That terrible, lying, hypocritical, murderous edict against the Christians."

"Until yesterday," he smiled, "that would have been *læsa majestas*."

"I don't care what it would have been yesterday, and I don't care what anybody says. You should know me well enough for that. I have come here because I cannot believe that you will identify yourself with crime—yes, crime,

Constantius. With the organized murder of innocent people whose whole guilt is that they assemble for prayer."

She burst into the story of Hilary, of Albanus. She told him what the military governor had said and the town official. She told him the story of the prison's being stormed.

"I've seen the people who were murdered in one of your prisons, Constantius. There were young women among them and even children! And Hilary, whom you liked and whom I loved very dearly. And Albanus—"

Constantius avoided her eye. "Hilary—that I understand", he said. "But what did this man Albanus mean to you? A simple man, you tell me—just one of the crowd. He'll be forgotten tomorrow."

"Perhaps his name will be forgotten, Constantius. But not his death. Christians remember their dead; they call them 'witnesses' because they have given evidence of their faith through dying for it. No, I don't think Albanus will be forgotten so easily.

"But what about your own name, Constantius? Will it go down in history as the name of a man who tolerated such persecution? And this isn't a personal issue, although I knew some of the people who were murdered. They are dead now. I have not come to plead for them—they are beyond the reach of human injustice. I could not prevent their end. I have no power. But what I felt I had to do was to try and prevent more crimes being committed in the name of the Emperor. Cancel that edict, Constantius! You are the Emperor now—you can do it. Cancel it—or—or—I shall have to organize groups to resist the attacks against the Christians. I've done it before, when Carausius ruled over Britain. I can do it again and perhaps with better results."

"You haven't changed at all, have you, Helena?" smiled Constantius. "As impulsive as ever. Threatening me with mutiny and revolution, are you?" And then, suddenly in a serious tone, "You haven't become a Christian yourself—like Curio?"

"No. And I didn't know Curio had. I'm glad about it, though—he was always a great-hearted man. Are you going to execute him?"

Constantius rubbed his chin. "I have been wondering for some time what to do with him", he said slowly. "He is too old for active service and too good a man to send back to his little estate in Italy. Now I know. I shall make him governor of Verulam ..."

She looked up in wondrous surprise. "Oh, Constantius—"

"As he is a Christian, he will see to it that my orders are carried out. Christians, I know, believe in authority."

"They do—they do; but—"

"But what are the orders he will have to carry out—is that what you mean? Well, the first order is the cancelation of the Edict of Nicomedia."

"Constantius—"

"Just in case you are interested," drawled the Emperor, "it is already being copied. Strabo is looking after that; very efficient man, my Strabo. We'll pay him a visit together after supper and see how far he has got."

"You mean—you *had* canceled it already?"

"That's what I'm trying to tell you", he nodded patiently. "My dear, it was very difficult for me to be just, as long as I had old Diocletian sitting on top of me—to say nothing of my—of Maximian. You didn't think I *liked* that idiotic edict, did you? But after all, why shouldn't you think so! You had every right to. I can't make the dead alive, as their Jesus is supposed to have done. But I can stop any further nonsense, and perhaps there are ways and means of making good some of the injuries—"

She rose, her eyes swimming. "I am a very happy woman", she said. "Doubly happy because you did not wait for me before doing the right thing. I—I *have* doubted you, you know, and—"

"You are not by any chance going to apologize to me, are you?" asked Constantius with a whimsical smile. "My dear, you are worse than the Christians! Of course you have doubted me! I've been doubting myself for years. But now, I think, I know where I stand. At least I know which was the best and which the worst thing I have ever done. No, I'm not going to tell you. I'll tell you something else instead—I have good news about someone you know."

"More good news? You've given me all the good news I want. I have had my fill."

"Then you are a bad mother."

"Constantine? What have you heard about him? I've been without news for many months now—"

"Not surprising. He's been at the frontier. Done a good bit of fighting and got himself decorated for valor. He was the first one on the wall of an Arab fortress; they gave him a wall crown. He's back in Nicomedia now. Galerius thinks of making him a legate."

"What! At the age of thirty-one?"

"Think it's wrong?" asked Constantius innocently. "I'm inclined to agree with you. Don't forget that I said 'Galerius *thinks* of making him a legate.' Quite between you and me, he won't."

She was up in arms at once. "Why not, after all? Just because he's young—"

"Oh, it isn't that. But I have other plans for him."

Her brows twitched. "I didn't know you had any plans so far as Constantine is concerned. And frankly—I don't think—"

"I had no plans until today. To put it even more exactly, I had no plans until a quarter of an hour ago. Now I have."

"I don't understand, Constantius."

"That's right, stamp your foot", said the Emperor cheerfully. "Oh, it's all so much like old times. I didn't think my first day as Emperor would be like this."

"You are mocking me."

He frowned a little. "That's the last thing I want to do."

"If you think Constantine's going to accept any favors from you, you're mistaken."

"Well, he will accept the throne, I think——"

There was a pause.

"What—did you—say?"

He seized her hands. "Helena, my dear—twelve years ago I did a shameful thing, the worst thing I have ever done in my life. I was mad for power and power only. I had always been an ambitious man, as you know—Do you remember that last day, the last night before I left for Rome and Milan?"

Her lips were white. "I do, Constantius——"

"That night—I never told you—that night, I dreamed that I would be Emperor. And when I awoke, in the morning, I remembered every phase of my dream as clearly as if it had been stark reality. I took it as an omen and decided to strive for that goal by all the means in my power."

My fault, she thought. My fault. All my own fault.

He released her hands and rose. "In Milan I heard the news about the Carausian revolt. I had only one idea: to get the command of the troops to reconquer Britain. But that command was not given to the man who was considered to be the best man for the task. These things were being handled in a different way at the Court of Maximian."

Her body was like ice. She could not move.

He began to pace up and down the room.

"When Vatinius failed, Maximian sent for me and offered me the command, together with the rank of Cæsar—on condition that I marry his daughter. I had spent five years fretting, kicking my heels. Five years! If I refused, I was finished. I accepted. They made me go through the abominable farce of repudiation in the temple of Jupiter. It was then that I learned to despise the gods. In the temple of Juno they had joined us together, you and me. In the temple of Jupiter they put us asunder."

His pace quickened. "I married Theodora", he said almost savagely. "And it might have been as great a crime toward her, almost, as it was toward you. For I did not love Theodora. Fortunately she is—not like you. She is a good woman, but—"

"Don't", said Helena. "Please, don't. She has given you children—"

"Oh, yes. I have six children from her. And the oldest is eleven. The oldest boy is eight. Am I going to make him Cæsar at that age? And then—it must be said, Helena. They are attractive children, good children, all of them. But—Theodora is not Helena. There isn't a ruler among them, believe me. And Rome must have a ruler."

He stopped dead in front of her. "I have learned a few things, Helena. I have learned a few things about power. I saw them all, the men who can fill thrones, when I was in Milan. Galerius and Maxentius and Licinius and all of them. Lean tigers, yapping for power, sick with greed and ambition. We've been breeding bloodthirsty animals to rule us, we Romans. Are we going to have another dragon's seed: more Neros, Caligulas, and Caracallas?

"I have become an old man, Helena, and my health is not what it used to be. I have the responsibility for the western Empire now. But for how long? And who is going to be my successor? Diocletian and Maximian had again introduced the rule of adoption. Let's see whether that rule cannot work out well for Rome, as it has done before, with Nerva and Trajan and the Antonines."

He chuckled. "It must have been a bitter blow for old Maximian", he said. "He always adored power—it's his only god. But Diocletian was too clever for him. When he accepted him as co-ruler, he made a pact with him: that when one of them should abdicate, the other would do so, too. Poor old Maximian was only too willing to oblige— then. He just could not imagine that anybody would give up the throne, and the pact seemed to make his position absolutely secure. But Diocletian knew already, then, that he was going to get sick of it all—he's not a bad man at heart, despite his many failings, and not half as cruel as Galerius, the true father of that despicable edict against your Christians. Now Diocletian knew that Maximian was impossible as sole ruler of the Empire, and so he bound him to himself, knowing full well that he was going to quit in a few years' time. And now he's done it. He's gone to Dalmatia, to plant cabbages in his garden and play the simple farmer. Or rather, after having played at being an Emperor, he now reverts to type and *is* a farmer. And Maximian has had to follow suit, little as he likes the idea. It's a huge joke, really."

He began to pace up and down again. "Now it's up to Galerius and myself", he said. "And Galerius is younger than I am—and a dangerous man. Unless I choose a successor, and a good one at that, he will become sole ruler of the Empire. And he will be a bad ruler. Therefore I need a successor. Theodora's children are too young—and not fit to rule. There remains Constantine—my eldest son anyway."

Again he stopped in front of her. "I know very little of him—as he is now", he said gently. "He is a good soldier and the father of a strapping son. That's all I know. That is—all except one thing. He is *your* son. The son of the finest woman I ever knew. Had I needed any proof of that—you have given it to me today. . . ."

"What do you mean?" whispered Helena tonelessly.

He gave a short laugh. "Do you think I do not know what it must have cost you to come and see me, after all these years? I should think I know you and your pride! And what is more, I agree with everything you did. There was a time when I wished, yes, wished that for once you would do the wrong thing. It would have helped me to feel just a little better about the way I had treated you. But you'd rather starve than accept anything from me. And today you come to me—to ask, not for help, not for favors, but for justice. And even that justice you want, not for yourself but for those Christian friends of yours. Well, a woman who can do that is fit to be the mother of the Empire, and by all the gods if there are any, the mother of the Empire you shall be! I shall despatch a man to Nicomedia at once to fetch Constantine back. I want him here, at my side. I want to see what a son of Helena and Constantius is like. Galerius won't like it, of course. But I don't think he'll dare to refuse. And I know the man I shall send, too. It was Favonius whom I saw at the entrance of this room, wasn't it? Very well—can you spare him a few months, Helena?—Good."

He strode over to the door and opened it. "Come in, old friend."

Favonius came in, stood to attention, and saluted.

"Do you know me still, Favonius?" grinned Constantius.

"Yes, Emperor."

"Emperor? And how do you know I am?"

"I listened at the keyhole, Emperor", was the grave answer.

Constantius roared with laughter. "He hasn't changed much either, has he, Helena? Well, Favonius: I am sending you on a bit of an errand. Want you to get your old pupil back to Britain. I shall give you your instructions before you leave—and a letter. And remember this: I don't mind what you hear! But I do mind very much what you say. Keep you big mouth well shut, understand? Good. You may go now."

Favonius made an immense effort to suppress the wild joy that threatened to split his face into an unceremonious grin. He saluted again and tramped out of the room so that the chairs trembled.

"I must go now, Helena", said the Emperor gently. "And you must have a rest. I shall let Curio look after you, while you are here. Come back in the evening—I want you to have a look at the new edict about the Christians. What did you say? The Empress? Theodora is in Aquæ Sulis. She can't bear Eburacum. I want you to be present at the official proclamation tonight. Even if it is your wish to return to Verulam—"

"It is my wish, Constantius."

"—even so: I want my Court to show their respect to the mother of the future Emperor. Until tonight, Helena."

He bowed to her, smiling, and left. His steps were firmer now than when he had come in, much less like those of an old man.

Slowly, Helena too walked toward the door.

A sea of voices seemed to rise from all sides, and she did not feel the ground she trod on.

"Now that you have lost everything, you will gain love— and you will have power.... Keep nothing for yourself, and you will be rich", said Albanus.

"Love him beyond disappointment and sorrow. It will bear fruit, when the time comes. Let love be stronger than pride—don't forget that: let love be stronger than pride, when the time comes", said Coel the Wise.

And somewhere higher up, like a strange sweet melody: "Blessed are the meek; they shall inherit the earth."

As she passed him, Favonius looked at her in dumbfounded awe.

Never in her life, not in the days of her most radiant youth, had she been so beautiful.

CHAPTER 4

FUMES OF WINE and perfume; the noise of voices drowning the music of a small, invisible orchestra; the reek of anointed, perspiring, wine-heated human bodies.

When the Tribune Constantine entered the banqueting hall with a group of young officers, all invited to the imperial *coena*, the older and higher-ranking guests had already worked their way through thirty courses of tidbits, accompanied by thirty different wines.

Above the noise, his ear caught the voice of a woman: "I tell you it's maggots—a sort of maggot is eating the life out of his body; his nights are horrible, I hear . . ."

"My dear, when one has the constitution and the strength of Galerius—"

"Are you mad? Who has mentioned names—"

Maggots. The young officers drew up in front of the imperial table and saluted; slaves then led them to their places.

There was no individual reception. Galerius hated unnecessary formalities at his banquets.

Maggots. Eating his life out. This was the Persian banquet room—arranged in Persian style, with trophies captured in the last war; its contents equaled the revenues of a province over a period of thirty years; yet somehow the orgies of silk and tapestry, blood-red and yellow prevailing, made one think that this was not a room at all, but the inside of a man, blood and entrails, swarming with male and female maggots, greedily sucking.

An immense purple mushroom, Galerius, surrounded by lesser fungi. The liver of the organism rather than its heart, swollen and dangerously alive.

To the Styx with that woman and her maggots!

Cæcuban or Massican? Cæcuban, of course. He had good vintages in his cellar, the imperial mushroom. The hearts and tongues of larks and nightingales, wrapped in thin petals of bacon and flavored with some unknown spice that tasted like—like—ambrosia.

It was a man's banquet, but women were serving and again doing that trick of hiding under the tables and coming out dancing-girl fashion: a slim arm shooting up, jingling with bracelets, then a lovely young head, large-eyed and beautifully made up, white shoulders, young breasts quivering under transparent silk, supple hips weaving. All the old dotards enjoyed it, some of them more than the meal itself, more even than the wine. It was a damned nuisance, really; Galerius just couldn't realize that anybody might prefer his own wife to this sort of ready-made love trickery. There were always a few men who objected to it and were jibed at for being hypocrites, or for having peculiar tastes. The best thing to do was to try and treat the girl gently, and when she became more and more—when she came more to the point, to tell her that one was tired or didn't feel so well or something asinine like that. Then one could let her curl up and go on eating. The main thing was not to get too much into the limelight.

The next course was a plate with about fifty or sixty different sorts of sea fruit. No, he didn't wish to change his wine; there was nothing wrong with the Cæuban. The fellow opposite, a young Syrian noble, proposed an exchange of girls; all right, let's exchange. Surprised by so much generosity, the Syrian amended his suggestion to throwing dice for them; he had beautiful dice, of Indian ivory and encrusted with emeralds. They diced, then; the Syrian won, and being both very polite and very drunk, he chose his own girl, and proceeded to kiss her and feed her with the remnants from his plate.

Constantine tried to see who was sitting at the Emperor's table, but a swarm of Gaditan dancing girls had entered and were now performing their antics. One could not get more than an occasional glimpse of Galerius himself—and of a tall, haggard man next to him, Licinius, who they said was out for the purple. At any other time within the last three hundred years this would have been akin to "being on the list"—even a vague rumor would have been quite sufficient for that. But nowadays a man did not strive for the purple, but rather for one of the purples. Two men had been Emperors many a time before, but now there were—how many? Well, Galerius here and Maximinus, Galerius' cousin lording it over Egypt and Syria—and they said Cæsar Severus in Italy was screaming for the title of Emperor; that's three. Licinius would be the fourth and Father the fifth. Or rather Father *was* the fourth, and Licinius was trying to become the fifth, though what he should be Emperor of, the sun god alone knew—*if* he did.

They didn't know about Father yet, of course, but they soon would, and in the meantime they were bound to suspect it. Four Emperors and a potential fifth—no empire could stand that sort of thing for long.

Damn that girl and her love making. Can't you keep quiet, you little slut. Wait, I'll show you—

He drew the slim body over his knees, turned it over, jingling armlets, bracelets, earrings, and all, put his freshly filled plate on her back and went on eating.

A wave of laughter ran along the tables and reached Galerius.

The Emperor had been amusing himself, playing with a fifteen-year-old Circassian girl of exquisite beauty; his fat white fingers were all over her, caressing her tiny ears, her dainty little nose, and the rigid nipples of her small breasts. He was not really very much interested in her; but it gave him a good excuse not to hear what he did not wish to hear—and Licinius had an infernal habit of arguing about his ideas and plans at the most inconvenient times.

"What are all those asses braying about?" he asked gruffly.

"Some young officer trying to be funny", said Licinius. "As I said before, Sire, it is intolerable for a man of my experience and rank to content himself with—"

"It's young Constantine", said Galerius. "He's using the bottom of his girl as a dining table. Good soldier, young Constantine. Send him a goblet of my own wine, somebody. I like the young scoundrel. Was like that myself when I was young. Damned young rascal. Like him."

He's drunk, thought Licinius angrily. Either he is drunk or he's pretending to be—you never know with Galerius.

A slave took the heavy golden goblet over to Constantine, who got up so abruptly that the girl on his knees fell to the floor.

He did not seem to notice it, but took the goblet and marched straight up to the Emperor's table: Licinius; a couple of high officials he did not know; Chanarangesh, the newly appointed prefect of the guards, a Persian by birth.

"The August Emperor's health", he said and emptied the goblet in one long draught.

"Good boy", laughed Galerius. "Good at fighting—good at drinking."

Constantine handed the goblet to the nearest slave, took a step forward, and stood stiffly to attention.

"Meaning?" asked the Emperor, frowning slightly.

"Your Majesty, I have had news from Britain—my father's health is declining, and he has expressed the wish to see me, if Your Majesty will consent to grant me leave."

Galerius pursed his thick lips. It was true, then, Constantius was getting old—like Diocletian—like Maximian—none of them was made of the real stuff—leave. The young fellow wanted leave. Filial piety? Possibly, possibly not—anyway, he was a youngster—why was Licinius blinking at him like that? What did he think he was doing? Been a bother the whole evening. Damn Licinius. Show you—

"You have our leave, young man—" nodded Galerius. "Tell your father we hope that your presence will speed up his recovery. Tell him we know that he is our loyal servant—"

A sharp look of the inflamed little pig's eyes—but Constantine did not show any resentment, and the Emperor continued, "—but we are hearing with regret that he is more than lenient with the Christian plague in his provinces. Leniency with these people is weakness and worse than weakness. We have not proclaimed our edict against them for nothing."

"No, Sire", said Constantine, parrotlike. He knew Galerius' pet aversion was that superstitious Jewish sect—everybody knew that.

"He is underestimating them", went on the Emperor. "He does not know them as we do; we were compelled to take measures against their organization—and what was the effect? These fanatics conspired against our very life. We had to leave our palace, this very palace here in our good city of Nicomedia, because fires broke out, twice within fifteen days after the proclamation of the edict...."

Galerius' face became redder and redder; there were livid patches on his cheeks and forehead, and his voice became shrill.

"We have seen many dangerous follies in our time, but none more dangerous than the Christian folly. Many of them are adepts of dark cults, magicians, sorcerers. There is only one way of dealing with them, and that is the swiftest extinction. Tell your father that—and we expect better news from him, in future. We wish to keep our confidence in the action of our Cæsar Constantius; it is up to him to see to it that we can do so. And we can think of no better way of showing our friendly feelings than by sending him his own son to tell him so—instead of choosing a more official way, as we have been advised to."

Suddenly his right arm shot out, and the Circassian girl's face was pushed deep into a dish of creamy salad; Galerius roared with laughter, and everyone else chimed in dutifully. Constantius and the Christians were forgotten.

Galerius, brought up in the barracks, had always loved horseplay. The pretty girl's discomfiture amused him.

"Go and drink, my boy", he said. "Have a good time—your Emperor commands it." He poured another dish over the unfortunate girl's head, wobbling with laughter, and then had her carried away. "Dirty girl", he said. "Needs a wash—dirty girl." His tongue was heavy. There was no longer any doubt that he was drunk.

Constantine bowed deeply and returned to his seat at the other end of the room, where he started drinking heavily.

"Divine Emperor—"

Galerius, turning, saw Licinius' face; it was deathly white.

"What's the matter with you, friend? You look as if you had seen a ghost!"

"I have, Sire", whispered Licinius. "I have seen the ghost of rebellion. This young man is dangerous, Sire."

"Nonsense. Drink, man, and stop torturing yourself with m-morbid ideas. Dangerous! Half a child."

"He is thirty-two years of age, Sire. But if my Emperor says that he is not dangerous, he is not dangerous—yet. However, if a young snake cannot yet bite, the old one can. How ill is Cæsar Constantius, I wonder. . . ."

Galerius' underlip quivered a little. "What do you mean? I hate riddles. Speak up, man. What do you mean?"

"There is such a thing as diplomatic illness, Sire—" Licinius' eyes had an almost hypnotic stare now. "Supposing Cæsar Constantius had plans more ambitious than to be the faithful servant of his Emperor—what would he do? Leave his son at the imperial Court? Or try to get him home safely—and out of reach of imperial vengeance?"

"N-nonsense", repeated Galerius wearily. But his brain, sluggish and intoxicated as it was, began to work again.

Licinius saw the glint of suspicion and attacked at once.

"Perhaps his—leniency toward the Christians is not just weakness", he whispered. "Perhaps there is a system behind it: these people are pretty numerous, as you know, Sire. Already there is a general migration to Gaul and Britain, where they feel safe from Your Majesty's just laws. Young Constantine may be half a child, though I'm not so sure about that, but he certainly is a valuable hostage in Nicomedia—and a great temptation for his father, when he is in Britain."

Galerius sucked his teeth. "Your advice, Licinius?"

"My advice is that he should not arrive in Britain, Sire—"

Galerius grunted. His bloodshot eyes turned in the direction of Constantine's table. The young tribune was lying half on his couch, half on the floor; he was dead drunk.

The Emperor grinned. "No, no, friend—not the most drastic means. You are just a little too keen on the western provinces yourself, aren't you? No, don't say anything. I know you are. I'd be, too, if I were in your place. Don't worry. Your time'll come. I'll see to it that it comes. I'm your friend, Licinius—your very g-good f-friend. But we won't kill the young snake yet. You yourself said that he'd be useful here in Nicomedia. We believe you're right. But not the most drastic means. Chanarangesh . . ."

The prefect of the guards approached. "Sire?"

"Send an officer to Tribune Constantine's house tomorrow morning—when he's slept off his present state—and tell him I have changed my mind. He is promoted to the rank of legate and will take over the Eleventh Legion. We are very fond of this young man, Chanarangesh. We do not wish to lose his services; we cannot afford to lose his services—just now. We shall send his father one of our most experienced physicians instead. That will be of g-greater value to him, as he is ill. Ha-ha-ha—what do you say, Licinius?"

"The Emperor is most wise", said Licinius with a thin smile.

Two sturdy slaves helped Constantine to leave the room. He was not the only one—there were a number of gaps in the rows of couches.

"Goo'chaps", murmured Constantine. "Nice chaps—must have fresh air—no, don't wanna go *there*—wanna go to the courtyard—wanna have fresh air. Thatsh right—goo'chaps. Where's my ch-chariot?"

They helped him into it. The charioteer grinned cheerfully.

"Mus'n laugh", his master reprimanded him. "H-home, you son of mischief—"

The charioteer took the reins, cracked his whip, and drove off.

When the imperial palace was out of sight, he heard his master say, "Give me the reins now, Fidus."

The charioteer looked up, startled; this was an entirely different tone, clear and metallic and not in the least drunk.

Constantine, impatient, took the reins out of his hands. He clicked his tongue. "The whip, Fidus." He cracked it over the heads of the horses. The chariot thundered through the midnight streets.

Within a quarter of an hour they reached the little house.

"Put the horses away, Fidus, and saddle Boreas and Zephyr."

"Saddle them, Master?"

"You heard what I said. Do what you're told! I'm riding down to the coast, for a night swim."

"Yes, Master."

The way he jumped off and walked into the house! And at the palace three men had been necessary to get him into the chariot! A night swim, indeed. There was something odd going on here, and it might pay to tell old Tetras about it tomorrow morning—it was just the sort of thing that might interest him, and he paid in good silver when he was interested. Fidus made off for the stable.

In the atrium Constantine whistled softly, and a huge shadow came forward. "Here I am, sir."

"Everything ready, Favonius?"

"Everything ready my end, sir."

Constantine chuckled. "Well, my end too, now. Got my leave from Galerius. He was a little drunk—not much. Not as much as he thought I was. And not drunk enough not to listen to old Licinius, who was very emphatic about something. So emphatic that Galerius got hold of Chanarangesh and gave him certain instructions. Where's my belt with the jewels? Got my traveling clothes? Good—"

He had undressed and stood stark naked in the room.

Favonius produced the traveling clothes and helped him dress. "Fidus will talk", he said quietly.

"Certainly he'll talk. But not before tomorrow morning."

As strong as Milo of Croton, thought Favonius. The arm and shoulder muscles are perfect; so are the legs. And not an ounce of superfluous flesh.

In less than five minutes Constantine was ready: strong sandals without any ornament, a simple dark tunic, a simple dark cloak, the belt with the jewels safely tied around the naked waist.

"Your sword, sir."

"Thank you. Fidus should be ready with the horses by now—yes, I can hear them. Let's go."

The charioteer led the horses along. They were Constantine's campaign horses; he had given them the same names as those of his favorite horses in childhood. Spanish bred, they were, strong and lasting.

"All right, Fidus. You needn't sit up. I'll be back late in the morning. Good night to you."

"Good night, Master."

As soon as the house was out of sight, they fell into a gallop.

"Mistake", murmured Favonius. "Should have thought of it."

"Of what?"

Ears like a lynx, thought the old soldier. "These clothes", he said. "We shouldn't have changed, or rather you shouldn't have changed, into traveling clothes. Fidus won't believe whatever the story was you told him."

Constantine laughed. "I didn't expect him to", he said, spurring his horse. "In fact, I wanted him to find it strange. That's why I told him we were going for a night swim."

"I don't understand", grunted Favonius.

"Well, he can't do anything tonight. No one's going to listen to the babblings of a slave as long as his story is not really established. It will only be established tomorrow morning when we are not back. Then it will be strange enough—especially as I have reasons to believe that the Emperor is going to send for me. And then Fidus is going to be asked questions."

"Exactly—"

"Good old Favonius—don't you see? They'll be suspicious by then anyway. It will only confirm their suspicions that we have made off, dressed in traveling clothes—"

"Quite—and they will know how we are dressed, too!"

Constantine laughed. "They will *think* they know how we are dressed. And that's exactly what I want them to think. But we shall leave our horses and clothes in Byzantium in the house of a friend of mine and then depart for Hadrianople with different horses and in different clothes. You'll see. It's all prepared."

"It's easy", grinned Favonius. "As long as one thinks of everything."

"Well, that's why I sent Minervina to Byzantium, with my son. She's seen to it that everything will be in good order for our arrival and has gone on to Dyrrachium—to take the cure there."

"The gods be with her", said Favonius. "Domina Minervina is a lovely woman and a great lady."

"Pity she had to take Crispus along with her", said Constantine. "I wish I could have taken him with us—it's out of the question, of course. He's only eight. You'll have a good pupil there in a few years' time, Favonius!"

"Difficult to teach him any tricks—with you as his father", growled the old soldier.

Constantine laughed. "Come on—gallop again."

They had left the town behind them now, and there was the white road, straight as a sword, flanked by cyprus trees and olive groves. On their left the moonlit sea rushed by as they thundered along.

One hour after midnight they reached a tiny fishing port, and Favonius drummed an old fisherman out of his bed and house. They knew both him and his boat; it was big enough for them and the horses for the short crossing over the Bosporus—no more than fifty stadia. It would have been thirty across the narrowest point, but the customs officials were always on the lookout for incoming ships there, and they did not wish to be questioned.

A few gold coins from Favonius' saddlebag, and the old fisherman became wide awake, and what was more, he awakened his three sons. "Listen," said Constantine, "you know me—just forget about this little trip of ours tonight, as soon as you are back in port. You haven't seen anybody. You slept right through the night—is that clear? I shall know whether you've talked or not. One more piece of gold for everyone, when we have landed at the other side. And ten more for each of you in one year's time—if you have kept your mouths shut. That's all. Get going."

The horses behaved well—they had stood up to more difficult things in the Persian campaign. Favonius fed them dried dates, their favorite food.

In Byzantium, in the house of the freedman Perennis, they found that Minervina had forgotten nothing of the long list of things that Constantine had made her learn by heart. Besides, Perennis had got special instructions directly from his former master, Constantius himself. "There'll be fifteen men at your command, sir", said old Perennis. "We did not expect you tonight, as you know—"

"I know—I had to choose the first opportunity. Didn't know myself. I had to get leave from the Emperor, or else he could send an order of arrest through the regular army channels, and that's too often fatal. Can't risk it."

"I know only one Emperor, and his name is Constantius", said Perennis, and Constantine knew that he had had news from Britain.

"Keep it quiet for a while", he said. "When will your men be ready? Mark you—I want three of them to be dressed as well-off merchants and the rest as slaves, and I want slave clothes for Favonius here and for myself."

Favonius gasped, but Perennis only nodded. "I know, sir. And the three who are to pose as merchants are carefully chosen—their description is bound to be unlike that of yourself and of the noble centurion. There will be thirty mules with merchandise. Will you need them for the whole journey?"

"Of course not—we would travel too slowly. All I want is to mislead our pursuers—if there'll be any. But I think there will be. We shall leave the caravan as soon as we have left Hadrianople, and they'll go back to you in due course."

"Not to me", pleaded Perennis. "It might cause talk. I shall give them their instructions; they'll go on to the country seat of a business friend of mine. He can do with the merchandise, too."

"Very good. And when will your men be ready?"

Perennis blinked. "You'll be traveling in a merchant's caravan, sir", he said smiling. "That means you'll have to travel by day. It's two hours after midnight now—at dawn they will be ready, in the Street of the Coppersmiths."

"Excellent. That gives us a few hours' sleep. I can do with it. Only a short time ago I had to drink a fair amount of Cæcuban at the Emperor's banquet."

"I'll show you your rooms—and that of the noble centurion. The Domina Minervina sends you her fondest love, sir. She left us two days ago for Dyrrachium."

"Thank you, Perennis", nodded Constantine. "Did my son behave well?"

"He is the very image of his father", smiled Perennis.

"That means he has broken at least half of your vases." There was pride in Constantine's laughter. "Come on, Favonius—to bed. The last good bed we shall have for a long time, too. Tomorrow morning we are slaves."

CHAPTER 5

"AND SLAVES WE WERE", said Favonius, soaking his naked legs in the hot water and groaning with relief. "And believe me, it wasn't funny at all. Rub my back, will you?"

Old Rufus proceeded to do so. There was not too much strength left in his lean arms, but what he had, he gave. "Slave yesterday—getting a first-class massage today", he said.

"You were always one for a luxurious life. How did you like being a slave?"

"It's good to be back in old Verulam", said Favonius. "Rub a bit harder, can't you? And I wasn't a slave yesterday. That was weeks and weeks ago. Careful with the plaster on my shoulder, you old son of a Ligurian cattle thief—"

"Got another scratch there, by Mars Repulsor", said Rufus. "Now how did *that* happen, I wonder? Shield side, too. Since when don't *you* know how to keep your damned shield in position? You must be getting old."

"I *am* getting old", grunted Favonius. "Though not as old as you, with your cheese fingers. Will you let me tell my story, or will you not? Now, then, where was I? Oh, yes—when we were slaves in Byzantium. He liked the city, you know—sniffed around all the time and said he was going to do something with it in his own time. He didn't like the way the walls were built, and he said he would see to it that smugglers could not get away with things as easily as we had, the night before. And he said—somewhat keenly, with a flash in his eyes, 'This city is built on seven hills—it will be a second Rome.' "

"He did, eh?"

"Yes, and then an old woman threw a basketful of very old fish out of her window and caught him on the head, and he forgot about his plans for a while. He's picked up a few fine ones in the east, Rufus—he really can swear, I'll say that for him. Then we got to the Street of the Coppersmiths and joined our caravan. Slaves of wool merchants we were, until we had left Hadrianople. Ate the food that slaves get and drank water to make it go down."

"No!" said Rufus with disgust.

"Slept like slaves, too—on the pack saddles of our mules. And they treated us like slaves—he insisted on it. One of those asses they'd disguised as merchants was polite to him once, in front of some village people; at night when we'd camped, he kicked the fellow around until I thought he'd break his bones. 'That'll teach you to be polite to me when I'm supposed to be a damned slave', he said. Next day the fellow had his revenge—showed off and kicked *him*, and he took it like a lamb. The night after, he beat the fellow up for it. Sound enough thrashing, it was. 'You mustn't overdo it', he told him. 'I said you mustn't be polite—I didn't say you should kick me.' After that all went very well."

"It would", said Rufus.

"In Hadrianople he made them buy a couple of horses— the best they could find—and when we were alone on the road, we changed back into uniform, mounted, and made off. Would have been better if we'd kept some of the mules, though—ye gods, what mountains they have in Thracia! And when we had reached the top of the pass I looked down, miles deep into an abyss, and there was the road we had been coming up, serpentine after serpentine, and deep down there was something glittering, like a small snake crawling its way up, and I showed it to him, and he said, 'That's it—off we go.' "

"They were after you, then?"

"Were they! If we weren't sure then, we were the next afternoon, when my horse broke a leg. He made me mount his own horse—there wasn't a horse around for miles. Well, I'm pretty heavy, as you know, and he is six feet, so we didn't make much headway. But would he let me go my own way?"

"Not he", said Rufus.

"Man, think before you babble like that. He's the master, isn't he? He's going to get himself a cæsarship, isn't he? He'll be the Emperor one day. And who am I? An old war dog with nothing to look forward to but six feet of brown earth—and a goblet of wine from *you*, if you want me to go on with my story."

"I'll get you that", grinned Rufus.

"Same as before—Falernian. Yes, that's the right amphora. You aren't a bad boy, Rufus. Well, after half an hour his horse thought it was enough and broke down, just like that. So he said, 'Come behind this bush with me and wait a bit.' 'What for?' I said. 'They'll catch up with us, and then good night. They are thirty or more and we are two.'"

"'We can't help that', he says. 'Besides, I want to find out whether they really are after us. We don't know yet for certain, do we? They must be pretty clever to have found us out that quickly. And anyway, *they* have horses—and we need horses.'

"Now how do you like that? He wanted their horses for us to go on with! Well, they came sure enough, an hour later. Forty-six men under a young tribune.

"When they saw our dead horse in the middle of the road, they stopped, and the tribune and a few others dismounted, to have a look, see? And the tribune says, 'That's the other—they can't be far now. There's something left in the saddlebag here—'

"There was, too—gold coins, two handfuls of them. *He'd* left them there. He knew that would catch their interest.

"So up we came, as quick as lightning, and jumped on the nearest horses, and off we went in a thundering gallop before they could so much as sneeze. It was easy. They were after us like the plague, of course, but, by Jupiter's beard, can he ride! I almost fell off my horse, I laughed so much.

"Got another goblet of this stuff, Rufus? Come on, don't be mean. You don't hear a story like this one every day, I'll swear. That's better.

"Well, then we *knew*, see? And from then on it was one long manhunt. Now that's where our gold came in and the belt with the jewels that I'd brought all the way from Britain. Wherever we went, we bought the best horses and the second-best ones, too—and we killed the ones that the owners did not want to sell us, because the one thing that mattered was that we held up the pursuers. Wherever we went, we left a trail of dead horses behind us and a handful of gold coins for the owners. He insisted on that, always.

"The places we slept in—old farms, deep forests, village inns—there was one night in streaming rain and thunder and lightning with nothing over our heads but our own rugs, and another in Dacia, not far from Nicopolis, in a barn, when the farmer with his four slaves tried to get our gold. I woke up with one of them sitting right on top of me, with a knife in his hand."

"Up went your knee", said Rufus with expert interest.

"That's right—just as in Hippo, you remember, when that big negro tried his knife stuff on me? That was with the Twelfth, wasn't it? We had—"

"Never mind the Twelfth and Hippo and the negro. What happened in that barn?"

"Well, my knee did the trick, and Constantine was up at once; they tried to get hold of his sword, but he was too quick for them, and then I drew mine, and we had a lo-ve-ly time. Left them all trussed up like fowl. They didn't have many teeth left, either. He is damned good at scrapping—and you know me, don't you, Rufus?"

"I know you", said Rufus. "Take your big feet out of the water. You've soaked them long enough."

"He didn't like Dacia much. Full of Germans and Sarmatians. He doesn't like either, and I don't blame him. An ungodly pack of barbarians they are, and no mistake.

We need more fortifications there, he said, and the old ones must be reconstructed. He drew up a plan about that, too, one night, when he could not sleep. He was worried about those Germans. 'There are too many of 'em', he said. 'They breed like rabbits. The thing to do is to take their best men into our own service and employ them out east, against the Persians. Tiberius was quite right', he said. 'Always cut diamond with diamond. There are too many Persians, too.'

"In Pannonia he didn't like the forests. 'This is a better race here,' he said, 'but there aren't enough of them, and why not? Because the whole country is one big forest. We shall have to cut it down and transform the province into an agricultural one. I must see to that.' And he had a plan to lead the waters of a lake there—Lake Pelso they call it—into the Danube."

"No more fights?" asked Rufus, who was getting bored with Constantine's empire planning.

"Plenty. We had the choice of crossing right through Noricum and over the Alps into Gaul, or of reaching Gaul by way of Italy. He decided for Italy, where the roads are much better. He didn't want to lose time. But in Italy old Severus got wise to us; he'd just got his new title and was as proud as a peacock at calling himself Emperor. He knew that he'd get it from Galerius, though, if he let us get through, and he tried hard to stop us. So we killed Italian horses now, instead of Pannonian and Dacian and Thracian horses. We raised a whole band of cutthroats in Istria, where they are two for half a denarius, and fought our way through. Just before we crossed into Gaul we had to fight our cutthroats— one of them had caught sight of his jewel belt and promptly told the others. We had to kill three and chase off the rest. That's how I got this thing here in my shoulder. You don't *have* a shield, when you are just having your breakfast, do you, Rufus?

"Once in Gaul everything was dead easy, of course—our Emperor, *the* Emperor, had seen to that. Fresh horses at every station and no payment or complaint. We cut through Gaul like a knife; there was a ship waiting for us in Gessoriacum, we landed in Anderida, rode up to Londinium and from there here and that was that. But, Rufus, never have I made a ride like that—"

Neither of the two old soldiers saw the tall figure of a woman in her long, dark-gray dress appear in the door. Favonius' next words made her stop and stand motionless.

"We rode across the whole of bloody Europe", said Favonius. "We rode across Bithynia, Thracia, Dacia, Pannonia, Noricum, Italy, Gaul, and Britain. We rode across the whole bloody Empire, we did. We had a bloodthirsty old Emperor after us, and another one waiting for us. Once we were in the saddle for thirty-two hours in one go—by the legs of Mars, Rufus, there aren't two men in the Empire who could have done it as we've done it. Am I going to sleep tonight! I'm going to sleep for thirty-two hours on end, that's what I'm going to do. It's easy. And—"

"Favonius", said Helena, and the two men got up and looked at her as children look when they have been caught stealing sweet meats in the kitchen.

"Favonius, my son wishes to proceed to Eburacum immediately. He wants you to be ready as quickly as you can."

"Yes, Domina", said Favonius, stony faced.

She gave him a wan smile. "I'm sorry, Favonius—I know how tired you must be—but they're already saddling the horses."

"Horses", said Favonius, when the door closed behind her. "I'm getting sick of them. We haven't killed enough of 'em, it seems. He must go and ride a few more to death, must he? Two hours we've been here—two hours he's got for his mother, and off he goes. What's the man made of, that's what I want to know?"

"It's cruel hard on you", nodded Rufus. "It's all very well for him, when he's half your age, and——"

"What do you mean? Think I'm an old dodderer like you? Hand me my riding sandals—give me my tunic. I've got to get ready, haven't I? What are you waiting for? Ouch, my feet. Horses. Wish we'd killed the lot. But that wouldn't help either. He'd run the whole way on his own feet—and so would I. Help me into my armor. What is it you say? Of course, I'll wear armor. We're on our way to the Emperor. Want me to appear before him like a damned civilian?"

Upstairs, in the atrium, Constantine kissed his mother.

"I'll send for you if there is any danger", he said. "I promise you I will. But I don't think there is. He has the constitution of a bear—you know that. Now I'd better see what they are doing about the horses."

His nod, as he clanked out of the room, was so like his father's that she smiled a little. But she was still in that strange trancelike state that had gripped her when she heard Favonius' words, and behind his words was the tired old voice of King Coel the Wise—not as she had heard him last, on his favorite stone near Coel-castra, but many years before—when he stood at her bed, looking at her newborn babe. "He will do as his father, though he will be greater than the father. He will own all land he rides on——"

"Own all land he rides on. . . ." "We rode across the whole of bloody Europe. . . ." Yes, he would be Emperor—and in him all her dreams would be fulfilled.

She shivered. How he had grown, grown in every sense. He was a man now, a man to whom Favonius looked up, the

258

same Favonius who had taught him the use of sword and shield. And there were in him an ambition and a drive that seemed to dwarf anything she had ever felt. There was greatness in him—but no warmth. He had hardly mentioned his wife at all—except to say that her second pregnancy had ended in a stillbirth and that she was now taking the cure at Dyrrachium. He seemed concerned about her only in connection with his son. "He will be bliss to his mother and death to his son"—how could that be? And yet it seemed that Father was right in all the other parts of his prophecy.

Favonius, fully armed, passed her with a grin and a salute.

She smiled at him. "I have missed you", she said. "Come back soon." Favonius' grin widened, and his strength was doubled by her words, as she had wanted it to be.

Slowly she moved toward the entrance. They had just mounted.

"You have my promise, Mother", said Constantine, and he waved at her. Then they rode off, into the future.

Suddenly she knew what she had to do. "Go and fetch Rufus", she said to the nearest slave. And as the old man appeared: "Rufus, I want the Gallic wagon. I am going to Eburacum—at once!"

CHAPTER 6

"The Tribune Constantinus", said the ceremonious voice of the chamberlain.

Constantius could hear the firm footsteps before the tall, slim, soldierly figure became visible, marching across the large room, blurred first, then clearer and looking more and more as the Tribune Constantius had looked, thirty years ago.

The Emperor was sitting up in bed, his thin legs supported by half a dozen cushions; he had had a bad night—another heart attack, the third within the last four weeks, and it had left him weak and dizzy. So often before he had feared that he would not live to see his son again—never more than last night. Then in the morning after a breakfast of bread and wine and a little porridge he had felt that perhaps he could go on for a few more days—and just then they announced that Constantine had arrived, and he had ordered them to show him in at once.

At the customary distance of three paces the young tribune halted and gave the salute.

"The Tribune Constantine at Your Majesty's orders."

The Emperor acknowledged with a weary solemnity.

That is I, thought the father.

He is dying, thought the son. An old, old man, dying.

The chamberlain had withdrawn on tiptoe.

Eighteen years, thought the father. He was a child, then. They have made a soldier out of him; it's all they could do. What else is he...? And he hated himself for not finding the bridge between his soul and that of this young man.

I have hated him all these years, thought the son. I should hate him now, but there is nothing left for hatred.

Son, Son, Son, thought the father, will you be spared what I have not been spared?

For a long time neither spoke a word or made a gesture.

Then the young man's eyes widened; the Emperor was raising himself from his cushions with an immense effort and bowing his head to him, a balding head the color of old parchment, half covered with damp wisps of gray hair.

Something broke in Constantine, and he rushed up to the bed and fell on his knees; he felt the touch of thin fingers on his head.

"Get up, Son", said Constantius in a trembling voice. "Don't let the feelings of the past pain you. I caused them; they are mine."

Constantine obeyed. "You did what had to be done—for Rome's sake."

The Emperor frowned. "Motives are always suspect", he said bitterly. "A man is rarely black or white—gray is the color of most actions. And gray action leaves gray thoughts, and gray thoughts become live animals, when a man comes to die."

He stopped his son's protest before it was uttered.

"However much it may have been for the good of Rome, Constantine—it was still wrong. And I can't set it right—there is no bridge between the past and the future. We can do—but we cannot undo. No action can be dissolved. Injustice can never become justice. Whatever I may do now—I have failed you. And injustice is horribly fecund, son—her children are many."

He slumped a little, and his eyes closed for a moment.

Constantine wondered whether he should not call for the physician, whom he had seen waiting in the anteroom.

But as though the Emperor had guessed, he made a sharp little gesture. "I wish to be alone with you", he said. "I have many questions to ask—give me that goblet—yes—hold it for me—wine is the best medicine, though Chrysaphios doesn't think so. He is an ass. To be a doctor means to fight battles that must be lost in the end. Ah, that's better. Put it back. Now then: Did Galerius let you go, or did you flee? Report, Tribune Constantine."

When the carriage bounced into the courtyard of the Domus palatina and stopped in front of the main portal, a swarm of slaves was waiting for it, and officials ran up with torches.

Helena had only just managed to set foot on firm ground, when Constantine appeared in the doorway.

"Mother! How could you do it so quickly—"

"Am I in time?"

"Yes, Mother, yes. But how did you do it? The messenger I sent to fetch you left only four hours ago ..."

"We met him on the way—or rather he flashed past us with such speed that I suspected what it was about. It was an imperial special messenger. How is my—how is the Emperor?"

"You are in time, Mother—that is all I can say. He is getting very weak. I still don't know—"

"I felt it. Come, to him. That is—if the Empress—"

"Empress Theodora", said the young man in a hard voice, "has not been called to the Domus palatina. She is still in Aquæ Sulis with her children. I shall summon her—later."

For one short moment Helena hesitated; then she entered, silently, and Constantine followed her.

Inside the palace a great many officers of high rank were waiting in little groups with a number of Court officials.

The chamberlain's long silver staff came crashing down on the floor as Constantine appeared; everyone looked toward mother and son and bowed or saluted.

Up the broad staircase, along the corridors, where everybody was going on tiptoe.

It was no secret among the courtiers that the Emperor's first wife had regained much influence on him; six months ago she had actually presided at an imperial banquet; the way Constantius had treated her, she might have been the ruling Queen of a powerful country rather than his former wife, repudiated at a formal ceremony in the Jupiter temple. There were even some who said that the leniency of Constantius toward the sect of the Christians and his revocation of the Imperial Edict of Nicomedia were due to her influence—an influence the more understandable as the Christian religion did not recognize divorce. Of course the Princess Helena would be for the Christians—according to them she was the only lawful wife of the Emperor!

Now this influence was backed by a young man who looked as if one would do well not to underestimate his presence—a young man who had spent hours alone with the dying Emperor and who happened to be his firstborn.

Eloquent looks were being exchanged; it was known that the Emperor had strictly forbidden them to send a message to the Empress in Aquæ Sulis or to his younger children, who were with her.

Helena felt the waves of all their thoughts, wishes, and feelings, hopeful and doubtful, admiring and sneering, simple and cunning, as she walked at the side of her son toward the door of the Emperor's suite. There were still more courtiers in the small anteroom; a group of physicians in whispered consultation dissolved in a series of clumsy bows.

Then Constantine said, "He asked to see you alone—as soon as you arrive. I shall be waiting here."

She bowed her head and walked into the dimly lit room, bared of all furniture except for the huge golden bed. The curtains closed behind her.

Like the shadow of death, Chrysaphios, chief physician to the Emperor, vanished from the room at her approach.

Silently she sat down at the foot of the bed.

Yes, he was dying. His face, always pale, was now the color of old, old ivory; the eyes were closed, surrounded by purple circles.

But as though her presence charged him with power, he stirred, and, still with his eyes closed, he murmured her name.

"I am here, dear", she said quietly.

The specter of a smile went over the shrunken face.

The bloodless lips began to move. She read from them—for there was no sound: "I—knew—you would not—fail me."

Her strength began to pulsate in him. He opened his eyes and said quite audibly, "Give me wine."

And she gave him wine in a small bowl, which she filled from a golden decanter on the low citrus table next to his bed.

He swallowed a few drops—then more.

". . . sit up", he said.

She helped him into a sitting position. The very touch of her fingers made strength flood through his body. His voice was almost normal, as he said, "I had—the report of—Constantine. A good report—he has—seen much—with the eyes of—a leader. I had—Favonius' report, too. I am—most—satisfied."

"He is very young", she said, against her own will. "And he is—hard. He will suffer much—unless he changes."

Again the specter of a smile. "You will be with him", said the Emperor. "You will—watch—over him. He is—safe. Remember—that last night—before I left—for Italy? My dream—of emperorship—"

"I remember—"

"I wasn't—an Emperor—for long, was I? Like in the book—of the—Jews—their Moses—who saw the land—but was not—allowed to enter. Constantine—will enter.

Remember—what your father said? 'He will be—greater than the father'—and so—he will be.... I am going—now—very soon, Helena. Call him—in...."

She rose silently, to obey.

A minute later Constantine stood next to her, tall and quiet.

The Emperor nodded to him. "You will rule", he said. "And I entrust you—with the fate—of my younger—children. I shall bless you—for—all you will do for—them—and—the Empress. Yours is—the responsibility."

Very pale, Constantine bowed deeply.

"More—wine", whispered Constantius. Helena gave it to him, and her fingers did not tremble. In her heart was the innocent pride of a bride. Once more she was his wife; nay, she had never ceased being his wife. He had understood her inner fear and dissolved it by entrusting her son with the sacred dignity of a guardian.

"Enough", said Constantius. "Call in—my officers."

When the young man had left the room, the Emperor said, "I will do more—for you." There were tears in her eyes now, and he smiled a little. But already the clanking of armor approached, and the room began to fill itself with the world of Mars.

The legates and prefects of twelve legions ranged themselves in a semicircle around the Emperor's bed.

There was a breathless silence, as he spoke to them.

"Friends—I am leaving you. It is my wish—and yours, as I believe—that the finest soldiers—of Rome—should not be ruled—by some obscure—stranger—imposed on you—by the sovereign—of Asia. You will find my son Constantine worthy not only of his father—but of his mother, Flavia Julia—Helena—Augusta."

The deep-throated murmur of assent of many voices cast a last spell of strength over the dying man.

"I leave you—my son—as my successor in the Empire. With the assistance of—the godhead—he shall wipe away— the tears of the Christians—and avenge the tyranny— practiced—against them. . . ."

Helena fell on her knees, hiding her face in her hands. He had not forgotten. . . . This was what he meant when he had said that he would do more for her—it was his parting present. She raised her head, and a look of unutterable love shone on her husband.

With a last effort, Constantius said, "In this above all do I place—my hope of—felicity."

A sudden spasm went over his face; there was a faint tremor going over his body under the thin rug. It was all over before Chrysaphios reached him; all the physician could do was to close the Emperor's eyes.

Helena remained on her knees. Towering over her, with his back to the assembly, stood Constantine. No one stirred. Then past changed into future. Slowly, very slowly, the young man turned, first his face, then his whole, powerful body toward the men behind him.

He looked at them—at every one of them in succession, as though he weighed every single commander's strength and power and courage; and in his eyes were gray steel and the dawn of triumph.

BOOK FIVE

❧

A.D. 312

CHAPTER 1

"NOT THAT IT matters much," said the Legionary Crocus, "but can anybody tell me what this war is about?"

Bemborix, of course, was the quickest to answer. "A young Emperor must always wage war. That's obvious to anybody but an Alemannic blockhead."

Crocus grinned, looking down at the little Celt from the height of his six and a half feet. "War is obvious to everybody, where I come from", he said.

"Then what are you complaining about?"

"I'm not complaining. I've joined this army because I want to do a bit o' fighting. We haven't had much of it lately, where I come from."

"Too bad", said Bemborix. "It's well known that you Germans can't feel well unless you are fighting somebody. Not happy until you've got your skull cracked, as well as what's in it."

"Bad tempered, little man? Tired, I suppose. Shall I carry you a while, baby? This is lovely country."

"Horrible country", grumbled the Celt. "Look at all those bloody mountains—like ulcers. You ought to see my country: all beautiful and smooth as a woman's skin. And you march along with ease, instead of losing your breath climbing all the time as we're doing."

They became silent as Aper the centurion passed by; Aper was a busybody and had been known for punishing a man just because he talked on the march—which was ridiculous. Everybody talked on the march, if he had breath enough—except, of course, when one was too near the enemy. But they knew that this was not the case. Not now and probably not for many days to come.

Aper's helmet disappeared in the distance, then appeared again at the end of the cohort in front; perhaps he wanted to talk to the primipilar, who was with the first cohort, about a mile ahead and at least a thousand feet higher up; which was about as much as they were ahead and higher than the third cohort; and then came the fourth and fifth and sixth and then the first cohort of the Eighth Legion. No one in the Twenty-First knew what came after that; Gallic horse, maybe, or some of the troops from Britain. There were tens of thousands of troops from Britain.

The biggest dragon the world had ever seen was worming its way through the forest; huge portions of its limbs disappeared between the clusters of pines and firs whose dark green belied the season.

"I hate 'em", said Bemborix. "Green, green, always green—you never know whether it's summer or winter; like some women who paint their bloody faces so much, you can never see a change."

"Everything's like women with you Gallic pigs", grunted Crocus. "Clean forest this is—nothing messy about it."

"Nothing messy? I've slipped four times since Aper passed by us; the ground's full of the damned needles. Some country, where the trees haven't even got leaves! I think Aper's got the evil eye—I haven't slipped once before."

The flaxen-haired German readjusted his pack, wiped a few beads of perspiration off his nose and forehead. "I'd still like to know what this war is about", he said ponderously.

"But I told you, fool—young Emperors must always wage war."

"Why?"

"Why! Because they aren't old and sensible enough to enjoy a quiet life. That's why. They must go out and get laurels. That's why."

Crocus meditated about that one. "So, if people want peace, they must choose an old Emperor", he said gravely.

Bemborix giggled. "No. No. That wouldn't help at all—because an older Emperor would have to go to war at once to prove that he is still young enough."

Crocus shook his head. He never knew quite what to make out of Bemborix' remarks. The Celt always seemed to say something that looked true from a distance and not so true when one came nearer to it.

But he got help. "I don't think you're right, you know", said the Legionary Vitus, a tall, lanky man with deepset eyes. "Young Constantine is not as you say he is. He's kept the peace well enough, these five years."

"What? After all we've been through in the north—"

"That was warding off an attack of robbers—Franks. That's not war."

"Not war"—Bemborix laughed. "I got a lovely sword cut in my left shoulder—and you've been having trouble with a bit of an axe wound, Vitus. What do you think that was—fun? All right, it was fun. We've just been playing about a bit. But now there is a war, isn't there?"

"Sort of", said Vitus. "Civil war. Just one more of them. It isn't the *real* thing. Not unless the signs come."

"Signs?" asked Crocus. "What signs?"

"Don't listen to him", murmured Bemborix. "He's queer. Always talks about such things—signs."

"When the signs come", insisted Vitus. "When the sun and the moon show signs, and for all to see—then there will be the new time. And it'll start with war."

"Christian nonsense", growled the Celt. "You make me sick, you people—always full of secrets and mysteries—nothing behind it. I've never seen such superstitious people. What is it you're praying to, you people? An ass's head, they tell me."

"I still don't know what this war is about", said Crocus obstinately. "Who are we fighting against?—that's what I want to know."

"Fellow called Maxentius", explained Bemborix. "Emperor Maxentius. He's in Italy. In Rome. That's where we are going."

"Emperor Maxentius?" Crocus scratched his head. "I thought *we* were for the Emperor!"

"So we are, you buffalo. For Emperor Constantine. By Hesus and Teutates, you shouldn't be allowed to be so stupid."

"Two Emperors? How can there be two Emperors?"

Bemborix roared with laughter. "Two! There are six! Six or seven. Wait—I'll tell you. There's Constantine, he rules Gaul and Britain and Spain, see? Then there's Licinius, who rules somewhere out east, in Thracia and Illyria and wherever; then there's Galerius, who rules still farther east, in Cappadocia and Syria. And that's not a nobody either, let me tell you. Four years ago he made a terrific row because of Maxentius and Maximianus, who'd killed Emperor Severus in Italy, and he landed with a considerable army in Italy and gave battle—but that wasn't a real war either, was it, Vitus? There were no signs, were there? Well, anyway, Maxentius and Maximian beat him off, and he went back where he'd come from."

"Maximian?" said Crocus. "Who's that? Another Emperor?"

"Yes—no—yes. He's dead now. He was an Emperor once. Then he abdicated; then he helped his son Maxentius to

272

become one instead. Then he joined up with him. Then he wanted to become Emperor again himself, but his son wouldn't let him."

"That's wrong", decided Crocus. "Father goes before son."

"In your forest at home, perhaps. Well, Maxentius didn't like it, and so old Maximian came over to Gaul and stayed with us for a while. And he took his daughter with him— the youngest. And that's the loveliest woman you ever saw— she's even the loveliest woman *I* ever saw, and I've seen some, believe me! So our Emperor Constantine goes and marries her. And she's now the Empress, Empress Fausta. Gave him a couple of children, too, and third one's on the way. I'm not joking. I *know*."

"Emperor Constantine", said Crocus. "Emperor Maxentius—that's two—" he began to count on his fingers— "Emperor Ga—Ga—"

"Galerius, that's three; Licinius, four; Maximinus is the fifth—"

"But you just said he was dead!"

"That's Maximianus, not Maximinus. Maximinus rules over Egypt and Africa."

"Max—Max—Max—" said Crocus, shaking his head. "I'd never be able to know which is which. That's the trouble with you Romans—you're all so comp—comp—"

"Complicated", assisted Vitus. "I'll make it easier for you, Crocus. Friend Bemborix isn't quite as well informed as he thinks he is. Emperor Galerius is dead now, too. He died last May."

"How do you know?" enquired Bemborix, incensed. "Never heard of it. What did he die of?"

"Worms. Maggots. Some beastly disease. He died a horrible death. God has punished him for the harm he's done to us."

273

"Well, we all have to die one day."

"So it's much simpler now", went on Vitus. "There are only four Emperors: Licinius and Maximinus in the Orient. Maxentius in Italy. And our Constantine. And the trouble is that Maxentius wasn't content with his share. He always talked about him being the only *real* Emperor. Now as long as it was talk, Constantine didn't do anything about it. But when Maxentius started massing his army near our frontiers—that wasn't so good. So we got going—and here we are."

"How do you know it's true?" asked Bemborix hotly. "I've heard stories like that before. You *say* the other fellow is going to make war on you, so you have to march first, to get the first blow in and hurt him before he hurts you. How do you know it's true?"

"I don't know", said Vitus calmly. "But I've seen Constantine, and he's not bad. He is the right sort. So I believe him. Why shouldn't I?"

"I don't believe anybody", said Bemborix. "Sometimes I don't even believe myself."

"Neither would I—if I were you", said Vitus pleasantly. "But I'll tell you another reason why I believe in Constantine. It's because Maxentius is lying."

"What about?"

"He says he's coming to avenge his father's death on us, and that's a lie."

"Well, Constantine did kill old Maximian, didn't he?"

"Yes, Bemborix, he did. Don't know whether he feels so good about it, either."

"Killed his own father-in-law, ha?" asked Crocus, open mouthed.

Vitus shook his head, sadly. "Ambition—that's what it was. Not Constantine's ambition—Maximian's. First he resigns. Then he puts his son on the throne. Then he wants his son to abdicate in his favor. So the son drives him out. Then he goes to Constantine and becomes his father-in-law. As soon as Constantine is busy fighting the Franks, what does he do? He spreads the rumor that Constantine has fallen in battle and assumes the purple himself. You can't do that sort of thing all the time, can you, now? Old Max—he just couldn't live without that purple cloak. Had to have it. Mind you, it isn't at all certain whether Constantine had him killed or whether he killed himself. I don't know. I wasn't there. But they do say he had him killed, and perhaps he deserved it, too. I wouldn't like to judge. But what I do know is that Maxentius is the last man to talk about avenging his father! He'd driven him out of Italy himself. What's up now?"

The sound of a trumpet from afar. Then another trumpet, nearer.

Rough voices began to bark orders.

The column, loose and disjointed, began to close its ranks. The huge body of the dragon became thinner and its scales glistened in the evening sun.

"Somebody coming up", whispered the irrepressible Bemborix. "It's a wagon—no, a carriage with mules. Four mules. No, more. Six. Eight."

"Quiet in the ranks!" bellowed the Centurion Aper, appearing from nowhere. "Helmets—up!" They had been wearing them loose, on the chinstrap, hanging down their necks.

"Sa-lute!"

The tramping hoofs of the mules. Four mules—then the carriage; then another four mules, heavily packed. Who was in the carriage? It could not be the Emperor; they knew he was a long way ahead with the Thirtieth Legion.

"Wodan! It's a woman!" Crocus could not help himself.

It was fortunate for him that at that moment Aper turned his back to him and that the carriage creaked.

A tall, gray-haired woman was sitting in it, alone.

"Let the men be at ease on the march, Centurion", she said with a smile that even Aper could not resist. Quite unceremoniously he broke into the nearest approach to a friendly grin. "Yes, Domina", he said, turned round, and roared, "Helmets—down! At—ease—everybody!"

The carriage rolled on. After the four mules with their pack saddles there followed a huge officer whose armor and uniform caused a good deal of interest. "I know what it is", whispered one of the older centurions. "That's the regular armor—as it was twenty-five years ago. African badge—Syrian badge—ye gods—the man's a historical monument."

"Would you believe it?" said Bemborix. "Know who that was?"

"Yes", said Vitus.

"No", said Crocus.

"That's the Emperor's mother—that was", explained Bemborix. "By Epona, what's the old lady doing here, in the middle of a campaign? And I thought she'd walked out on her son, years ago—"

"Why?" asked Crocus.

"Because of him marrying the Princess Fausta. He was married to another girl, I've forgotten her name now. The old lady didn't like that. It had happened to her, too, when she was young. So she knew how it felt. She wasn't at the wedding."

"Stop jabbering", said Vitus, and the little Celt, looking up, saw tears in his eyes.

"What's the matter with you, Vitus? Got stung by something?"

But Vitus beamed. "Did you see her face?" he murmured. "Did you see her smile? 'Let the men be at ease'—did you hear that? Have you ever seen such a face, and such a smile and such a tone of voice? What a woman she is. . . ."

"But she's an old lady—" Bemborix was perplexed—"what are you going all funny about, you superstitious old ass?—Oh, *I* know, of course: that's it. She's one of your faith, isn't she?"

Vitus nodded. "So they say. I don't know for sure. Or rather I didn't until just now. Now I do know."

"How do you know?" prodded Bemborix.

"She's a Christian all right—I could see it", said Vitus.

"Do they wear badges or special dress?" asked Crocus.

"They say she carries a golden chalice with her wherever she goes", whispered Vitus. "And the Bread of Life is in the chalice. And wherever she comes, the place is blessed."

Bemborix looked up in despair. "O Teutates!" he said. "Vitus, you're in a bad way, you are. Of all the ridiculous stories . . ."

They fell silent, then; the road before them became steeper and steeper. The forest opened before them, just as the sun set behind the glowing tops of the Alps. For a while they could see the valley deep down below—then the road led them into a new world, a world of naked rock. It was much cooler now. The monotonous tramping of thousands of feet kept up its rhythm, but the sound had changed; it was harder, sharper.

A long drawn "ha-a-aalt" came from afar and was taken up by staccato commands in quick succession. The huge dragon stopped, its scales glowing in the last reddish light of the dying day.

"No fires allowed."

They grumbled, of course. It was not only that they could not cook a decent meal. There was something else, something strangely oppressive in the stony darkness of the landscape. A thin mist was coming up, too. And it was cold. Cloaks were unwrapped and slung over shivering shoulders. They sat and munched their dry bread, a handful of olives from the plains, a bit of hard cheese; stewards went from man to man, filling their goblets with a mixture of wine and water. Somewhere lower down, a maniple or two started to sing—one of their old, ribald camp songs. But they didn't sing for long.

They stopped quite suddenly. Probably some officer had told them off. Strangely enough, it was almost a relief when they stopped. This was not a good place for singing.

"I don't like this place", said Crocus suddenly.

Bemborix laughed. "I don't think anyone does", he said. "Cold rock under your backside and no warm food in your belly. No woman around for miles—except old Helena, of course."

"Shut up", said Vitus.

"You do stick together, you Christians, don't you?" said Bemborix. "Why don't you go and denounce me for talking loose about Her Importance, the Empress-Mother?"

"Because you are a fool," said Vitus cheerfully, "and fools don't know better."

"This is an ungodly place", said Crocus. "I don't like it."

"There is no such thing as an ungodly place on earth", said Vitus. "God is everywhere."

The German was interested. "Is that what Christians believe? What sort of a God is yours?"

"He's *the* God", explained Vitus. "And he is one and yet three."

278

"How can that be?" asked Crocus, frowning deeply.

"I don't know", admitted Vitus. "I don't think anybody knows."

"Why believe it, then?" laughed Bemborix.

"That's just why", said Vitus gravely. "I believe it, because I don't know it. If I knew it, I wouldn't need to believe it, would I?"

"You're mad", sighed Bemborix.

"And he became man once", continued Vitus. "He lived a regular human life."

"Why?" asked Crocus. "Did he want to know how it feels?"

"I'm not sure about that", said Vitus doubtfully. "There may be something in that, though. But he did it also because he wanted to put us right, see? Because we'd gone wrong, all of us. He had to die to put us right, and he did die for us, like the lamb they slaughter as a sacrifice."

"We do that with our enemies, where I come from", nodded Crocus. "Seems more sensible."

"Good old Crocus—" Bemborix rubbed his hands with glee.

"Christians don't slaughter their enemies", explained Vitus. "Matter of fact, we shouldn't have enemies. We must try to love them."

"Love them?" Crocus fairly goggled. "Your enemies?"

"It isn't easy", admitted Vitus. "I've tried hard, more than once. It isn't easy."

"It's impossible", shrugged Bemborix. "Why, it's against human nature!"

"Well, and if it is?" asked Vitus. "Is human nature so good that you can take it as a yardstick? That's just what Christ came for—to better human nature, to change human nature."

"He'll have to do an awful lot of changing," grunted Crocus, "if we're supposed to love our enemies. I think I'll stick to Wodan. He's not that difficult."

An excited group of soldiers came clanking down the rocks; they were crowding around one man who was carrying something that looked like a round cap.

"What's the excitement?" asked Bemborix. "What are you carrying? A helmet?"

"Yes—but look at it! Ever seen a helmet like this before?"

"Can't see much in this bloody darkness. No—what is it—copper? Funny shape."

"Yes—showed it to old Calpurnius, you know—primipilar of the Eighth. Know what he said? 'Go and see that you find the Emperor and show it to him. That's a Punian helmet, that is—it's five hundred years old.' He'll probably buy it off me."

"Five hundred years old? You're being funny. Or old Calpurnius is."

"I suppose he sends me to the Emperor with it because he thinks it's a joke? He'd get it good and proper from the Emperor, wouldn't he? It's a Punian helmet all right, if old Calpurnius says so."

They went on and soon had disappeared in the misty darkness ahead.

"It's not impossible, you know", said Vitus thoughtfully. "This is the way Hannibal crossed the Alps, too, with the Punian army. Maybe that was five hundred years ago. Could be, easily. He lost a lot of men, crossing the mountains."

"Punians?" asked Crocus. "Who were they? A Gallic tribe?"

"No fear"—Bemborix was full of contempt. "Punians were Africans—weren't they, Vitus?"

"That's right. He came over to conquer Rome, just as we are doing. He had a good-sized army and many elephants."

"Elephants?" asked Crocus, frowning again. "What are elephants?"

"Animals", explained Bemborix. "Huge animals."

"As big as horses?"

"Much bigger."

"As big as buffaloes? They can't be as big as buffaloes."

"Can't they? An elephant is three times as big as a buffalo, you German numbskull. His ears alone are about as big as you!"

Crocus shook his head.

"I'm telling you", cried Bemborix. "And its legs are thicker than your body. And its nose is longer than your body—"

"Look here, Bemborix—"

"Much longer than your body! And it uses its nose like an arm, see? Stretches it out and takes things with it—heavy things—and lifts them with it. And it takes its food with its nose and pushes it into its mouth with it."

"Listen", said Crocus, and for the first time there was real anger in his voice. "I'll believe that there is a God who is one and yet three. I'll believe that he became a man and maybe even that people can love their enemies. But I will *not* believe that there is such an animal!"

"But I've seen it!" cried Bemborix, raising up his hands and shaking them violently. "I've seen some with my own eyes!"

"Then you're mad," said Crocus, "or you're a liar. Good night." And he wrapped himself into his cloak and turned away.

Bemborix stared at him in despairing disgust; a clucking, gurgling noise made him turn his head toward Vitus. He found him rolling to and fro on the rock, convulsed with laughter.

CHAPTER 2

"A Punian helmet", said Constantine. "Do you think it's an omen that they should have found it and brought it to me? But I suppose you do not believe in such things—or do you?"

He was standing with his face toward the entrance of the tent they had pitched for him; it was a regulation tent, the ordinary army issue. They were pitching another for Mother now—where he was standing he could hear them working on it.

She had not answered, and somehow he did not dare to look back to where she was sitting, in his own little field chair wrapped up in a rug, with the dim light of the oil lamp shining on her face. She did not seem to have changed much, from what he had seen—the few times that he had looked at her since she had arrived.

Suddenly he spoke again, quickly, as though he were afraid that she might say something before he could. "I am glad you have come, Mother; very glad. It's madness, of course— you shouldn't have done it. But I'm glad all the same. Just like your father—aren't you? Always turning up at the decisive moment."

There was still no reply.

"After all, I owe my life to the fact that your father turned up when things went wrong at my birth, don't I? I'll never forget that story as long as I live. And then when you arrived at the Domus palatina just in time again, when my father died; how did you know that I needed you, Mother? You have known that, haven't you? It's that gift again. You know, some people are afraid of you. But I am glad you have come.

For a long time I've wanted to talk to you—about many things. I know you didn't want to talk to me—don't say anything, I know you didn't. That's why you buried yourself in the country. For a long time I didn't even know where you were. Even now I am not sure. Where were you, Mother?

"I had to do it, Mother. I couldn't help it. I knew it would hurt you; you were fond of—Minervina. So was I. I still am, you know. But that's how life is, Mother. I know now exactly how Father felt, when he had to do it, too. One—one is not free when one is Emperor. One must do things—things one wouldn't do, if it were not for—well, you see, Mother, either this Empire is nothing, or it is something. And if it's something, one must bring sacrifices, even—even if they are agreeable! I'm not being a cynic about it, Mother, I hate cynics. It's easy to bring a disagreeable sacrifice; makes you feel big, somehow. Like the way I felt when I got my first wound; I never told you about that, it was in the next to last skirmish with Arabs. But an agreeable sacrifice stinks, Mother. You feel people are pointing their fingers at you when you're not looking. See what I mean?"

The silence weighed and weighed. The very mountain-top over there, glittering in starlight, was not more silent than the old woman in the tent.

"I know", he said angrily. "It isn't only Minervina. It is Maximian, too. He had to die, Mother—I couldn't help it. I don't know what they've told you about it. Probably the worst. Do you know he had gone so far as to bribe some of my best officers? It was he who spread the rumor that I was dead—he was not deceived about it himself. And I knew: the old man had to wear the purple even if he had to kill his own child for it. He had broken his word to Diocletian;

he'd broken it to me—he had to go. Surely you must understand that, Mother—"

At long last he turned toward her. Her eyes were closed, and for a brief moment he thought, in burning fear, that she was dead. So violent was the shock that the relief to find her breathing made him stagger at her feet. He knelt beside her. She was sleeping as peacefully as a child. He could see the pulse throb in the blue veins of her temple. How long had she been asleep? It was no more than half an hour, no, less than that, since she had been announced to him by Valentinus. At first, he had thought it was a silly joke. Then they had led her in—in the middle of the war council it was. Well, there hadn't been much to be discussed, it was all routine stuff. Still, it was hardly the occasion for a sentimental scene between mother and son. They'd behaved very well, anyway; very polite and understanding; and old Asclepiodatus had shortened the procedure so that Constantine could be alone with her. Just at the end of it they had brought the Punian helmet. Why, he still had it in his hand!

He put it on one of the tables, still laden with maps and plans; and Helena opened her eyes with a deep sigh and saw her son on his knees beside her; she stirred, and looking up he saw her face above his own, the eyes that had looked down on him in his cradle. Such a long pause there had been between them, after the officers had clanked out of the tent—such a long pause before he spoke at last and told her how he felt—and she had never heard it; she had fallen asleep. The accused had made his apologia—and the judge had fallen asleep, dead tired after the long ride in the carriage.

Constantine had an intense feeling of relief; he knew suddenly that all he had said had been weak and unconvincing. It was true, but it was deplorable truth. It was an excuse, a string of excuses for which condemnation should have been the answer. He smiled with relief, and in sudden joy, saw the answering smile on the face of his mother.

And they embraced. She was still using verbena as a perfume—for a brief moment the tent changed to her room in the villa in the south. The maids were combing her long, black hair and sprinkling it with verbena from a delicately cut phial of amber, tipped with gold.

Her hair was gray now, and her skin was getting wrinkled.

"Mother—where have you been all this time?"

It was not at all what he had wanted to ask her. But he had said it now.

"I was in Camulodunum most of the time. And in Verulam—I had important business in Verulam."

He suddenly remembered that he had not even offered her something to eat. "You must be hungry, Mother—"

"No, Constantine. I had my supper in the carriage. Favonius has been looking after me. I have lacked nothing."

He nodded. "Not if Favonius was looking after you. But what about wine? Shall I—"

"No, no. I don't need anything. I think I was a little tired, just when I arrived. That's over now. I am quite fresh."

He looked at her. "Five years, Mother—and what years—"

He wondered whether she was going to talk about Minervina—and about Maximian. He wondered even more why she had come.

She said, "I have been talking to many of your subjects, son—and as many as I've talked to gave me blessings for having borne you."

He looked up, in beaming surprise. "Mother—"

"You have ruled wisely and well, son. And I am adding my blessing to theirs."

"You are making me very happy, Mother—I thought—I—feared—well—you—disapproved of—"

"I have been praying for you all these years, Constantine. But I hope you did not think of me only as one who disapproves. I would have no right to disapprove, if I didn't value all the good you do—and there is only one voice about your rule in Britain and in Gaul. Time and again I wanted to write to you—and as often as I did, I felt that I had to say it to you."

"But why wait so long, Mother—"

"You were never alone, Constantine. I had to wait until you were alone."

Fausta, thought Constantine. It was strange how she and Mother disliked each other; it was not only a matter of principle, he knew that. There was a natural enmity between the two—as between fire and water. And Fausta would never forgive his Mother for leaving Aries two days before the wedding.

But for Mother to wait until he had left for a major campaign and then to join up with him, carriage, mules, Favonius, and all—

Suddenly he laughed boyishly. "You're incredible, Mother. You haven't changed a bit, have you?" But he knew that he was wrong. She had changed. He could not fathom it, really. But there was something in her he did not understand. Perhaps it was due to that queer faith of hers—yes, very likely it was that.

"You do not disapprove of this war, Mother, do you?"

She shook her head. "No, Constantine. War is terrible—but Maxentius is a bad ruler and treacherous. Even so I was deeply worried—until I heard about Sophronia."

Constantine nodded. Sophronia, wife of the prefect of Rome, had stabbed herself to escape the violence of Maxentius.

286

"She was a Christian, Mother, wasn't she?"

"Yes."

"Another Lucretia", said Constantine. "Strange that the old tradition of Roman virtue should be upheld by Christians."

Her eyes flashed. "You are the avenger", she said. "God will be with you."

"God—" said Constantine. He began to pace up and down, just as his father used to do when his thoughts were racing each other. "God—you know, Mother, I was never much of a scholar. The only thing I really understand is soldiering. I was never much of a templegoer either. But when one gets to the top of things—well, it's difficult to believe that oneself should really be the highest. I have a pretty high opinion of myself, but I am not stupid enough for that. Of all our many gods and goddesses Apollo alone appealed to me as *real*—the sun god. The sun—that's life, isn't it? Without the sun, nothing will grow."

"The sun is part of creation, Constantine."

But he did not listen. "There is one thing," he said, "the one thing that really makes sense to me in the belief of the Christians—and that's that they believe in *one* God. There is something in that, I think. It makes sense. There should only be one God—just as there should only be one Emperor."

She smiled a little. She said nothing.

"When Father left that—last command of his," Constantine went on, "that I should make good what injustice had been done to the Christians, I had to go into that question to some extent. So I know something about what they believe—of what you believe, Mother. But I'm afraid that about God being one is the only thing I can swallow. You'll forgive me for being so frank, won't you, Mother? It's no good pretending, is there? I know you would like me to share your belief. But I know also that you would not like me to be hypocritical about it. I just can't believe it, Mother."

She was sitting quite still. "What is it that you cannot believe, Son?"

"Oh, well—everything. That about God becoming man, for instance, and being born of a virgin, and living among men, and dying on the Cross to redeem the world. It's—it's asking a little too much to believe all that—all those things. He's a touching figure, this Jesus. But—it's such an unlikely story, Mother. And all that about paradise and the serpent and this poor unfortunate young Jew being the Son of God— no, Mother, I can't. It's a Jewish story—it is utterly un-Roman. Yes—that's it. It has nothing to do with our world."

He stopped in front of his desk. "Rome means too much to me for that", he said. "I know we have produced monsters in the thousand years of our history. But we have also produced the finest men on earth. It is not true that we had to borrow and to steal from the Greeks. Rome is not sterile. To me Titus Livius is as great a historian as Herodotus. And Virgilius as great a poet as Homer. I was reading the *Æneid* last night—he sings of arms and of a hero: that is my world, Mother—and not the story of the poor little Jew."

He thumped the scrolls on the desk, and one of them fell off; he bent down and picked it up. It seemed a little like an anticlimax, and he smiled. "You are not angry with me, Mother, are you? You know I'll do all I can for your Christians—I need not be one myself for that."

She looked at him intently. "I know you will do all you can," she said, "but it's nothing compared with what Christ can do for you—and for Rome." She got up. "I am tired."

"Your tent is ready for you, Mother. Valentinus!"

The aide-de-camp appeared.

"The Augusta Helena wishes to retire, Valentinus."

The sturdy, thick-necked officer bowed deeply to her. He had provided torch bearers; he had sent a subaltern to inspect the new tent only a few minutes ago. Rugs and cushions and a few tables and chairs, a field bed, an oil lamp. And a few amphoras of wine, snow cooled. The luxury of snow-cooled wine was easy to provide—some of his men had found snow in a ravine a little higher up.

"I'm afraid it's all a little rough, Domina", he said with an apologetic smile as they entered the tent.

"Young man," said Helena, "this is a campaign and not a banquet. Where did you get all these rugs and cushions from? Tell me one thing, and don't you dare lie to me: Am I depriving anybody of his rug or anything else?"

Valentinus hastened to protest that the things in the tent were from the stores of the Emperor himself. He did not lie—and he felt it would have been very awkward to lie with those large black eyes searching one's thoughts. He was forty-five years old, married, and the father of three strapping sons, but he felt a child of six in front of this incredible woman.

"Where are your ladies?" asked Constantine, who had come with them. "I've seen a big hulking shadow outside—Favonius, of course. But where are your ladies?"

She faced him abruptly. "Do you think I'd drag my girls up the mountains and make them go on a campaign? They would be a nuisance to me all the time."

"But you yourself, Mother—"

"My boy, I tamed horses before you were born. I don't know whether I could do that now, but I'm still strong enough to ride a mule. And I want to see this campaign."

"You mean—you're coming with us—all the way?"

"Certainly", was the firm answer.

Constantine and Valentinus looked at each other.

"But, Mother—this is war! What if—"

"Of course this is war. What do you think I thought it was? Come, come, Son: you're the Emperor, aren't you? And this is Roman territory, isn't it? Well—what should stop the Emperor's mother traveling through Roman territory? I won't be a nuisance, don't you worry about that. And now good night."

"Good night—Mother", said Constantine, and this time he did not dare to look at Valentinus.

The grandmother of the Empire, thought Valentinus, as they left the tent. She's as good as a goblet of wine before the battle.

He saw the huge man at the entrance stand to attention; he was wearing an old out-of-date uniform.

"Well, Favonius," said the Emperor, "I didn't think you'd let Mother go on a mad expedition like this."

Valentinus saw the man grin as Hercules might have grinned, or one of the Titans.

"Couldn't hold her, sir. Don't think anybody could."

"Meaning me, I suppose", nodded Constantine. "Good night, Favonius—look after yourself."

"Good night, sir. Sir!"

"Yes, Favonius?"

"The third cohort of the Twenty-First is badly equipped, sir. Sandals in bad condition on every third man; armor faulty on every fourth."

"Make a note of that, Valentinus", said Constantine. "Anything else, Favonius?"

"The blacksmith of the Second and Third Gallic horse doesn't know his business, sir; I saw eleven riders who'd lost an iron."

"Note it, Valentinus. Anything else?"

"No, sir."

"Very good. Thank you, old friend. Good night."

"Good night, sir."

As they arrived at the imperial tent, Constantine said, "Wake me half an hour before dawn, Valentinus. By the way—send an amphora of my best wine to Centurion Favonius."

"Yes, Sire. An extraordinary man, Sire. Must have eyes like a hawk."

"Favonius? He's *the* soldier, Valentinus. I'm proud of having had him as my teacher when I was a boy. Good night."

"Good night, Sire."

The sentries saluted stiffly. It was bitterly cold inside the tent now. When he approached his desk he found, not without surprise, that he was still holding the scroll in his hand—the one that had fallen off the desk. Looking at it, he saw that it was not the *Æneid*, but a collection of other poems, the *Bucolics*. It was rather a shame, really, that he had to read them for the first time in his life at the age of thirty-eight. He remembered dimly that old Philostratos had tried to make him read a few of the poems when he was a boy—but on the whole Philostratos had made him concentrate on Greek rather than Latin poetry. Not that he'd had much success with that, either.

Well, it was natural that old Philostratos should prefer his Greek poets. But there was something about Virgil that made them all look pale and bloodless, whether he sang of a hero's deeds or of the sweetness of Latin soil. Virgil—he was the soul of Rome.

He spread the scroll on the desk, and it brushed against the dull copper of the Punian helmet. There was the remnant of African glory: a piece of dead metal, useless and ugly—and it was all that was left of Hannibal's magnificent adventure. It was a good symbol—for it had never got there—just as its unfortunate bearer's general had never got to Rome. Nothing had survived of Carthaginian power—not even a line of poetry to sing of its greatness and fall. Perhaps it was Destiny—the icy goddess, greater even than the sun—that nations had their lives just as did individual men, that they were born and grew and became old and died. As the Assyrians had died—and the Babylonians—yes, and the Greeks.

How had he felt, the great Punian, when he had camped here, under the snow-capped summits of the Alps, the grim one-eyed hater of Rome, whom his father made swear as a boy of nine to be Rome's implacable enemy? Had he come to avenge his father's fate? Or did he feel that it was left to him to avenge an earlier wrong: the fate of Dido, whom Æneas had deserted, to become the father of—Rome. They had something to say to each other, Virgil's *Æneid* and this helmet. . . .

But Carthage was dead, and Rome lived. And would live and see still greater greatness, perhaps, than in the past. One could not have a stronger belief in Rome than Virgilius had. And had not someone said that a true poet was also a true prophet? No, Mother. I leave you your Jewish prophet or God—give me my Rome and Virgil.

And he took the scroll and read.

Ye Sicilian Muses—let us sing of higher things
—For vineyards and lowly tamarisks delight not all
If rural lays we sing, let them be worthy of a consul's ear
The last era of Cumæan song is now arrived,
The great series of ages begins anew . . .

Begins anew! That wasn't a bad omen. Childish, perhaps, to think like that, but still—

292

> Now, too, returns the virgin Astræa
> Returns the reign of Saturn
> Now a new progeny is sent down
> From high heaven ...

Better still! But whom did he mean? Augustus? Hardly a new progeny—and as for being sent from high heaven—

> Be thou but propitious to the infant boy
> Under whom first the iron age shall cease
> And the golden age over all the world arise
> O chaste Lucina
> Now thine own Apollo reigns ...

The Emperor stopped for a moment and passed his hand over his forehead. Thoughts rose and had to be chased away. Foolish thoughts. It was idiotic to combine things that had no connection. It was idiotic even if mankind had made a habit of it, calling it omen or—or perhaps even religion. Let Virgilius give us his own interpretation of Virgilius—

> While thou, Pollio, art consul,
> This glory of our age shall make his entrance
> And the great months begin to roll ...

Pollio—a contemporary. The golden age to start under the rule of Augustus? Three hundred years ago, or a little more?

> Under thy conduct
> Whatever vestiges of our guilt remain
> Shall be done away,
> The earth released from fear forever;
> He shall partake of the life of gods,
> Shall see heroes join the society of gods,
> Himself be seen by them
> And rule the peaceful world
> With his father's virtues ...

293

Pale as death, with trembling fingers, Constantine read on. And Virgilius burst into a wild paean of praise: the earth would blossom forth its fruits as never before—all poisons would vanish and

> the serpent also shall die

He read and read, as a thirsty man will drink water, hastily, in wild, uncontrolled gulps; again and again he had to go back to reassure himself as to the meaning of the text. All would not be well for a time with the golden age, he read. Some marks of the ancient vice would remain—

> there shall be likewise other wars ...

Yet the felicity of the world was assured—

> The ram himself shall in the meadows tinge his fleece
> Now with sweet-blushing purple, now with saffron dye.
> Scarlet shall clothe the lambs as they feed.
> The Destinies, harmonious in the established order of
>   the fates
> Sing to their spindles:
>   Ages—run like this!

And here the Promethean poet went down on his bended knees and worshipped

> Dear offspring of the gods
> Illustrious increase of Jove
> Set forward on thy way to signal honors
> *The time is now at hand*
> See how the world with its convex weight is nodding to thee
> The earth, the regions of the sea and heavens sublime:
> See how all things rejoice at the approach of this age.
> Oh, that my last stage of life may continue so long
> And have so much breath as to suffice to sing thy deeds!

Neither Orpheus nor Apollo Linus should surpass him in song, nay, not even the great Pan himself—and all the poet begged for at the end of his last stanza was a smile from the lips of "the sweet babe"—a smile "to make his Mother rejoice".

Feverishly, Constantine began to read the poem again, from the beginning. The Fourth Eclogue it was. The virgin Astræa—wasn't that the ancient goddess of justice, who had fled from earth, horrified by the impiety of mankind—of whom it was said that she became a constellation of stars, called the Virgin? Thus they were speaking of Isis in Egypt, too. Her offspring—a virgin's offspring to be born on earth—and to take away the guilt of the world and partake of the life of the gods—and the death of the serpent.

But the most decisive thing was that Virgil had seen all that in the very near future—that he himself had hoped to live to see the beginning of it. His friend Pollio would see it—

"Valentinus!"

The aide-de-camp rushed in, bare sword in hand, terrified.

Constantine forced himself to a smile. "No, no, Valentinus, no one's trying to kill me. It's—something else. Valentinus—I want you to call me one of my Christian officers—anyone—Tullius, or—anybody. But he must be a Christian."

Valentinus smiled. "I am a Christian myself, Sire", he said. "Will I do?"

"What—you, too? You never told me! Never mind—of course you'll do. Tell me—when did this Christ of yours live, and when did he die?"

By now Valentinus had overcome his first shock. "He was born in the year 753 of the City, Sire. And he died thirty-three years later, in 786."

"Under Augustus, then."

"He was born under Augustus. He died under Tiberius."

"Yes, yes—of course. But tell me—do you know when Virgilius died, Valentinus?"

"Virgilius, Sire?"

"Yes, yes, man—the poet. Surely even a Christian has heard of Virgilius. In any case, Virgilius seems to have heard of—well, do you know, or don't you?"

"Yes, Sire. He died in the year 734 of the City."

"That's—that's—nineteen years before your Christ was born, isn't it?"

"Yes, Sire."

Who was it who said that a true poet was also a true prophet?

The Emperor sank back in his chair. "Very well. Thank you, Valentinus. You may go now. I—I must think."

CHAPTER 3

"I KNOW the Fourth Eclogue of Virgil", said Bishop Osius with a slow smile. "There is no doubt to my mind that it is prophetic—just as the words of inspired men in the Old Testament. Who are we to demand that God should inspire men of the Jewish nation only. . . ."

Helena nodded. "I knew you would say that, holy Bishop—or at least I hoped you would. You see, my own father sometimes said that things would come to pass—and they did come to pass. And there are moments when I myself—"

She broke off.

The plain chant started again; there were many people praying in the Basilica. She could see only the last rows of chairs and benches through the small window of the vestiary, but even they were filled.

"At last we can serve God in the open", said the bishop. His dark eyes seemed too youthful for the graying beard. How old was he? Fifty-five? Sixty? His complexion was dark, even for a Latin—some said that he had Egyptian blood. "We haven't been as happy as the subjects of your great son", he went on. "We could meet only in secret—at night; and many of us were killed. It was as bad as in the grim old days, when the Edict of Diocletian was first published. At that time it was bad in Britain, too. I remember it well. I was traveling through Britain then——"

"I know", said Helena. "It was you who ordained the Deacon Hilary in Verulam, wasn't it?"

He looked at her in surprise. "Quite right", he said. "You knew him, then? What has become of him, I wonder?"

They were singing away lustily now.

"He is dead", she said. "He died, shielding the Body of our Lord with his own."

The bishop crossed himself. "May he rest in peace", he said. "I didn't know that he, too, had become a martyr. I knew of my old friend Albanus——"

"I had a church built in Verulam in Albanus' memory." Helena's voice was quiet and firm. "I want his memory to live through the ages. I am sure that is what Hilary would have liked me to do—he was so modest, almost like a girl. I am sure he wouldn't have wanted me to name a church after him, and Albanus was his teacher."

"He has a church of his own—in your heart", said the bishop softly, and he saw her smile for the first time. But it did not last long, and he knew that there was a deep struggle going on in that extraordinary woman, who had become something of a legendary figure in the Western Empire. There were some who said that she was the daughter of a wizard; that an angel had assisted at the birth of her son; that she carried with her, wherever she traveled, the chalice that Christ had used at the Last Supper. He had been rather curious to see what she was really like; she had arrived a few days after the occupation of Verona by Constantine's troops, and her first visit had been to the head of the Christian community. She had found him dying and with him "the traveling bishop", as Bishop Osius was called. A few days later they had met again—here at the Basilica.

"What is it that is worrying you, my daughter?" he asked. "You mentioned Virgil's Fourth Eclogue—but you did not tell me the connection—"

"My son read it—some weeks ago, in the night—just after we had met again. He read it by sheer—accident. If it was an accident. Constantine was never much of a scholar. He is a soldier first and foremost. He even had to rediscover Virgil. The poem impressed him vastly—whenever he found time, he discussed it with me and with his aide-de-camp, Valentinus—"

"A Christian?"

"Yes. It is all quite new to him, of course, and—very different from his own trend of thought; but he did say to me that he felt now that the world was altogether different from what he had thought it to be. But that was all—"

"It is a great deal—don't you think, my daughter?"

She breathed heavily. "It is a great deal for an ordinary man; it is little—much too little—for the man whose mission it is to submit the Empire to the Kingdom of Christ."

The bishop took a step backward. Years after he would remember this moment as one of the most startling of his life.

"Empress—my daughter, what makes you think that he has a mission of such magnitude?"

"His dying father's last words—and more than that. Don't ask me now, please. There is no time, I fear, for much explanation."

What did she mean? Her tone was nervous, almost desperate. The bishop asked himself whether the strain of the last weeks might not be the real cause. For a woman, and a woman of her age, to have crossed the Alps with an army was a tremendous achievement—and a terrible exertion. He had heard that she actually was in the fighting area throughout the battle of Turin; if that was true, she was likely to have seen things that few women could see without grave damage to their health. Perhaps she was mentally unhinged. Yet he felt strongly that the main source of her nervousness was the natural unrest of someone who feels that he is losing valuable time instead of taking action. What action?

"I gather that you are worried about your great son's spiritual development", he said cautiously. "Why not let it take its natural course? You feel, I believe, that he did not come across that poem by accident—that our Lord is drawing him. Very well, then—why not leave it to our Lord?"

Enormous eyes—and an expression in them that made it easy to believe in all the legends spun around her.

"No, holy Bishop, I fear it is not so easy as that. Our Lord has been drawing him for some time now—and it is for him to respond. How can he expect the right to win this war otherwise? I have read in the Scriptures that it is the tepid ones that God has spat out of his mouth. And

Christ said, 'Who is not for me is against me.' There is no in between."

The bishop nodded gravely. "I cannot contradict you", he said. "But doesn't it seem as though our Lord *is* with him? He has succeeded in crossing the Alps, he has taken the mountain fortifications almost with ease, he has beaten Maxentius' troops at Turin and Pompeianus at Verona—I am not trying to diminish his merit as a general; I know very little about military matters, but I am told that his leadership was inspiring, and his personal bravery—"

"Yes, his own officers had to send a deputation to him, imploring him not to expose himself to such an extent. I know. But these victories were paid for—and paid for heavily. His army is no longer the army he set out with, and there is no time for reinforcements to arrive. I've seen the troops—I've been living with them all these weeks—not one of them is the man he was when he set out. They've lost much equipment, too, and had to replace it from what they found in enemy stores; but it was not always the type of weapon they were accustomed to, and that makes a great difference to a fighting man."

His astonishment made her smile once more. "It is not so surprising, holy Bishop; I've been living with the army half of my life. I do know how a soldier feels and what is important to him."

"So it seems", admitted Bishop Osius. "And I do understand your worry now, I think. Besides, there is the numerical superiority of the enemy. From what I heard, Maxentius has an army of over 120,000 men, and perhaps still more. . . ."

But she waved that argument aside. "Numbers are not so important—it isn't that. Numbers will not decide this war. It is Constantine's *mind* that matters—and the minds of his men. And it is just that—the state of their minds—that makes me worry so much. You have felt the worry in *my* mind, holy Bishop—and you've thought of me as of a poor nervous old woman who needs a few good words of encouragement. No, don't protest, I *know* that that is what you thought. But what you have felt was not really my worry at all—it was *their* worry, their doubts and uncertainty that were reflected in my soul."

The experienced old fisher of souls looked at her keenly; it was he who usually read the thoughts of others, and he had to overcome a slight feeling of irritability and then another of annoyance at his irritability. He knew now that he had underrated her—that he had talked down to her, when, perhaps, her mind was high above his own.

She did not seem to be aware of that. She went on, "You see, my son and his army are like one body; he is the head, the brain, and some of what he thinks and feels will be imparted to the last of his men. I am his mother—and in a way I am the mother of his men as well. Their worries are mine—I hug them to my heart and *make* them mine."

For a moment it was on the bishop's mind to warn her against the sin of spiritual pride—but then he felt with acute certainty that he was wrong, that she had simply stated what to her were facts. And to his own astonishment, he heard himself say, "Some of us have our Gethsemane, my daughter." She became very pale, so pale that he thought she was going to faint. But she asked in quite a firm voice, "And does Gethsemane always lead to crucifixion?"

Again as though against his own will, he heard himself say, "No victory can be achieved without suffering, my daughter." At that moment it seemed to them that they were no longer alone—that faces, many faces were staring into the little room, and both of them looked about, instinctively. And there were faces, many of them—gliding past the small window looking into the nave of the Basilica, dim, with unseeing eyes—for the service had come to an end, and the community had turned round and was leaving.

The bishop decided that it was time to break the spell. "We are fortunate to have our Basilica back", he said in a lighter tone—"and that it was not burned down as so many others have been. It was used as a sort of warehouse for Maxentius' army. I had to consecrate it anew, of course. Do you wish to see it?"

Helena drew herself up. "Yes, holy Bishop, as soon as these good people have left."

A few minutes later they entered the nave; it was a huge room, almost without ornaments. There were flowers at the altar. On the right—

"I've had that cross erected in memory of our martyrs", said Bishop Osius. "Every church should contain a large cross like that, don't you think? It's about the size the Cross of our Lord must have been—but you don't hear me, do you?"

"It is too dark", said Helena; her voice sounded so strange that he glanced at her sharply. She was looking at the cross, very steadily. The expression of her face had not changed. But what did she mean?

"The wood is too dark", said Helena. "It should be much lighter. It was much lighter."

She walked over to the cross, slowly and firmly; yet it seemed as if she were being drawn toward it. She knelt down at the foot and began to pray.

Bishop Osius remained where he was for some time; then he saw Deacon Gallus coming up to him, a mild little man who had been in charge of the evening service. Deacon Gallus whispered that Domina Metella had just come to see him—her husband was dying. Would the holy Bishop come and comfort him in his last hour?

Bishop Osius gave a hesitant look in the direction of the woman kneeling before the cross. He did not quite know what to do. Should he disturb her prayer by excusing himself—or should he leave and make his excuses tomorrow, in the form of a special visit at the house in the Via Roma, where she had taken quarters during her stay in Verona? He decided for the latter course. "Very well, Deacon Gallus. I shall go at once. Stay here in the meantime, and when the Empress-Mother has finished her prayer, give her my apologies and tell her why I've been called away. Say I shall come to her house tomorrow morning to offer my excuses. In no circumstances leave the church before the Empress-Mother has left."

The deacon made his obeisance, and Bishop Osius walked out on tiptoe. It took him the better part of half an hour before he arrived at the house of Domina Metella; about two hours later her husband died peacefully, and the bishop spent a considerable time in consoling the widow and her two children. When he finally made his way home, it was almost midnight. As he was passing the Basilica, he saw the figure of Deacon Gallus near the door and heard him call out.

He went up to him. The mild little man was trembling and quite unable to speak.

"Pull yourself together, man", commanded the bishop. "What is it?"

Then, with sudden suspicion, "Has anything happened to the Empress-Mother? Speak, Deacon Gallus!"

"I—I don't know", stammered the little man. "She—she is still here ..."

"What?!"

The bishop rushed up the stairs and entered the Basilica.

The light of a solitary little oil lamp was holding its own against the silvery flood of moonlight assailing it through the windows. There was a dark figure kneeling in front of the cross.

The dead don't kneel, was his first thought, under the inrush of a breath of relief. Yet there was no motion in her—there was a rigid, wooden stillness about her that made him fear again.

He approached her—and found himself slowing up the nearer he came. Deacon Gallus was at his elbow all the time.

Now he could see her face—now her eyes; he stopped dead in his tracks, giving the deacon an imperious sign to do likewise.

Helena's eyes were wide open, but there was no knowing of what they were perceiving. Her hands were raised as in supplication, but the force that kept them up did not seem to be her own. There was an expression of rapt tenderness on her face; yet all that was life in her seemed projected on the huge moonlit cross—as though it were a vital organ, the vital organ of her body, pulsating with a bloodstream of moonbeams, glittering and scintillating in perpetual motion.

CHAPTER 4

"THE MAIN POINTS", said Constantine, "are simple enough and I want every commander to keep them in mind. This is going to be a battle of the wings; in other words, it is going to be a battle of cavalry."

"They have three horses to each of ours", said the Legate Asclepiodatus.

"I know that. But their cavalry consists of Numidians, whose horses are tiny and whose armor is negligible—and of their new invention, the same type of heavy cavalry we've encountered at Turin and Verona: both men and horses covered with armor so that they can't maneuver. Our Gallic horse will deal with either type—what say you, Vindorix?"

The little cavalry general grinned. "Crush the Numidians and play around with the heavies", he said.

"Exactly. You've done it before. You can do it again."

"Perhaps", said Vindorix. "There are more of them, this time. And there are fewer of us."

"They are nearer to Rome", warned the Legate Trebonius. "In fact, they are covered by their capital. They will fight better."

"On the contrary", exclaimed the Emperor. "It may well become fatal for them. They have had too good a time there. They're overfed, and it'll take a better man than Maxentius to keep them off wine and women. What's the matter with all of you? We've beaten them wherever we met them. One more effort, and the war is over."

There was silence. Then Asclepiodatus took a deep breath. "Emperor, I had the honor of fighting under your august father as well as under you, and I'm proud of it. I think I'm safe in saying that my counsel has never been on the side of too much prudence. But this is not an easy situation, Sire. We are outnumbered to such an extent that the very idea of attack is—boldness, indeed. The enemy has lost some of its strength at Turin and Verona—but this time he's fully prepared. Our greatest ally in the past was the moment of surprise. He didn't expect us. Now he does. In round figures he's a 140,000 against our forty thousand."

"Numbers", said Constantine contemptuously. "One of my veterans is worth six of his green levies."

"He has seasoned troops as well, though", parried the old legate. "And what is more, he has the Pretorian Guards—the best fighters of the Empire."

Constantine jumped to his feet. "The Pretorian Guards!" he cried. "That bunch of callous scoundrels who've sold the Empire to the highest bidder throughout the centuries. By the gods, I shall smash them and destroy them so they will never rise again. If this expedition had no other effect than abolishing that nest of vipers, it would be well worth undertaking! Maxentius has restored and even augmented their privileges—they'll fall with him, I swear it. And I shall lead the attack against them myself. So much for the Pretorians."

Asclepiodatus shrugged his shoulders. "The Emperor is the Emperor", he said in his deep, rumbling voice. "I'm a simple soldier; I do as I'm told."

"We're all doing as we're told", agreed little Vindorix. "Many lovely horses will die tomorrow. It's a pity." Obviously it was the only thing he was preoccupied about.

Constantine looked from one face to the other. There were many of them who had been with him in Eburacum, when his father died. He knew them well, now. Trebonius, who had stormed the mountain fortress of Susa; Ulpius, whose attack against the enemy's left wing had done so much to decide the battle of Turin; Asclepiodatus, whose knowledge and foresight had been invaluable at the siege of Verona; and little Vindorix, a centaur rather than a man—and so many others. They had done the impossible more than once. But now they seemed to have lost their impetus: they were tired. They were thinking of all the great men whose attempt to conquer Rome had failed in the past. Only a few years ago Galerius had tried and failed against the same enemy.

Somehow they all seemed to have lost faith. Faith! And you've got to believe in victory if you want to achieve it. For a moment he thought of making a speech to them—to rouse them from their deadly lethargy. But he knew he had nothing to say. He had heard Trebonius saying an hour ago, "The gods will be on our side." And Vindorix had laughed shrilly, like a horse neighing, and countered, "The gods? They like a safe bet, the gods. They're always on the side of the stronger army and the better equipment."

What if he was right? The memory of countless hours spent in torturing doubts arose and crystalized in the form of impatience.

"That will be all, friends", he said. "We shall meet again tomorrow—at dawn. Good night."

He did not like the way they left the tent: the hunched shoulders, the hesitant walk, the way they avoided looking at each other.

A wave of wild, uncontrolled fury shot through him, and he would have liked to send an arrow through each of them, but at once he felt that it was all his fault, that it had been up to him to inspire them with the confidence they lacked, to breathe strength into them, and to throw a spell over them. That was what he was their commander for. That was why he was their Emperor. He had failed them.

And tomorrow was the day of battle. Tomorrow was the day that decided everything. If Maxentius won the day, the war itself was lost. Ah, if he had been able to take his entire army with him—but that would have meant to denude the eastern frontier; it would have meant that the Franks and the Saxons could have entered Gaul without finding resistance. Maxentius, perhaps, wouldn't have cared. But he had cared, and now this would become his downfall. Where was justice?

Was it true, then, that justice, that Astræa had left the earth in despair? Or was Virgil right when he sang that she had returned?

Justice ... when we feel weak, we invoke justice as our due. But justice presupposed the existence of the gods—or of a God. If there is no God, why should there be justice? From whom, then, demand it? From men? Why? Why shouldn't they do exactly what they wanted?

Anyway, if the battle tomorrow were lost, it would mean death for the Christians in the Empire. So *if* there was a Christian God, he, at least, should be for Constantine's army.

But was there? And if so, he was not likely to be a God of war. He didn't like swords, did he? And there was the shrill voice of little Vindorix: "The gods? ... They're always on the side of the stronger army and the better equipment."

Mother, of course, was sure in her belief. And everything had gone well, as long as she was there. Pity, she wasn't here now. Stupid thought—the little boy whining for his mother at the eve of battle. If the troops should know ...

But she was an extraordinary woman. It would be better if she were here.

He sauntered toward the entrance of the tent, where he found Valentinus staring at the sky. "What's the matter with the sky?" he was going to ask. But he did not ask. He looked.

The sun was just setting; and above it was a strange, luminous excrescence, as though the sun was shooting out an enormous ray, as though the sun was giving birth to another sun—no, it was like a long beam of fire, two-forked ...

"That's a strange thing, Valentinus."

"Yes, Sire", came the awestruck reply.

A long, long beam of fire, two-forked: it was still growing.

"It's—it's like a cross", said Constantine, and he heard Valentinus beside him gasp.

He averted his eye, looked over to the thousands of tents—that was where Trebonius' troops were camping. He could see the countless little columns of blue smoke; they were cooking their supper, and for many of them it would be the last supper. But now there was the shape of a dark cross over their tents—and when he looked in the opposite direction, where the silvery band of the Tiber was visible between smooth hillocks overspun with olive groves, there too was that dark cross, the reflection in his eye of the queer, flaming apparition above the sun.

"Good night, Valentinus", he said abruptly and went back. They had arranged supper for him, but he did not feel hungry. He poured himself a goblet of wine, but he forgot to drink it. He threw himself on his field bed and tried hard to think of the battle plan he had worked out. The enemy had deployed at least half of his strength along the Tiber—this side of the river, not the other side. That meant he intended to fight the battle with the Tiber at his back. Therefore he would bring the rest of his army over, either now or in the early hours of the morning—or both. It was essential, then, to attack him as early as possible—perhaps before he had got all his troops over, so that the bridges would be congested. If only one had more cavalry—some of his best men were rotting in the northern plains . . . it had looked like a cross . . . Valentinus had felt that, too . . . strange thing . . .

Pulsating with life, glittering and scintillating in perpetual motion.

He could still see it as he awoke, and he heard himself repeating the same words over and over again. "By this thou shalt conquer. . . . By this thou shalt conquer."

He rose, stumbling. "By this thou shalt conquer."

Who had said that? Had anybody said it? Or had he seen it written? "By this thou shalt conquer."

"Valentinus! Valentinus!"

When the aide-de-camp entered, half drunk with sleep, he found the Emperor standing at his field desk, erect and wide awake.

"Make a note, Valentinus. General order to the army ..."

The morning mist of the twenty-eighth of October was rising.

Bemborix, waked up by the clanking of armor, rubbed the sleep out of his eyes and stared dully at Vitus, who was fully dressed and readjusting his helmet.

"What's the matter with you—we haven't been called, have we? What is the time? The sun isn't even up yet! Is there an alarm?"

Crocus was coming to, now. So had two or three others; there were over twenty in the tent. Somehow they were all staring at Vitus, who was looking after his shield and his two spears now, the *pilum* with its long iron hilt and the pike with its short sharp blade.

"What's the matter with him? Is he walking in his sleep?"

"You'd better get ready", said Vitus gravely. "This is the day."

"The day hasn't even started yet. Aper hasn't called, has he? You must be mad."

"This is the day", repeated Vitus. "You know what I mean. You've seen the signs just as well as I have. I told you there'd be signs, and there were signs."

"Oh, you with your superstitions, can't a man have his sleep? What's the army coming to, I'd like to know. All because there was some sort of a queer sunset—"

"It was the sign of the Cross", said Vitus quietly—"and that's the sign. There'll be more to come. This is the day."

"Hit him", said Crocus, yawning. "Hit him, Bemborix."

"Wa-a-ake up!" came the deep voice of Centurion Aper from outside. "Wake up! All men ready as quickly as you can!"

He came in, in full armor and with him a man carrying a pail filled with a white liquid.

"Attention", he said.

They all stared at him in bewilderment. A crude white cross was painted across his helmet.

"By order of the Emperor: every man will paint a cross on his helmet and another one on his shield. And don't splash! Be careful about it, you scum. Come on, get your armor. What are you waiting for? You there—you're ready. You first!"

They saw Vitus walking up to the man with the pail; he was walking very slowly, and Bemborix expected Aper to break into a stream of abuse; in fact, the centurion took a deep breath to do so and then didn't. Instead, he was watching Vitus kneel down at the pail, put down his shield and take off his helmet with an almost sacerdotal gesture. Aper's face was expressionless. But those soldiers who could see Vitus exchanged a quick look. There was a heavy brush in the pail. The work was done in a few moments. Vitus rose.

"All right", said Aper gruffly. "Get on with it. Next! Same way, all of you. As soon's you're ready, assemble outside in front of the tent." He left, and as he was opening the canvas covering the entrance, they could see half a dozen men with pails of paint waiting for him.

Then over a dozen voices spoke at the same time. "Order of the Emperor, eh? ... What's it mean? ... Some sort of a spell, I suppose.... Yes, but—... Come on, get it done, it doesn't hurt. Yes, but—... What's the idea?"

"I know", cried Bemborix. "It's that sunset—the Emperor has taken it as an omen."

"It's the Christian sign, isn't it?" asked Crocus. "You should know all about it, Vitus!"

Again they were looking at the tall man with the deepset eyes.

"Yes", said Vitus. "It's our sign. And this is victory."

"It's a charm then, is it?" asked one of the legionaries.

"It's all the charms of the world together", said Vitus. "It's victory. It's the new age. I knew it. I told you so, Crocus—and you, Bemborix!"

"That's true enough", admitted the German. "He did say that. Hand me that brush."

"I told you so when we were crossing the Alps", said Vitus, and his voice broke in excitement. "And now it has come. We'll drive them before us like the storm. *He* is with us—do you know what that means? I'll tell you: he is the One who scatters armies before him. He is the One who overcomes the world, and no one can resist him. Maxentius is as good as dead."

"Have you seen them?" argued Bemborix. "Have you counted their tents at the banks of the Tiber? I have! They're two or three against one of us!"

Vitus broke into loud, cheerful laughter. "If they were ten to one of us," he cried, "if they were twenty to one—they're finished. You'll see!"

"Madness", said Bemborix with his usual shrug; he had the brush now and he was painting away furiously. "A cross—! I'd rather have another oxhide on my shield. That's protection! And not a bit of paint."

"Ox yourself", said one of the legionaries. "Always talking big, aren't you? That fellow knows something about it—that's clear to me. Give me that brush."

"What's wrong with Jupiter?" asked a bitter voice. "Are we going to offend the gods by going in for this foreign stuff?"

"Oh, shut up! My wife's brother is an augur at the Jupiter temple, and he lies every time he opens his mouth, she says."

"Yes, and the priests of the Mars temple at Autun give you amulets that are supposed to make you safe against arrows and spears. My old pal Aulus bought one—cost him two months' pay!—and he got an arrow right into his throat in the first battle."

"About time we had a change."

"Besides," said a thickset man, struggling with his armor, "*they* believe in Jupiter and Mars and bring sacrifices to them before the battle, don't they? And they're three to one of us, as Bemborix says. Therefore they'll offer them three times more. And if we stick to Jupiter and Mars we're just done for. We might as well try someone else!"

"Something in that!"

Vitus had left the tent and was standing in front of it with gleaming eyes. They were coming out of all the hundreds and hundreds of tents around him, all with white crosses on helmets and shields.

He recognized a few brother Christians and waved at them with his spear, vertically first and then horizontally; they immediately answered in the same way, and their greeting was taken up by other Christians in other formations. There weren't very many—only about one in fifteen or even twenty—but every one of them knew that this was the day they had been waiting for.

There was scarcely a tent in the Emperor's army in which similar discussions were not taking place.

The morning rations were being distributed—*pulsum*, bread and water mixed with a little vinegar; there was an extra goblet of unwatered wine, too. One of the men serving it had a strange story to tell: he knew why this white cross business had been ordered. He knew it from Heraclianus, the wine steward of the Emperor, who knew it from Valentinus, who knew it from the Emperor himself. The Emperor had had a vision in the night: the Christian God had appeared to him in a dream and promised him victory if he would carry the emblem of the Christians into battle. Victory over Maxentius and over all his enemies! And Heraclianus had told him that Valentinus had said that the God of the Christians was an absolutely sure bet. You just couldn't go wrong. Why, once when he had promised his help to an army trying to take a fortress, all they needed to do was to blow their trumpets and the walls of the town just crumbled. . . .

In this, the steward was challenged. Where did that happen, and how did he know it had happened? But the steward knew: it had happened somewhere in Syria or Palestine, and Valentinus himself had seen it with his own eyes.

This was cheerful news.

They had just finished their breakfast when a flourish of trumpets was heard. It came from afar, but grew in strength and with it the thunderous murmur of acclamation, rising to a roar of thousands of voices.

"Is he blowing them down already?" asked Bemborix, but the Centurion Aper bellowed, "Attention!" and they formed a double column; double columns sprang out of nowhere right and left, and now a cavalcade of riders appeared from the north end of the camp. Fifty trumpeters on horseback. Then the Life Guards, picked men. Every one of whom had shown his valor at least three times in the field. Usually the eagle carriers would follow. And they came, well-known figures most of them—but instead of the

314

eagles they carried huge pikes, intersected by a transversal beam. A purple veil of silk hung down from the beam, and the summit of the pike supported a crown of gold, enclosing a mysterious sign, like a monogram.

"The name," whispered Vitus, "the holy name!"

"What is it? What is it?"

"It's the name of the new God!"

No centurion would interfere with their talking this time—everybody around them was shouting and roaring at the top of his voice. Here came the Emperor, beaming, on a heavy chestnut. The cross on his helmet and shield was painted in liquid gold.

"He looks like Mars himself!"

"Shut up! Mars is a foul demon. There is only one God, and he's with the Emperor. Look at him! Can't you see it?"

Large silver crosses were painted on helmets and shields of the staff officers following the Emperor.

"We're a new army", shouted Vitus. "We're God's own army."

Somehow he had said what most of them felt instinctively—though very few of them really understood why. There was the element—primitive and effective—of feeling that the Emperor was up to something new, something of which he felt very sure; that he had known their secret plight, their hidden worries, and that he had found some way of his own to tap new sources of strength. There was the feeling—again primitive and superstitious—that there was something in the nature of a spell about these glaring crosses everywhere. It was like putting on a new uniform. There was a feeling of union, of a new pact made that welded them all together in a new sense. Many of them remembered the strange sign they had seen at sunset yesterday. The old sun had gone down, but even after it had gone down, the fiery cross had remained for some time. No doubt it was an omen, and the Emperor had accepted it with the same alertness and swift action that had made him victorious at Susa, Turin, and Verona. The belief in the old gods had become weak and corrupt a long time ago. This was something new arising. Most of them had heard of, and many of them had seen, Christians dying for their faith—and often enough they had asked themselves secretly whether they would have died with equal fortitude for Jupiter, Mars, or Apollo, if such had been required of them. A man must be damned sure of his faith if he is ready to die for it!

There was no need for primitive and sluggish brains to think of all this by themselves—the Christians in the army saw to it that they thought of it. True, there were only a few thousand of them, but every one of them became the hero of the hour, as Vitus did. They were jubilant; they shrieked, screamed, and roared their enthusiasm. They had known it all the time, and now it had become true for everybody to see. This was the new age, the golden age, the new reign, the victory of God. The hour was now at hand. . . .

But the non-Christians, too, had all been longing for something to happen, and now it had happened. They were soldiers, and a soldier wants to feel that he is on the winning side. Now all those mild, quiet, rather mysterious and secretive fellows among them opened up and yelled their sure belief in victory. That by itself was an omen if ever there was one. The news that fifty thousand reinforcements had arrived could not have impressed them more. They had wanted to feel sure of victory—they had wanted nothing more—and this was the opportunity to feel sure, and they grasped it avidly.

On went the magnificent cavalcade, from tent street to tent street. Behind the Emperor and his staff came again Life Guards and then an endless stream of cavalry, Gallic horse, thousands of them. It was one hour after dawn.

CHAPTER 5

"OFFICER COMING—on horseback", said the soldier Priscus. The half-dozen sullen men relegated to keep watch over the baggage wagon looked up. It was not an amusing time sitting around here and listening to the noise of the battle, only a mile away. They and their comrades—about five hundred of them—were not allowed to fight, some of them because they had showed cowardice in front of the enemy at Turin or Verona, others because they were ill or invalid.

"Look at him—what sort of a uniform is that? Never seen anything like it. A centurion—but—"

"By the beard of my aunt, he's as old as Troy!"

"Must be over seventy. What's he dressing up as a soldier for?"

"Perhaps he's a ghost. There've been battles here before—"

"Shaking all over, Cacus, aren't you? Just like at Turin!"

"Shut up, you louse, or I'll murder you."

"He *is* a centurion. Get up, chaps, or we'll get it."

They stood, as the centurion rode up, and they saluted sullenly and with ill-concealed insolence.

"At—ease!" said the old officer, dismounting. "This the wagon with the eagles? Right."

He walked toward it and lifted the canvas. Yes, there they were—seven of them. The eagles of the seven legions.

The six soldiers were looking on in malevolent bewilderment. There was no doubt now that this was an officer, though his uniform was as strangely out of date as his age. But what was the idea of caressing the bloody old eagles as if they were pretty women? Cacus pointed with his dirty finger toward his forehead and blinked; the others grinned. That was it. The old man wasn't quite right in the head. Priscus laughed outright.

The officer turned round; the very movement of his huge body was so threatening that they recoiled. "Fifty steps back with you", he snapped. "If I hear one more noise, there'll be hades to pay. Off with you!"

They knew that tone and they obeyed.

Favonius turned back to his eagles. Yes, this was the one of the Thirtieth—he'd seen Africa and Syria and Pannonia and Dacia. He had been carried into swarms of Sarmathians, and he'd seen the death of Publius Draco, who'd carried him for twenty-two iron years. And this was the eagle of the Nineteenth, who'd seen Germany and Spain and Persia; he had been captured once by the Persians, when half the legion had been killed by Arab horsemen and recaptured by Aurelian in the war against Zenobia, though how he came to be there was a riddle that no one had solved or would ever solve. And this was the eagle of the Eighth, and they'd marched him into Parthia and into the Nubian desert, and little Gumnorix had carried him twenty years ago, no, twenty-seven years ago, a man from Autun he'd been, but with a Roman mother, and one of the best; they had to give him the eagle despite his smallness and he'd died with a German spear in his stomach. He hadn't let go, though, not Gumnorix! For half an hour he'd carried on until relief came, with the damned spear hanging out of his belly. What men they were, who'd carried them, silly gilded things, through anybody's country—and just as well they hadn't lived to see them as they were now, heaped on top of each other, in a baggage wagon.

Holy things they were! Made holy by the death of brave men. Senate and people of Rome—well, everybody knew that the inscription had no meaning; the senate was a group of gray-haired dodderers, jabbering praise to whoever was sitting on the throne; and the people—bah, they'd long ceased being a people. The inscription was nothing. But the eagle—that was different. It wasn't so much that it was Jupiter's holy bird. There wasn't much holy about birds—and maybe there was nothing holy about Jupiter. Mars Repulsor—he wasn't such a bad god, though when it came to real fighting one didn't think of him either. Perhaps he existed, perhaps he didn't—who could tell. Perhaps Domina Helena was right about her new God. It didn't make the eagles less holy. It was the blood that had soaked into them, that sanctified them, the spirit that had carried them from Rome to Persia and from Persia to Britain and from Britain to Africa.

Good-bye, eagles.

He kissed them, all seven of them. And stood back and saluted. And turned round and went back to his horse and mounted and rode off, without so much as a look at the group of soldiers.

As he was riding on, the noise of the battle became louder.

He knew he'd be in time, though—and it wasn't the only thing he knew. He passed the waiting columns of the Eighth Legion, which was kept in reserve. Strange they all looked, with their white crosses on helmets and shield. Quite different. Then came a formation of Gallic horse, and another, and still another. The Emperor had massed them here on the right wing. And there was the clumsy little group of reddish rock that had given the place its name, *Saxa Rubra*. There was a way up, he knew that. Crowds of staff officers, mounted, staring toward the Tiber. Somewhere on top there would be the Emperor himself.

No one tried to stop him as he rode uphill. Most of the high-ranking officers knew him by now—or had known him from previous campaigns.

Yes, here was the Emperor, on his chestnut—he even had half a smile for him, though he went on gazing straight ahead. Then he asked, "Mother all right, Favonius?"

"Yes, sir."

The Emperor nodded and stared ahead. He didn't ask questions. It was a natural thing that old Favonius could not have a battle fought without him. Besides, there was no time for questions.

The old centurion breathed heavily with delight. This was a sight after his own heart. To the left three legions were standing like a wall of iron, motionless, waiting for the enemy to attack them. And there, at about three miles' distance, came the enemy infantry—advancing very slowly. It was impossible to count them—but far behind them the Tiber was clearly visible.

Still further to the left all was dust and storm. There the battle was in full swing; the speed in which clouds of dust were chasing each other disclosed that cavalry was fighting cavalry.

But directly in front a strong formation of Gallic horse had deployed—about three thousand men. The country before them was fairly flat, and again at a distance of perhaps three miles was the enemy—cavalry, too, but of quite a different caliber. The glitter of their armor was clearly visible, and it seemed to cover them down to the ground:

Maxentius' pride, his heavy cavalry. Both men and horse were covered with armor.

Favonius whistled softly; he had begun to understand. The three thousand Gallic horsemen in front were supposed to appear as the Emperor's right wing—a thin cover, just enough to hold the ground until reinforcements arrived, if they were attacked by stronger forces. But in reality they were a spearhead. There were thousands of others waiting behind the rocks; he had just passed them. The Emperor's right wing posed as a defensive wing—but it was from here that the main attack would be made.

Constantine himself looked intently in the direction of the left wing; the dust columns were still pursuing each other madly. Vindorix was having a difficult time with the Numidians, chasing them about like a wolfhound with sheep. There were glittering lines *behind* the Tiber—the enemy was bringing up his reinforcements. If only Vindorix would get on with the job. . . .

Now that he saw the whole thing in its true proportions he felt that he had much to be thankful for. If Maxentius had played a more cautious game and kept within the walls of the city, the situation of the attackers would have been exceedingly dangerous, perhaps even desperate. Rome was well supplied with food and could have stood a siege of many months—and there was nothing more difficult than to keep such a giant city under siege with so few men. Sortie after sortie would have decimated the attacking forces, and in the end they would have shared the fate of Hannibal—to leave Rome behind them, unconquered. . . .

It was obliging of Maxentius to come out of his hole and to give battle—but then, of course, he felt safe with his giant army, three times superior in numbers.

Again Constantine looked to the left. It was essential that Vindorix beat the Numidians before Maxentius' center had seriously come to grips with his own.

Galloping hoofs—a young tribune arrived, his horse was foaming—he did not dismount, but rode straight up the hill.

"Yes, Aufidius?"

"Report from Legate Vindorix, Sire: the Numidians have lost over a thousand dead and are beginning to give in. At latest in half an hour they will be in full flight."

"Very good. Stay with us, Aufidius."

At latest in half an hour. He began to calculate. It was just right—if Vindorix' opinion could be relied upon. It couldn't always.

Another officer rode up. "Report from Legate Trebonius, Sire. The Pretorian corps is approaching the Tiber and will cross the river immediately, at the Milvian Bridge."

"Good. You may stay, Faber."

Favonius grinned. A good commander in the field should know the names of his officers; he was satisfied with his pupil.

The Milvian Bridge, thought Constantine. So that was where the enemy's center would be at the main action. That was where Maxentius would be. The Milvian Bridge.

"Valentinus!"

"Sire?"

"An orderly to Asclepiodatus: the Eighth and Twenty-First will attack in the direction of the Milvian Bridge in two hours' time."

Valentinus made a hasty note.

"I may need him earlier. If so, I shall fly six white pennants on my own standard, and give the signal C on the tubes. He will have the honor of defeating the Pretorian

Guards—if it is an honor. Tell him I'm making him a present of the Pretorians. Tell him I want him to eat 'em, and I hope he's got a good appetite."

"Yes, Sire."

Valentinus completed his note and dispatched a junior officer to ride over to Asclepiodatus. Then he made sure that there were six white pennants about; there weren't, so he took his own white coat and had the pennants cut from it.

Once more the Emperor was looking at the left wing. Slowly but inexorably the dust clouds proceeded in a southerly direction. Good old Vindorix! He was keeping his word after all.

"Valentinus!"

"Sire?"

"Give the signal for the Gallic horse. The first wave."

"Yes, Sire."

An orderly rode down to them. A minute later they were waving their lances and had begun to move. There was no need for more detailed orders. They knew exactly what part they had to play against the heavy cavalry.

Valentinus' eyes were on the Emperor's lips. Surely he would give the order for the second wave to follow the first now. The three thousand simply hadn't got a chance— they were one against five.

What was he waiting for?

The Gallic horse had fallen into trot now; soon they'd be galloping straight into the tremendous mass of iron that awaited them, men and horse covered with armor so as to be almost invulnerable. It was like a pack of courageous dogs attacking elephants—and there were five elephants to one dog. It was madness.

And still the Emperor hesitated. Even Favonius was looking worried. The Gallic horse were galloping now. They were lost, as good as dead, every one of them.

At last Constantine seemed to wake up.

"Valentinus—the second *and* third waves. The auxiliaries to follow at once."

Valentinus barked orders.

"Just right", said the Emperor calmly. "Must give 'em time to stir 'em up a bit."

Valentinus understood suddenly. The first wave was a sacrifice, a deliberate sacrifice—and it had to be made to create disorder enough in the ranks of the terrible armored horsemen to give the second and third waves a chance. He was an experienced soldier, but he looked at Constantine almost with horror. The young Emperor's features were calm and unmoved. There were friends of his and of Valentinus among the First Gallic horse. He seemed oblivious of that.

The dispatch rider came back from Asclepiodatus; he brought a letter. Valentinus cut the strings and gave the tablet to Constantine.

"I'll eat as many Pretorians as I can", wrote Asclepiodatus. "If I get a bellyache it won't be my fault."

Constantine would tell the story of that letter a hundred times in years to come, and always he would roar with laughter. He did not laugh now. He had no time to laugh. He was looking intently at the first wave of Gallic horse, which just now clashed against the iron wall of the armored cavalry. The attack seemed to be a complete failure. Not a single Gallic horse could penetrate.

But he knew that was not so. He knew that his horsemen had jumped off and were crawling now under the bellies of the enemy horses, killing them off one by one. It was a desperate thing to do, but he had seen it done before, at Turin, and had decided to make use of the idea in big style. They had had to train themselves for it these last days; it was what little Vindorix had called "playing around with the heavies".

Something like a slight weaving to and fro was going on within the first third of the armored cavalry.

That was when the second wave of Gallic horse thundered past the Red Rocks. There would be no belly creeping for them—their task was to crash into whatever hole the first had made for them. As for the third—

For the last time Constantine looked toward the left wing.

The dust clouds were retreating toward the Tiber and massing—in a few minutes they would become one single cloud hanging over Maxentius' right wing. It was time.

"Valentinus! The Guards; we are taking our place between the second and third waves of the Gallic horse. What? You didn't think I was going to sit still and do nothing, did you? Trumpets, the A-sign! Come on, friends."

Valentinus was riding on his shield side, Favonius on his sword side; about half a hundred picked officers closed round the Emperor, swords drawn. Valentinus had learned his lesson from past experience; if the Emperor *had* to ride right into the enemy, he'd at least see to it that he was properly protected.

Life Guards, three hundred strong, started the imperial attack—then came the Emperor and his fifty-two officers—then another three hundred Life Guards. "Tubes with us!" yelled Valentinus, and the trumpeter corps joined in.

Now the last formations of the second wave were galloping into the plain. Already the thunder of the hoofs of the third wave could be heard.

"Now, Valentinus", said Constantine. "Up the standard! Off we go. Trot!"

They rode downhill in perfect order, swung round, and followed the whirling dust of the second wave. A thousand yards behind them came the third wave, already galloping.

"Gallop!" roared Constantine. "Hi, Favonius—same as in the old days, ha?"

The old centurion grinned; he did not answer. When one is seventy-two, one does well to save one's breath at a gallop. Some might do that even earlier. He was not a staff officer and never had been. He had no qualms about the general-in-command trying to get in a few sword thrusts in person. This was good sport. Besides, Constantine was quite right. Everything depended upon this attack—it was just as well that the Emperor himself should be there. It was just as well for him to be in it, too—for this was without doubt the last battle of the war, and he could scarcely hope to fight in yet another.

He kept his horse steadily half a length behind Constantine; as long as he was there, Domina Helena would not receive that one message she must not receive.

There was a terrific crash a few hundred yards in front of them—the second wave had broken into the armor. This was a grand world—now the three hundred Life Guards in front were getting their spears ready. In the next minute they were in a fighting alley, almost a hundred yards deep, with the Gallic horse still pressing on in front: their task was to split the enemy cavalry into two halves and then to go on where the first wave had left off, on their way back. The enemy was far too unwieldy to be able to maneuver— all they could do was to hail spears on the intruders in the alley from both sides, and that they did, very thoroughly. Within half a minute Favonius had four spears in his shield— they were aiming for the Emperor, of course. The first wave, he saw, had done excellent work. There were fallen horsemen everywhere, and the very weight of their armor prevented them from getting up; and still a few hundred battle-mad fellows of the First were crawling about among the enemy, slitting open the bellies of the horses from underneath. Each time it was as if a little fortress was going down, and there were little fortresses going down everywhere. They were helpless against this sort of attack, and if only there had been more men in the first wave, the issue would have been clear enough within half an hour. As it was, there was bitter fighting. The Life Guards especially had their hands full—their shields, uplifted, were forming something like a porcupine's skin round the Emperor; the moment came when they had to free their small round cavalry shields from the countless spears of their attackers.

Valentinus saw two Life Guards go down, one with a spear in his throat, the other because his horse was hit. He was just in time to ward off a well-aimed spear and then himself was wounded in the shoulder.

"Look after him", ordered Constantine. "And let me get at this fellow with the golden helmet. Leave him to me—he's mine."

Favonius beamed—he dropped his shield with the four spears in it—he could not lift it any longer—and rushed up at the Emperor's side against the man with the golden helmet. In the next moment the man fell with Constantine's sword in his throat; Favonius grasped his shield and swung it into position.

"Like getting horses in Thracia", he laughed. A swarm of Life Guards galloped between them and the enemy, and they could breathe for a moment. "Only point you can get them", said Constantine with great satisfaction. "Just where the helmet ends and the shoulder armor hasn't started yet. Takes a bit of aiming."

Then he looked about and saw the third wave crashing in. Their impact was too much for the weaving, seething, roaring mass, and it split wide open....

With tremendous joy Constantine saw the last formations of the armored cavalry break away and make off. Nothing could be better—they were riding, were forced to ride straight into the lines of their own infantry. . . .

He looked at the sun—it was not even an hour since he had sent his messenger to Asclepiodatus. Say, half an hour for the roundup, no more. No, it had to be done in half an hour, it was essential—for Maxentius would by now be in the middle of the work of getting the Pretorians over the Tiber, and the Milvian Bridge was bound to be congested. He must allow no time to get them all across, or else Asclepiodatus would get his bellyache after all. . . .

"Give the trumpet sign, the C sign", he commanded. "And up with the white pennants. Let's hope they can see them. . . ."

They saw. And they came—and with them the three legions that had been waiting for the enemy's attack in the center—an attack that never took place. It is not easy for seasoned troops to stick it out when the two wings have caved in and they find themselves pressed at both sides by their own cavalry—for the young legionaries of Maxentius, most of whom had not seen much fighting and some of whom had seen none at all, it proved too much. By the thousand they simply tried to escape from the hoofs of the Numidian horses on the east and, worse still, from the armored horsemen on the west, by running back toward the Tiber bridges, just as Maxentius was trying to get his cavalry reserves over. The terrified legionaries had horses hemming them in from all sides but one, and from that one side came Asclepiodatus with five legions, all fresh troops, twenty-five thousand men, each of whom had seen battle—and what is more, victorious battle—before. The white crosses were gleaming in the sun. Strange standards were carried before them. No wonder that the day after the battle the rumor went round in Rome that an army of warriors of light had come to the help of Constantine and had decided the day for him.

But six thousand Pretorian Guards had got over the Tiber and stood like one man. Unlike the rest of Maxentius' army, they knew they could not expect clemency from Constantine; besides, Maxentius himself was with them.

The Gallic horse had to attack again and again, to support Asclepiodatus' men. Around the Milvian Bridge the butchery was horrible. Far more men died from drowning in the Tiber and from being trampled to death by their own comrades than from spear thrust and sword cut.

Four times Constantine had to fight his way through with the bare sword—twice he had to be rescued by his Guards. He was indefatigable—leading sometimes a detachment of Gallic horse against the nearest formation of Pretorians, sometimes a cohort of infantry. He had lost sight of most of his original followers; Valentinus was wounded, and so were Aufidius and Faber. Old Favonius, too, had had to stay back and pluck an arrow out of his left arm. It was quite irresponsible on the part of the Emperor to go on fighting in person, for the battle was won—but he could not resist the lavish opportunity offered. . . .

At last even the stoicism and valor of the Pretorians began to give way, and Constantine was collecting a few cohorts for a last furious attack, when the report came that Maxentius himself was dead—and he had not fallen in battle. He had tried to escape across the bridge, and his own soldiers had swept him off into the Tiber. He had drowned, dragged down by his armor, and they were now fishing for his body. . . .

"Maxentius is dead!" shouted the troops of Constantine. "Surrender, you fools! Old Max is dead!"

That discouraged even these brave men—and only little groups went on fighting grimly.

Constantine saw one of them warding off attack after attack—until one man jumped right into them, cutting about right and left and seizing something glittering, a golden lance, no—an eagle. The eagle of the Pretorian Legion!

"Help that man and bring him to me!" he ordered and threw himself into the last sparks of fighting. He came too late—already the group was disarmed, and everybody was waving spears and swords at him and giving the imperial salute.

Then he saw the man who had conquered the eagle—he had lost his helmet, and blood was covering half of his face and staining his uniform. But what hair one could see on his head was white—it was an old man: it was Favonius.

He rushed up to him. But Favonius drew himself up to his full height and gave the salute with the eagle. The one eye he still had was burning. "The last eagle, Emperor", he cried. "Keep him well—and safe: he was a valiant one—"

As Constantine, pale with emotion, took the eagle from his hand, Favonius fell dead at his feet.

The Emperor knelt down and laid the eagle at his side.

The jubilant shouts ebbed away, and for a moment a great stillness prevailed.

"Marcus Favonius Facilis", said Constantine in a trembling voice. "Farewell, old friend."

He rose. "Bury him in Rome", he said loudly. "And bury the eagle with him—the last eagle of Rome."

They roared again, now—and they understood. Tomorrow they would bury the dead hero in Rome—for the way to Rome was free.

BOOK SIX

❦

A.D. 326

CHAPTER I

CONSTANTINUS IMPERATOR AUGUSTUS, by the Grace of the
Blessed Savior Jesus Christus, sole Emperor of the Roman
world from Britain to Persia and from the Danube and the
Rhine to the Nile . . .

. . . to Flavia Julia Helena Augusta, his venerable and saintly
mother greetings and filial obeisance.

It is now almost thirteen years ago that our arms, sanctified by the name and sign of the Redeemer of glorious
and eternal memory and supported by our mother's prayer,
were fully and decisively victorious at the gates of Rome.

In the annals of the City there is no victory compa-
rable to that of our troops against an enemy so much
stronger in numbers.

We were indeed fortunate to have at our disposal the
advice and guidance of our august mother, admonishing
us to clemency toward the vanquished enemies and spreading the spirit of love over the whole of our Empire, by
founding institutes for orphans, widows, and other afflicted
people and laying the foundations of many churches, of
which the Golden Church in Antioch and the Church
of the Twelve Apostles are luminous examples.

By the Edict of Milan we have fulfilled the last wish
of our august father and given back to the Christians all
rights which the injustice of former monarchs had withdrawn from them.

For many years we have kept the peace, contenting
ourselves with warding off the attacks of barbarians at
our frontiers and dedicating all our time to the thorough

reorganization of our dominions. For twelve years, we can say that without either pride or undue modesty, we have been eager to give to our peoples that new and golden age of which Virgil prophetically sang in his immortal poem.

We could not, however, blind ourselves to the ambitious intentions and plans of the Emperor of the east, and we decided to forestall them. Once more we were allowed to be victorious, and the battles of Hadrianople and Chalcedon decided the outcome of the war and the fate of Emperor Licinius, to whom we gave sanctuary, but who could not or would not survive his defeat for long.

From then on the throne of the Empire was once more firmly established, and the same just laws encompass the populations of all our provinces.

Thus we would enjoy the peace and the multifold blessings given to us and passed on by us to the multitudes—were it not for the one thing that gives us the cause for deep anxiety and grief and of which it is our wish to write to our august mother, so as to plead for her understanding, her appreciation, and her compassion.

Our august mother will remember what care we have always given to the education and upbringing of our eldest son, Crispus.

We surrounded him with the best teachers of our time, including the wise Lactantius, and we have had much pleasure also in his military talents, which induced us to confer the high dignity and rank of Cæsar on him as early as the seventeenth year of his life.

Nor did we seem to have to regret such a step: for not only did he excel himself in the frontier wars, when we submitted our beloved province of Gaul to his youthful command—but he fought also with the utmost valor and success in the war against the tyrant Licinius and had no mean part in the achievement of victory.

But then it became more and more evident that so many accomplishments in one so young and the subsequent flattery of certain self-seeking men had a nefarious influence on Cæsar Crispus' mind. For a long time we listened silently to the reports of those who are watching over our security and of our friends about the opinions of the young Cæsar, expressed with steadily growing bitterness and violence. Several grave admonitions given to him with paternal kindness proved entirely fruitless, and we had to abstain—for the time being, as we thought—from putting him in charge of another province. We preferred to keep him at our Court.

Now, however, a situation of the most serious aspect has arisen. We have been informed by the most reliable sources that the young Cæsar, blinded by ambition, has become the head of a conspiracy directed not only against our throne, but our very life.

We are pained beyond expression to have to relate such things, but the dignity of the Emperor as well as the security of the State demanded that firm steps were taken immediately.

It is only natural that, confronted with such decisions, we appeal to our august mother once more, as so often in the past, for her spiritual succor and that loving understanding that has proved to be to us a source of invaluable benefit.

Given in Rome, in July of the year one thousand seventy and seven of the foundation of the city.

Constantinus

This was the letter Helena had been given when she returned from her father's grave to her little house in Camulodunum. She had walked all the way there and back, and it had taken her over an hour to come home. She remembered that she had once needed only a third of that time.

When she had seen the imperial messenger waiting, she had known at once that bad news was in the air.

She had always had that sort of foreknowledge; it seemed to have grown rather than diminished as life advanced. Sometimes she could feel that a certain person was about to enter the room, and he did. Sometimes she felt with a deadly clarity that the person she was talking to was going to die soon; in earlier years this had caused her much fear. Now she was resigned to it, knowing that she herself was nearing the end of her life. There was a message of death in the hands of the imperial messenger—she had known that the moment she set eyes on him, standing in front of the house and giving the imperial salute. She had taken the sealed parchment from his hands, had ordered Terentia to look after the man and then to join her, and had sat down in her favorite corner, under the three statues.

The one in the middle showed Constantius as he was in his youth.

The one on the right showed Hilary; that on the left Favonius.

All three were of dark bronze.

She had sat down abruptly, placing her strong black cane with the ivory knob at her side: a letter from Rome. From Constantine. And it spelled death. Whose death? Not his own, surely. He was not ill. She would have felt it if he were ill. Whose death?

She cut the strings, opened, and read. What a perfectly nauseating, pompous style the Emperor affected. That was not the way to write to one's mother. Patting himself on the back, giving her sweet-smelling compliments—he must have a bad conscience. Ah—there it was. Crispus. . . .

She threw the letter on the floor and stamped on it. "Those who are watching over our security"—miserable informers. Serpents. And "our friends", too. Friends who set the father against the son.

"Terentia!"

But she was not going to ask the lady-in-waiting to pick up the letter. She was going to do it herself. Seventy-four years of age and still so irascible. Pay your debts to your anger, Helena—pick it up, even if it hurts a little, bending the old back. There you are.

"Terentia!" How long does it take to order something to eat and drink for a man! Ridiculous. There she was at last.

"Terentia, my carriage. Pack my things. We're going to Rome. Yes, to Rome, don't ask silly questions. Send a dispatch rider to Anderida, to the port authorities, and see to it that a ship is ready for us when we arrive—no, not a large ship, anything that can float. We're crossing the channel, and then we travel by land. Off with you, child—there's no time to be lost."

The child Terentia, aged fifty-seven, rushed out of the room.

Helena smiled wanly; one didn't need to have foreknowledge of any kind to foresee what the next weeks would be like. A tiny nutshell of a ship to cross the channel in—then the state mail carriages, six horses or eight, the endless roads, nights at all sorts of inns, Terentia vomiting all over the place as she invariably did, the idiotic deputations at every town, trying to slow up her journey and not succeeding—roads in Gaul, roads in Italy—and when she arrived it would be too late.

Crispus. What a magnificent youth he had been when she saw him last!—the very image of his grandfather, strong and dignified, with a touch of genius in those dark eyes, Constantian eyes. Twenty-five he was now—

The idea of Crispus conspiring against his father's throne and life! At the age of twenty-five! What had come over Constantine to believe such an absurd story? It was not like him. There was someone else's influence there. It was not difficult to guess whose: Fausta's. The same, of course, the same poisonous influence that had made him repudiate Crispus' mother, the gentle Minervina.

However often she had promised herself not to think evil of the Empress—something always happened that made it inevitable. Crispus in disgrace—and the way was free for Fausta's own children. The red-haired witch was not one for taking chances. What had happened to Empress Theodora must not happen to her—that the son of a first marriage was made Emperor and the guardian of her children. . . .

Was Constantine blind? If so, Fausta had blinded him.

She got up, not without difficulty. Old bones, old bones. She seized the black cane and walked into her sleeping room, where the maids, alerted by Terentia, were waiting for her orders.

"No more luggage than goes into one carriage", she commanded. "No useless things. No vases or statues. Make haste, children."

She took a hand herself, bent and a little creaking, upsetting most of what the maids were doing and instituting her own order. The maids knew her well enough not to interfere.

"That's the way", she said. "Get on with it. The carriage will be ready any moment now. You'll have months and months of free time from today onward. Now I want you to be quick."

She walked back to her favorite place. Underneath the three statues, next to her old armchair—oak, the sacred wood—was a chest of iron to which she alone had the key. She produced it and opened the chest. It contained a golden goblet or chalice, covered with a lid of the same metal that had been fixed most carefully. She rubbed the chalice gently with a piece of her veil of silvercloth and, having closed the closet, put the chalice on top of it. Slowly and with difficulty, she went down on her knees before it and prayed silently. She got up just before Terentia came in to announce that the carriage was waiting and that the maids had finished packing.

"The blue silk cover for the chalice, Terentia. And what about your own things? Didn't think of them, did you? You are a good woman but a little stupid sometimes. Go and have your things packed. Give me the blue cover first. Thank you. Now run along—I'll wait for you in the carriage. You needn't take *all* your face creams and things; there's only a little space left."

She smiled a little as Terentia fluttered away and then carefully covered the chalice with the veil. As she was walking toward the carriage, it occurred to her that the thought of death that crossed her mind might concern her own death and not that of Crispus.

Well, what of it? Had not her work been done?

But Crispus had to be saved—if it was still possible.

"Too late", said Bishop Osius sadly. "Caesar Crispus was killed in Pola, in Istria, a week ago. I did my utmost to prevent it—I am not without influence on the Emperor, as you know—but this time he was adamant. He even refused to discuss it."

The old Empress did not flicker an eyelid; she was sitting bolt upright in her chair, both hands crossed over her cane. They did not seem to have aged with her, these hands— they had kept their slimness and pallor. Her face had shrunk a little, and deep furrows led from her strong nose to the corners of her mouth. Strangely enough, her forehead was almost free of wrinkles—a young forehead to an old face—and it was crowned by a challenging peak of silver-white hair.

"Too late", she repeated after a long while. "I have driven here with all the speed possible. When we arrived, they had to lift my poor Terentia out of the carriage and to carry her indoors. She is still sleeping. And I am too late." She tapped the ground with her cane. "It seems to be my fate to be too late in saving the lives of people I love", she said grimly. "Hilary—and Albanus—and now Crispus."

The bishop was pouring wine into a goblet. "It happened a week ago, as I said, Domina—you could never have been in time. You tried your utmost—that is all that is demanded from us. And God's time is not our time, you know. . . ."

"Providence", said the Empress bitterly, "is all too often invoked to excuse our own weakness. I had heard rumors before, of course—I should have listened. But I preferred to pay no attention to them. I wanted to go to my father's grave, as every year. It would have been a very disagreeable thing to go to Rome instead. I am a fool, holy Bishop. Instead of going to my father's grave, I should have remembered his words about Constantine. 'He will be death to his son'—that's what he said, when Constantine was born."

"—and bliss to his mother", nodded the bishop. "You told me that once, in Verona." He passed her the goblet of wine.

She gave a sad little laugh. "I'm repeating myself—well, I am an old woman now." She drank a little of the wine, then more. "'Bliss to his mother—'" she said. "I was always afraid he would become too hard. I told Constantius so, even on his last day."

"When are you going to see him?" asked the bishop.

"There is no hurry now, is there?" was the weary answer. "I'm glad I came to see you first at your house. I did want to know what the situation was—and now I do know. And my son cannot take it amiss that I did not visit him immediately. I am not an invited guest. I shall go and see him tomorrow. 'Bliss to his mother . . .' Tell me, holy Bishop—how did the poor boy die?"

Bishop Osius sighed. "We don't know for sure", he said with some hesitation. "—There is a rumor that he was poisoned—another that he was killed with the axe of the lictor. But why torture your mind with such sad pictures, Empress? It is all over, and . . ."

She leaned forward, and her eyes had a steely shine. "And was he really guilty?" she asked. "Did he conspire against his father's throne—and life?"

"Against his life?" exclaimed the bishop, horrified. "I had not heard that—nor do I believe it for one moment. He was an ambitious youth—and no wonder. But to conspire against his father's life—no, no, I cannot believe that. Who told you that, Empress?"

"The Emperor", said Helena firmly. "And he believes it, too. Can you imagine who made him believe it?—Well?— Your silence is very eloquent, holy Bishop. You hate serpents as much as I do, I take it."

Bishop Osius remained silent. He knew, of course, to whom the Empress-Mother alluded—and he was inclined to agree with her. But just because he was so inclined, he did not wish to speak out. For he had no proof.

She rose, trembling. "Holy Bishop, my God forgive me through his Blessed Son! I have failed in my mission in this life."

Now the bishop, too, rose. "How can you say such a thing, Empress! You, whose prayers have been answered with victory! You through whom the Edict of Nicomedia was supplanted by the Edict of Milan. If we Christians can worship God freely and live for Christ without fear of torture and death, it is largely thanks to you!"

But she shook her head. "What does it help me if I win the whole world—if my child loses his soul? I am a mother, holy Bishop. If I can forgive Fausta for what she has done—"

"You have no proof, Domina—"

"I have the voice of my heart, and it has never deceived me. If I can forgive her, it is because I feel that she has done what she has done for her own children's sake. I am responsible to God and my dead husband for Constantine. And I have let him repudiate his first wife for ambition's sake. I have let him kill his father-in-law for the sake of the throne. And now I have let him kill his own son. Have I given birth to a monster, then?"

"Domina—Domina!"

But she was not to be stopped. "Can it be that such hands, such bloodstained hands, will be allowed to build the Kingdom of Jesus Christ on earth? Have I been deluded in everything I tried, all these years? Have I done Satan's work, instead of God's?"

"Sit down", said the bishop sharply. "And listen to me."

No one had dared to speak to her like that in decades. She obeyed. Osius' strong, dark face was towering over her.

"You are overwrought and tired", he said quietly. "Or else you would not speak such words. You are in grave error—so grave that it can well endanger your own soul. Guard that—before you take the responsibility for the soul of another, be it even your own son. What a proud woman you are—to think as you do! Do you really believe that only an entirely faultless man can be the instrument of God? Think of the Apostles—did they not desert their Lord—all

342

of them—when the guards came to capture him? Did not Peter himself, the leader of the others, commit treason against our Lord three times in one night? And yet it was he whom our Lord called the Rock and on whom he has built his Church! I tell you, there has been only one faultless Man throughout all the ages of mankind. All of us can only *try* to follow his footsteps as best we can. . . ."

He seemed to grow as he was speaking. "We have been born with the stain of original sin", he said slowly. "That means that since the fall in Paradise—whenever that was, and wherever—human nature has become corrupt. We have been praying to the gods of self-love and of force, of violence and lust and greed. To Jupiter and Venus, who committed adultery; to Mars, who enjoyed the butchery of war as the element of his life. To Pan, who enjoyed lust, and to Bacchus who enjoyed drunkenness and cruelty. Do you think our nature—not as an individual, but as a whole—the nature of mankind can be changed within a few hundred years so radically that the earth becomes a paradise again? All we can do is to lay the foundation for the Kingdom of Christ—to see to it that more and more people are released from the curse of the Fall by the sacrament of Baptism and that the teaching of the Lord is hammered into their young souls as soon as they can think. For thousands of years the world has believed in force—it has become as hard as iron. We must melt that iron in the fire of love—but it will take a long time to kindle the flame to such heat that this will be possible. . . ."

"I shall not live to see it, then", said Helena tonelessly.

"Why should you live to see it?" exclaimed Osius relentlessly. "What right have you to claim a privilege higher than that of the Apostles?" But his face lost the expression of almost threatening severity, and his voice was milder as he continued: "You have seen the beginning of it, however—and you were allowed to become God's instrument. I am a practical man, Domina, and not easily given to the high-sounding verbiage of the mystic schools. When your son, the Emperor, introduced the sign of the Cross to his army, there was a wave of enthusiasm, inspiring his troops to victory. It was not a holy enthusiasm altogether, Domina—I know the nature of man too well for that. It has not changed much yet. They are still ready to shout 'hosanna' today and 'crucify him!' tomorrow. They—many of them—will follow the Cross today and another emblem tomorrow. It is not only the power of good that can spread enthusiasm—believe me. Even at the time when our Lord was walking on this earth there have been some who were zealous for his teaching at first—and then denounced it. Do not think that I am not deeply grateful for the victory of the Milvian Bridge, Domina—and do not think that I am fool enough not to see the finger of God when its imprint is as unmistakable as it was then, at that great turning point of the history of mankind. But a cross on helmet and shield does not necessarily change a man's heart. It was you yourself who once said to me, in Verona, that you felt how strongly and closely your son's mind was linked up with that of his soldiers'. Well, there is still much that is pagan in Constantine—and there is still much that is pagan in his Empire. Slowly, slowly he will overcome it. There will be relapses—we stand in sorrow and grief in front of such a relapse now. But that does not give us the right to despair of our task—we must go on, even if we shall not be allowed to see final victory. The power of evil is strong and may well remain strong for many generations to come—but God does not build in centuries—perhaps not even in thousands of years. He builds in his own good time...."

"I have sinned", said Helena, still in the same toneless voice. She was deep in thought, and now he refrained from interrupting her. But the interruption was to come from outside.

A young cleric entered, despite the bishop's warning frown.

"An urgent message from Bishop Timeon", he said in a low voice. Osius looked quickly at Helena, then back to the messenger. "From the palace?" he asked.

"Yes, holy Bishop. All audiences have been canceled—the Emperor refuses to see anybody."

Helena awoke from her thoughts.

"And the reason?" asked Bishop Osius impatiently.

"It is not known for sure, holy Bishop, but there is a rumor that the Empress has—has died quite suddenly."

Helena rose. "Lead me to the palace—at once", she said. Her face was ashen, but her hands did not tremble now.

CHAPTER 2

THE DOORS OF the huge palace opened one by one before the old lady with her black cane. No one dared to resist her, as she walked on, inexorably through flight after flight of rooms and halls. At first there were still officials, both men and women, bowing to her from all sides. Then they became fewer and fewer, and finally only grim-faced guards were standing in front of the doors, guarding a dark, eerie solitude of golden chairs and silent tapestry.

Gradually those who had come with her faded away—the chief chamberlain, the Emperor's physician, and in the end also Bishop Osius and his young cleric.

In front of the door, leading to the room, where whispering terror-stricken voices had indicated that the Emperor was, two huge bodyguards were crossing their pikes.

The old woman, without a word, lifted her cane and struck the crossed pikes with it.

The two guards saw her eyes—and what they saw there even more than the frantic beckoning of the chief chamberlain from the other end of the large hall made them lift their pikes in a bewildered salute.

And Helena walked on, into the room no one else in the Empire would have dared to enter at this moment.

From the stale, cloying perfume that filled it she knew at once that it was one of the Empress' own suite. Everything in it was feminine in the extreme—the dainty furniture, the ornament-ridden curtains, the oversoft deep carpets.

But, sprawled over a bed filled with cushions of all forms and colors was the motionless body of a man.

Helena stood still—and felt at once the silence of the room assailing her with terrible force.

Now the man on the bed looked up—

"Mother!" screamed Constantine, and reeling like a drunken man, he tried to rise to his feet.

She rushed up to him, and hugging him, pressed him gently back into the cushions; she felt his arms, his hands clutching her as if he were drowning; she heard his voice murmur words, always the same words, always, always the same words, and although she could not hear them—for he was murmuring into the folds of her cloak and she had been growing just a little deaf lately—she knew exactly what he was saying.

"I've killed her, Mother—I've killed her, Mother—I've killed her—"

She felt an icy hand touching her heart and squeezing it; she could not breathe. O Jesus Christ, grant that it isn't true, grant that it isn't true, it mustn't be true, not that—

But she knew it was true, and she knew it had to be. And nothing that he now would tell her could be new to her or terrifying, for she knew it all, and really she had known it all from the beginning, when she had set eyes for the first and only time on the proud, beautiful daughter of Maximian. She had deserted them two days before the wedding; it had been an intolerable thought for her to see her son's destiny bound up with that lizardlike woman, whose eyes were tireless in seeking the admiration of all and sundry, whose mouth seemed to offer itself not to the highest bidder, but to every bidder—and whose one aim next to lust was power.

Now all that was required of Helena was to be the mother of her child.

This is it, she thought; this is why I had to come to Rome—not Crispus, for whom I came too late. Constantine—for whom I came just at the right time. "In God's own time"—oh, dear great friend Osius.

She said nothing; she just went on caressing the dark head, slightly graying and balding.

When at last he had recovered sufficiently to sit up, she saw with overwhelming compassion that his face was ravaged and furrowed—a field freshly ploughed by the most merciless of ploughmen; hopelessness and fear and despair had been sown into the furrows.

Oh, the blessing of having come in time . . .

"Tell me all, my son. Tell me."

But it took time before he was able to speak and more time before he could speak coherently. He had found the

347

Empress—he himself had found her in the arms of a slave from the stables. The slave had been killed at once. The Empress . . .

"Mother, I came to her, because I—I couldn't sleep. I haven't slept since Crispus died. I wanted to ask her—to ask her again whether she was quite sure about what she had told me about him—she had told me that he had tried to make her sleep with him, Mother—that he had laughed at me and said that a good son had to make up for what his father neglected. She told me that he wanted to win her for his own aim—that he had promised her never to marry, but to regard her as his true Queen. . . . Oh, she was very indignant. I talked to Crispus for a long time, I examined him again and again—alone, of course. Should I myself spread the story of my shame? He denied it—who wouldn't? He denied everything. Even those things I knew to be true, things he had said to men I trust, ambitious things—he denied it all. If he lied here—why not there, too?

"Only Fausta could give me certainty. I knew that she was ambitious for her children, of course. I knew that she was as hard as nails when it came to that. I was not so blind as not to see how she behaved when I had to have her father killed. She hated him. She always did. She was afraid he might marry again and have other children and give them preference over her and the children she had given me. . . ."

"Where are they?" interrupted Helena quickly. "Where are your children?"

"None of them is in Rome, Mother—fortunately. How ever shall I tell them—"

"We'll talk about that later. You went to see—her—and you found her with that slave—and you had the slave killed."

"Yes—yes. Then I gave orders to prepare a bath for the Empress and to heat it with triple heat and go on heating it until her guilt had melted away. That's what I did. And she died. She suffocated. She is over there now—in the next room. The men who know about it I had sworn to secrecy. The Empress died in an accident. Mother, Mother—why must I do all this? Maximian—and Crispus—and Fausta! Why, why?"

Helena groaned. Why was it indeed that men always punished others for their own faults and mistakes? Fausta had always been what Constantine saw in her now—only he had seen her differently—and when in the face of facts he had to change his mind, he killed her—killed her for being different from what he had wanted her to be. Killed Fausta for being Fausta. "The world had become hard. We must melt the world in the fire of love"—the end was aeons away, beyond reach.

"I was beside myself, Mother—you know, sometimes it takes me like that—I could have killed not only her, but—"

"Quiet, Son, quiet—"

"—sometimes I think it is not really I who have done this—that it is someone else doing it in me and through me—"

She lifted his head up to her own, and her eyes fastened on his.

"If you do not accept the responsibility for your sins, you cannot claim responsibility for the good. You have done what you have done—and you cannot undo it. Don't blame the dead—blame yourself. You asked them to be what they couldn't be. You see where that has led you. There is only one thing for you to do now."

He began, at last, to regain control over himself. Mechanically he tried to tidy his hair and to readjust his dress. She saw the thin red of shame rising in his cheeks and knew instinctively that this was just another demon, after that of hurt pride, vanity, and fury. Many a crime had been committed because a man felt ashamed.

She knew that this was not the time to listen to her own feelings—that this was his worst hour, and that she must not fail him. The moment when she had been allowed to be his mother and nothing but his mother was over irrevocably. This man of almost fifty was the absolute Emperor of the Roman world, the victor of the Milvian Bridge, of Hadrianople, and of Chalcedon.

"No one is going to make you responsible for killing your—for killing the Empress, Constantine. Both as the head of the state and as the father of the family you are beyond anyone else's jurisdiction. Even if you weren't—there'd be many who would acquit you for what you have done today. But you yourself cannot acquit yourself. And you cannot undo what you've done. Therefore what remains, but action!"

"Action", he repeated automatically. "What action?"

She rose, painfully, seizing her cane. "To my son I have nothing but love to offer", she said. "To the Emperor I say: the shadows of Maximian, Crispus, and Fausta have darkened your victories in the sight of history. To the man I say: contrition without retribution is not enough in the sight of God."

He looked up. "What can I do, Mother?"

"You can do good—you can work for the glory of God. You don't need an old woman to tell you how to go about that. . . ."

She stopped. Suddenly and for no apparent reason her heart began to beat tumultuously; she could hear the beat like a wild gong, thundering and thundering a flaming appeal; louder and louder, until there was nothing but that beat, filling the room and the world.

She herself was nothing but that beat, and there was nothing in the world that was not that beat. It was all over almost before she was really aware of it, like a chariot thundering by so quickly, one could get only a glimpse of manes and tails and wheels as it vanished in a cloud of dust.

"Mother—Mother—what is it? Are you ill?"

She took a deep breath. "No, Constantine. But the time has come to tell you—my secret. I have been keeping it faithfully, for many, many years. You know that at your birth, my father foresaw strange things that would happen to you and about you. You would own all land you'd ride on, he said. You would do as your father, but you would be greater than your father. You would be death to your son and bliss to your mother. I told you some of that—not all of it. But when he was dying, he said to me, 'There is a strong tie between you and your son—stronger than blood—stronger even than mother love, of which the poets say that it is the strongest force on earth. You and he—together you will find the tree of life—yea, the living wood itself. . . .' And these were his last words on earth, Constantine. . . ."

The Emperor was looking at her in awe; so Coel the Wise had foreseen almost the whole of his life—even the death of Crispus. But even more than that knowledge, the sight of his mother made him feel suddenly insignificant and small, as though she were a superior being.

"When I heard of your victory at the Milvian Bridge," went on Helena, "I thought that even that part of my father's words had been fulfilled. For the tree of life, the living wood, is the Cross of our Savior. And on that day you made it the emblem of your entire army, and it was in this sign that you conquered."

He nodded silently.

351

"I was wrong", she continued. "Only now I see how wrong I was. I thought of a symbol—not of reality. And with Christ it is stark reality all the time. I forgot what Hilary had told me, just before he died. 'It is said that Christ's teaching will encompass the Roman world only when the Cross is found again. For it has disappeared—and no one knows where it is.' "

She took a step forward, her eyes radiant. "When I heard of your victory, I thought my task was fulfilled", she said. "It was not. I must find the Cross—the True Cross!"

He jumped to his feet. "Mother, it's been lost ever since his death. How can you hope—"

She smiled now. "I shall find it, Son. And I want you to give me unlimited power—ships, men, money must be at my disposal. Will you give me such power, Emperor of Rome?"

Deeply moved, he bowed his head. "Your power comes from a higher source than any I can give you, Mother. But what power I have is yours."

CHAPTER 3

BISHOP MACARIUS of Jerusalem was in despair. He had been worried ever since that first letter had arrived from the Emperor, announcing that the Empress-Mother would sail for the Holy Land in a few weeks' time and would make her headquarters at Jerusalem. The Emperor had requested him—in the most polite and respectful way, but it was an order all the same—to help his mother with her task, to build a church on Mount Calvary and to find the True Cross of Christ.

A church on Mount Calvary—when not a single soul in Jerusalem knew even where Mount Calvary had been at the time of the Blessed Lord. The surroundings of Jerusalem were full of little hills and hillocks, any of which might have been Mount Calvary three hundred years ago.

As for the True Cross, it was simply hopeless to find it. Where to begin? Whom to ask?

He had a fairly big community in his diocese by now, convert pagans, convert Jews—there were Syrians, Phoenicians, Arabs, and Copts among his flock, Greeks from the isles and from Greece itself. And there was, of course, the small nucleus that had always been Christian and, since the Edict of Milan of blessed memory, could worship Christ in the open.

He had his hands full—there was work enough to be done from sunrise to a long time after sunset, day after day, without this additional burden of seeking for something that had disappeared three centuries ago.

Besides, now at long last one could openly communicate with one's colleagues; experiences and ideas of the most far-reaching importance had to be exchanged, articles of faith had to be interpreted and the interpretation submitted to the Bishop of Rome. True, the Council of Nicea had done wonders, last year, and much had been settled there that would stand like a rock to the end of time. But no council, however much inspired by the Holy Spirit, could solve all the problems; correspondence with other bishops was essential.

The welfare work had to be supervised; some seemingly very pious people had proved to be self-seeking and corrupt, and some of the younger clergy were too inexperienced to see through such people. The great problem of confession had to be tackled—if only Pope Sylvester had given clear directions about it. There were many who advocated that remission of sins could be given only once in a lifetime and that a relapse into the same sin was unforgivable. Surely, that was not so! If one was to forgive one's brother not seven, but seventy times seven, could not at least equal mercy be expected from Mercy itself? A little time must be given to a bishop for meditation on problems of such magnitude, however much practical work had to be done.

Then there were some members of the community who had shown signs of spiritual pride and overbearing lately, understandable, perhaps, after so long a period of depression and persecution, but nevertheless wrong and even dangerous. When a man has had to conceal his faith before the world, or has been jeered at and vilified for it by the world, and then suddenly the Emperor proclaims his faith to be true and the true faith of the Empire—well, then he has to be a very good man indeed, if such radical change is not to go to his head!

The rapid growth, the expansion of a religion from a subterranean cell life to a tremendous world organization, all in the course of a few years, was bound to have a thousand different consequences and to raise a thousand new problems. To a bishop it meant a flood tide of hard work.

Into all this thundered the incredible old Empress-Mother with her self-styled mission of finding the True Cross. It had been clear from the beginning that she was going to be a very substantial nuisance. But no one could have foreseen quite what magnitude of nuisance she would be. . . .

Within the course of a week she had turned Jerusalem upside down.

She had arrived with half a dozen shiploads full of experts, agents, and investigators, who had spread all over the city

and were riddling everybody with questions; they were con-
ferring with oil and wine dealers, with priests of the Christian and rabbis of the Jewish faith, they tackled the keepers
of hostelries and the owners of shops, and they listened to
the stories of high officials and beggars with equal zeal and
attentiveness.

It was easy to foresee what would be the outcome: they
would be told vague rumors at best, but more often simply
a pack of lies. It was just asking for trouble. What an opportunity for a cunning Syrian, a shrewd Jew, a Greek—always
with the tongue in his cheek, anyway—to provide the dear
old Empress-Mother with all the stories she so obviously
wished to believe!

One cannot be a bishop without knowing a good deal
about human nature; Bishop Macarius was no exception,
and he groaned every time he was asked into the Imperial
Presence—which happened daily.

She was nearing her seventy-sixth year—but she seemed
to have the energy of a man half her age—and a most energetic man at that. She was treating him with the respect
due to his office—but she made it unmistakably clear that
she regarded her purpose in Jerusalem as of prime importance and that she would not tolerate any slackness in the
help granted to her.

She herself interviewed a host of people without distinc-
tion of rank, sex, nationality, or creed; she wandered about
in the city, in the company of a few ladies-in-waiting and
at most one or two guards. And she had a most disconcerting preference for the less respectable and therefore more
dangerous quarters, the streets of low-class inhabitants, of
thieves, beggars, and prostitutes.

She spent hours quite alone, on the slopes of the Mount
of Olives, praying or meditating; it was spring now—the

month of May—and the fig trees were budding; the garlands of cypress trees were gleaming in fresher green, topping the groves of silvery olives. The monotonous yellows and browns of Jerusalem blossomed forth into myriad shades of color. Even the ruins of the city—and there were many, especially at the periphery—seemed to look less austere and forbidding. The scent of jasmine, lavender, and oleander was over all the city, mixing with the odors of spices and dung fires.

It was warm—and the prolonged hours on the Mount of Olives would not do damage to the Empress-Mother's health, but they were dangerous all the same. The Roman chief of police, Sulpicius, was beside himself about the whole thing. His men were working overtime, watching the many criminals, following the formidable guest around like silent shadows, as worried about being barked at and chased away by the old lady as about her safety. Five times in a fortnight, in rising despair, Prefect Sulpicius went to see Bishop Macarius.

"Can't you do something to put an end to this?" groaned the perspiring official. "It's putting years on my life. I can't sleep. You know what she did yesterday? Went out of the walls, into the slum quarters near the old camel gate. With one—one!—lady-in-waiting and no guards at all. I had six men guarding her—she found them out and chased them away! She has the firm idea that the presence of police officials, even without uniforms, prevents the people from being frank with her. Frank with her! Camel drivers and spice merchants! She's been told that Mount Calvary was everywhere and in every direction. There is no story so stupid that she will not follow it up. I am at my wits' end."

"I know, I know—" Bishop Macarius was nothing if not compassionate—"it's a terrible ordeal for you; it isn't easy for me either! I get the latest news directly from her, when I go to see her after the midday meal, every day! I hear all the stories. Even I didn't know that people could be so inventive. There was one old merchant who'd told her that Mount Calvary has been mysteriously raised up and transplanted to Jericho after the conquest of Jerusalem by Titus. There was—"

"Excellent idea!" Sulpicius became quite excited. "Can't you confirm that? Or at least say you've heard a similar thing? She'd go over to Jericho and give my colleague there something to do for a change! Or, better still—can't you persuade her that this thing isn't *meant* to be found? After all, you're a bishop—if she's such a good Christian, she should believe you!"

"Which is just why I cannot tell her a lie", said Macarius, suddenly very stiff. "My dear friend, I also find my activities sadly curtailed by all this—hum—research, but that does not mean that I can take it upon myself to dissuade the Empress-Mother—much less to mislead her with deliberation."

The prefect was apologetic. "But you must admit, holy Bishop, that the whole thing is stark madness! It's like trying to find a—a needle in a haystack! There are no less than eight different hills where she has started excavation work! Hundreds of workmen are busy at it, and hundreds more are added every day—if this goes on much longer she'll dig up the entire neighborhood. And even if she finds the—the hill in question, how is she going to find that Cross! Why, it's hopeless, and you know it as well as I do!"

"You never know", said Macarius, a little to his own surprise. Perhaps it was the attitude of the police chief that had driven him into such opposition, but he felt that it could not be that alone. The untiring, almost ferocious energy of the old woman seemed to be contagious. He laughed suddenly. "I'm afraid I can't help you, Sulpicius.

She is as overwhelming to me as she is to you. And after all there is just the chance—the off chance—that she is right! You cannot expect me to dissuade her. If she wants to dig up the neighborhood of the city, the very least I can do is to let her dig! And there is something to be said for so many workmen finding a job to do—and also for the house for orphans she is building in the southern district and for the new hostelry for poor travelers. No, no, this thing, wise or foolish, mad or inspired—it must go on. Bear it like a man, Sulpicius. I'll do the same...."

Actually, Macarius did more than bear it. It was he who had given Helena the information that according to Jewish law, the bodies of executed criminals had to be buried at the very place of execution, together with the implements of the execution. This had not been the case with Jesus' body, as was clear enough from the Gospels. But the Cross itself was more than likely to have been buried on Calvary itself. Therefore, if only she could find that little hill....

But the surroundings of Jerusalem were just one little hill after the other—that was the main difficulty.

"Good evening, Simon", said Helena, lifting her black cane in a friendly salute. Terentia smiled a little wanly.

"Good evening, Lady", replied the boy, with a grave little bow; he was about fifteen years old. Almond-shaped black eyes in a thin face with well-cut features, curly black hair—he would have been a very good-looking boy, thought Terentia, if it had not been for that withered right arm that hung lifelessly at his side, a useless excrescence rather than a human limb. She could never help shuddering a little when she saw the boy's arm, but she was careful not to show it—Domina Helena had little patience with that sort of thing. They had met the boy several times on their excursions into the neighborhood outside the destroyed walls of the city. They always found him standing calmly in front of the little hut where he lived with his mother, a woman old before her time through ceaseless work. He was looking after her as well as he could, doing odd jobs, mostly as a messenger. He could not very well do manual work—not since the lightning had crashed into the tree under which he had sought refuge seven years ago, striking him unconscious and leaving him as he was now—a cripple.

Helena had taken a fancy to him; he was intelligent, and his dignified little ways amused her. Twice before she had made use of him as a guide, and each time he had taken a gold coin home, which he had accepted with a respectful indifference that Terentia found rather irritating. As if a brat like that saw gold coins every day!

"We'll try another direction today", said Helena. "Care to lead us again, Simon?"

"With pleasure, Lady", said the boy. "But you've been almost everywhere around here now; there are two more hills over there—it's not very far. But I don't think you'll like them much."

They were walking on now. "Why not?" asked Helena.

The boy shrugged his lean shoulders. "There is nothing to see there", he said. "They're just hills."

Spring was in full bloom—they were walking on flowers all the time; the air was full of their scent. The strange old lady was looking for hills. Well, they were two a penny near Jerusalem; but time and again, when she was standing on top of one, she would shake her little white head and say, "No—not here—not here—" as though she were trying to find a place where she had been before. Yet she had told him that she had never been in this country before. She was a very old lady.

No doubt she was a little mad—not so mad as Mordecai, the hunchback, whom they had to tie up when he had one of his fits, but like Rahel, who sometimes said things that didn't make sense and sang in a queer voice. Yet most of the things that the old lady said did make sense.

More than once he had wanted to ask her what she was really looking for, but he had not dared. She wasn't the sort one could question just like that. Even the haughty, well-dressed lady who always came with her never asked her questions, never even spoke before she was spoken to.

He rather liked her. She did not give him pitying looks as old women often did because of his arm. She never referred to his arm at all. She treated him as though it were the most natural thing that he should be as he was. It made one feel natural, too.

Also, she was a good walker and did not seem to get tired—the other one, although younger, became tired much easier.

"We've been here before, surely", said Helena.

A brook, oleander bushes, sweet-smelling grass that reminded her of Britain. At some distance a shepherd was watching his little flock; it was grazing quietly.

Simon shook his head. No, they hadn't been here before. But one hill looked very much like another. His Latin was a little halting, but not too bad. How had he come to learn Latin, Helena wanted to know. He had learned it from his rabbi. Many boys did. He had had a very good rabbi. But now he had no time for studying because mother was getting old. He would have liked to go on, yes—but what was the good of thinking of that? It could not be.

And here were the two little hills he had mentioned—this one, here, full of grass and flowers with a lonely cyprus tree to watch them—and that one with the ruins on it.

Yes, the ruins of a temple. It had been built a long, long time ago, by an emperor called Hadrian. Simon was a little proud of what he knew. It was the temple of a Roman goddess, the one to whom doves were sacred—Venus was her name.

But to his surprise, he found that the old lady was not listening.

She was standing still, looking at the hill with the ruins. Her breath was heavy, and perhaps she felt tired today after all—there were beads of perspiration on her forehead. Or—or was she ill? Her eyes were so wide—it wasn't natural. And the other one was staring at her and she was worried and didn't know what to do.

Helena stood and stood; once more her heart was thundering in flaming appeal, louder and louder, until she herself was nothing but that beat of her heart—until all the world was nothing but that beat of her heart. Then she began to move, slowly, across the meadow and uphill, up to the summit of the hill with the ruins of the temple. She did not know that she was moving—there was a soft, tingling feeling all over her body, as if the wind were rushing up to her. Fiddlers were playing, and flutes and drums, and the music was getting louder and louder; all the world's flowers were bowing toward the hill; all the world's trees were bowing toward the hill.

Step by step, and every step was thunder coming from the center of the earth. Thorns tearing at her, nettles, thistles; a snake fled through the bushes.

The ruins of the temple, overgrown by weeds, barred the way.

When Terentia and Simon reached the summit of the hill, they found Helena standing in front of them; her eyes were still wide open, and there was not a single drop of blood in her face. With her cane she pointed to the ruins of the temple. Her voice, as she spoke, was unnaturally calm.

"This—will be torn down today!"

In the afternoon of the following day Simon made his way back to the hill with the ruins; around him there was continuous coming and going; hundreds of people were on the road, where yesterday only a lonely shepherd had been seen. Most of them were workmen with picks and shovels, and a number of heavy carts, drawn by bullocks, accompanied them. But many were officials of all ranks; there was a detachment of soldiers under a centurion and a little group of Christian priests, marching steadily through a weaving, milling mass of sightseers.

Simon was wondering what they had come to see—there wasn't much in seeing a few old temple ruins cleared away.

When the old lady had uttered her strange command on top of the hill, he really had thought that she was quite mad after all. She had looked mad—and why should anybody tear down the old ruins, just because she wanted it?

Yet no more than two hours after their return the first workmen arrived, and they worked till sundown under the supervision of soldiers. And they did not content themselves with tearing down the temple ruins—they had begun to dig up the soil underneath. And at night, the soldiers had stayed on, keeping watch on the summit of the hill, as if they were guarding a treasure. Perhaps that was it! Perhaps they *were* guarding a treasure!

Even so—how was it that the old lady could command all these workmen and even soldiers to do her will? It had puzzled him greatly—until he had found out the truth from some of the workmen. An old lady—with a black cane?

Stumping about and looking for hills? Why, of course, that was she, the Empress-Mother Helena, didn't he know? She was having excavations made at a dozen places around Jerusalem—this was just one more of them.

The Empress-Mother . . .

He had to have another look at her, now that he knew who she was. He had known that she was in Jerusalem—even that on her command excavations had been made. But somehow he had visualized her all dressed up in gold and purple and surrounded by swarms of slaves and officials—not as a very old, bent woman, walking on a black stick and talking to him as she had done.

He followed the crowd streaming in the direction of the hill; it was easy with his slim body to slip through where others could not; there was a cordon of soldiers around the summit, and he knew he wouldn't be able to slip through that. But now he could see the old lady, this time with a half dozen women behind her; at her side was a priest in resplendent robes.

Cautiously he steered his way through the throng; everybody was staring at the place, where until yesterday the temple ruins had been. Now the ruins had disappeared, and in their stead was a huge hole dug deeply into the soil and seething with the activity of the workmen, like an ant heap it looked.

"Back with you, boy", grumbled one of the guards.

But at the same moment, Helena looked up and gave a sign to let him through; timidly he walked up to her and bowed. The fingers of her left hand were touching his head. "This is Simon, holy Bishop—he led me here yesterday."

Bishop Macarius gave a nod. "Perhaps he, too, will change his name to Peter sometime", he said gently. He was feeling rather ill at ease; this morning a messenger of the

Empress-Mother had summoned him to her, and from that moment on he had become caught in the whirl of events around her. She had insisted on his coming with her to this hill; and, of course, her women had not been able to keep their mouths shut—half of the city was assembled here. What if all was in vain? It would not be good for the dignity of the Empire if the Emperor's mother made a fool of herself. It would not be good for the young dignity of the Church either. To say nothing of having stood here for three solid hours already. Well, he was a man and not yet sixty. How she could endure it, at her age, was more than he could understand. Really it was almost bound to be a wild-goose chase. Hadn't there been a number of minor earthquakes in the vicinity of Jerusalem? That sort of thing made hills out of the plain and flat land out of hills. It was an absurd thing, to stand here and see workmen digging a deeper and deeper hole. . . .

A deputation of three young priests approached him, and their spokesman, bowing, murmured something about letters having arrived from Antioch; his presence in the city was urgently required.

"My place is here", said Bishop Macarius. "Go away, friend."

And he went on staring at the hole in the earth.

It couldn't be, of course. It was out of the question. But even the slightest, the most nebulous of chances . . .

There was one point, only one, that had appealed to his sharp forces of reasoning, and that was the fact that Emperor Hadrian had had a temple of Venus built on this hill. Hadrian—that was two hundred years ago; he hadn't been a friend of the Christians. In fact, he'd hated them, as much as a man of his curiously twisted sort of mind could hate. Hadrian and his pervert friends—he would be just the man to conceive such an idea: to have a temple of Venus built on Calvary. The goddess of lust was abomination to the Christians—to build a temple for her here was to prevent the place from becoming a sacred meeting place for the hated sect. . . .

That made sense. But it was the only thing that did in the whole matter, and if—what was the matter with the Empress now? She was trembling all over. . . .

Suddenly from the depth of the hole in the earth came a long-drawn cry—and then another—and still another—

"Wood! Wood! Wood!"

Helena fell on her knees; instinctively her ladies followed her example.

Bishop Macarius stared at the hole; his breath came heavily. There were so many workmen in the excavation ground that one couldn't see anything. Or—or—could one?

The crowd had become silent, and their silence hung in the air like a live thing. There was no wind.

The very birds and insects seemed to have become mute.

Only the occasional clang of an iron spade was audible.

And then Bishop Macarius fell on his knees with a brief, hoarse cry. An instant later everybody was kneeling.

Up from the depth of the hole grew three crosses.

Slowly they grew—shaking and swerving a little, as the workmen carried them up to the surface.

Now they had reached the surface, and a cluster of men followed with their spades and shovels—one was carrying something that looked like a strip of parchment. Still more men were coming up. There they stood, hesitating, like dumb animals, as though they did not dare to come nearer to the Empress.

Helena tried to rise; she could not. Macarius on her left, little Simon on her right, had to support her. Her knees sagging under her, she stumbled forward until she stood at the foot of the three crosses; she was sobbing now, and her body was shaking convulsively.

Despite his overwhelming excitement, Macarius' brain was working with an uncanny clarity. He saw the parchment in the workman's hand, and he recognized the remnants of Hebrew, Greek, and Latin characters on it ... the proclamation of Pilate. Therefore one of these crosses really was the True Cross. But which one?

Before he could think this thought to an end, Helena was clasping one of the crosses as a mother might clasp her child. Then, with a sudden movement, she grasped little Simon's shoulder and drew him nearer to her. Wide eyed, the boy looked on, as she seized his withered arm and touched the stem of the Cross with it.

Simon wailed. A tongue of fire seemed to go up inside of his arm, burning and burning. With a jerk he withdrew it, and—it obeyed his will. Utterly bewildered, he stared at it—and for the first time in seven years he saw the fingers of his right hand move. He tried it again—and again they moved. He tried to swing his arm—up first—then sideways—

To the multitude it looked like the sign of the Cross.

There were many present who knew Simon, the cripple—a wave of whispering went across the onlookers.

Helena's and Macarius' eyes met. Slowly the bishop bent down and kissed the upright of the Cross.

The return to Jerusalem was one long, triumphant prayer.

Most of the crowd were Christians: they were singing.

Macarius himself, with two of his priests, was carrying the Cross; Helena followed, supported by young Simon, who was walking as in a dream. Halfway, the old bishop had to give in, overcome by emotion as much as by the frailty of his body. But as they approached the gate of the city, he took over again. With tears streaming down his face, he thought that it might well have been this self-same gate—now half-destroyed—through which the Cross had been carried out, almost three centuries ago. . . .

CHAPTER 4

"SHE IS SLEEPING now", said Constantine in a low voice. "Tell me more about it—everything."

Terentia looked once more toward the little terrace; the Empress was sleeping peacefully in her armchair—her face had shrunk almost to the size of a child's. The sun, setting over the tops of the pine trees, threw its last spell of gold and red and purple over the Roman hills.

Both the Emperor and Bishop Osius were listening tensely. The report of Bishop Macarius had arrived by the same ship as the Empress, and he was a very thorough man. But every detail mattered in this story; the Empress herself was too ill and exhausted to talk—and Terentia had been with her all the time.

"The holy nails were found, too", whispered Terentia. "And a spear. Perhaps it was the spear that opened the side of our Lord—I don't know. The Domina left a large piece of the Cross with Bishop Macarius: he is to build a basilica for it. It is set in a beautiful silver shrine. One of the three nails got lost during our sea voyage. We could never find out what had happened to it. The Empress has the other two with her. We had a terrible journey back—storms were raging, and once we thought we would be shipwrecked. But then quite suddenly it became calm again. . . ."

Bishop Osius nodded slightly. There was a rumor in Rome already that the Empress had calmed the storm by throwing one of the holy nails into the sea.

"The Empress fell ill", went on Terentia, "as soon as we had set foot on land. But she insisted on traveling on to Rome. I think she wanted to go on still farther—she said something about Britain this morning—but her voice was very weak. I couldn't understand it clearly enough."

"She is the greatest woman ever born in Britain", said Osius.

"In the afternoon," continued Terentia, "she made me unpack the golden chalice she always carried with her—and open it."

"What was in it?" asked Osius quickly.

"A little bit of white dust—she looked at it for a while, and I think she was praying. Then she took the chalice—quite firmly, and it's heavy—and held it to her lips and ate the content."

Constantine looked in surprise at the bishop, who was nodding in silent understanding. But suddenly all three of them looked toward the terrace. There had been no sound, no movement—yet they rushed up to the Empress in her armchair.

Helena's eyes were wide open, but there was no knowing of what they were perceiving. There was an expression of rapt tenderness on her face.

On the other side of the terrace, the huge Cross was touched by the last rays of the sinking sun; it seemed to glow, pulsating with a bloodstream of sunbeams glittering and scintillating in perpetual motion.

The End

Author's Note

These dates are historically correct. Only the time of Book One, which is more or less a prologue to the others, is doubtful. We do not know for sure exactly in what year Constantius and Helena met, fell in love, and married. I made it coincide with the fall of Palmyra, which was in 272.

274 is the correct historical date for the birth of Constantine;
289 for the acknowledgment of the Carausian regime by Rome;
294 for the assassination of Carausius;
296 for the liberation of Britain;
303 for the famous Edict of Diocletian and Maximian against the Christians;
306 for the death of Constantinus (July 25);
312 for Constantine's campaign against Maxentius and the battle at the Milvian bridge (October 28);
326 for the death of Crispus and the finding of the True Cross (May 3).

This is a novel and does not claim to be accredited history in all points. Where historians are at loggerheads with each other—as for instance about the birthplace of St. Helena, and her original rank in society—I was free to choose the version I preferred. But most of the events of the book are based upon historical fact, and so are most of the personages in it—even down to the Centurion Marcus Favonius Facilis, of whom a bronze statue is still extant in Britain.

L. de W.

There follows a list of the Roman cities most frequently referred to and least easily identifiable in their Latin forms, with their English equivalents:

Camulodunum—Colchester
Eburacum—York
Aqua Sulis—Bath
Verulamium—near St. Albans
Gessoriacum—Boulogne